A Code for

Tomorrow

A CODE FOR TOMORROW

JOHN J. GOBBELL

ST. MARTIN'S PRESS ❦ NEW YORK

A CODE FOR TOMORROW. Copyright © 1999 by John J. Gobbell. All rights
reserved. Printed in the United States of America. No part of this book
may be used or reproduced in any manner whatsoever without written
permission except in the case of brief quotations embodied in critical
articles or reviews. For information, address St. Martin's Press, 175 Fifth
Avenue, New York, N.Y. 10010.

Maps by Mark Stein Studios

OVER THE RAINBOW, by Harold Arlen and E.Y. Harburg
© 1938 (Renewed) Metro-Goldwyn-Mayer Inc.
© 1939 (Renewed) EMI Feist Catalog Inc.
All Rights Reserved. Used by Permission.
WARNER BROS. PUBLICATIONS U.S. INC., Miami, FL 33014

Library of Congress Cataloging-in-Publication Data

Gobbell, John J.
   A code for tomorrow / John J. Gobbell.—1st U.S. ed.
     p.   cm.
   Sequel to: The last lieutenant.
   ISBN 0-312-20511-2
   1. World War, 1939–1945—Campaigns—Philippines Fiction.
2. World War, 1939–1945—Campaigns—Esperance, Cape (Solomon
Islands) Fiction. 3. World War, 1939–1945—Campaigns—Santa
Cruz Islands (Solomon Islands) Fiction. 4. World War, 1939–1945—
Naval operations, American Fiction. I. Title.
PS3557.016C63   1999
813'.54—dc21   99-21991
                                               CIP

First Edition: July 1999

10 9 8 7 6 5 4 3 2 1

*To the Allied forces who courageously
defeated the enemy in the Solomon Islands
campaign of World War II*

PACIFIC THEATER, WORLD WAR II

August 7, 1942–December 31, 1942

0   400   800

Mercator Projection
Scale of miles according to latitude

U.S.S.R.

China

Vladivostok

Korea

Seoul

Pusan · Kure

Shanghai

Tokyo · Japan

Okinawa Island

Formosa

Luzon

Philippine Islands

Manila

Nasipit

Mindanao

Iwo Jima Island

North Pacific Ocean

Midway Island

Tropic of Cancer

Hawaiian Islands

Wake Island

Mariana Islands

Guam

Caroline Islands

Truk Islands

Marshall Islands

Tarawa Island

Equator   CENTRAL PACIFIC AREA — NIMITZ   *Equator*

SOUTHWEST PACIFIC AREA — MACARTHUR | SOUTH PACIFIC AREA — GHOMLEY/HALSEY

New Guinea

Bismarck Archipelago

Rabaul

Port Moresby

Dutch East Indies

Soerabaja

Darwin

Solomon Islands

Guadalcanal

Espiritu Santo Island

Coral Sea

Vanuatu Islands

New Caledonia

Noumea

Fiji

Tropic of Capricorn

Australia

Brisbane

Sydney

South Pacific Ocean

New Zealand

N
W · E
S

© Mark Stein Studios, 1999

120°E   135°E   150°E   165°E   180°

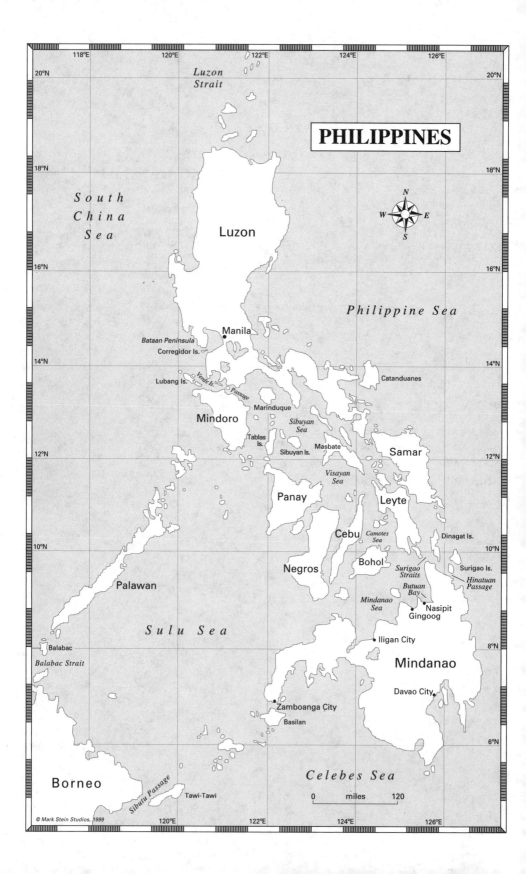

PHILIPPINES

Luzon Strait

South China Sea

Philippine Sea

Luzon

Manila

Bataan Peninsula
Corregidor Is.

Lubang Is.
Verde Is.
Passage

Mindoro

Marinduque

Sibuyan Sea

Tablas Is.

Sibuyan Is.

Masbate

Samar

Visayan Sea

Panay

Leyte

Cebu

Camotes Sea

Dinagat Is.

Negros

Bohol

Surigao Straits

Surigao Is.

Hinatuan Passage

Butuan Bay

Palawan

Mindanao Sea

Nasipit
Gingoog

Catanduanes

Sulu Sea

Iligan City

Balabac

Balabac Strait

Mindanao

Davao City

Zamboanga City

Basilan

Borneo

Celebes Sea

Sibutu Passage

Tawi-Tawi

0   miles   120

© Mark Stein Studios, 1999

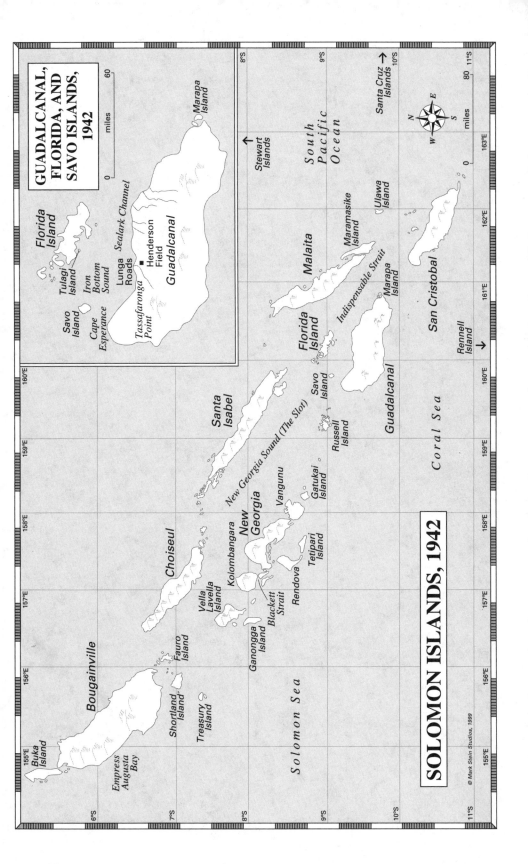

GUADALCANAL, FLORIDA, AND SAVO ISLANDS, 1942

0   60
miles

Florida Island

Tulagi Island
Iron Bottom Sound
Savo Island
Cape Esperance
Tassafaronga Point
Lunga Roads
Henderson Field
Guadalcanal
Sealark Channel
Marapa Island

8°S
Stewart Islands

9°S

10°S
Santa Cruz Islands

80
miles
0

11°S

N
E
S
W

160°E   159°E   158°E   157°E   156°E   155°E

6°S

7°S

8°S

9°S

10°S

11°S

South Pacific Ocean

Malaita
Maramasike Island
Ulawa Island
Marapa Island
Indispensable Strait
Florida Island
Savo Island
Russell Island
San Cristobal
Rennell Island
Guadalcanal
Coral Sea

163°E   162°E   161°E   160°E   159°E   158°E   157°E   156°E   155°E

Santa Isabel
New Georgia Sound (The Slot)
Choiseul
Vella Lavella Island
Kolombangara
Blackett Strait
New Georgia
Vangunu
Gatukai Island
Rendova
Tetipari Island
Ganongga Island
Bougainville
Fauro Island
Shortland Island
Treasury Island
Empress Augusta Bay
Buka Island

Solomon Sea

SOLOMON ISLANDS, 1942

© Mark Stein Studios, 1999

CAST OF CHARACTERS

Alton C. Ingram, Lieutenant
"Todd"

Executive Officer.

Jeremiah T. Landa, Commander
"Boom Boom"

Captain.

Leonard P. Seltzer
"Leo"

Boatswain's Mate Second Class.

Luther T. Dutton, Lieutenant

Gunnery Officer.

Henry E. Kelly, Lieutenant
"Hank"

Chief Engineer.

Jack W. Wilson, Lieutenant (JG)

Fire Control Officer.

Howard Skala

Chief Fire Controlman.

Ronald T. Lavery

Shipfitter First Class.

Eric Monaghan
"Bucky"

Pharmacist's Mate First Class.

L. A. Briley

Quartermaster Second Class.

Willard F. Justice

Yeoman Third Class.

Thomas N. Hopkins

Machinist's Mate Third Class.

Howard T. Thomas

Seaman First Class.

John T. Wilcox

Seaman First Class.

Oliver P. Toliver III, Lieutenant (JG)
"Ollie"

Gunnery Officer, U.S.S. *Riley*
(DD 452).

Theodore R. Myszynski, Captain,
USN
"Rocko"

Commodore, Destroyer Squadron
Twelve.
Flag in U.S.S. *Porter* (DD356).

W. M. Gobbell, MD,
Lieutenant, USN (MC)

Doctor aboard U.S.S. *Zeilin* (APA-3).

Joseph R. Prentice

Pharmacist's Mate Third Class, U.S.S. *Zeilin* (APA 3).

Antonio De Silva

Aviation Ordnanceman Second Class.

U. S. NAVY, ASHORE

Raymond A. Spruance, Rear Admiral

Chief of Staff to Admiral Chester W. Nimitz, Commander in Chief, Pacific Fleet.

Maynard T. Falkenberg, Captain, USN

Spruance's Staff Intelligence Officer.

William F. Halsey, Jr., Vice Admiral

Commander, Task Force 16.

Miles Browning, Captain, USN

Halsey's Chief of Staff.

Julian Brown, Major, USMC

Halsey's Staff Intelligence Officer.

Robert L. Ghormley, Vice Admiral

Commander, South Pacific Area and South Pacific Force.

John T. Mott, Major General, USMC

Staff Intelligence Officer under Vice Admiral Ghormley.

Robert A. Jessup, Captain, USN

Ghormley's Chief of Staff.

Earl Babcock

Seaman First Class and elevator operator.

U. S. ARMY

Helen Z. Durand, First Lieutenant

On Mindanao, Philippines.

Otis DeWitt, Major

Aide to General Sutherland.

Richard K. Sutherland, Major General

Aide to General Douglas MacArthur.

OTHER AMERICANS—CIVILIANS

Wong Lee

On Mindanao, Philippines.

Suzy Lee

Wong Lee's daughter.

Frank and Kate Durand

Helen's parents.

George K. Atwell

Vice President Research, Winslow River Corporation.

Cassidy

FBI agent.

FILIPINOS

Don Pablo Amador	Ex-Deputy Finance Minister under President Quezon and leader of resistance, northeastern Mindanao.
Emilio Legaspi	Resistance guerrillero.
Felipe Estaque	Resistance guerrillero.
Manuel Carillo	Resistance guerrillero.
Carlos Rameriez	Resistance guerrillero.
Carmen Lai Lai	Collaborator.

IMPERIAL JAPANESE NAVY

Hayashi Fujimoto, Rear Admiral (Shōsō)	Father of Katsumi Fujimoto.
Yoshi Tomo, Lieutenant	The Shōsō's aide.

SERVICE BARGE 212, NASIPIT, PHILIPPINES

Katsumi Fujimoto, Lieutenant Commander	Captain.
Hisa Kunisawa, Warrant Officer	Salvage Officer.
Koki Jimbo, Lieutenant	Intelligence Officer.
Kenji Ogata, Lieutenant	Repair Officer.
Yawata, Seaman	Fujimoto's orderly.

SOVIETS
U.S.S.R. SAN FRANCISCO CONSULATE

Eduard Ianovich Dezhnev, Senior Lieutenant, Soviet Navy	Naval attaché.
Sergei Zenit, Captain Third Rank, NKVD	*Zampolit,* political officer aboard the *Dzhurma,* TAD to consulate.
Georgiy Voronin	NKVD enforcer.
Yuri Moskvitin	Telegraphist Second Class.
Michael Fedotov, Captain Second Rank	Captain of the prison ship *Dzhurma.*

MOSCOW, U.S.S.R., LUBYANKA PRISON

Lavrenty Pavlovich Beria, Commissar	NKVD—*Narodnyi Kommissariat Vnutrennikh Del*—State security police. Second most powerful man in the U.S.S.R. under Premier Josef Stalin.
Vasiliy Laptev, Colonel	NKVD, Beria's assistant.
Dmitriy	Beria's bodyguard.

GERMANS
REICH EMBASSY, TOKYO, JAPAN

Doctor Dieter V. Birkenfeld	A Soviet spy posing as a newspaper correspondent for the *Frankfurter Zeitung*.
Karl Schmidt	SS thug.

FOREWORD

Major General Alexander M. Patch, U.S. Army commander of the Americal Division on Guadalcanal, sent the following radio message to Admiral William F. Halsey, headquartered aboard the command ship U.S.S. *Argonne* (AG 31) in Nouméa, New Caledonia:

TOTAL AND COMPLETE DEFEAT OF JAPANESE FORCES ON GUADALCANAL EFFECTED TODAY ... TOKYO EXPRESS NO LONGER HAS TERMINUS ON GUADALCANAL.

Halsey sent a copy right away to Admiral Chester Nimitz, commander in chief of the Pacific Fleet (CinCPac), in Pearl Harbor. At the time, Nimitz was in the hospital with a serious dose of malaria. Halsey's action was wise, for his boss brightened considerably upon receipt of the message and was back at his desk within a few days.

Thus ended a series of bloody land, air, and sea battles contesting an island critical to the Japanese's southward advance toward Australia, where they planned to at least sever American supply lines, if not invade the continent.

With Guadalcanal stabilized, Halsey turned his attention to securing the rest of the Solomon archipelago, while General Douglas MacArthur began his thrust into New Guinea and on toward his promise of "I shall return" to the Philippines. Simultaneously, Rear Admiral Raymond A. Spruance, hero of the Battle of Midway, and later chief of staff to Nimitz, commenced his campaign across the Central Pacific, starting with Tarawa in the Gilbert Islands.

The battle for Guadalcanal served not only the Allies' strategic interests, but their tactical interests as well, relative to the land, air, and sea battles fought over the island. Both sides lost about the same number of ships and airplanes. But the Japanese suffered large losses in personnel: an estimated 24,000 (with thousands more dying en route) out of 36,000 committed— compared to the United States' casualties of 1,600 killed and 4,250 wounded out of 60,000 directly involved.

At sea, the Japanese had fine ships with crews highly skilled in night tactics. They were supported by their vastly superior Type 93 torpedo, later dubbed the "long lance" by Samuel Eliot Morison in his fifteen-volume work *History of the United States Naval Operations in World War II*. With the Churchill/ Roosevelt "Europe First" policy, new U.S. Navy ships entered the area at a trickle, with the United States' naval forces at best on parity with the Japanese and many times far less in numbers and tonnage. This was especially so after the loss of the heavy carrier U.S.S. *Hornet* in the Battle of the St. Cruz Islands on October 27, 1942, leaving the U.S. Navy with only one operational carrier in the entire Pacific.

The naval campaign for Guadalcanal began with the Battle of Savo Island and ended with the Battle of the Rennell Islands, with seven major sea battles fought during the period. Both sides slugged it out like punch-drunk boxers, one having extraordinary eyesight (radar) but not utilizing it well, while the other side had a solid roundhouse punch (the Type 93 torpedo) but didn't capitalize when major victories were within grasp.

Relating details doesn't come easy for those who have fought in sea battles, whether their opponents were on the surface, in the air, or underwater. The carnage is unimaginable. For example, visualize what a two-thousand-pound explosive projectile does as it smashes into a compartment full of men at a velocity of twenty-six hundred feet per second. From the times of Phoenician swords to Lord Nelson's twelve-pound cannons to today's Harpoon missile, war at sea is a bloody business. Crews don't just fight for flag and cargo. They defend their ship, their home, their only source of food and shelter, their only tangible connection to the safety and comfort of their hearths.

The sea battles described herein are real. Almost all of the flag officers and senior officials are real; the other characters are fictitious. Except for the *Fletcher* class destroyers *Howell* and *Riley,* the four-stacker *Stockwell,* and the submarines *Needlefish* and *Turbot,* the ships did exist. The suicide plane scene in chapter thirty-seven is a dramatization of an actual occurrence during the Battles of the Santa Cruz Islands when Lieutenant Commander Hunter Wood, Jr., heroically saved his destroyer, the U.S.S. *Smith* (DD 378). The U.S.S.R. maintained a consulate in San Francisco during World War II; it was closed in 1946, since they wouldn't allow the United States to set up a consulate in Vladivostok. However, the U.S.S.R. reopened a San Francisco consulate in a different location in the mid-1970s. During World War II, the Soviets had other consulates in New York City and Mexico City, which, along with the Washington, D.C., embassy, were bases for major espionage activities against the United States, much of it targeted to the Manhattan (atomic bomb) Project. Any mistakes are mine alone.

As before, I have been truly blessed with the help of many fine people. In part, they are: In matters of aviation, Richard Bertea, Gordon Curtis, and Robert Schlaefli. Dr. Frederick J. Milford, an expert in naval torpedoes, contributed priceless advice in naval ordnance and operations. In matters of Russian culture and language, Susan Kechekian at USC's Department of Slavic Studies and Professors Vladimir and Victorina Lefebvre, Department of Russian Programs, at the University of California at Irvine. Concerning historic San Francisco, Howard Mutz of the St. Francis Hotel and my old friend Richard L. Heilman. For medical information, Dr. Fred Meister and Hartley

J. E. Turpin, M.D., on pharmacology; Russell J. Striff, M.D., on traumatic medicine. In World War II matters, Alvin P. Cluster, Dr. Norman R. Fertig, Dr. Irvin F. Gellman, and H. Dale Hilton, Captain, USN (retired). Also, I couldn't have accomplished any of this without valuable support from Blair Armstrong; the Reverend David P. Comegys, Jr.; Valerie Finch, Roland R. Speers, Esq.; and Captain Jerry Sullivan, USN (retired); as well as the Orange County Fictionaries and the Newport Beach Public Library. And thanks to my agent, Todd Keithley, whose unselfish attention to many, many details stands in evidence of what synergy is all about. To Joe Veltre, my editor at St. Martin's Press, my unending appreciation.

Special friends and readers who threw me a line as I went down for the third time include Willard E. Dunlap III, Richard M. Geiler, Donald L. Phillips, Larry T. Smith, and again, Russell J. Striff, M.D. Special thanks to Dr. and Mrs. Robert L. Bennett and Gerald L. Govan. And always, to Janine, my wife, my love, who unselfishly edits my material.

JJG
Newport Beach, California
July 1998

*Truth is lacking, and he who departs from evil
makes himself a prey.*
ISAIAH 59:15

PROLOGUE

"There was a phone call for you a few minutes ago." Karl Schmidt unsnapped the top lock. As usual, the tall, mufti-dressed SS thug, with short orange-blond hair and thin lips, had formed his statement like a question.

"What?" Dieter Birkenfeld set his briefcase on the parquet floor, took out a handkerchief, and mopped his brow. The side door vestibule was furnished with a heavy, dark, side table bookended by two ornate upright chairs, weighing a hundred kilos each.

Schmidt took his time with the triple locks, making the cramped space seem hotter. "The telephone?" He reminded Birkenfeld. "Say, are you all right?"

"I got the call. Thanks," stammered Birkenfeld. *Slow down.*

With a shrug, Schmidt finished the locks and swung the door open. Sounds of Tokyo wafted in, with Berkenfeld hardly noticing the fetching glow of the late afternoon sun. It had been a warm, cloudless day, with a moderate breeze clearing the smoke from the steel furnaces and automobile exhaust. Usually they combined to form an oppressive, lung-searing haze as the factories around the great city ground out the tools of war twenty-four hours a day.

Get hold of yourself.

Schmidt leered. "And who is the lucky girl tonight?"

Birkenfeld tried to flash an even row of snowcap-white teeth. "Tanya." For years he'd joked with Schmidt about loose women.

Schmidt stepped out of the way, gave Birkenfeld a conspiratorial nod, and whistled. "Ahhh, Tanya. *Ja, ja?*"

Birkenfeld, a reporter for the *Berliner Zeitung,* drew to his full height of six feet four inches. His worst feature was a pockmarked face and, at forty-six, his weight had ballooned to 225. However, this was well overcome by his best features: a full head of dark graying hair, a thin mustache, and a piercing, near-professorial countenance that overwhelmed the German diplomatic staff—and their wives. Indeed, his rich baritone voice allowed him to easily penetrate the tightest of Tokyo's inner diplomatic and social circles. And with the lights out, Birkenfeld usually got what he wanted where women were concerned, be they German or Italian or American.

"Ja, ja?" Schmidt repeated, letting Birkenfeld pass.

"All right, Karl. All right. If you must know, she works at the Italian Embassy."

Schmidt gave a low whistle. "You mean Tanya Gabrielle?"

A surprised Birkenfeld stopped halfway down the steps, oblivious to Tokyo's cacophony. Horns honked, brakes screeched, and there was a constant thump-thumping somewhere two or three blocks away. "How did you know?" Schmidt really did amaze him. At times, the thug actually displayed small flashes of insight.

"She's the only one there worth dating. The rest are all animals."

"Yes. She's different, all right." Birkenfeld wondered if Schmidt was on to Tanya.

Schmidt's eyes narrowed. "Different, yes. Isn't she Armenian?"

My God! How does Schmidt know that? "On her grandmother's side." Changing the subject, he sputtered, "Tonight, she cooks roast goose."

"Just for the two of you?"

Birkenfeld did his best to screw on a pixie grin as he walked down the steps. "I'm all she needs."

"I'll make sure the quack checks you tomorrow for crabs. We must have none of that on sovereign Reich territory." Schmidt laughed as he closed the door.

"Sieg Heil, you pig," Birkenfeld muttered under his breath.

"Doctor Birkenfeld!" Schmidt's voice was like a thunderclap.

"Yes?" He turned around, his heart skipping a beat.

"You forgot this." Schmidt's leather heels quickly tapped down the marble steps. With a curt bow, he handed Birkenfeld his briefcase, said, *"Wiedersehen,"* then went up the stairs and slammed the door.

This morning, the day had been so beautiful that he'd decided not to ride his motorcycle and had walked the two kilometers to the embassy. And now he cursed himself as he stepped into the faceless, shoving crowd.

The trouble was, with all that was going on, he didn't realize he really loved Tanya until last night. She'd cried and talked about things that awakened his own past and what the Germans did to his family in World War I. The same thing had happened to her, it turned out, and they held on to one another, desperately, until it grew late and they had to encode for tonight's broadcast.

Birkenfeld ground his teeth in frustration. He had to get to Tanya's apartment fast, but he didn't have the damned motorcycle. And it was too dangerous to return to his apartment. But the good news was that there was a ship out tonight. He'd checked the papers. The *Vera Cruz,* with a cargo of farm equipment, was sailing for Valparaiso, Chile, at eleven o'clock and he'd managed to book passage for two. The agent had demanded cash. Five thousand American. Each. That would be no problem. Neat packages of fifty-dollar bills lay under a false bottom of the briefcase that Schmidt had just handed over. *Hurry.*

The embassy phone call Schmidt had referred to was on an open line, so Kiramatsu, one of his operatives, had to be cryptic. As Birkenfeld nodded in shocked silence, Kiramatsu relayed that the Tokubetsu Koto Kaisatu Bu (Tokko—civilian secret police) had come within a hair's breadth of arresting Major Abe, his mole on the Japanese General Staff. In panic, Abe had left Tokyo on a flight for Manchuria, returning to the relative safety of the amorphous Kwangtung Army. God only knew, Birkenfeld had learned, one could get lost in that organization, a political entity all of its own.

In a near-screech, Kiramatsu added that he'd just learned the Tokko's monitors were standing by on Birkenfeld's frequencies, ready to triangulate. Then Kiramatsu said he was headed for the country and rang off abruptly. His warning was clear. Stop Tanya before she tapped out her six o'clock broadcast to Moscow.

Roast goose. He wondered if he and Tanya would ever enjoy roast goose again. Maybe on the *Vera Cruz* after she cleared port.

Birkenfeld rounded a corner, seeing Tanya's apartment building halfway down the block. Here, in the middle of Tokyo, the sidewalk narrowed, forcing the people into a crush. His height saved him from being one of them, like one of a million-billion salmon charging up the river, fighting the rapids, crashing onto rocks, being thrust back only to try again madly, flapping its tail, pumping its gills, and gasping for oxygen. Only to return to—

Someone rabbit-chopped Birkenfeld in the back of the neck. The next thing he knew, he'd been shoved face-down on a car's floor—it smelled like a mixture of grease and American chewing gum. The car was a big one—a four-door sedan, Birkenfeld sensed as he wheezed and struggled. But, comically, his long legs still stuck out the door and people had to walk around them. Someone's knee dropped into his back, muttering in Japanese, smelling of garlic. Birkenfeld renewed his efforts and, with a loud groan, raised his 225-pound bulk off the floor. Just then another pair of knees crashed onto his shoulders. Through the man's legs (this one wore white trousers), Birkenfeld saw the crowd push past, not missing a step, moving silently on, unfazed, eyes straight ahead, not daring to leave the impression the scene was at all observed.

With a mighty gasp, Birkenfeld again raised to his elbows and began rolling over.

"*Chikusho!*" growled one of the men. Something smashed into Birkenfeld's temple and his head thumped to the floor.

Then something else was shoved over his nose and mouth, a rag. It was damp and—chloroform! Even without breathing, Birkenfeld felt the brittle tendrils biting into his nasal passages, his lungs.

In panic, he beat his feet on the sidewalk. Someone tried to slam the door on his long legs but only succeeded in bashing his ankles in the doorjamb. He gurgled and struggled and again beat his toes on the sidewalk in a macabre tattoo while the faceless crowd pushed past—like salmon.

And when his head felt like it burst, Birkenfeld heaved a frantic breath. . . .

PART ONE

Let a man once overcome his selfish terror at his own finitude,
and his finitude is, in one sense, overcome.
GEORGE SANTAYANA
THE ETHICS OF SPINOZA

I am willing to believe each of us has a guardian angel,
if you fellows will concede to me that each of us
has a familiar devil as well.
JOSEPH CONRAD
LORD JIM

CHAPTER ONE

The ship's running lights were switched off. Steaming in ponderous circles on the windless night, she slogged through dark swells five miles west of the Farallon Islands. The moon was down, yet nervously she waited for her Coast Guard escort to lead her through the minefield into San Francisco Bay. After a sixteen-day, 4,570-mile trek from Vladivostok, the freighter was tired and nearly out of fuel oil to feed her ancient boiler. Without cargo she was top-heavy, rolling awkwardly in the swells, her crew cursing and holding on as she creaked from side to side.

Displacing 6,908 tons, the ship was built in Schiedam, Holland, in 1921. Cyrillic letters spelled DZHURMA on her curved transom, from which drooped the red and gold ensign of the Union of Soviet Socialist Republics, a neutral in the Pacific war. Lazy wisps of smoke meandered from a narrow stack on her midships superstructure high above pale yellow decks. Long, reddish brown streaks ran down her gray superstructure, trickled across her decks, and finished the trip to her faded white boot-topping on the waterline. Countless storms had dished in her hull plates, making the *Dzhurma* look every bit of her twenty-one years, almost as if she were a stooped old woman hobbling down the hall, a hand braced on her hip.

She hailed from a large fleet of prison ships whose holds were stuffed with thousands of pitiful wretches who had survived Stalin's execution squads. Instead of dying, their greater misfortune was to be shipped by rail to Vladivostok, then boarded on the *Dzhurma* or one of her sisters, for a hellish trip through the Bering Strait to Ambarchik at the mouth of the Kolyma and on to the gulags above the Arctic Circle.

Nevastroi, Indigirka, Dalstroi, Dneprostroi, Nikolai, Felix Dzerzhinsky, Igarka, Kulu, and *Sovlatvia*: Each ship's name was a death sentence. Among them, they averaged five thousand prisoners per shipment, with the *Dzhurma, Dalstroi,* and *Sovlatvia* acknowledged as the core of the slave fleet.

The stench of misery, perspiration, excrement, and death lingered among the ships, but the *Dzhurma*'s odor was unusually fetid. It was most noticeable on those warm evenings when a soft wind grazed her quarter, the ship steaming in her own stagnant air. Even so, her crew, unrotated for three years, grew accustomed to the rank smell, impossible to wash away or eradicate with chemicals.

On this trip there were no prisoners, only a crew of twenty. In the pilothouse, her skipper, Kapitan Vtorovo Ranga—Captain Second Rank—Michael Fedotov, braced himself against the roll, wearing a stained Navy surplus pea coat. He was stocky, with virtually no neck, bald, a Van Dyke beard, and the largest and blackest eyes east of the Urals. With Fedotov was the ship's first officer and three enlisted watch-standers gulping the last of their ersatz coffee. Five others stood watch in the engine room, with the rest of the crew lying in their bunks, some listening to a San Francisco jazz station, others pretending to sleep. But with the ship's motion and the visage of a Japanese submarine firing a torpedo into the engine room, one could only look at the rusted overhead and hope for a quick rendezvous with the American escort or a quick death in the cold Pacific.

The bridge intercom buzzed and Fedotov reached for the handset. After three low grunts, the *Dzhurma*'s skipper hung up and trudged to the hatchway. Eduard Dezhnev stood on the port bridge wing, binoculars to his eyes, scanning the ocean, his body rigid with concentration as if expecting to find an entire fleet lurking behind the Farallon Islands. At five-eleven, Dezhnev had dark red hair combed straight back, and was fair-complected with a medium build. His chest and arms, although not prominent, were well defined, conveying a sense of power and alacrity when he moved. It was difficult to disguise a limp, and most of the time his left foot twisted out when he walked. It was a prosthesis, Fedotov knew; Dezhnev, commander of a patrol boat, had lost his left leg in a battle with German E-boats last winter in the Gulf of Riga.

Fedotov had orders to treat Dezhnev like a VIP. After all, the man was a Starshiy-Leytenant in the Voyenno Morskoy Flot—a senior lieutenant in the Soviet Navy. But the man kept to himself and Fedotov knew little of him, except for the Gulf of Riga business. But fighting boredom, Dezhnev had volunteered for everything during the tedious voyage from Vladivostok, practically becoming a member of the crew. For the past three hours, he'd been port lookout, this time filling in for able body seaman Lodoga, ill in his bunk after drinking homemade brew.

"Dezhnev."

Dezhnev, wearing a black turtleneck sweater, pea coat, and dark work trousers, walked over and leaned in the pilothouse hatchway. "Yes, Sir?"

Fedotov nodded to the phone. "Zenit wants to know why you aren't in the wardroom."

"Had to stand a watch, Sir." During the voyage, Dezhnev had more than subtly demonstrated contempt for Sergei Zenit. Even though he tried to avoid him, there were times when he actually had to snub the man to stay out of his path. For Zenit was the ship's *zampolit,* or political officer: a politician who wore the naval uniform and stood first in line to suck up the glory. *Zampolits* were not regular Navy. They were NKVD—Narodnyi Kommissariat Vnutrennikh Del—state security police, who hid behind their rank when the going grew difficult. Zenit had no idea what made a ship run, was of no use while under way, and openly defied the captain by refusing to stand watches of any kind.

The ship slowly circled, letting a small breeze catch up to sweep across the fantail, bringing once again the strange sweet-foul odor.

Fedotov said, "Go on down. I'll fill in until your relief comes."

Dezhnev stood there, his eyes burning.

The air was moist for this time of year. Fedotov sniffed and wiped his nose on his sleeve.

A curtain seemed to rise above Dezhnev's face. "Thank you, Sir. No sign of the American escort yet." He handed his binoculars to Fedotov and headed for a companionway.

"Eduard."

Dezhnev turned. "Captain?"

"Go easy."

"Yes, Sir." Dezhnev hobbled down a ladder, his cane clattering on the steps.

On the main deck, the wardroom was perhaps five by ten meters, with a long table running athwartship. On the starboard side, a serving buffet stood against the aft bulkhead, where a pass-through window gave way to a small galley just aft. Two tattered couches, a chipped metal game table, and folding chairs were scattered about the port side. Dezhnev walked in, finding Zenit seated alone, wearing the coat of a *kapitan tret'yevo ranga*—captain third rank, one grade senior to him. He had dark curly hair, was much taller than Dezhnev, and was a bit on the heavy side, at least as much as a Soviet diet would allow. Zenit's nose was long and drew to a fine point, as if carved by a wood whittler. His blue-gray eyes were close together, and he wore a thin mustache above a protruding upper lip. As the *Dzhurma*'s *zampolit,* Zenit was charged with the cultural, moral, and political development of the *Dzhurma*'s officers and crew. But Dezhnev knew that half of Zenit's time was spent collecting the crew's mandatory contribution to the Merchant Seaman's Retirement Fund, then raking ten percent off the top. It was a way of life in the Navy and the grumbling crew eventually gave in, lest they end up on the beach, rifle in hand, marching off to fight German tanks.

After too many peppermint schnapps one night, Fedotov told Dezhnev the San Francisco trip presented new challenges to Captain Third Rank Sergei Zenit. After a layover for much-needed repairs to the *Dzhurma*'s boiler, she was due to take aboard a yet-to-be-specified cargo financed by Lend-Lease dollars, courtesy of the American Congress. Then she would sail for Vladivostok. Except . . .

. . . the Americans didn't know she would stop first in Yokohama, Japan, where Zenit would sell much of her cargo to the Imperial Japanese Army. Zenit was counting on another shipment of penicillin, the wonder drug now mass-produced by the Americans, that cured everything from gangrene to gonorrhea. Fedotov knew Zenit would demand that his Japanese broker pay in gold bullion. Next, Zenit would rake off another twenty percent, kicking back ten to the Japanese broker and keeping the other ten. The rest of the proceeds would go to the NKVD. All in gold bullion, of course.

Zenit leafed through a file as Dezhnev sat, propping his cane against the table.

"You're fifteen minutes late." Zenit withdrew a flimsy from the folder; it looked like a radio message.

"I was standing watch."

"Sir." Zenit gave him a cold stare, expecting a reply.

"Sir."

"Yes." Then Zenit returned to his folder.

The ship careened on a swell to port. Dezhnev caught the cane just as it threatened to spin away. After securing it, he tried again. "Fedotov is filling in for me."

Zenit folded his hands and looked around the wardroom before focusing on Dezhnev. "Well, now. How do you like our part of the Navy?"

"To tell you honestly, this ship stinks."

"Of course. Did you ever wonder why, comrade?"

"Actually, yes." *What the hell is this?*

Leaning forward, Zenit drew a deep breath and said, "Three years ago we boarded a load of prisoners in Vladivostok, cleared the Bering Strait, and sailed into the Arctic. But it was late autumn and we'd had a boiler break-down. We were two and a half weeks late getting underway, you see."

Dezhnev scratched his head, wondering why Zenit was telling him this.

Looking into space, Zenit continued, "Winter came early, and we were trapped in the ice pack near Wrangel Island. We carried only two thousand people on that trip—all of them criminals of some sort: murderers, rapists, thieves, and political malcontents, you see. They were in the forward hold."

Dezhnev closed his eyes momentarily, trying to visualize what it would be like living with two thousand souls in a stinking, cramped hold.

"After four weeks in the ice, a fire broke out. The prisoners"—Zenit lit a cigarette, took a long puff, and exhaled—"well, with this fire they rioted, you see. We had to hose them down and keep them battened in the hold. But we couldn't control the fire." He leaned forward and speared Dezhnev with his eyes. "The water boiled and they were roasted alive."

Dezhnev gasped, "All of them?"

"Every last one. I . . . I still hear their screams in my sleep.

"Then . . . then, it was sixteen weeks until the icebreaker reached us. Only the crew remained. Thirty-five in all. Thirty-three, actually. Two committed suicide, you see."

An emptiness swept over Dezhnev.

"That is why the ship stinks, comrade." After a pause, Zenit asked, "Does anything else bother you? Perhaps you would like a tour of the forward cargo hold?"

Dezhnev tried to comprehend what sort of men crewed the *Dzhurma*. Living with constant death and human misery, he wondered how they maintained their sanity. Or did they?

Suddenly the ship's motion changed to a deliberate rolling. Both could tell she now steamed on a straight course. "On to San Francisco," Dezhnev said.

Zenit stared at Dezhnev for a moment, then let his eyes fall to a folder on the table. "This says you commanded a torpedo boat and, hmmm"—he made a show of flipping pages—"and you shot it out with two German E-boats in the Gulf of Riga, sinking at least one."

"Yes."

"But then you lost your boat?" It sounded like an accusation.

It was in his file. All the fool had to do was read on. "Yes."

"And your crew was lost, too?"

"Yes."

"Yes, what?" Zenit snapped. He wanted another "Sir."

"A direct hit, Sir. I remember nothing except being fished from the water."

"And your leg?"

Dezhnev raised his left leg and thumped it twice on the deck. "That, too. Just below the knee. Sacrificed for the glory of the *Rodina*."

Zenit didn't miss a beat. "Yes, an artificial leg. Made in Britain, I understand. Mmmm. Very privileged. Lets you get around very well. Does it still hurt?" His eyes sparkled.

It hurt like hell, especially in this damp weather. And it still wasn't fully mended. But Dezhnev wasn't about to say anything. "What is it you want, comrade?"

Zenit wasn't ready yet. "And you carry the Order of Lenin?"

"They gave that to me, yes."

"Hmmmm. And your mission now?

"I'll be leaving the ship . . ."

"Yes?"

". . . to be assigned as naval attaché to the San Francisco consulate."

"Doing what?"

Dezhnev shrugged. "What all naval attachés do. Discovering the latest in your host's tactics and technologies."

"Come, now. Doesn't Beria have something else in mind for you? Your English, for example, is perfect. Aren't you Bykovo-trained?"

Dezhnev sat back. Zenit trod on dangerous ground, invoking the name of Lavrenty Pavlovich Beria, NKVD commissar, one of the most powerful men in the Soviet Union and second only to Premier Josef Stalin. Also, he had referred to Bykovo, a school for spies sixty kilometers north of Moscow, established by Beria in 1938. It was a large camp of gifted youths in their late teens to mid-twenties, from pianists to athletes, who were Americanized, learning everything from baseball to *What's up, doc?* Dezhnev had spent six months there, training and recouping from his leg wound.

With the slightest of smiles, Zenit prodded further. "An actor in peace-time?"

Now the fool was showing off. Dezhnev picked up his cane and tapped it on the deck.

Zenit reached to a chair beside him and produced a thick packet of papers. "Your assignment has changed, comrade." He tossed the packet before Dezhnev. "And I am to be your control. You will find the authorization in there."

A cold sickness grew deep in Dezhnev's stomach. He picked up the papers, finding a long transmittal. It was signed by Beria. "I see nothing here about you being my control."

"I wasn't supposed to say anything until our arrival in San Francisco. But because of this message"—he held up the flimsy—"we have to talk now. It came in two hours ago: priority. I've been decrypting the damn thing. So there you have it." Zenit handed over the radio flimsy.

Dezhnev read:

BURN WHEN READ

TOP SECRET—OPERATION KOMET—TOP SECRET
EYES ONLY—EDUARD DEZHNEV, LT, VMF.,—DZHURMA 11 AUGUST 1942

1. KAPT/3R SERGEI ZENIT APPOINTED YOUR CONTROL.

2. RADIO INTELLIGENCE LAST TWO DAYS INDICATES U.S. NAVY SUFFERED MAJOR DEFEAT IN SOUTH PACIFIC IN SOLOMON ISLANDS. STILL CONFIRMING BUT IT APPEARS THEY LOST ONE POSSIBLY TWO CRUISERS AND ONE DESTROYER IN NIGHT ACTION NEAR SAVO ISLAND. JAPANESE TYPE 93 TORPEDOES APPARENTLY DID THE TRICK. BE ADVISED TO LEAD WITH THIS ONE. MESSAGE ENDS.

LAPTEV FOR BERIA

BURN WHEN READ

Dezhnev was flabbergasted. The thought of following orders from this dreg ran counter to everything he believed in.

Zenit must have read his thoughts, for he said, "If not for me, comrade, for the *Rodina*."

"*Da,*" Dezhnev replied. Wait and see. That was the only thing to do.

"Finished?"

"Yes." Dezhnev handed it over.

Zenit held the pages over a large ashtray littered with brackish Russian and Egyptian cigarette butts. Drawing a gleaming American Ronson cigarette lighter, he flicked it into life. As the document burned, Dezhnev asked, "What's this about leading with this one? And what is a Type 93 torpedo anyway?"

Zenit cocked his head slightly, adopting an officious air. "Let's begin at the beginning." He waited, giving Dezhnev an unfocused stare.

Dezhnev almost laughed aloud. "Very well."

"As you saw from the message, you are assigned to Operation KOMET."

"Yes?"

Zenit checked his notes. "It's in two phases. The first involves General Douglas MacArthur, who is running for president in . . ." He flipped pages and looked up. "When is it?"

Play along. "Their next presidential election will be in November 1944."

"Yes. November 1944. Now, the Japanese think there is an enormous potential to disrupt the American leadership. That's phase one."

Thoughts of Lend-Lease and American convoys bringing badly needed supplies to Murmansk to fight the Nazis swirled through Dezhnev's head. "They're supposed to be our friends."

"That's just the point. They are our friends, you see. But it won't hurt to slow them down a little. Beria is convinced the Japanese will ultimately lose the war in the Pacific, and it looks like they're beginning to realize this, too." Zenit rolled Beria's name off his tongue as if he'd been out drinking vodka with him just last night. "Especially after the Battle of Midway. His best estimate is that it will become a war of attrition, with the Americans outproducing the Japanese and defeating them in 1948, perhaps 1949."

"Midway?"

"In June, the Japanese lost four large attack carriers in one decisive blow near Midway Island. This essentially nullified their ability to remain on the offensive. Now they feel off balance."

"I hadn't heard."

"You were in Bykovo, listening to jazz and sucking up chocolate milkshavings."

"Milkshakes."

"Yes. And with the Birkenfeld fiasco, we owe the Japanese a favor."

Dezhnev raised his arms and flopped them to his side.

Zenit nodded. "All right. Dieter Birkenfeld and Richard Sorge. Spies, they worked for us. In Tokyo, they posed as newspaper correspondents in the German Embassy for the past five years. They were brilliant, uncanny. They penetrated the highest levels of government and unearthed an enormous amount of top secret data. Then"—Zenit's voice softened—"they were caught last October. They confessed, you see. Birkenfeld has been executed; we don't know about Sorge. That's why we owe the Japanese a favor. And we're trying to do something for them without violating our neutrality."

"What is it, precisely, that you want me to do?"

"Monitor MacArthur's campaign. You see, like you, he's an actor, very dramatic. The Japanese figure MacArthur's speeches can undermine confidence in President Roosevelt's government by blaming him for the disaster at Pearl Harbor. They're hoping world opinion will swing against Roosevelt if MacArthur does run for president. It doesn't matter if he wins. Enough damage will have been done. But if MacArthur should win, it will be very disruptive to the American political and military systems, since he would have to vacate his post in Australia while kicking Roosevelt and his cronies out of the White House.''

"And if MacArthur doesn't openly blame Roosevelt for Pearl Harbor?''

"Then you are to look for ways to make it appear so. You see, the Japanese need the disruption to buy time.''

Dezhnev leaned forward, his hand on the table, balling into a fist. "I'm not a politician, damnit.''

Zenit shrugged.

"What about the staff there now? Why can't they do this?''

"Apparently Beria thinks you're more qualified. A combat veteran trained in American nuances.''

Dezhnev spun the cane handle between his palms. "KOMET.''

"Yes, KOMET.'' Zenit opened another file. "On to phase two. A part of being a naval attaché requires that you gain the trust of your American Navy counterparts. At your discretion, you are authorized to release Japanese secret technical data to appropriate American personnel. This will give you credibility with the Americans. Then you, in turn, may be able to learn some of their secrets. Some that we may want to pass on to the Japanese.''

Screw the Americans while screwing the Japanese. What sort of game is Beria playing?

Zenit jabbed the table with his middle finger, something that would have looked comical in America. "Let me be clear on this. You are to go to the meetings, attend the parties, and listen. You will stay alert. You will stay sober. You will not chase women. You will make friends by dropping the little Japanese eggs where appropriate. And you will gain their confidence.''

"What do I have to give them?''

Zenit ticked on his fingers: "Included in your package is microfiche on such things as Japan's new M2597 light tank, their 240-millimeter howitzer, their current naval order of battle. And as the cherry on top of the pie''—he pointed again with his middle finger—"there is some rudimentary data on the Type 93 torpedo.''

With his forefinger, Dezhnev stirred the ashes in the tray. "The radio message said the Type 93 had been used in the Solomon Islands battle.''

"Yes. Apparently the Type 93 is the best torpedo in the world.''

Dezhnev sniffed. "Nonsense.''

"Check for yourself. It's all there.''

"I plan to.''

Zenit looked from the hatch to Dezhnev, then to his folder. "Like you say, this ship stinks. I'll be glad to get off, too. When we get in San Fran—"

The roar was terrific. The whole deck seemed to lift, and a great light flashed before their eyes. Dezhnev was knocked to his hands and knees. Then he rolled to his back, realizing there had been an explosion.

CHAPTER TWO

Smoke enveloped them. And he felt the rush of deep, humid, hot steam.

Then there were horrible, gurgling screams while the ship's whistle sounded six short blasts: the danger signal. It started another series but wheezed into silence.

Coughing and choking, Dezhnev rose and stumbled into the passageway. Lights flickered, smoke gushed. He couldn't see. Grabbing a battle lantern, he lurched to the engine room hatch, hearing more screams. Just then a wraith crawled up. Dezhnev helped pull him out onto the main deck. He peered down and looked into the scalded face of Kharbov, the assistant engineer. Singed flesh hung from his scalp. "Anybody else down there?" Dezhnev yelled.

"All done for," the man gasped. "Scalded."

"What happened?"

Kharbov's eyes rolled, then he focused. "Fuel oil. The feed pump shot too much oil in the fire box. Regulator didn't . . ." He passed out.

Dezhnev eased the engineer to the deck. Grabbing Zenit's coat, he shouted, "Hurry!"

Zenit stood frozen, his face dead white.

"Hurry, you stupid sonofabitch! Do you want to die, too?" He spun Zenit and pushed him stumbling out on the main deck. In the half-light, they found four large deck-mounted emergency fire-room valves. Dezhnev leaned over one, perhaps thirty centimeters in diameter. "Fuel-oil feed valve." He tried to rotate it. "Rusty," he shouted, and dropped to his knees for a better purchase. Looking up to a wild-eyed Zenit, he gasped, "Help me."

Yelling sailors poured on deck, jumbling about. Four started lowering a lifeboat.

Dezhnev again yelled to Zenit, "Come on!"

". . . can't . . ." Zenit moved to join the men milling near the lifeboat.

Dezhnev jumped up and grabbed Zenit by the collar, kicked him in the butt, and shoved him over to the valve. "Start turning, you dumb bastard, or we all die!"

Somehow, Zenit got the idea the valve was important: that turning the valve might keep the ship from blowing up and sinking, his efforts thus saving him from the inconvenience of boarding a lifeboat and bobbing up and down in the Pacific's cold waters. He stooped, and began twisting with Dezhnev. With groans and squeaks, the valve turned, the going easier the more they rotated. Two minutes later, it was done.

"That should do it," wheezed Dezhnev. For confirmation, they saw another assistant engineer stand over the engine-room hatch and say, "Fire's out."

Just then Fedotov dashed down the companionway, his eyes bulging.

Zenit looked up and made a show of breathing in quick gasps. "All finished, Captain. The fire is extinguished."

"Quick thinking," Fedotov said. "You'll get a commendation, Sergei."

Zenit bowed deeply.

Fedotov rolled his eyes at Dezhnev.

Someone yelled from the rail. There was a commotion as the American Coast Guard escort nosed alongside, also running without lights. Figures could be seen outlined on her bridge. A megaphone sounded, ". . . what's your problem?"

Fedotov stood on a ladder and shouted in shrill, accented English, "Boiler explosion. No power. Soon, do we drift into your mines?"

The reply floated back to them, ". . . we can tow . . . stand by to take a heaving line . . ."

"*Da.* Thank you. God bless America." Fedotov waved and rushed up the ladder to the bridge.

Zenit looked at the moaning Kharbov, then walked to the rail and stared in the distance. "This is long overdue."

Dezhnev followed him. "What do you mean?"

"Ironic, don't you think? Our turn to be scalded. Just like those wretches in the Arctic." Then he focused on Dezhnev. "You call me a dumb sonofabitch? You call me a bastard?" Veins bulged on Zenit's forehead as he thrust a forefinger at the bridge. "There's your dumb sonofabitch. Your bastard!"

Dezhnev yelled over the commotion, "Who are you talking about?"

Men stood all around them. For such a small crew, their noise was incredible. It seemed everyone wanted to crawl in the starboard lifeboat. Zenit waved a hand toward the bridge. "You know why we were late getting underway from Vladivostok in 1939?"

Dezhnev shook his head.

"Fedotov, your dumb sonofabitch. He had all the parts he needed to overhaul his stupid boiler. From America. Everything he needed. But he sold the stuff: feed pumps and the fuel pumps and whatever else you call it, all on the black market. Then he made the engineers remachine the old parts with lathes and whatever else. They had to use cardboard and tar and chewing gum for gaskets. It's a wonder the damn ship hasn't sunk. He does this all the time.''

Dezhnev glanced at the Coast Guard ship as it eased forward. Someone on her fantail spun a monkey fist over his head, then released it. It arced though the air perfectly and thunked on the *Dzhurma*'s fo'c'sle.

On the bridge, Fedotov jammed a megaphone to his lips and screeched at his foredeck crew, ''Hurry!''

Needing no urging, the *Dzhurma*'s men started hauling across the messenger, which was connected to the tow line.

Zenit began laughing. ''And guess what he did with the money.''

Dezhnev looked at him dumbly.

Leaning back, Zenit laughed again, almost Homerically, and once again cast a long, bony finger up to the bridge. ''Your stupid sonofabitch up there bought barrels of lye to kill the smell in the forward hold. And with what was left over, he bought clothes and boots and blankets for his crew, that's what he did!''

CHAPTER THREE

It was a crisp and cool sunny morning, wind stirring whitecaps on the bay. Wearing dress khakis, Lieutenant Todd Ingram shivered as he walked into the lobby of the Federal Building. An elevator door yawned open and he stepped in quickly, pressing his six-two frame against the rear bulkhead, luxuriating in the relative warmth. He had an angular face with steel-gray eyes; perspiration on his forehead evaporated quickly with the breeze that trailed after. A giddiness ran through him and he still wasn't sure if the shivering was due to an intolerance to cooler temperatures or to the weight he'd lost. Until last June, he'd been in the tropics for over two years and the doctor said he would still feel light-headed for a while. He'd been at Corregidor, in the Philippines, and had dropped to 130 pounds. After a five-month siege, the Japanese finally took Corregidor, with Ingram escaping the night it fell.

Now he was back to 165, ten pounds less than normal, and had been told to avoid rich foods. In a hurry this morning at the BOQ, he hadn't given a thought when the gravel-voiced cook boasted the pancakes were made with cement, the sausages from ground-up bird beaks. Now Ingram believed him, his stomach doing flip-flops. With each agonizing contraction, he was convinced the cook was some reprobate boatswain's mate just out of the brig.

A seaman apprentice wearing dress whites was seated at the elevator control panel. "Floor?"

The boy hadn't faced him or called him "Sir." But Ingram could only think of keeping a lid on the mini-eruptions in his belly. "Umphff."

"Floor?" the sailor repeated.

"Sorry," gasped Ingram. It was an effort to speak and all he really wanted to do right now was dash for the nearest bathroom and yield to his misery.

The sailor turned and gave Ingram a foul look. His face burst with pimples and he couldn't have been more than eighteen. "Floor." It sounded like an order.

For a moment, Ingram panicked. He couldn't remember where the damned meeting was scheduled—only that he had been ordered to be at the Federal Building and show up for a meeting at 1130. He reached in his pocket to find out, just as someone else—an officer—stepped in and turned, facing forward.

"Good morning, Sir! Floor please, Sir!" The elevator operator squeaked loudly.

"Seven, please."

The doors closed, cutting off the curses of at least two other officers who attempted to board.

All Ingram could see was the back of the passenger's neck, and from the look of his close-cropped dark hair he was older, perhaps late forties or early fifties. Tall, thin, he wore a khaki shirt with tie, but no blouse. He carried a briefcase, and his Navy combination cap was tucked under his arm. It was impossible to determine his rank without seeing the devices on his collar, but he must have been fairly senior, judging from the elevator operator's reaction.

With groans and rattles, the elevator began its ascent. The operator gave Ingram another cold stare, his eyebrows raised, still demanding an answer.

The churning in his stomach subsided for a moment and Ingram was able to blurt, "Seven." Thank God the other passenger had said seven.

The elevator jerked to a stop. The lights went out. Somewhere in the labyrinthine system of elevator shafts, a bell clanged as the other elevators stopped. Then another. In the shafts, someone's voice echoed, "Not again."

Enough light leaked in to let Ingram know his fellow passenger remained anchored to the center of the compartment.

"Uhhh," went the operator.

At first Ingram thought he'd lost control, that it was his own voice that had betrayed him.

"Ohhh, God," moaned the kid at the control panel.

Ingram was too busy gulping and fighting with his stomach to add anything.

The lights flashed on and the elevator jerked up. Then the power went off once again, plunging them into darkness. Ingram slid to the corner and loosened his tie. Suddenly it seemed hot and close and he wished he were back in the Bethlehem Shipbuilding Company on San Francisco Bay. Squeezing his eyes shut, he mustered every bit of conscious energy to conquer his digestive tract's demands. He didn't have to bother with claustrophobia.

"Ohhhh, please." The sailor jabbed at the emergency button, the bell having the same urgent, shrill ring that Ingram had heard so long ago in Echo, a little railroading town in northeastern Oregon. He'd gone from the first to the twelfth grade in the same building, where class size never exceeded five.

"Jesus . . ." The kid wheezed, and began punching an urgent dit-dit-dit, dah-dah-dah, dit-dit-dit—SOS. Other elevator bells chimed in, their passengers shouting and banging on the compartment walls.

Ingram suppressed a belch, forcing himself to think of the whitecaps and seagulls he'd seen on the bay this morning. He wondered if easing his belt a notch would help and reached to do it, just as the kid blasted his SOS again.

Then the kid began punching out a series of dots and dashes. It was fast, but Ingram caught some of it: . . . I . . . H-A-T-E . . . T-H-I-S . . . C-H-I-C-K-E-N-S-H-I-T . . . J-O-B . . . W-H-Y . . . C-A-N-T . . .

"That's pretty good, son. You thinking of striking for radioman?" said the other passenger.

"Wh-what?" squeaked the sailor.

"Radioman." The passenger's voice was steady, cool, fetching. "Sounds like you know your stuff. And our fleet needs good radiomen. They're hard to find."

"I dunno. God, I—"

"What are you striking for?"

"Nothing, I guess . . ."

"Where'd you learn to do that?"

"High school. Radio club. Uhhh, you mean you understand what I said, Sir?"

"Yes."

"Sorry, Sir."

"How many words do you take?"

"Used to do twenty."

"You know, a radioman worked for me once when I was a little older than you. It was on the *Aaron Ward,* my second destroyer, and we hit a storm coming out of Batavia. It's shallow down there and the water's all choppy and the ship really bounced around."

The kid went, "Grhffff."

"What?" asked the officer.

"Yes, Sir . . ."

"It was so rough we had to tie everything and almost everybody down who wasn't on watch. Anyway, one of my sailors fell down a hatchway. It looked like he'd broken his neck, and there wasn't a doctor aboard." The man paused and the kid no longer goosed the bell. In the meantime, the temperature felt as if it had risen ten degrees. Ingram unbuttoned his blouse.

The man went on evenly, his voice echoing in the hot compartment, "So we needed help, and guess who saved the day?" In the faint light, he turned and looked at Ingram, as if to size him up. Something glinted on the man's collar tabs. In fact, a lot glinted there. But because of the low light, it was impossible to determine exactly what.

The man tapped the sailor on the shoulder and repeated, "Guess who."

The kid struggled for self-control, "I dunno, uh, Sir. All I know is I don't wanna die."

"Ummm." The man paused and stroked his chin. "Well, anyway, it was my radioman who saved the day. He tapped his CW key like there was no tomorrow. We actually brought the injured boy up to the radio shack and laid him out on the deck. Then we did exactly what the doc on the beach told us to do. Lucky for us there was an English-speaking doctor in Batavia. But our man, Higgins was his name, lived. And later, we found out, he did have a broken neck. He turned out okay."

"Yes, Sir."

"What's your name, son?"

"Babcock, Sir."

"Well, Babcock, what do you think about—"

The lights went on and the elevator jerked into motion again.

"Hey, hey." Babcock grinned, jamming his control lever all the way to the stop.

The passenger turned and winked at Ingram. Then both were surprised, examining one another for an extra second. They looked very much alike. The man could have been Ingram's older brother. Then Ingram realized he had two stars on his collar: a rear admiral. Ingram stood to attention, loose belt and tie, unbuttoned coat, and everything. All he could think of to say was, "Good morning, Sir."

"Morning."

The elevator stopped and the doors clanked open, admitting a blessed cool breeze. "Seven," chirped Babcock, as if nothing had happened.

The admiral nodded and stepped out. But then he drew to a stop and moved back. Ingram almost ran into him.

The admiral looked at the sailor squarely. "Radio School." Imperceptibly, his eyebrows went up.

"Uh . . . yes, Sir. Apply to Radio School, Sir."

"Good. Then I won't be seeing you anymore. Good luck." The admiral quickly merged with the crowd. He slowed and Ingram found himself walking alongside.

The admiral noticed him and gave a thin smile. "Never did like going up in elevators. High places bother me. Maybe that's why I didn't try for a pair of wings."

Ingram said, "You did a good job with that kid, Sir. For a moment there, I thought he was going to crack up."

The admiral shrugged. "Well, like they say, better to be killed attacking the enemy than to be frightened to death."

A gaggle of Navy and Marine officers rushed up to surround the admiral.

They smiled and guffawed at the incident and then turned toward the entrance to a room with large double doors: 722. Just then, a lanky Army major brushed by to join them. "Excuse me."

Ingram nearly shouted, "Otis! For crying out loud." It was Major Otis DeWitt, who had escaped with Ingram from Corregidor. He hadn't seen him since Australia. Outside of regaining some weight, DeWitt hadn't changed much. He was still bony, not a shade over 160 pounds. He had a craggy, lightly pockmarked face and a thin mustache that underlined a large hawk-billed nose. Even though he used cigarette holders, his teeth bore the evidence of a three-pack-a-day habit. Also, it seemed strange not to see DeWitt in his signature campaign hat and jodhpurs; he was now dressed in Army light khakis. But even with his weight gain, dark circles punctuated DeWitt's deep-set eyes. Working as an intelligence officer on MacArthur's staff could do that to you, Ingram supposed.

DeWitt spoke in his thick Texas twang, "Good to see you, Todd." With that, he turned to catch up with the group.

Ingram was astonished. After twenty-nine days at sea with Otis DeWitt while fighting off starvation, the elements, the Pacific, and the enemy—that was it? Major Otis DeWitt, sliding past a shipmate as if he were covered with shit and saying, "Good to see you, Todd"?

Ingram called after him, "Hey, Otis! Whaddya say we go get drunk tonight and pick up some women?"

More than a few ranking passersby gave DeWitt and Ingram cold stares. DeWitt turned and, spreading his arms in exasperation, said, "Out of time, Todd. But I'll see you later. You're on the program in an hour or so—1130, I think." He stepped to a water fountain for a drink.

Ingram moved close to him, "Are you part of this?"

DeWitt finished slurping. "Yes. An Army-Navy joint planning session. I'm aide to General Sutherland." He started to walk away.

Ingram pointed to the admiral moving with the group of men through the double doors. "Who is that?"

DeWitt looked Ingram up and down as if he were crazy. "Why, don't you know? That's Admiral Ray Spruance."

DeWitt pushed toward the doors to room 722 while Ingram dashed for the men's room.

CHAPTER FOUR

Ingram's orders stated he was to be at Room 722 at 1130. To be prompt, he walked in at 1126, feeling much better. It was a large lobby with a Marine sergeant seated behind a linoleum-topped metal desk. A sign read:

ADMITTANCE BY INVITATION ONLY.
TOP SECRET CLEARANCE REQUIRED.

The sergeant didn't mince words. "ID, Sir?"

Ingram handed over his card. The Marine took it and compared it to a schedule on a clipboard. "Sir?"

"Yes?"

"You're not scheduled until 1130, Sir."

Ingram checked his watch: 1127.

"You'll have to—"

DeWitt walked in. "Okay, Todd, you signed the log yet?"

"It seems I'm early."

DeWitt gave the Marine a stare as Ingram signed in. "What a shock. I didn't realize how much you looked like Spruance until I saw you side by side."

"I hope he doesn't fire me or something."

"I don't think so."

"Uhh, you are cleared for top secret?"

Ingram's security clearance paperwork had caught up with him three days ago. "That's right. Otis, what's your job here, anyway?"

DeWitt pulled open a set of double doors and lowered his voice. "Circus man."

"What?"

"I'm the joint Army-Navy facilitator who gets to clean up all the shit after the parade goes through town." He put a forefinger to his lips and went, "Now . . . shhh."

Room 722 turned out to be a large, darkened auditorium. Strident voices echoed from a stage illuminated by footlights. There were ten or so flag-rank officers: Navy, Army, Army Air Corps, and Marine, everyone talking at once. They were seated around a long table and, like medieval sycophants, their aides sat behind them, opening briefcases and nervously shuffling papers. Collars were undone, ties loosened, coffee cups littered the table. In spite of red-illuminated NO SMOKING signs on each side of the room, they smoked cigarettes and one or two puffed cigars, an enormous blue cloud hanging overhead.

Just then, the man at the extreme left end rapped his knuckles. "Enough!" It was Spruance.

The silence seemed heavier than the tobacco smoke as DeWitt and Ingram tried their best to walk softly down the aisle. Even so, their movement turned a few heads. Spruance must have noticed them, too. He raised his eyebrows and squinted through the haze.

DeWitt called out, "Errr . . . I have Lieutenant Ingram, Admiral. Next one on the agenda. He's cleared." They made the front row and DeWitt nearly shoved Ingram into a seat.

As he settled in, Ingram quickly glanced around, seeing light flash off the brass collar devices of twenty or so silhouettes scattered about the first five rows. Then he sat back to watch Spruance, hero of the Battle of Midway. The U.S. Navy hadn't yet released the story because they had lost one of their own carriers. But word had flashed around the fleet that the Japanese had lost four attack carriers. And Spruance, outnumbered in ships three to one, was the genius who had led the victory. Now he was chief of staff to Admiral Chester Nimitz, commander in chief of the Pacific Fleet (CinCPac).

At the other end of the table sat an Army general with thin sandy hair. His coat was off, collar and tie were loosened, and shirtsleeves were rolled up. His nameplate read, MAJOR GENERAL SUTHERLAND. Besides being Otis DeWitt's boss, Sutherland was chief of staff to General Douglas MacArthur in Brisbane, Australia.

Ingram felt an oblique pang of ineptitude. Before him were some of the most powerful men in the Pacific war. And the shadowy figures scattered around him were, most likely, players like himself, summoned to deliver bits and pieces so the admirals and generals could plan their attacks against the enemy. But as a matter of pragmatics, Ingram knew that, like the others, he was really a pawn in a power struggle between MacArthur and Nimitz; their representatives now engaged in battle up on stage.

Two days ago, he'd received a cryptic temporary additional duty (TAD) assignment signed by the Commander Twelfth Naval District. Paragraph three ordered him to attend an Army-Navy chiefs of staff conference, and deliver a verbal report about his experiences fighting the Japanese in the Philippines. Paragraph four stated the time limit: FIVE MINUTES.

On stage Spruance nodded, then spoke to a Navy captain, his name tag read, CAPT. M. T. FALKENBERG, who stood before a large blackboard. "Go on, Maynard."

The captain, holding a portable microphone with a long extension cord, looked up at the chart labeled SOLOMON ISLANDS. "Nothing more to add, Admiral." The captain slapped the chart with a pointer, making it sound like a rifle shot. "That's how they did it."

Spruance asked, "And the *Blue* just let them go by? How can that be?"

The captain replied, "Well, Sir. They needed permission to open fire. And, er . . ." He coughed and looked at the floor. "Well, Admiral Crutchely couldn't be reached."

"Why not?" demanded Spruance.

"Yes, well, ah, he was not aboard his ship. He was in conference with Kelly Turner on the *McCawley,* anchored in Lunga Roads."

"Where's that?" asked Spruance.

"Here, Sir." The captain pointed to Guadalcanal and stepped off the distance from Savo Island. "Uh, I'd say about seventeen miles."

There was a collective gasp at the table. Someone gasped, "Good God!"

Spruance said, "Fine time for a conference."

A burly Marine general—his nameplate read MOTT—half-rose and pointed a finger at the captain. "To begin with, the Navy turns tail our first night on Guadalcanal and leaves us without supplies or reinforcements to fight the Japs. Then you go off and lose your damned fleet. What about my boys, now? Who's going to take care of them?"

A murmur broke out that turned into a clamor. Spruance rapped his knuckles. After it subsided, he turned to Mott. "It seems to me, John, that your boys are alive today and are doing just fine. Perhaps it's because our ships at Savo Island turned away a major Japanese invasion force. May I remind you that when our ships went down that night, we lost many of our boys defending your boys. And if memory serves me correctly, we're now landing your supplies."

The general sat and took his time lighting a cigar. "Point taken, Ray. So, what do we do now? Wait until they reprovision and chop us up?"

Spruance drummed his fingers and pondered.

Ingram tapped DeWitt again, this time nodding to the chart on stage. "What happened, for God's sake?" he whispered.

"Mmm. A battle at Savo Island."

"Solomons?" Ingram asked. He'd heard the First Marine Division had landed on Guadalcanal about two weeks ago. The fighting had been bloody.

DeWitt nodded, then muttered in Ingram's ear, "Yeah. We lost four cruisers and a destroyer to Jap torpedoes. In one night, they got away scot-free."

"Jesus!" It slipped out. Ingram wished he could have tied a string to the word and yanked it back. DeWitt slapped a hand over his eyes and groaned. The auditorium fell silent and Ingram knew every eye was stapled to him as if he were the only beacon of light for hundreds of miles around.

Spruance looked in Ingram's direction. "Yes, indeed. We need His help." Then he turned to General Mott. "No, John. The Japanese Navy is not going to chop you up. We won't let it happen. Believe me. Now, you have a job to do and we're here to help you do it—"

"How can you do your job if your damned torpedoes don't work?"

With a nod to the audience, Spruance said sharply, "John!"

"Okay. So even if you can fix that, what about—"

Spruance held up a hand. "The pipeline will fill up, John, but it takes time. We'll have the ships. We'll have the men. For now, we can defend. We can supply you as well. It's not going to be easy, but we'll do it. Not easy for any of us, but then war is like that." Spruance sat forward and splayed fingers across the table. "We'll do it."

Sutherland spoke. "Granted that you can do that, Ray, that you can defend. Then what are we doing here?" He waved a hand around the table. "I thought this was a strategy meeting."

Spruance replied, "Indeed it is a strategy meeting, Dick. We're here to define it for the Southwest and Central Pacific campaigns."

"Good. I'm sure General MacArthur will be glad to contribute."

Mott jabbed his cigar at Sutherland. "Contribute what, Dick?"

"Well, anything that—"

Spruance interrupted, "We have to agree on some things."

All turned their heads.

"Right now it seems there are three broad questions." Spruance rubbed his chin. "The first is about logistics and how we can support the Marines on Guadalcanal and Tulagi with what they need and when they need it. The second question is related. How do we keep our lines of communication open in order to accomplish the first? Third, how do we obtain control of the air?"

Sutherland added, "And the sea."

DeWitt glanced at his watch. "Ahem."

Spruance looked up, stone-faced. "Perhaps there is something you would like to add, Major DeWitt?"

DeWitt shot to his feet and stood at near-attention. "Not at all, Sir. Except that we're ten minutes behind schedule. I see the cooks are ready. So if I may suggest, Sir, that we let them serve chow while our next speaker takes the stand. Then he can return to his regular duty assignment." He sat and whispered to Ingram. "What do you call your food servers?"

Ingram smiled. Same old DeWitt, long on pomposity, short on substance. "Steward's mates. Otis, didn't you learn anything about the Navy during our trip?"

"Steward's mates, yeah, that's right. I get them mixed up with ship captains."

There was a collective mutter around the table. Spruance took that to be a positive. "Good idea, Major. We'll be served here while the other gentlemen in the audience are invited to take their noon meal on the . . ."

"Third-floor cafeteria." DeWitt's Texas accent resonated about the auditorium.

". . . third-floor cafeteria," said Spruance quietly, as if refining the phrase so that it could be more clearly understood.

The lights went up and the officers in the audience stood, stretched, and filed for the doors.

DeWitt checked to make sure the steward's mates were properly setting up for the meal. "Okay, Todd, you're on. Sing for your dinner. Remember, just five minutes. There's someone else right after you. Okay?"

"Where do I stand?"

"By the blackboard. Use the mike if you want. See you later. I have to herd the cattle." With a wave, DeWitt followed the last of the officers out the door.

The meal began as Ingram took the stairs to the stage and walked to the blackboard. He'd brought a clipboard and arranged his notes. Then he turned and faced his audience, ready to begin the talk that he'd practiced over the past two nights.

They shoveled from plates laden with breaded pork chops, mashed potatoes and gravy, and peas, only taking time to slop butter on their bread and slurp iced tea. Except, Ingram noticed, Spruance had just tomato soup, salad, and a roll.

"Ahem," Ingram began.

Cutlery clanked.

"Good morning, gentlemen. I'm supposed to tell you about my escape from the Philippines."

They kept scraping and munching. To Ingram, it seemed a contest to see who could eat the fastest. One had already finished his pork chop and motioned to a steward's mate for seconds.

"The night after the Japs took the Rock, we jumped into a thirty-six-foot P-Boat and made it to Australia."

He paused as another two officers signaled for seconds.

"People ask me why we did that. Why we just didn't give up."

No one looked at him.

"Well. I was skipper of a minesweeper, the U.S.S. *Pelican*. With very little fuel, we had been stranded at anchor off Corregidor since last December."

They ate and ate and ate.

"Here's why we decided to escape. On the tide, many corpses floated past my ship over those weeks and months. Some were Army, some were Marine. A few Navy. Many Filipinos. A lot of them had their hands tied behind their backs. Many were without heads."

CHAPTER FIVE

They stopped eating, forks poised midway. Sutherland pushed his plate aside. "I don't think that's funny, sailor."

"Nor do I, General," said Ingram.

Sutherland waved his hands in frustration.

Ingram said, "Your aide, Major DeWitt, can confirm this. He was on the trip with us."

"I know what Major DeWitt did, Lieutenant," said Sutherland. "It was Major DeWitt who suggested you speak to us. As far as what happened at Corregidor, don't forget I was there, too."

"You jumped ship with Doug," said Mott, referring to General Douglas MacArthur's escape from Corregidor by PT-Boat on March 11, 1942.

Sutherland shot to his feet, "Damnit! I don't have to put up with—"

Spruance rapped his knuckles. "Gentlemen! Please remember Lieutenant Ingram has the floor."

Sutherland and Mott glared at each other, then slowly sat. Mott turned. "Sorry, son. We've been at it for two days now, and there is a lot of ground to cover." He swept an arm around the table. "All of us here admire your bravery. We're happy you've returned to set an example for others who must face what you've gone through."

Ingram paused for a moment. "I have a confession, General."

Mott scooped up the last of his peas and nodded. *Go ahead.*

"I didn't feel brave. I was just doing my job."

"Doesn't surprise me," said Mott.

"As a matter of fact, I was scared to death. I really—"

Spruance said, "Nobody expects you to come out with a smile on your face, Lieutenant. War is a dirty business—like Sherman said, 'War begins when the music stops playing.'"

"Yes, Sir."

Spruance snapped his fingers. "I remember you. Wasn't it in the elevator this morning? With the kid who's going to strike for radioman?"

"Yes, Sir."

Spruance gave a tiny smile. "Well, I was scared. How about you?"

"Out of my pants, Admiral."

They all laughed.

Spruance checked his watch. "We're almost out of time, Lieutenant. Please forgive me, but I'd like to cut to the quick."

"Yes, Sir." Ingram put down his notes.

"I'm interested in what you have to say about the Jap fighting capability."

Ingram rubbed his chin, thinking Spruance would have heard a ton of comments from the pilots who flew at Midway. *Why me?* "Well, Sir. We were on the receiving end most of the time. Either Jap artillery or their Air Force."

"Tell us about the naval air."

"Well, they bombed the Rock, too. And they finally got us off Caballo. A string of bombs ran right down the island and into our engine room."

"Ummm." From an aide, Spruance retrieved a paper stamped TOP SECRET in large red block letters. He examined it for a moment, then looked up. "Have you ever seen a Japanese torpedo?"

"No, Sir. Except . . ."

"Except what?" prompted Falkenberg.

"Our own torpedoes," Ingram said tentatively.

They sighed. Spruance prompted, "Go on."

"A couple of weeks before we escaped, I took a launch out to meet one of our submarines off Corregidor: the *Wolffish*."

They all looked at the floor for a moment, knowing the *Wolffish* was later sunk near the Surigao Strait. Ingram went on. "For a few minutes I talked to Foggy Sutcliff, her engineering officer. We were at the Naval Academy together. He told me their torpedoes were no good. Duds, he said. Apparently they fired three point-blank at an anchored cruiser and they didn't go off. Jap destroyers followed the torpedo tracks and held them down for eleven hours with depth charges."

Nobody spoke. A little breeze stirred an auditorium drape. With a glance to Spruance, Falkenberg prompted, "Anything else? From the Japanese, I mean?"

"Bombs. Lots of them."

"How was their performance?" Spruance asked.

"Very accurate. Of course, they were unopposed. But then . . ."

"But what?" asked a thin, hollow-eyed Army Air Force general.

". . . well, Sir. They were very predictable, always flying in tight, three-plane vee elements that never varied. Those elements flew in a tight, three-vee formation—nine planes in all. They always held their place, even when another was blown out of the sky. They were easy to track. Sometimes they got cocky and came in too low. We got one that way—a Betty. We held our fire until they were directly overhead. Then we let 'em have it."

Spruance tried again. "I see. But no torpedoes?"

"No, Sir. Sorry."

Spruance asked, "Your action report said you were at close quarters with a destroyer?"

Ingram pinched the bridge of his nose, trying to remember. "Well, that's true. It was the second night of our escape. She was a Japanese destroyer, *Hubuki* class, I believe, patrolling off Fortune Island. She nearly ran us down. We were able to spin inside her turning radius and lose her in the dark."

"Nothing else?"

Ingram wondered what they were fishing for. "Not that I can recall, Admiral."

Spruance nodded to Captain Falkenberg.

"Did you engage her, Mr. Ingram?"

"Engage?"

"Like open fire?" said Falkenberg.

"Well, er, yessir. We had a couple of BARs, a rifle or two. Popguns, really. They caught us with a searchlight and opened up on us with small stuff. Twenty-millimeter, I think. So . . . we returned fire. Right into their pilot-house. Now that I remember, we doused their searchlight with the BAR. That's how we got away."

"How close were you?"

"Ummm, fifty, seventy-five yards."

"Amazing." Falkenberg strapped on a pair of reading glasses and shuffled through papers. "Ah." He looked over his glasses. "I have permission to share with you a fleet intelligence report. The destroyer you engaged was indeed a *Hubuki* class. Her name is the *Kurosio* and her skipper is . . ." Falkenberg flipped to another paper—"Yes, here it is . . . Lieutenant Commander Katsumi Fujimoto."

Ingram blinked at Falkenberg. *How the hell does he know all this?*

Falkenberg looked at Ingram over his glasses. "Do you know what *Kurosio* means, Lieutenant?"

"No, Sir."

"*Black Tide,* Lieutenant." He scratched his head and continued. "Actually, Fujimoto went from the penthouse to the outhouse because of you. He was born to the purple, so to speak, to a three-generation Navy family. His father sailed victoriously with Yamamoto at the Battle of Tsushima Strait. Fujimoto went to Etajima Naval Academy and sailed through the junior ranks as favorite son with a promising future. Up until last February, he was aide to General Yoshitsugu Tatekawa, Japan's ambassador to the Soviet Union. Then it was time for his own command, so they gave him the *Kurosio*. But your gunfire put the *Kurosio* out of commission for three weeks. It seems she ran aground, although that's not confirmed. All this earned Fujimoto a letter of reprimand and, I suppose, shame and embarrassment. Now they got him on dog duty, running a repair barge and code station in northern Mindanao. So watch out. Your Lieutenant Commander Fujimoto is one pissed-off sailor."

A few chuckled.

Ingram said, "It's my turn to be amazed, Captain, at how you know all this."

Falkenberg sat back, poker-faced.

The rear door opened and DeWitt stepped in with a figure in tow who walked with a limp.

Spruance eyed them on their way down the aisle. "Could you cover that chart, Lieutenant?"

Ingram turned around to the SOLOMON ISLANDS chart; the upper left- and lower right-hand corners bore the legend TOP SECRET in red. As he reached to flip the blanket, he couldn't help but see several ships' tracks plotted. They converged around Savo Island and at least four tracks ended abruptly with a cross. Just as the blanket rumpled over, he caught two of the crossed names: *Vincennes* and *Canberra.*

Spruance asked, "What's your duty station now, Lieutenant?"

"U.S.S. *Tingey,* Admiral. New *Fletcher* class can under construction at Bethlehem Shipyard."

"And your billet?"

"Exec."

Spruance nodded. "Good. Very good. Thank you for your time. We appreciate your help. Major DeWitt will take care of you."

"Yes, Sir. Thank you." Ingram headed toward the steps.

Spruance said, "Lieutenant Ingram."

He stopped. "Yes, Sir?"

"You're being recommended for the Navy Cross."

My God. Give it to the guys that are still out there. "Thank you, Sir. I really appreciate it."

As the admirals and generals finished lunch, Ingram walked down the steps and found DeWitt standing beside another officer, a foreigner, wearing a well-tailored dress-blue uniform with two stripes. Fair-complected, he had a square face, dark red hair combed straight back, and he leaned on a polished mahogany cane, his combination cap tucked under his arm.

DeWitt held out his hand. "Congratulations, Todd."

Ingram took it. "You should have one, too, Otis. Everybody should. After all—"

"Nonsense. You're the one who brought it off." Then he glanced at the stage. "I'll give them another minute or two. Here, Lieutenant Ingram, say hello to Lieutenant Eduard Dezhnev of the Soviet Navy."

"A Russian? I mean, a Soviet? Welcome." They shook.

Dezhnev spoke in his clear baritone, "Soviet, yes. But Russian, no. I'm from Georgia."

Ingram tried to place Soviet Georgia on the map but gave up. "What brings you here? My God, your English is better than mine."

Dezhnev smiled easily. "Thanks. I'm assigned here as naval attaché. And please let me add my congratulations on your Navy Cross."

"It's only been recommended."

"Nonsense. If Spruance recommends it, you're decorated." DeWitt spread his hands and looked toward the sky. "Turn on the searchlights, Hollywood. Here comes Ingram."

"No, thanks," Ingram protested.

Spruance looked down and gave DeWitt a nod.

DeWitt waved a hand toward the stage. "Okay, Lieutenant Dezhnev. You're on."

"*Spasibo.*" Thank you.

As Dezhnev hobbled up the steps, DeWitt asked, "Want to stick around? You might find it interesting."

"Okay," Ingram took a seat next to DeWitt. "Say, how 'bout dinner? Ollie's in town."

DeWitt whispered, "Tied up till next Monday."

"Monday it is, then."

On stage, Falkenberg began the afternoon program by introducing Dezhnev.

DeWitt whispered, "You don't really want to get drunk, do you?"

"Keep a secret?"

DeWitt nodded.

Ingram whispered, "Still have no tolerance for the stuff. I pass out at the sniff of a wine cork."

"I'll be damned. Me, too. Okay, you're on. You mind if the Russian comes along? I'm his watchdog for a while."

"Sure." Ingram sat back to watch Dezhnev step before the blackboard.

Ingram was surprised at how relaxed Dezhnev was. With a solid command of English, he quickly summarized the status of the Soviet Union's fight against Hitler, which he repeatedly referred to as the "Great Patriotic War." Then, after waiting for a good five seconds, he went into detail about Marshall Zhukov's plan to form a line along the River Don with hopes of throwing back the Nazi advance in the south, stemming their thrust for the oil fields in the Caucasus. If successful, Premier Stalin and Marshall Zhukov believed the Great Soviet Armies could go on the offensive and wipe out the vermin on their soil. But this could only be accomplished if the Allies opened a second front in Europe.

Someone sat in the row behind Ingram and tapped him on the shoulder. "Sir?"

He turned to find the elevator operator—Babcock. Close up, the seaman apprentice seemed even younger. Ingram raised his eyebrows.

Babcock whispered, "I'm glad I found you. The chief didn't believe me."

"Believe what?"

"That the admiral recommended me for Radio School." Babcock plopped a sheaf of papers on Ingram's shoulder.

Ingram took them, astounded to find a freshly typed set of orders detaching Seaman Apprentice Earl (n) Babcock from the Twelfth Naval District Services Command to Fleet Radio School in San Diego. At the bottom was an illegible scrawl by a chief boatswain's mate. Beneath that was an endorsement section calling for the signature of "Raymond A. Spruance, Rear Admiral, USN."

"How'd you get this done so fast?"

"We're self-contained here and the yeoman is a buddy of mine. So he typed the orders up for me. Er, in fact, he wants out, too."

Looking from side to side, Babcock leaned closer. "My chief thinks it's all BS, Sir. Dares me to get 'em signed by the admiral."

The people on stage heard Babcock and turned their heads momentarily. Dezhnev, too. He cast his eyes at him but kept talking.

DeWitt leaned over and hissed, "What the hell is this?"

Ingram held up a hand. "I'm not your CO, Babcock."

Babcock leaned close, his voice desperate. "Sir, please help me. The chief, well, his last duty station was the Bremerton Stockade. He's a sadist—a real jerk. It's hell working for him, Sir. I'd rather fight Japs."

DeWitt glared at Ingram. "Get him out of here or I'll tell that Marine to stuff him down a manhole."

In frustration, Ingram grabbed the orders. "Wait back there."

"Yes, Sir. Thank you, Sir." Babcock walked quickly to the back of the auditorium and took a seat.

Dezhnev was winding up. ". . . as to the B-25 crew from your Tokyo raid who landed in Vladivostok—they are in good health and spirits and send their love to their countrymen and families. My government regrets that we must intern them for the war's duration since we are a neutral to your Pacific conflict. Of which"—he spoke sotto voce—"we commiserate with you mightily."

"Hear, hear," said Mott.

Dezhnev braced himself on his cane. "There is a saying in my country that goes: 'Men with clenched fists cannot make friends.' Thus we hope you'll understand that, while we are engaged in mortal combat against Hitler's thugs, who daily slaughter thousands of our civilians, we may seem unresponsive at times, even insensitive. But I want you to know that the people of the Soviet Union do appreciate what the United States is doing for us. You are our friends and we hope you'll forgive us just a little for our preoccupation until our final victory. Thank you."

Dezhnev gave a perfect bow as the men at the table clapped.

Spruance said, "Ten minutes for head call, gentlemen."

"Damn it all. Why don't you just call it a latrine?" protested Sutherland, scraping back in his chair.

Falkenberg zipped down the steps and headed up the aisle.

"Captain," Ingram called.

Falkenberg stopped, his eyebrows raised.

"You're not going to believe this, Sir, but . . ." Ingram told Falkenberg about the morning's elevator incident.

Falkenberg rubbed his chin for a moment. "Why not? The kid has balls coming in here." He grabbed Babcock's orders and took them up the steps to Spruance, who was talking to Mott and Sutherland. While waiting, Ingram turned to see Babcock still in the back, sitting on the edge of his chair and twisting his white hat in his hands. Then his face broke into a broad smile. Ingram spun to see Spruance take the orders, prop them on the table, sign them, and hand them back to Falkenberg. With a nod to Ingram, he rejoined his conversation with Mott and Sutherland.

Babcock rose from his seat, the smile on his face even broader. But then he slipped and fell, bumping his forehead. Seconds later, he scrambled to his feet and ran down the aisle. "Sir," Babcock puffed to Ingram. "I can't tell you what this means to me."

"Not at all. Good luck. Say, looks like you cut your forehead. Better have it looked at."

Babcock held out his hand. "So damned happy to be getting out of this hellhole. Thanks again."

Ingram shook it. "Not at all. You better stop by the head. That thing's bleeding."

Babcock grinned. "It's worth it." He waved and mouthed *Thank you*, trying to get Spruance's attention. But the admiral was still talking to General Mott and ignored him.

DeWitt growled, "Get moving, Babcock."

"Ye-yes, Sir." Babcock spun and dashed for the door.

Just then the lights went out. The men instantly turned into vague shadows. There was a collective groan. "Who's keeping score?" someone grumbled.

Spruance's voice rang through the auditorium, "We need you back in the elevators, Babcock."

Babcock's voice echoed back, "Sorry, Admiral. I'm a radioman now."

A roar of laughter followed Babcock as he blasted through the doors.

CHAPTER SIX

19 AUGUST, 1942
U.S. FEDERAL BUILDING
SAN FRANCISCO, CALIFORNIA

A buzzer howled. The Marine sergeant stepped into the auditorium waving a battle lantern and bellowed, "They just called up, gentlemen, with orders to evacuate. If you will follow me to the fire exit, please?"

"What about our classified stuff?" asked Falkenberg. "There's more than we can carry."

"A security squad is on its way up, Sir. We'll dig it out for you."

Spruance glanced around the stage. "Anything here we can't afford to leave, Maynard?"

"I got most of it, but I wonder—"

"Sir. We should leave now, if you please, Sir?" The Marine propped the battle lantern on a projector table, its beam penetrating the tobacco smoke and throwing a ghostly hue through the auditorium's vastness.

"Oh, what the hell," muttered Falkenberg.

"The exercise will do us good, gentlemen," said Spruance. "Let's go."

There was a collective groan. Nobody could keep up with Spruance, who walked three miles a day. Muttering and grumbling, they passed through the door, following Spruance down the hall.

The double doors swung shut. With their voices trailing off, the auditorium fell into silence.

After a few seconds, a solitary figure slowly moved from behind the curtains. Dezhnev's heart beat fast. He was taking a terrible chance. *Sixty seconds at the most.* He headed for the blackboard and swung the blanket over the top, exposing the chart. *They hadn't had time to take that.*

His skin tingled as he read the casualty report in the lower left-hand corner. The Japanese had sunk *three American cruisers and one Australian cruiser* and one destroyer at Savo Island, not just two cruisers, as Beria had supposed.

What else? He quickly replaced the blanket, walked to the table, and scanned the notebooks scattered about. Falkenberg's loose-leaf folder was atop something, he saw. Easing the folder aside, he saw that it was stamped TOP SECRET and labeled: TORPEDO FAILURES: MARK 13, MARK 14, MARK 15. Quickly flipping pages, he noted columns of figures, some having a common label: FAILURE RATES. His heart skipped a beat when he saw that the torpedo failure rates exceeded sixty percent in some cases.

He checked his watch. *Twenty-two seconds.*

Dezhnev kept browsing, wishing he'd brought his Minox. He tried to figure if—

"Sir?"

Dezhnev spun. Babcock!

"You forgot to write the date in, Sir. My chief is a stickler on dates. Could you—Say, where is everybody?"

Dezhnev closed the report, grabbed his cane, and thumped down the steps to Babcock. "They had to evacuate. I came back for my notes." With a flourish, he scooped his hat off a seat. "We'd better go, too. Quick, now."

Babcock squinted as he drew close. "Holy Toledo. Aren't you . . . ?"

Dezhnev smiled at the kid with the pimples. "That's right, er, Babcock? I was backstage picking my notes off the floor when the lights went kapoof! Let's go."

Together, they walked up the aisle. Dezhnev exaggerated his limp, letting Babcock get a little ahead. His grip tightened on his cane as his mind raced. Should he do it?

They went through the first set of doors and into the empty lobby, Babcock leading the way, walking ahead to hold the outer door for Dezhnev.

Dezhnev was going to raise his cane and whack Babcock across the throat, but for some reason hesitated. Just then, the door slipped from Babcock's hand.

"Oh, sorry, Sir." Babcock fumbled and reopened the door, letting Dezhnev through.

Dezhnev squinted in the half-light. "Your head's still bleeding. Come on in here and let me fix it for you." He walked toward the men's room door.

Babcock dabbed the cut with a handkerchief. "Later, Sir. Gotta run." He quickly walked down the hall and through the fire exit at the other end.

Damnit! Dezhnev banged open the men's room door with an open palm and walked in. *What the hell to do?* He stood against the marble wall to think, the sounds of the city drifting through an open window.

"Lieutenant Dezhnev?" DeWitt's Texas accent caromed through the hallway.

Shit.

"Hello?" DeWitt's voice echoed.

Do something. "In here, Major," Dezhnev yelled, unzipping his pants. He backed into one of the open stalls and flushed the toilet.

DeWitt rushed in, with Ingram just behind. "Thought we'd lost you," he shouted.

The toilet gurgled convincingly as Dezhnev stood before Major Otis DeWitt and pasted on his best sheepish grin. His voice echoed on the black and white tiles as he pulled up his trousers. "Looks like I got caught with my pants down."

"Oh, damn! Sorry," wheezed DeWitt. He leaned against the wall, out of breath.

Ingram said, "We were worried as hell. Got down to the fourth floor before we realized you weren't with us."

Dezhnev raised his eyebrows. "What's going on?"

DeWitt replied, "It's this damned building. Load's always tripping out. They gave orders to evacuate. You never can tell when—"

The lights went on.

"Well, how do ya like that?" DeWitt jammed his hands on his hips.

Dezhnev finished arranging his clothes, walked to the mirror, and ran a comb through his hair.

Ingram led the way into the hall.

DeWitt was last and asked, "Elevator, anybody?"

"If it's all the same to you, Major, I'd rather not risk another power failure today. Besides, I need some exercise." Dezhnev walked through the doors marked EXIT and started shuffling down the stairwell, thankful this was the west stairwell. Babcock had taken the east stairwell, making it unlikely he would have run into DeWitt or Ingram when they ran back up. But still, it nagged at his mind. *Had Babcock seen anything in the auditorium's darkness? How long had he been standing there?*

DeWitt walked through the door. "You all right with that cane?"

"You will be surprised." Dezhnev began to hobble his way down, supporting his left side with his left arm, doing fairly well. As DeWitt and Ingram clattered behind, he still wondered what to do about Babcock.

At eight o'clock that evening, the Soviet duty radio operator in Moscow Center took traffic from the San Francisco consulate. One message, double encoded, was routed to Dzerzhinskiy Square and the Lubyanka Prison, where it found its way to Vasiliy Laptev's office on the second floor. Laptev was slender, totally bald, and wore the green flashes of an NKVD lieutenant colonel on his olive uniform.

Having been up since five, Laptev was exhausted and wanted nothing more than to go home. Yet here was a message to decrypt. And his staff, knowing he would be irritable at day's end, stepped quickly past his open door with exaggerated purpose. It took three tries spinning the safe's dials to open the damned door and extract the code books. Laptev smashed the volumes on his desk and began his decryption in earnest. Twenty-five minutes later, he was finished. He bristled when he saw that it was from Captain third rank Sergei Zenit, the man forever contaminated with the *Dzhurma* fiasco.

No matter. There was business to conduct. Time to see the man. He unbuckled his holster, hung it on a peg behind the door, grabbed his cap, and walked out, two privates in tow, their uniforms trimmed in the same green NKVD insignia, PPSh submachine guns slung over their shoulders.

It took three minutes to walk the distance to the east wing of the Lubyanka. Eventually they entered a large lobby with a shiny green linoleum floor. Two guards passed Laptev and his entourage through double doors and into a small carpeted anteroom.

As usual, Karachek sat at his desk, stamping papers with an enormous rubber stamp. Karachek looked at the guards, then back to Laptev.

Laptev turned and excused the guards with a wave of his hand. "Top secret KOMET message from San Francisco."

"I see." Karachek picked up a phone and dialed. After a moment he looked up. "He'll see you. Are you armed?"

It was plain Laptev wasn't wearing his holster. "No."

Karachek's eyes lingered on Laptev for a long moment. "Very well."

Laptev knocked on the door and was admitted by Dmitriy, a rail-thin, pockmarked man, who wore a dark suit with a plain yellow tie. As Laptev stepped in, Dmitriy kept his eyes on every move Laptev made. Compared to Laptev's modest office in the west wing, this one was enormous. It was perhaps eight meters square, painted a pale yellow, its four-meter-high ceiling trimmed with scrolled crown moldings and finished in pastel green. Victorian furniture, Persian rugs, and original French art were tastefully arranged in the room. To his left was an ornate partner's desk, while directly ahead, a log burned in a two-meter-high fireplace. Casting a yellowish gold glow, it was the room's only light, except for a small reading lamp on one end of the couch.

And there sat Lavrenty Pavlovich Beria, NKVD Commissar, second only to Premier Josef Stalin, reading from a thick folder, pages tumbling about him and onto the floor. Beria took his time, more papers scattering to the floor as he sipped coffee from a fine china cup, while the fire crackled and Dmitriy's eyes drilled though the back of Laptev's head. As long as Laptev had known Beria, the Georgia-born man outwardly seemed quiet and inner-directed. He never smoked or drank, and his voice was a soft baritone. He stood at five-ten, weighed nearly two hundred, was balding, and this evening wore a light brown suit with a neutral tie.

Beria turned an oval face to Laptev, displaying deep-set light-blue eyes shielded by rimless gold-framed glasses. He held out a hand, palm up. "You have a VOSTOK message?"

"No, Sir. Just a KOMET message from San Francisco." Laptev handed the flimsy over.

"Ah, yes." Beria adjusted his glasses and read:

TOP SECRET—OPERATION KOMET—TOP SECRET
TO: L. P. BERIA
FROM: S. ZENIT, KAPT3R, SAN FRANCISCO
19 AUGUST 1942

DEZHNEV REPORTS CHIEFS OF STAFF CONFERENCE PENETRATED, BE ADVISED: USN LOSSES BATTLE OF SAVO ISLAND THREE, RE-PEAT THREE CRUISERS, I.E.: ASTORIA, VINCENNES, QUINCY, AND DESTROYER JARVIS. AUSTRALIANS ALSO LOST HEAVY CRUISER CANBERRA. JAPANESE TORPEDOES FAR MORE SUCCESSFUL THAN WE BELIEVED. ALSO, AMERICANS HAVING MAJOR TORPEDO FAIL-URE PROBLEMS. MESSAGE ENDS.

ZENIT

Beria looked over his shoulder. "Dezhnev, the one from Bykovo?"

"Yes, Sir."

"Make sure Tatekawa gets this in its entirety." General Yoshitsugu Ta-tekawa was the Japanese ambassador to Russia.

"Yes, Sir."

"Any word on VOSTOK?"

"No, Sir."

"We may have to put Zenit on that one, too. Think about it."

"Yes, Sir."

Beria picked up a document, then pivoted his whole body, his eyes boring into Laptev. "Didn't we pick Dezhnev for VOSTOK West Coast?"

"Yes, Sir."

Beria kept his eyes on Laptev for a whole three seconds. Then he returned to his reading. "I see."

Laptev headed for the door, avoiding Dmitriy's eyes. Tomorrow, he would think about Zenit. Tonight, he would sleep.

CHAPTER SEVEN

21 AUGUST, 1942
RAMONA, CALIFORNIA

The afternoon's heat embraced Ingram as he drove the sky-blue convertible into the filling station. Pulling the brake handle, he stepped out, noticing the thermometer dial in the station's window read ninety-eight degrees. He'd been on the road since yesterday, the trip to northeastern San Diego County taking far longer than he had planned. Even so, he took solace that the heat was dry, not the humidity-soaked, near-saturated hell of the Philippines in summer. And as he looked around, it seemed the only thing alive here was a long-haired sheep-dog snoozing under the shade of an oak tree, forty feet away.

A stooped attendant walked out and leaned against the doorway. "Nice jalopy. Cadillac?"

"Packard."

"Oh, yeah? And lookie that: four doors. You don't see many of them around. Brand-new, huh?"

"Actually, I think it's a 1940."

"Ain't it yours?"

The car belonged to Oliver Toliver III, a born-to-the-purple shipmate. "A friend."

The attendant stepped out and walked around the car, running a gnarled hand along the fenders. In greasy coveralls, the scarecrow-shaped man looked like a panhandler in B Westerns. His name was stitched above the pocket: ED. He stooped, squinted at the license plate, then took out a pencil stub and wrote the number, 92 M 288, on the back of a match box. Then Ed rose, and noted a sticker on the rear window. "All the way from San Francisco, eh?" It sounded like an accusation.

"Yes."

"Fill'er up?"

"Please."

"You got the stamps?"

"Here." He handed over the ration stamps.

Ed was soon pumping gas and wiping the Packard's windows. After being paid, he gave change. "Anything else?"

"How do I find the Durand Ranch?" Ingram blurted. He wondered if he shouldn't turn around and head back to San Francisco. But he'd put this off for so long.

"Which one?" Ed smacked his lips and spat thick juice into the dust.

"I don't know." He opened the top two buttons on his shirt, wishing he hadn't come.

A crooked finger pointed down the road. "Frank Durand's spread is that way. He raises avocados." Then his thumb jabbed in the opposite direction. "Lamar Durand is back there."

Ingram waited. Finally, a fly buzzed at his neck. In frustration, he slapped at it, saying, "What's he raise?"

"Lamar Durand raises alfalfa." Ed's eyes narrowed.

"Where does Helen Durand live?"

"Ooooooh." Ed stepped away from the Packard and looked it up and down, hands on his hips. "Who wants to know?"

Damnit! He snapped open his billfold and flashed his U.S. Navy ID card. "Lieutenant Todd Ingram. War Department. Official business." Then he looked from side to side, lowered his voice, and covered his mouth. "Office of Naval Intelligence. She's been helping us out and now we need to talk to her mom and dad."

Ed's mouth dropped. "You mean spies?" he almost shouted.

"Shhhhh."

Ed's voice dropped obligingly. "Where's your uniform?"

"How can I catch spies if the enemy sees me walking down the street in dress blues?"

Ed pondered that for a moment. "If it's spies you're looking for, you oughta check on old Steiner over there." He swung his arm and lined up a forefinger on a shop across the street where a sign announced, STEINER'S CLOCK REPAIR. "I swear, the bastard's sending messages to them Nazis every day. Look at the damned place. Shades all drawn. Probably in there right now with Gerta takin' notes and tapping out code to that there Schicklgruber—"

"Helen?" He pasted on his best smile.

Ed was unstoppable. After Steiner, he ranted on about Betz, Bugg, Frankenberg, and Althoff, spies all of them, whose daily actions, indeed their drawing of each breath, were activities gravely prejudicial to the security of the United States of America. Then Ed's eyes narrowed again. "Say, what's your name?"

"I told you. Todd Ingram."

"Mmmmm." Ed rubbed his chin.

"It's English. My ancestors sailed with Sir Francis Drake." Ingram had no idea who his ancestors consorted with.

That seemed to satisfy Ed, for he took a deep breath and gave Ingram directions to the Durand Ranch, which turned out to be the one where Frank and Katy lived; the one who raised avocados.

"Helen's been gone for near two years," Ed added as Ingram got into the Packard.

"I know."

"Hold on." With a conspiratorial wink, Ed dashed in his little office, rattled around for a moment, then came out with a frosted Coke. Popping the cap off, he handed it to Ingram. "On the house, sonny. Just keep rounding up them Nazis." His arm swept across Ramona's main drag toward Steiner's Clock Repair.

"Thanks." Ingram took the Coke gratefully, jammed the Packard into gear, and turned around. Soon he was jiggling down a potholed narrow road with the asphalt giving way to dirt. The afternoon had grown hotter, and Ingram mopped his brow as the coupe bumped and thumped over the washboard lane. But the neatly planted trees were tall and green and they seemed, in a way, to suck the heat out of the air, and there was a sweet scent, although he couldn't place it. Soon he pulled into a driveway where the mail box read DURAND. The house was a low, brick, rambling ranch style with a long porch surrounded by walnut trees, their trunks painted white. A combination work shed and garage stood off to the side, empty, its doors gaping open.

As soon as he stopped, a woman walked out and stood on the porch. She was in her late forties or early fifties, hair dark ebony and gray-streaked. Yet her face was well defined and she had Helen's eyes, with the same crinkles in the corners that conveyed humor and patience and a tinge of temper. She wore a simple short-sleeved dress with an apron, and held a long wooden spoon, mashed potatoes clinging to it.

He stepped from the Packard. "Hello, I'm Todd Ingram." He tried to appear relaxed, but with another look at the woman, Ingram felt light-headed again. She looked so much like Helen.

"Navy?"

"Well, er, yes." *Amazing.* Helen had just about said the same thing to him when they'd first met on Corregidor.

"You've come about Helen." The woman grabbed her wrist.

"How did you know?"

"She's my daughter. I'm Kate Durand."

This is going badly, thought Ingram. "She's alive," he blurted.

"I know that." She closed her eyes for a moment and exhaled. "But I'll tell you. We've been worried sick since Corregidor fell."

My God. She really does know. "She's fine. She really is."

Kate walked up and stood close, her eyes searching. "How do you know?"

"I was there. I was with her." Ingram felt like taking Kate into his arms.

"Thank God. Then . . . then where is she?"

"Mindanao."

"What's that?"

"Big island in the southern Phillippines. About five hundred miles south of Corregidor."

"Oh." She paused for a moment. "The Japs have that, too, don't they?"

Ingram stepped in the shade of the porch and rubbed a hand over his face. "I'm afraid so. But she's fine. She's with the resistance."

"You mean she's living in the weeds?"

"In a manner of speaking."

Kate gave a little snort. "If that's all there is to it, then she'll be fine." She swept a slender arm. "That's all she did around here. Couldn't find her half the time. But then she had to grow up and go to college and become a nurse and join the damned Army. I wish—Say, are you all right?"

Ingram leaned against a post. "I'm fine. Just a little hot."

"Look. Come in and cool off. Frank will be home soon. He's out trapping gophers. You might as well stay for supper." It was almost a command.

"Well, I don't—"

"Don't worry. The food's good. We have enough." Her voice was exactly like Helen's. And she had the same brown eyes. *Amazing.*

"You okay, Todd?"

"Never better."

"Well, then, get inside and run some cool water over your wrists. And you can tell me all about Helen."

He clumped after her through a screen door. The house was small, utilitarian, but cool. The living room was arranged around a used brick fireplace, long since blackened to the ceiling by burning wood. To his right was a dining room with a large table where two places were set. But at one time, Ingram could tell, four or five had gathered. Kate pushed aside café doors and walked into the kitchen. "Back here, Todd. Make yourself useful."

"Right away. And I do love mashed potatoes."

"Good."

They insisted he sit at the head of the table, Frank Durand to Ingram's left, Kate on his right. Frank, a tall, lanky man, had clear blue eyes and a long lock of whitish blond hair that swept over a surprisingly boyish face. That morning he had killed a chicken and that's what they had for dinner. Mashed potatoes and peas, both grown by his brother Lamar, and a salad of mixed greens completed the meal. The talk had been light, forced in a way.

After they finished, Frank sighed and stood. "Let's go outside." He led Ingram to the porch, where it was still eighty-two degrees. Overhead, a million-million stars shouted at them on a moonless night. Sitting in a rocker, Frank waved to another. But Ingram sensed the other rocker was Kate's and chose the bench. And he was right, for she came out a moment later carrying a tray of cups and a pot of coffee and sat. While she poured, a cat, a gray tabby, jumped in Ingram's lap, curled up, and fell asleep.

Frank and Kate looked at one another.

Ingram stroked the cat's head. "Anything wrong?"

Frank said, "That's Fred."

"Yes?"

"Well, he's Helen's. Usually he doesn't jump in people's laps."

All Ingram could manage was a muted, "I'll be damned."

Nobody spoke as Kate passed the cups around. Even then, they waited patiently, while Ingram absorbed the sound of the crickets, the evening's heat, and the same brilliant pinpoints of light overhead that had guided him through the Philippine archipelago to Darwin, Australia. And Fred. He purred when Ingram scratched his ears.

Finally, Ingram drew a deep breath. "A submarine took her from Corregidor a couple of weeks before it was captured."

"It must have been hell," said Kate.

"She's very brave, your daughter." Ingram tried to smile. "I almost socked her, once."

"What?"

With a forefinger, he tapped a jagged two-inch red-orange scar on his right cheek. "Right here. Don't know if you can see it. Shrapnel. The Japs sunk my ship off Caballo Island. They took me to the hospital in Malinta Tunnel. That's on Corregidor. There was no doctor available, so Helen sewed it up."

He waited. Then he realized why they didn't get it. "There was no anesthetic. Hurt like hell. Took three guys to hold me down. Even so, she did a great job. And I saw her handle far worse cases. She's very brave."

"You get a Purple Heart?" asked Frank.

Ingram shrugged. "I don't need one of those things. Helen and the others who are stuck out there—they deserve the medals."

"You don't have any medals?"

"No," Ingram lied. He didn't want to talk about the Navy Cross recommendation.

"You should," said Frank. "But then I was in the last one. I don't think a medal would have helped one way or the other."

"Where were you?"

"Verdun."

He knows what it's like. Corregidor, Verdun, Gallipoli. What a waste.

Kate and Frank sat back and rocked, their chairs squeaking as they looked up at the sky and waited.

Ingram continued, "She got out by sub, but they landed her party on Marinduque so they could run right back and grab some more people off Corregidor. Everybody knew it was going to fall any day. In the meantime, we got out by motor launch, and four nights later ran into her on Marinduque."

"Who's 'we'?" prodded Frank.

"My crew mostly, off my minesweeper."

"Oh." The rockers squeaked.

Sing for your dinner, Ingram. "We picked her up there, on Marinduque . . ." he droned on, telling the story as if it were a travelogue. What he didn't say was that Helen Durand had been captured by the Japanese on Marinduque and tortured by the Kempetai, the military thought police. When he'd found her, she was close to death, cigarette burns covered her body, and she was totally dehydrated. In fact, her heart had stopped beating at one time, giving them all a terrible fright. Yardly, their pharmacist mate, had saved her, brilliantly using the few primitive medical items in his kit.

". . . then we landed at Nasipit in northern Mindanao. We didn't realize Japs were garrisoned there."

"How many?" asked Frank.

"About a hundred." He waited, glad he had been able to get through telling them about Marinduque.

They rocked and sighed and sipped, with Kate occasionally throwing her head back, looking at the stars. In the half-light, Ingram saw tears well in her eyes and glisten on her cheeks. He wondered if he should dab them with his handkerchief, and pulled it out. But his own eyes were moist, so he wiped at them.

"We . . . we were separated. We had to shove off before more Japs showed up. But"—he sat upright on the bench—"she got away. The War Department will probably send a telegram saying she's 'missing in action.' But it's not true. And you mustn't tell anybody I told you. That's why I came here in person."

"You mean it's a military secret?" said Frank.

"All I can say is that she's fine. And she has my ring. I gave it to her." *My God, why did I say that?*

"What ring, Todd?" asked Kate.

Ingram closed his eyes, luxuriating in the sound of Kate's voice.

"Todd?"

"My Naval Academy ring. At the time, I'd lost so much weight that it would just fall off my fingers. Had to wear it on my thumb. So I gave it to her for safekeeping."

Frank asked, "Is she really living in the weeds?"

"She's with Pablo Amador. He leads the resistance."

In the darkness, he sensed they stared at him.

"Don Pablo Amador. He was deputy finance minister under President Quezon. His family has owned Nasipit's lumber mill for nearly a hundred years. And I think he's in the mountains now, setting up the resistance."

Frank and Kate rocked for a while. Then she rose from her chair and went inside, a hand wiping at her cheek.

Frank watched her go. "Thanks for coming."

"You should be very proud of her."

"I am. But that's not what I mean. Here." Frank dug in his pocket, pulled out a crumpled envelope, and handed it over. "This came three days ago."

Even in the faint light, Ingram could see it was a telegram. "War Department?"

"Ummm."

Ingram took it and read:

THE SECRETARY OF WAR DESIRES ME TO EXPRESS HIS DEEP RE-
GRET THAT YOUR DAUGHTER FIRST LIEUTENANT HELEN Z DU-
RAND HAS BEEN REPORTED MISSING IN ACTION SINCE SIX MAY
IN PACIFIC AREA IF FURTHER DETAILS OR OTHER INFORMATION
ARE RECEIVED YOU WILL BE PROMPTLY NOTIFIED PERIOD

                    T L ROBERTS THE ADJUTANT GENERAL

"My God."

"Yes." Frank nodded toward the living room. He rasped, "I just didn't know how to tell her. So like I said, thanks for coming. You saved her a lot of grief."

Ingram could see it had been tearing up Frank as well. "Believe me. She's okay. Just don't say anything."

"What are her chances of getting out?"

"Good. They're looking at ways to get supplies to them, but nobody is supposed to talk about it. All very secret. They don't want the Japs to find out."

A dim light flicked on inside and Kate silently walked out, backlighted. Presently, she stood close and held out something. Ingram opened his palm and she placed a ring on it. Turning it in the living room's pale light, he saw it was a class ring with a red stone—a garnet, he supposed. The legend around the stone read SCRIPPS COLLEGE—1929. Inside the band, a neatly scrolled inscription read HZD. Kate closed Ingram's fingers over it. Her voice was husky. "You keep this for her until she returns."

The next thing he knew, his head rested against Kate's hip and his chest was heaving and he was gasping and moaning and doing a terrible job of keeping it all in.

"It's okay, Todd. It's okay." Kate stroked his hair.

"Forgot to close the garage doors." Frank stood and walked into the evening, his boots crunching on gravel.

Ingram said a silent thank-you to Frank for moving off. "I hardly know you," he mumbled to Kate.

"Shhhhhh."

"They're going to send me back, sooner or later," he said softly. "And damnit . . . I don't . . ." He was tempted to tell her about the nightmares and cold sweats. But then he was afraid to say anything because memories would gush back in full clarity, of men with their arms and legs blown off, bloated headless corpses floating in Manila Bay. Some nights he would see young Brian Forester screaming when a soldier thrust a bayonet through his chest. He squeezed his eyelids tight, trying to keep out the visage of the living who would have been better off dead, men with no hope, no future except servitude and privation and atrocity under their conquerors; the ones he had left behind on his trip to freedom.

She ran a palm down the back of his neck. "No, they won't send you back. Not if you don't want to."

"I'm sorry." His fingers found the cat's fur. And the damned thing purred. He looked up. "Honest. We really tried to get her out."

Kate patted his shoulder. "I'm sure she's fine, Todd."

CHAPTER EIGHT

Helen froze in terror while two Japanese soldiers gripped her wrists, twisting her skin. Their officer—he looked like an Army captain—stood just three feet away. With the slightest of smiles, he drew his Nambu automatic pistol, chambered a round, and pointed it directly at her chest, his elbow locked. He said conversationally, "Good-bye."

It seemed her heart had a life of its own. Knowing it was about to be ripped apart by an eight millimeter bullet, it pumped at an incredible rate while she drew quick lungfuls of air and looked up for a final, earthbound glance at heaven. But that was impossible, since they stood under a thick canopy of sixty-foot narra trees. Helen tried to force an image of something beautiful, something like home. But with this ghoul about to end her life, she couldn't remember anything about home; not even where it was or who was there.

The Army captain raised an eyebrow and hesitated.

The little bastard was enjoying this, she realized, and her terror turned to rage.

With a smirk, he eased his finger off the trigger, then snugged it again and slowly squeezed—

Three explosions cracked through the air, followed by a guttural scream. Helen was on the ground and men twirled above her. Suddenly they had her wrists again, but this time they yanked and pulled her through brush as sharp branches snapped in her face. "What?"

Before her ran a man with a white flowing mane of hair, his planter's hat bouncing on his back by a lanyard. Quickly he looked around and shouted, "Helen, get your feet under you!"

Amador! The man before her was Don Pablo Amador. And a glance to either side showed that the crazy Chinaman, Wong Lee, and Renaldo, the front of his shirt spattered with blood, were the ones dragging and cajoling and kicking at her. *Amazing.* Both were only an inch or two over five feet. Where did they get their strength?

Gunfire rattled behind them and bullets zipped through the underbrush, some thunking into trees, others kicking up three-foot columns of dirt around them. She heard shouts, then an explosion; it sounded like a grenade. Someone screamed horribly.

"Helen. Come on!" urged Amador.

With a gasp, she did as Amador commanded, found her feet and ran.

They stumbled into a dark clearing after an hour of frantic scrambling through streams, down into deep gullies, over enormous fallen logs, through impossibly thick bushes and vines. Amador had led them halfway up Mount Maiyapay's mist-enshrouded 2,360-foot peak and into obscurity, while frustrated Japanese float planes buzzed in the distance.

Wong Lee stopped first, simply running out of breath and collapsing in a wheezing, gasping heap. The others gladly followed suit and flopped on their backs, splaying their arms and puffing and coughing, chests heaving. Helen, her face bleeding and lacerated by branches and thorns, lay among them feeling light-headed, drawing lungfuls of cool, saturated air.

Finding his strength first, Renaldo rolled to his belly, and with a grunt, raised to all fours, then stood. Nodding to Amador, he picked up his ancient bolt-action Springfield rifle and shuffled down the trail as rear guard.

Amador gasped to Helen, "They nearly had you."

"Another second or two and he would have pulled the trigger." Something popped into her mind. "I didn't see God. I thought you were supposed to see God at the last moment."

"That means He doesn't want you now."

"I'm not so sure." With a groan, Helen sat up. Wong Lee lay before her, still flat on his back, his arms straight out and his mouth open and his chest rising and falling. "Wong. Your tongue is hanging out."

"Ghhhhhsh," Wong moaned.

The man had just saved her life, but she couldn't resist. "Could I have a Chesterfield, please?" Everybody gave Wong a bad time about his cigarettes. The man smoked whatever he could—sometimes making do with dry shredded weeds. A month ago, he'd found a carton of American cigarettes on a dead soldier and smoked his way to near oblivion. But those soon ran out and after ambushing the next convoy, he found more cigarettes—not the smooth Lucky Strikes but a lung-searing Egyptian brand. But even those he smoked incessantly. "Ghhhhsh."

Gradually, the twirling in Helen's head slowed down. "What happened?" she asked Amador.

"Damned Hapons circled around and surprised us. While we were stalking them, they stalked us.'' They had been attacking a three-truck convoy. She'd been farther up the mountain, about two hundred meters, watching.

"Did you get anything?"

"There was nothing to grab. Just U.S. Navy crates shipped from Davao marked 'Torpedo Parts.' No guns, no ammo, no aspirin. Not even a damned carton of cigarettes,'' wheezed Wong Lee. "Then the Japs showed up and we dropped everything and ran."

"Where's Emilio?"

Amador shrugged, but just then they heard a whistle. Emilio Legaspi, thin, half a foot taller than the others, with a craggy face, emerged from shadows and trudged among them. Standing his Springfield against a tree, he unbuckled his cartridge belt, let it flop to the ground, and sat heavily.

Amador crawled over and clomped him on the shoulder. "Thank God. I thought I saw a bullet throw you down the mountain."

"Did damned right,'' said Legaspi in a high-pitched pidgin English. He grinned, showing a wide expanse of missing front teeth, and held up a crushed U.S. Army belt buckle between his thumb and forefinger, its brass still gleaming.

"Was it you who tossed that grenade?" asked Wong Lee.

Legaspi's grin widened. "Smashed four, maybe five of the sonsabits." Then he turned to Amador and spoke in rapid Tagalog.

As they talked, Helen leaned back on her hands and looked up at the trees, hearing a monkey screech, a good sign. It had been quiet when they first arrived.

Wong Lee's breathing seemed a bit smoother. "What time is it?"

"Nearly three o'clock,'' Amador said.

How can he do that? Helen wondered. Here, in deep shadows under the narras' canopy, the old land don could gauge the time to within ten minutes without a timepiece.

Amador turned to her. "Good news, dear. Emilio says they're not following. Not today, anyway. There were only fifteen or so. Of that, they lost four to Emilio's grenade, plus the ones who . . . who . . . had you."

Helen exhaled deeply, more from relief than from a need to breathe. This was the second time she'd been close to death in this living hell. The irony was that today the Army captain just wanted to shoot her. Capture by the Kempetai was far worse. Thanks to them, the cigarette burns were still evident, from her face to the bottoms of her feet.

She crawled over to Amador, finding his face smeared and caked with blood. Unclipping her canteen, she poured water over a rag and started wiping.

"Later," he growled.

She unbuttoned a small first-aid kit and dabbed at the cuts on his face. He'd taken the brunt leading the way up the mountain. He tried to push her away, but she held fast. "They'll get infected. Then you'll be on your back begging for mercy, begging for penicillin, begging for everything we don't have. Beside, you look like Lon Chaney playing Genghis Khan."

"Looked at yourself lately?"

She shrugged, wiping dried ooze off Amador's face.

Wong Lee jabbed a cigarette between his lips and lit it with a Zippo, gray-blue smoke swirling around his head. "Next time, drop me at Hollywood Boulevard." Wong, an American-born Chinese, owned two restaurants—one in downtown Los Angeles, the other near St. Mary's Square in San Francisco. With his mother running the Los Angeles restaurant and his wife and daughter running the San Francisco place, he'd traveled to Malaybalay in north-central Mindanao trying to bring his uncle and two nephews back to the United States. With the war's outbreak, they were stuck there and melded into the background, posing as Filipino kitchen workers. Somehow, the Kempetai got on to them and kicked their way into their one-room apartment one night. Wong barely made it out a back window, the others shot where they lay. It was something he never spoke of. Months later, he was still on the run when Amador found him at Nasipit's outskirts, skeletal thin, fishing and living off the sea.

"I may start smoking, too." Amador looked up, studying Helen's ebony hair and quick brown eyes. A pang of guilt struck as he took in the gaunt, overly sharp, angular features of her otherwise young face. He'd seen it in others, a sign of constant fear, of sleeplessness and depravation. And with Amador, she had to keep moving, day and night like a monkey, losing weight as she lived on near-starvation rations. And the cigarette burns. But there was nothing Amador could do about it.

The fighting troops had long ago shipped out to prepare for a major campaign in the South Pacific. In their place were the Kempetai—criminals, thugs, and malcontents wearing the uniform of occupation troops. Beheadings were commonplace in the streets, as were machine-gunning of civilians, robbery, the cruelest rapes and hangings, even crucifixions. In a way, Amador preferred living in the bush, so he wouldn't have to hear the screams that pierced the night. For Helen, it was worse. She was a nurse. Each time someone lived through the torture, Helen was called. She'd seen gruesome things and often didn't sleep. Amador heard her moaning in the night, dreaming her all-too-real dreams. He often wondered which was worse, the nightmares or the human wreckage Helen was called on to patch up. Living in the bush, the constant running from the Japanese, slapping mosquitoes, and pulling leeches off one's skin day and night was a harsh existence. Still, the alternative was far less attractive.

"Cigarettes will kill you."

"Better way to go than by the Hapons."

She grunted and kept dabbing.

Amador said, "He is very lucky."

"Who?" Without thinking, she patted her mud-encrusted blouse. Inside, his ring hung from her neck by a thick leather lanyard.

"Lieutenant Ingram. He is very lucky to have one so beautiful."

She looked away. "Please, don't."

He raised a palm to her cheek and ran a thumb over one of her cuts. "Why?"

"I don't want to think about it." She sank back and laid her hands in her lap.

"Why not?"

In a small voice she said, "Todd is probably in America now. And America is where people laugh and eat all they want and watch *Snow White and the Seven Dwarfs* on long Sunday afternoons." A tear ran down her cheek.

"Yes?"

To think of Todd and home was a luxury she couldn't afford, lest she let go and become a drooling lunatic. Someday, she would think about home when the enemy was dead; when she could once again step into broad daylight and walk down a sidewalk without fear. And think about her parents rocking on the front porch on hot summer evenings . . . "What?"

"I said, 'That's all that keeps me going.' " Amador put a hand on her shoulder.

"Yes?"

"Mariveles. My wife. And my son and daughter in New Mexico. I think of them. It helps."

"But you'll make it." She was convinced that Amador would survive to see his wife and children again. It just seemed that was the way things were to be.

He patted her arm and smiled. "And so will you, my dear."

A tightness pulled at her throat and her eyes welled. Forcing the images deep into her subconscious, she managed to say, "We're almost out of iodine. And we need quinine, and aspirin, and penicillin, and ether, and bandages, and . . ."

Amador let her ramble. After she ran out of things to say, he called over to Wong Lee, "Does Carillo's radio still work?" Now part of the resistance, Manuel Carillo had once been foreman of Amador's lumber mill.

Wong Lee took a long puff. "Batteries are flat."

"Then we steal batteries. It's time to get a message out."

"What about Japs?" asked Helen.

Amador nodded with determination. "We'll be more careful this time."

"I don't know," said Wong.

"Relax, Wong. I grew up here, remember?"

Wong took a long drag and blew smoke rings. "I don't know. Too many Japs."

CHAPTER NINE

Dezhnev stepped to the radio room door and looked in at Yuri Moskvitin, *a starshina vtroy stat'i telegrafist*—telegraphist second class—sitting at his typewriter, taking traffic effortlessly from Moscow Center. The NKVD had scooped a grateful Moskvitin off the Baltic Fleet destroyer *Tucha*, the night before she stood to sea and was blasted to the bottom of the Gulf of Finland, courtesy of a stick of bombs from a German Heinkel 111. In his short time in San Francisco, Dezhnev had discovered Moskvitin was not just a skilled telegraphist, but also accomplished on the guitar, played the piano, and was a near-master at chess. It seemed Moskvitin was one of those with a combination of strong intellect and good looks who could do anything well.

While typing the traffic, Moskvitin shouted to the coding officer in the next room, "Three messages, Sir." Finally, he signed off and, sensing Dezhnev in the doorway, nodded a greeting and winked—a signal meaning one of the messages was for him, and that he should wait until it was decoded. Moskvitin yanked the message forms out of his typewriter, shoved them through a wall slot to the crypto room, then leaned back in his chair and stretched. Dropping the earphones around his neck, he grabbed a softbound book of music and flipped pages. After a few moments, he picked up his guitar and softly strummed, seamlessly moving from one song to the next.

Dezhnev checked his watch to make sure there was time to get ready for the party tonight. He'd been invited to a farewell function given by Admiral Spruance at the St. Francis Hotel.

He hadn't seen the Americans since the day Babcock had surprised him. As soon as DeWitt dismissed him that afternoon, Dezhnev had taken a bus to the Hunter's Point Naval Shipyard and walked a half-mile to the pier where the *Dzhurma* was moored, undergoing extensive boiler and engine repairs. There he hobbled up the gangway and found Sergei Zenit. Quickly, he told the NKVD agent about peeking at the documents after the lights went out. Zenit actually smiled and clucked his tongue approvingly until Dezhnev added the part about Babcock walking in on him.

Zenit sat straight in his chair. "Are you sure he didn't see anything?"

"It was too dark, I think. It all happened so fast."

Zenit slammed his fist on the table. "You *think*?" he shouted.

Dezhnev shrugged.

"We must make sure," said Zenit. "I'll handle this."

Together, they went back to the consulate, where Zenit took the matter to the reclusive Georgiy Voronin, the beefy, pockmarked NKVD resident they found watering potted tomatoes outside his second-floor window. With a grunt, Voronin picked up the phone and dialed the Scapini Custodial Service. After a stilted six-minute conversation—Voronin's pidgin Italian was horrible—the NKVD resident hung up the phone and went back to watering his tomatoes. Leaning out the window, he had told them in so many grunts that the Babcock situation was in good hands and not to worry. The next evening, Voronin reported that Babcock would be missing from the U.S. Navy muster for a long, long time, that Zenit and Dezhnev had no cause for alarm. Ever.

Dezhnev's forehead became clammy as he thought about it. Babcock was most likely dead, while Zenit played with his crypto machines and Voronin watered tomatoes. He leaned against the doorjamb and closed his eyes, trying to separate Moskvitin's chords and melodies from the sound of clacking typewriters and jingling phones. After a while, he gave up and gazed out the third-floor window, where a renegade midday fog had finally burned off, giving a spectacular view of the city, the bay, and the reddish orange structure to his left, the Golden Gate Bridge.

Selected for its commanding view of San Francisco Bay, the Soviet Consulate was a thirty-one-room, four-story Georgian mansion. Built in 1910, it was located at the highest section of Divisidero Street in the posh Pacific Heights area. Squeezed into a special top-floor cubicle were two *Glavnoye Razvedyvatelnoye Upravlenie* (Chief Intelligence Directorate-GRU) officers who each day scanned the Bay with high-power binoculars. At this moment, Dezhnev was sure their logbook would reflect the passage of a cruiser, menacing in her dapple-gray camouflage, as she slid beneath the Golden Gate into the Pacific.

Moskvitin picked up a new piece of sheet music and strummed a compelling tune. In a low voice, he sang in Russian, "One day, under the rainbow."

Dezhnev recognized it as a selection from a new American musical. "Psst. Moskvitin."

Moskvitin, absorbed in his guitar, was startled, not realizing Dezhnev had remained in the doorway. "Sir?"

"In English, it goes, 'Somewhere, over the rainbow.'"

"Ahhh. Better." Moskvitin smiled and penciled a note on his music. "And does the next line sound right? 'Up in the—hmmm, sky?'"

"Way up high."

"Of course. 'Way up high.'" Moskvitin wrote again and looked up. "How do you know all this?"

Dezhnev shrugged. "I listen to the radio."

"It's because his mother is a gorgeous actress from Tbilisi, you see. She sent him to the finest schools in Georgia, teaching him flawless English." Sergei Zenit stepped from the crypto room next door and walked up to Dezhnev, handing him an envelope. He leaned through the doorway and winked conspiratorially to Moskvitin. "Don't tell me you haven't heard of René Dezhnev?"

Moskvitin, a mere *telegrafist,* knew when it was time for *molchi-molchi—shut up. Or you'll end up either in a gulag or with a bullet in your brain.* "I'm not sure, Sir," he gulped.

Zenit's eyes flicked to Dezhnev. "Ah, well, Moskvitin, René Dezhnev raised her son to be an actor. That's how he knows all about your songs."

Dezhnev looked at Zenit. *Where are you going with all this?*

Zenit smirked. "Tell us, Dezhnev, did she really have the affair with Viktor Sorokin that we all heard about? And what about Stalin's trysts in Georgia? I hope there isn't any truth to those rumors, either."

With Zenit's canard, a fire rose in Dezhnev's belly. He'd only been twelve years old at the time and hadn't seen his mother for weeks. But he was sure that gossip hadn't traveled to Moscow. René Dezhnev was not that well-known outside Georgia. It must have been in his folder with Zenit enjoying his demented form of amusement. Perhaps Zenit was still angry that he'd been snubbed by the Americans for the party tonight. Zenit would have given anything, Dezhnev knew, to attend a sumptuous cocktail party at the St. Francis Hotel.

Three days ago, Zenit had walked through the consulate's doors with a temporary appointment to the cryptography department. Word spread within minutes and the staff became morose, quiet, and avoided him. The *Dzhurma* was well-known in Soviet circles; Zenit and his special branch of slave ship *zampolits* carried the stench of the tens of thousands of wretched humans they herded to life's dark promise in the gulags. Perhaps Zenit was retaliating to everyone's reaction.

"Aren't you going to read the message?" Zenit raised an eyebrow.

It was all Dezhnev could do to suppress the living rage boiling within him.

"Report to me after you've done so." Zenit turned and walked to his crypto room, closing the Dutch door.

Dezhnev nodded to Moskvitin, then hobbled down the back stairs to his closet-sized room on the second floor in the back. Next to Voronin's room, it was about eight feet by five with a small window and tiny desk. But it was neat and, like Voronin's, was decorated in a light violet wallpaper. Next door was a bathroom, which was the bad and the good. The bad, in that all night, he was awakened to the groaning of ancient pipes and flushing toilets. But the good was the unlimited showers where everyone stood as an impresario, singing gloriously, with Eduard Dezhnev taking his turn, bellowing his songs and reveling in the steam and magnificent hot water, a phenomena rarely available at home.

His room was stuffy. He opened the window, locked his door, and sat to read his message:

TOP SECRET—OPERATION KOMET—TOP SECRET

EDUARD DEZHNEV, LT, VMF.,   SFO/CON
INFO: SERGEI ZENIT,   SFO/CON

24 AUGUST 1942

DATA ON U.S. SAVO ISLAND LOSSES VERIFIED. ALSO OTHER RE-
PORTS FAULTY AMERICAN TORPEDOES FILTERING IN, BUT ARE
SKETCHY. WE NEED MUCH MORE.

EXPECT COMPLETE REPORT ON WET OPERATION VIA SOONEST
POUCH. YOU WERE INSTRUCTED TO TAKE NO CHANCES.

LAPTEV FOR BERIA

Beria's admonition rang in Dezhnev's mind, "You were instructed to take
no chances."

How the hell did Beria find out about Babcock? Voronin would not have
spilled the beans. It wasn't his style and he simply didn't care about such
things.

Dezhnev jumped to his feet.

Zenit! The only other one on the consulate staff authorized to send messages at will.

He rammed his fist into the wall and glared at the mute, pale violet flowers.
Zenit! A man responsible for the deaths of thousands, perhaps tens of
thousands. And now the little bastard sat in his little cubicle upstairs making
jokes about Dezhnev's mother. He was typical of the NKVD bureaucrats who
killed by doing nothing, by indecision, by trickery and self-indulgence, while
contriving intricate schemes to cheat Americans, Japanese, and, worse, Soviets. Plus—Dezhnev ground his teeth—it was Zenit and Voronin who ordered Babcock's liquidation, the matter taken out of his hands.

Stuffing the message in his pocket, Dezhnev ripped open the door and
bumped and scraped up the stairs to the third floor. Three quick strides found
him at Zenit's office, the Dutch door open. But then he took deep breaths and
leaned against the hallway wall for a moment.

There is a better way to handle this.

Then he looked into the crypto room, seeing Zenit seated at his desk. "You
know, you just may be right about Stalin and my mother."

Zenit looked at Dezhnev suspiciously.

"May I?" Dezhnev opened the Dutch door.

"Stay out," ordered Zenit. He rapped on the wall and shouted, "Moskvitin,
call Voronin!"

Dezhnev held up the message. "It's all a sham, isn't it?"

Zenit's eyes darted around the room. "You disobeyed orders."

"It was you and Voronin."

"You failed. And it must be reported, you see."

"Voronin is the NKVD resident here. It's his decision to report wet operations. Not yours."

"Beria will decide. Now get to work on that report."

"You'll have it. It'll be plain that you lost your head."

"That's for you to find out." They glared at one another. Finally, Zenit found his tongue. "What's this about Stalin?"

Dezhnev stepped closer. "Have you ever met Josef Vissarionovich face-to-face, Sergei?" Premier Josef Stalin's real name was Josef Vissarionovich Djugashvili. He'd taken on the name Stalin, which means "steel," when he went into politics.

"St-stay back."

"Well?"

"No."

Dezhnev's shoulders slumped. He rested his buttocks against a low table. "I have." He stroked his chin. "Pulled guard duty for him while I was a senior warrant."

"What?" Zenit's mouth dropped open.

"You know. At his summer villa in Sochi in '37."

Doing his best to look nonchalant, Zenit lit a cigarette.

Dezhnev paused for five seconds. "One night a dog barked into the wee hours in an adjacent villa. Josef Vissarionovich couldn't sleep a wink. He called the guard shack. I was on duty and heard him tell the sergeant to find the dog and shoot it."

Moskvitin peeked in the doorway. "Comrade Voronin is in the garage greasing the car. Shall I tell him to come up?"

Zenit's eyes darted from Moskvitin to Dezhnev, who by now was totally relaxed against the table.

Dezhnev gave an imperceptible shake of his head. "Leave it, Sergei. You need me. I am your ticket off the *Dzhurma*."

Zenit thought that one over. "Tell Voronin to finish greasing the car."

With Moskvitin gone, Zenit said, "Now get out."

Dezhnev continued as if nothing had happened. "So the sergeant and I went out and found the dog's home. And his master. It was only an old man. Blind as a bat. His son was the commissariat of Georgia's Agriculture. The dog had been given by the son to help the old man through his declining years. So we threw dog and old man into a truck and sent them to the son's house on the other side of town."

Zenit took a puff. "Your story doesn't interest me."

"Next morning at breakfast, Josef Vissarionovich summoned my sergeant and asked if we'd shot the dog.

"No, Sir," said my sergeant. 'We sent them to his son's to stay.'

"Well, Josef Vissarionovich became very angry. Very angry." Dezhnev leaned toward Zenit. "Have you ever seen Josef Vissarionovich when he is angry?"

Zenit slowly shook his head.

"It's like looking into the soul of hell." Dezhnev wiggled a finger at Zenit. And summoned his crispest baritone. "Never, never make Josef Vissarionovich angry."

Imperceptibly, Zenit nodded, then, confused, shook his head.

"Do you know what he did?"

"No," squeaked Zenit.

"He ordered us to bring back the old man and his dog. An hour later, we returned with both. And then he told us to take the dog into the park and shoot it."

"Yes," agreed Zenit.

"Guess who had the honors?"

Zenit shook his head.

"Me." Dezhnev jabbed a finger at Zenit's chest. "The damned thing snarled and growled all the way outside. But then I shot it. One bullet to its brain. Then another for good measure. Goo all over the place."

A clock ticked in the hall as Dezhnev drew everything he could from the silence. Then he casually waved a hand toward Zenit. "So never, never make Josef Vissarionovich angry. Never. Do you understand?"

Zenit gulped.

"Good. Very good. Now, if you don't mind, it's time for me to get ready for my party at the St. Francis."

CHAPTER TEN

24 AUGUST, 1942
UNION SQUARE
SAN FRANCISCO, CALIFORNIA

A freak cold front slammed into the city, bringing a deluge that drenched Ingram and DeWitt as they jumped from the taxi. It was a miracle neither slipped on the slick sidewalk while dashing for the glistening revolving doors of the St. Francis Hotel. Shaking water off their overcoats, they maneuvered through the large, ornate lobby, crowded with men from all the services. Most outranked Ingram, and he avoided their eyes, keeping his head down and following DeWitt, who bulled his way along as if hacking a trail through a dense jungle.

"This way, Todd," DeWitt's resonance shimmered over the crowd as they threaded their way toward a corridor. The going was a little easier when they walked into the shopping arcade, but even so, Ingram was amazed at the number of people here on a Monday night. "Where does everybody come from, Otis?"

DeWitt called over his shoulder, "They have pockets full of money but no place to stay. It's rough in San Francisco when you're on furlough."

"Liberty."

"Whatever." DeWitt edged past two Navy captains and a Marine colonel, who watched in disbelief as he unhooked a red-velveted chain barrier, passing Ingram and himself through, then resnapping it. The two men stepped up to a small elevator, the mahogany doors finished in carved floral patterns and polished to a high gloss. A gleaming brass plate read, PRIVATE.

A Navy ensign walked up to them. "Sir?"

DeWitt cleared his throat. "Major DeWitt and Lieutenant Ingram for the Spruance party."

The ensign ran his finger down a clipboard and nodded sagely. "Of course, Sir. Here, allow me." He inserted a key, and soon the elevator doors eased open. A white-haired uniformed operator in bellman's cap stood inside, wearing gold round spectacles. The ensign stepped away. "Good evening, gentlemen."

DeWitt and Ingram walked in, the doors closed, and the elevator started up. There was only one stop, Ingram noticed. Another brass plate announced, TWELFTH FLOOR—POPE SUITE. Ingram had heard Nimitz stayed in the Pope Suite when he was in town, as did Roosevelt, Cordell Hull, and Charles Lindbergh, to name a few. DeWitt had called last night, inviting Ingram not only to a rescheduled dinner, but extending an invitation to attend a cocktail party hosted by Spruance for his fellow officers in the Army and Marines. Actually, they'd been summoned, DeWitt said. Spruance wanted to show off officers like Ingram and DeWitt; both had ribbons with battle stars, a rarity among the new ranks flooding the armed services.

The elevator doors opened and Ingram stepped into a marbled lobby, finding a desk and large set of dark mahogany double doors. Another ensign walked up with a clipboard. As DeWitt gave their names, sounds of tinkling glasses and laughter drifted from inside. The ensign pushed open a tall pair of double doors and they stepped into a drawing room perhaps twenty-five by fifty feet, with dark-paneled walls and a high, twenty-foot ceiling decorated in white plaster of paris relief. Heavy Victorian furniture had been pushed against the wall. With so many people, Ingram could hardly see across the room. Handing off his overcoat and cap to a butler, he felt the warmth leap from an enormous fireplace to his right, the mantel at least six feet high. To his left was a small bar, and stuffed in the corner were four musicians playing violins and a harp. Most of the guests were military, although Ingram spotted a few well-dressed civilians. One was an exquisitely dressed young redhead.

"She looks familiar," whispered Ingram.

DeWitt drawled from the side of his mouth, "Rita Hayworth. She's in town on a USO tour. We were lucky to get her. See the guy she's talking to?" He nodded to a curly-headed civilian.

"Yes?"

"That's the mayor, Angelo Rossi . . ."

"Ummm."

". . . of San Francisco. And the other guy handing her a drink is Colbert Olson."

Ingram gave a blank stare.

"The governor of California."

Ingram muttered under his breath, "How long do we have to stay, Otis?"

"What's the matter?"

"We're in over our heads."

"Ten minutes, tops. General Sutherland wanted me to check in and make sure—"

Ingram felt a nudge at his elbow and was surprised to see Admiral Spruance and Captain Falkenberg. "Welcome to the den of vipers, gentlemen." Spruance extended his hand.

They shook as a waiter stepped up, offering drinks off a huge silver platter. Taking his time, Falkenberg selected something dark, while Ingram and DeWitt took plain soda waters. Also taking soda water, Spruance raised his glass. "To the teetotalers of this world." He smiled at Falkenberg.

Falkenberg gave a mock bow. "Sorry, Admiral. Every now and then I must grease the machinery."

They drank and Spruance said, "I enjoyed your talk, Lieutenant."

Ingram had forgotten how tall the admiral was. He had to look up at him. "Thank you, Sir. I didn't think it was that compelling."

"Yes, it was. Right now men like you are all we have." He sipped his soda water and continued, "Forgive my curiosity, but why aren't you, like everyone else here, tanking up on the free booze?"

"Can't take it, Admiral. My stomach still hasn't recovered from the half-rations on Corregidor."

Spruance gave a thin smile. "A warrior's plight. But don't worry. The stuff will eventually kill you. At least that's what my mother used to say."

Falkenberg excused himself and ambled across the room to General Sutherland. As he did, General Mott, resplendent in his Marine dress blues, walked in and immediately stepped right in front of Mayor Rossi and shook hands with Rita Hayworth, clapping her on the shoulder. Colbert Olson held his ground, however, remaining a part of the circle.

Ingram and DeWitt followed Spruance to the fireplace, where they took in the warmth. Ingram glanced around, seeing more than one flag officer looking him up and down as if to say, *I'll be damned, that sonofabitch looks just like Spruance. I'll bet he has the easiest job in the Navy.*

Lowering his voice, Spruance said, "You're trying to be modest and doing a bad job of it."

"Sorry, Sir."

"No. I don't mean it that way. As I listened to you the other day, I realized the difference between men who've stood the test of arms and those who haven't."

Ingram and DeWitt exchanged glances.

Spruance continued, "One of our biggest problems out there is leadership. We need leaders who can fight."

DeWitt ran a finger around his collar.

Ingram couldn't help saying, "What do you think, Otis? You ready to go back out there and knock off some Japs?"

DeWitt was saved by Sutherland, who motioned from across the room. He parted with, "Excuse me, gentlemen, duty calls. Good seeing you again, Admiral. Thanks for inviting us." He walked away.

Now Ingram was alone with Spruance. Like reigning monarchs, they stood off by themselves in dress uniform at the fireplace of the Pope Suite in the St. Francis Hotel in downtown San Francisco, with Ingram thinking, *My God! What do I say?*

Spruance went on, "It's the senior ranks. The decision makers. They're just too many deskbound career types out there who are afraid to take risks."

"Yes, Sir." Ingram gulped half his glass. In spite of the driving rain outside, the fire suddenly felt very hot.

Spruance reached up to grab the mantel. "How far along is the *Tingey?*"

"Just laid her keel, Sir."

"Who's your skipper?"

"It's me, for the time being. I'm the senior officer. Sort of a ship supervisor as things get rolling."

Spruance stroked his chin. "And what about—"

There was a commotion across the room. General Sutherland announced loudly, "Excuse me. Pardon me, everyone." He turned to violinists. "Okay. Hit the fanfare."

The musicians did a plausible job bringing conversation to a halt. Then Sutherland stood on a footstool and, with his hands on his hips, surveyed the crowd. He paused for a moment. "For me, it's been an incredible week." Nodding to Spruance, he said, "And please accept our heartfelt thanks, Ray, for calling this conference, so we could iron out our differences in order to get on with the job. And that is to kill the enemy."

A few went, "Hear, hear."

Sutherland gave an officious smile. "I must say that I've come to appreciate the Navy a lot more and the fine job you are doing. And General MacArthur especially wants me to convey that you, the Navy, Marines and Coast Guard, have our fullest cooperation in the Southern Oceans and that together, we're dedicated to wiping out this tyranny in the shortest time possible." With a nod to Olson and Rossi, Sutherland went on, "the General also thanks you, Governor Olson and Mayor Rossi, for your fine leadership. And he sends special thanks to your loyal California constituents for the deep sacrifices made to pursue the war effort. Daily now, supplies and troops are pouring into Australia, reminding us of your great job and that the ball will soon be in our court, to go on the offensive. To take the fight to the enemy."

Sutherland turned to Rita Hayworth. "General MacArthur gave me specific instructions to thank you and your fellow workers in film and radio, for your fantastic efforts. In recent weeks, the general has noticed that our boys are coming out to us with smiles on their faces. And we know it's because the USO is doing its job."

This time, there was applause as Rita kissed Sutherland on the cheek.

Sutherland smiled and made a crack about not washing his face for a week while everyone clapped and hooted.

"And now..." They still whistled; Sutherland raised his hands until they quieted. "And now...on a more serious note." He paused for a moment. "There are special moments when we have the privilege to recognize achievement in times of adversity. I am proud to say that this is one of those moments. So, without further ado, it is my great honor to announce to you this evening that my superior officer, General Douglas MacArthur, has approved the promotion of Major Otis DeWitt to lieutenant colonel, effective immediately!"

DeWitt's mouth dropped as Sutherland's voice cracked like an artillery shell. "Front and center, Mister DeWitt. You're out of uniform."

DeWitt made a quarter turn and gained a semblance of attention.

"No, that way." Sutherland waved a finger in the opposite direction.

DeWitt didn't get it, so Sutherland commanded, "About...face!" After DeWitt spun, he continued, "Pinning on your new silver leaves, Colonel DeWitt, is Rita Hayworth! And may I say, Colonel, congratulations. Our country is proud of you and so is your Army.

"Ladies and gentlemen. May I present Lieutenant Colonel Otis DeWitt: hero of Corregidor."

A photographer knelt before them. Jammed in his hatband was a small tag that said PRESS: SAN FRANCISCO CHRONICLE. He snapped flash pictures while Falkenberg handed Rita Hayworth a small box. Opening it, she pinned the devices on DeWitt to more applause. Cheers and catcalls broke out when she kissed an astonished DeWitt fully on the mouth, leaving a gloppy red streak. Then she whispered in DeWitt's ear and he shook his head with a broad grin. Then, among all the clamor, DeWitt lifted Rita Hayworth's hand, kissed it, then turned to shake with Sutherland.

Sutherland signaled, the violins played softly again, and the party resumed its tempo.

Spruance smiled. "Good for him. He's doing a good job running things for us. And he was with you in your boat, wasn't he?"

"Yes, Sir."

Just then, Falkenberg mounted Sutherland's footstool and called loudly, "On deck. Attention to orders."

The music stopped, then the quintet did another fanfare as Falkenberg continued, "Lieutenant Ingram, front and center."

Oh, my God. Ingram walked over with Spruance, falling in beside Falkenberg.

Falkenberg raised a large piece of heavy bond paper directly before his face and read, "The Secretary of the Navy takes pleasure in presenting the

Navy Cross to Lieutenant Alton C. Ingram, United States Navy. Citation for extraordinary bravery during and after the siege of Corregidor and the fortified islands of Manila Bay: Lieutenant Ingram risked his life, fighting boldly, and with determination on six May 1942, to assist eleven shipmates to escape Caballo Island, at the mouth of Manila Bay, the night it fell to the Japanese. Through foresight and skillful preparation, he navigated a thirty-six-foot launch over nineteen hundred miles through the Philippine Archipelago, out the Surigao Strait, and into the Pacific Ocean, safely reaching freedom at Darwin, Australia, on seventeen June 1942. En route, he and his men unselfishly harassed the enemy at great risk to their own lives, causing serious damage to a Japanese destroyer. They also wiped out a Japanese Army garrison on Mindanao, inflicting a great deal of damage to equipment and loss of at least fifty enemy lives." Falkenberg looked over to Spruance. "For the Secretary of the Navy, Raymond A. Spruance Rear Admiral, United States Navy."

Spruance's eyes gleamed as he accepted the box from Falkenberg, then stepped up and shook Ingram's hand. "Congratulations, Lieutenant."

"Thank you, Sir." Ingram was trying to figure out what Spruance was going to do with the medal when suddenly Rita Hayworth walked up and gave him a big smack on the lips.

"Wooooah," went the crowd as the music struck up once again.

"Congratulations, sailor." Rita accepted the medal from Spruance and pinned it on his uniform. Then she stood on her tiptoes and whispered in his ear, "You have a sweetheart?"

"Well, yes." Ingram hoped she wouldn't ask where Helen was right now.

Flash bulbs lit up the Pope Suite as Rita stepped back and gave Ingram her famous blazing smile. Then she tapped him on the tip of his nose with her index finger. "Well, you tell her she's a very lucky girl and that if she doesn't grab on to you real tight, I'm standing next in line."

All Ingram could manage was, "Thanks, I'll tell her."

Spruance edged up. "Congratulations again, Todd. Excuse the theatrics, but I'm a strong believer in honoring heroes, whether the heroes like it or not. And right now, America needs heroes."

Ingram decided against saying something inane like, *Tell it to the guys who are still over there.* "I appreciate what you've done, Admiral, and—"

Governor Olson took Rita aside, letting a civilian edge up to them. "Evening, Admiral. Good to finally meet you. And congratulations, Lieutenant. What a marvelous achievement." In his mid-forties, the man had blondish meticulously bleached sun-streaked hair combed straight back and a square jaw. His build was like that of an Olympic gymnast and he wore a dark blue suit, red tie, and black wing-tipped shoes that outshone the brass plaque in the elevator.

Spruance gave an icy smile, "Ah, good to see you, George. Here, meet Lieutenant Todd Ingram. Todd, this is George Atwell."

Atwell's grip was like an aluminum extruding machine working at twenty thousand pounds per square inch. A look into the man's pale green eyes told Ingram he enjoyed giving it all he had. Ingram actually had to let go. "How do you do?" With difficulty, he kept from wiggling his hand.

Spruance explained, "George is vice president of technology with the Winslow River Corporation." He turned to Ingram. "George joins our meeting tomorrow to tell us all about torpedoes."

There was something in Spruance's tone, and it hit Ingram that the Winslow River Corporation manufactured the Navy's torpedoes. He'd heard dark rumors about faulty torpedoes and he didn't want to be close by when the sparks flew. Especially at this level.

Looking at Spruance, Atwell said, "You play golf, Admiral? I can get us a round at the Olympic Club. How 'bout Saturday morning? Say, ten o'clock, weather permitting?"

Spruance slowly shook his head. "I'd like to, but I'll be at sea Saturday and Sunday aboard the *Indianapolis*. We'll be watching our destroyers go through their paces, including"—he paused—"torpedo-firing exercises. Would you care to join us? We'd love to have you."

"Oh, my gosh, Sir. Thank you very much. I'd love to, but—my, what an opportunity—I wish I'd known an hour earlier."

Spruance gave a cold, thin smile. Ingram wanted to crawl into the fireplace.

Atwell gulped his drink. Ironically, it also looked like soda water. He pasted on his own smile. "But we have Admiral Norman and Ted La Grange—he's our technical hotshot—and myself. Actually, we're seeking a fourth."

"Thanks anyway. How about Lieutenant Ingram, here? Todd, do you play golf?"

Atwell's smile fell twelve floors to the lobby.

Ingram saved Atwell with, "No, Sir. Sorry. I don't play golf." In fact Ingram was a five handicap. But he hadn't played since last November in the Philippines.

"What a shame." Spruance waved a hand in Sutherland's direction. "Perhaps . . ."

"Yes, thank you, Sir. And many, many thanks for inviting me to your party. Perhaps we can talk later. Tomorrow for sure. Nice meeting you, Lieutenant." Atwell moved across the room toward General Sutherland.

Spruance downed the last of his drink. "Getting a little warm." He stepped away from the fire. "Gonna take a long time to build that ship of yours, Lieutenant."

"Yessir." Ingram didn't add that the BuPers officer had promised him at least six months in the States before reassignment overseas, knowing the hell Ingram had endured. Hiding him as a ship's executive officer in charge of new construction seemed the perfect solution.

"In six months, a year at most, I can give you your own can."

"Thank you, Sir."

"I need you out there for your command experience now. And I need you and plenty more like you, to replace the ones who are dragging their feet."

Suddenly the blazing log seemed like a superheated boiler pumping out seven-hundred-degree steam. "Yes, Sir."

Diagonally across the room were three mufti-clad civilians in dark suits quietly drinking in the corner. Among them was the red-headed Soviet Navy lieutenant Eduard Dezhnev, who broke into a smile and shook both hands over his head when he spotted Ingram.

Falkenberg walked up, and with a look at Ingram, said, "We'd best spend some time with the Russians, Ray."

Spruance waved to the Soviet consul. "You'll have to excuse me, Lieutenant. It's time for me to extend the hand of friendship to our Soviet guests." He nodded toward Dezhnev, who had moved off, inspecting a massive tapestry that ran from ceiling to floor. "Remember that one?"

"Yes, Sir. I do."

"Imagine that. Shooting it out with three German E-boats. He takes two with him as he's going down." He looked at Ingram. "Now, there's somebody I'd like to have in the Pacific Fleet. We need people like him out there. And people like . . . you."

Something popped into Ingram's mind and he blurted. "Like Babcock, Sir."

Spruance drew a broad grin at the memory. "That's right. Like Babcock. By the way, did you hear about him?"

"Sir?"

"Kid went AWOL. Hasn't been seen since last Wednesday. That elevator business must have driven him nuts."

"That's a surprise to me, Sir."

"Me, too." Spruance shook his head. "I thought I was a pretty good judge of character." He offered a hand. "Thanks for joining us." An Army Air Corps general moved up and started talking.

Falkenberg stepped close. "The admiral's not kidding. Wherever he can, he's digging up the right people for the varsity. You'll be getting orders in the not-too-distant future, Lieutenant. In the meantime"—he looked around the room—"enjoy yourself."

Ingram felt as if he'd been just pushed out the window. "Yes, Sir. Thank you, Sir."

Falkenberg must have known what he was thinking. "Don't worry. It'll probably be convoy duty or something very boring. Your Corregidor days are over, Lieutenant."

CHAPTER ELEVEN

"Can't see a damn thing on an empty stomach." Wong Lee lowered the binoculars.

Helen grabbed them and raised the lenses to her eyes. "Here, I'll show you." She knelt at the window and peered out onto Butuan Bay. But her view was into the setting sun, making direct sunlight dance in her eyes.

"Well?" demanded Wong Lee.

"Wong, step away, please," Amador barked. He sat at a little makeshift table in the back of the room. Due to the Japanese's indiscriminate torture, Don Amador had set a policy early on not to disclose their presence to the villagers.

"Sorry." Wong moved into the shadows.

"There it is." Helen pointed to the forty-seven-foot Japanese landing barge well into the bay, perhaps four or five kilometers offshore. "I can see them pulling in another one." Ever so gently, she rolled the focus knob, making the scene sharper. Working with block and tackle at the bow ramp, several silhouetted sailors hauled a black cylindrical object from the water. "That's three torpedoes so far."

"Let me." Wong Lee exhaled smoke, knelt beside Helen, and took back the binoculars. "Damn, you're right."

Helen stood. "What do you supposed they're up to?"

"They're getting ready for dinner, is what they're doing," said Wong Lee. He looked up to Helen, his blue-black hair blazing in the setting sun. "I'm famished. Isn't it your turn?" He looked back to Amador, who nodded in concurrence.

"Men and their stomachs," muttered Helen. She walked across the dirt floor for the rucksacks, which contained the *lechón*, roast pork, that Rosarita Carillo had packed for the evening meal. Rosarita had sent along a thermos of tea and, for a treat, another thermos of *tuba*, a beer made from coconut.

Their hideout for the evening was a four-room bungalow built in the 1900s by Fito Ruiz, a Portuguese gambler from Macao. In a mad dash, he consolidated his winnings and, craving solitude, sailed to the beaches of northern Mindanao, where he took in two Filipina concubines to augment his retirement. In 1922, Ruiz was beheaded by a Moro raiding party and his European-style bungalow stood empty for several years. Gradually, it was taken over as a common storehouse by Buenavista's fishermen. Now the rooms were stocked with nets, line, tackle, floats, and boat gear. Except for the left front window, the windows were nailed shut; the place stank of grease, rotted fish, drying netting, and fuel oil.

Naturally, it was convenient for a weapons cache. Over three weeks, Amador's people had dug a subbasement directly underneath, an area perhaps twelve feet square that, although advantageous for storage, quickly became a habitat for a number of creatures, large and small. It was damp and dark, with the vegetation renewing itself at an alarming rate. A week ago, Helen could have sworn Wong Lee's beautiful hair turned pure white for an instant when, after two short screeches, he erupted from the basement and dashed out the bungalow's front door. It turned out to be a ten-foot python, and it took two days to get rid of the thing with smoke bombs. The trouble was a myriad of holes and rotted roots riddled the earth. There was no way of keeping snakes out, save paving the whole mess with concrete, an impossibility with the Japanese and their surprise visits.

She gave Wong Lee and Amador each three slices of *lechón*, then sat to eat her own portion. Amador finished quickly and sucked juice off his thumbs and forefingers. ''Excellent, Rosarita.'' He poured some tea and nodded toward the window. ''What do you suppose they are trying to prove?''

Helen savored her pork. And after what seemed just a few bites, there wasn't much left. ''Torpedo testing station? I don't know. One would think they could pick a better place.'' Over the past few days, many Japanese ships had been standing in and out of Nasipit, six kilometers to the west. Even now, a small coastal *Maru* headed for the once-quiet lumbering village. Last week, the Japanese had towed in a floating dry dock along with something else that looked like a barge-mounted two-story hatbox. Amador called it a work barge, and from his runners, it sounded like Nasipit was being converted to a ship repair yard.

Amador had to shade his forehead as he looked out at the sunset's last rays. ''Manuel says they have a torpedo tube mounted on work barge's bow.'' Manuel was Rosarita's husband, who had been foreman of the Amador Lumber Mill until after war broke out.

''Well. It looks like they're firing right into Butuan Bay. Three yesterday. Three today.''

''Why? is the question.''

Helen took her last bite and shrugged.

Wong Lee lowered his binoculars and walked over. ''They're heading in. All done for the day. What time do we try?''

Amador checked his watch. ''Ummm. In about three hours. It should be quiet then.''

Wong Lee jabbed a thumb toward the window. ''Should we tell them about what the Japs are doing?''

Amador bent over a scratch pad and made notes. ''All I want to do is make contact. We can worry about that later.''

* * *

After the stifling, humid day, the night was warm, and, through the palms, Helen watched a quarter moon fall over Diuata Point and touch the western horizon of Butuan Bay. She marveled at the infinite shades of gray and deep blue and yellow; it was as if she had stepped into a travelogue.

Amador looked up from his writing pad. "What else?"

"Maybe some penicillin?" It was hard for Helen to see; the room was lit by only two candles, emphasizing deep fatigue lines under her eyes. Amador, too. They'd been up for the past twelve hours getting ready.

Even so, each hair of Amador's flowing white mane was in place, as if he'd just stepped out of a barber's chair. He muttered, "Why not? May as well ask for all the Hershey bars in Pennsylvania while we're at it."

"I only meant—"

"Sorry. I'm a little off center tonight. I think we all are." He turned to Wong Lee, who fiddled with the radio equipment. "How about you? Any requests?"

"MSG. These mountain lizards taste lousy."

Amador looked up from his little desk, an upturned crate. "I'm afraid it'll have to be just plain lizard soup and *lechón* for a while longer." Then he said to Helen, "We'll try for Otis again."

"Tell him hello."

"Of course."

As Amador worked, Helen's eyes darted around the little space.

Early this morning, Wong Lee, his teeth chattering in eighty degrees of heat and ninety-eight percent humidity, dutifully crawled into the pit, as they called it, and passed up a Japanese Type 92 radio transmitter. He also heaved up a Type 94 receiver; both items stolen from a truck convey. He clambered up quickly afterward, passing the last piece of equipment: a model "F" portable hand generator that weighed only sixteen pounds. But it required seventy revolutions a minute from a single hand crank to produce twenty-four watts. Now he sat stoically ready to grind, a cigarette dangling from his lips as he thumbed through a ten-month-old issue of the *Saturday Evening Post*.

Recently, the Kempetai had staged a surprise raid in Nasipit and uncovered a beautiful Halicrafters transceiver stored under the stairs of Ricardo Albano's house. After setting the house afire, the Kempetai hung Albano and his family upside down from a tree, setting them afire one by one, leaving Ricardo for last, the family's ear-piercing screams ripping through Nasipit again and again.

This left the Buenavista cache as the only radio equipment in the Butuan Bay area. But it had been frustrating. After days and days of broadcasting in the blind, there was no reply on the crackling airwaves, the Allies fearing a Japanese trick. But recently, Wendell Fertig, an American colonel who led the resistance in western Mindanao, had sent a messenger giving them the proper call sign for Otis DeWitt. Tonight was to be their first attempt.

"How about this?" Amador looked up.

Helen leaned over his shoulder and read:

TO: GMD
FM: DPA

URGENT NEEDS   WEAPONS AMMO NOW USE JAP GUNS
ALSO NEED MEDICINE ESP PENICILLIN PLUS RADIO US
CURRENCY OR GOLD   JAP SCRIP WORTHLESS   PLUS FOOD
CLOTHES   PREFER AIR DROP BUENAVISTA   HELEN SENDS
BEST   AMADOR

BT

Helen nodded. "How 'bout the Jap barge and torpedoes?"

"Later. Have to keep things simple."

"Okay."

"This time I'm going to try code."

"How can you do that?" Helen asked.

Wong Lee waved a hand with evident sarcasm. "Where's your secret book?"

"Before the war, when I worked in the Ministry of Finance, we used an emergency code when on travel. We had to use Western Union. It was the only way to communicate. It's simple, but effective."

Helen asked, "How do you do it?"

Amador was silent for a moment, then his eyes darted to the lanyard around Helen's neck. "Ah! The ring."

"What?" She drew back.

"May I see it, please?" He held out his hand.

Wordlessly, she lifted the lanyard over her head and handed it to him.

Like a jeweler, Amador bent over and examined Ingram's Naval Academy ring. "Okay. It'll be a checkerboard code with a simple key. Watch, you may have to do this sometime." Amador took a fresh sheet and sketched out an alphabet in five rows:

A	B	C	D	E
F	G	H	I/J	K
L	M	N	O	P
Q	R	S	T	U
V	W	X	Y	Z

Then he rolled Ingram's ring over in his palm. "His year of graduation is 1937. That's the key." Across the top, he wrote:

0	1	9	3	7
A	B	C	D	E
F	G	H	I/J	K
L	M	N	O	P
Q	R	S	T	U
V	W	X	Y	Z

Then he muttered to himself, "Now we need a key for the left-hand column. So we'll use the other digits from zero to nine, that don't appear in the top row." Thus, he wrote vertically:

	0	1	9	3	7
2	A	B	C	D	E
4	F	G	H	I/J	K
5	L	M	N	O	P
6	Q	R	S	T	U
8	V	W	X	Y	Z

"Each letter has two digits. You read across, then up. For example, the letter 'H' is 49. So 'Helen' is expressed as: 4927502759. And this conveniently breaks down to two, five-letter groups of 49275 and 02759."

Wong Lee said, "Pretty good."

"Simple. Experts can crack it, but it's the only thing I can think of right now."

Silence fell as Amador began encoding. Wong Lee sat at his generator and lit another cigarette while Helen replaced the ring and lanyard around her neck. She looked out the window once again, marveling at the evening's beauty, yet trying not to think of the United States or the people who lived there or what they did on Sunday afternoons. Everything seemed so long ago. What was it like to go into town for a root beer float? Or ride a horse? Or watch a movie? Or pull weeds? Or peel onions? Or—

Wong Lee was up and had his arms around her. "It's okay, hon, don't cry."

Helen wiped her eyes. "I'm only peeling onions, damnit." She pulled away and looked out, her arms folded.

"Huh?" Wong exchanged glances with Amador.

After ten minutes, Amador tore off his sheet. "All right, here it is."

Helen stepped over and looked at the page:

TO: GMD
FM: DPA
REF: INGRAM USNA + QUEZON

67614	12759	63592	72723	81272	05753	59632	05151	53595
38167	69274	34057	41675	96920	50695	35927	27235	12723
43294	35927	27695	75727	59432	94350	50435	95750	67696
12023	43536	76929	67616	12759	29835	36141	53502	34320
57692	96143	57638	15361	63495	02769	69575	06769	40535
32329	50536	34927	69576	12740	27612	04361	23615	35721
67275	92080	43696	32049	27502	75969	27592	36921	27696
32051	20235	36100						

BT

Wong Lee gave a long exhale. "DPA is . . . ?"

"Don Pablo Amador."

"Why Quezon?" wondered Helen. Manuel L. Quezon was the president of the Philippines who had escaped with MacArthur to Australia the previous March.

"It's the only way I know of tipping them that it's a government checkerboard code. And here"—Amador pointed to Ingram's name—"I'm betting they'll figure out that's his year of graduation from the U.S. Naval Academy, which gives them the top row."

"It's worth a try," said Wong.

Amador checked his watch. "You know, there's still time. Maybe I will add a bit about the torpedoes. What do you think?"

Helen nodded. "Can't hurt."

"Okay." Amador redrafted the message, then looked up. "This should fool the Hapons. Beyond that, we must hope DeWitt is good enough to figure it out. You ready to crank, Wong?"

Wong Lee stood at the generator. "Let'er rip."

"You'll poop out in two minutes." Helen walked over to stand beside him.

"Out of my way."

"Connect the antenna," ordered Amador.

Wong screwed down the antenna wire, then leaned over to grind the generator. It whined into life, and soon Amador switched on the transmitter and receiver, their gauges dancing and lights blinking. "Here goes . . ." Adjusting earphones on his head, he started tapping the cw key.

gmd fm dpa . . . gmd fm dpa . . . gmd fm dpa . . .

Five minutes passed. Helen said, "Okay, my turn."

A grateful Wong Lee stepped aside and Helen started grinding, surprised at the energy it took to maintain the proper level of revolutions. Two minutes later, she was about to give up when Amador shouted, "Presto!"

"You have them?" Wong and Helen said together.

Amador looked at his message sheet and tapped furiously. "I can't believe it. Weak, but clear."

Helen felt almost faint with the realization that a live signal, albeit tiny signal, was going into Amador's earphones. It was a signal generated by a live person—a live *free* person—thousands of miles away. American or Australian, man or woman, he or she would most likely be sleeping between clean sheets later tonight. The tiny inaudible pulses in Amador's earphones made Helen grind with a new spirit. While her muscles ached, she reveled in thoughts of Ramona, of movies, of horses and avocado groves and hot summer afternoons.

Wong stepped up. "How you doin', hon?"

She managed a smile, the first one in a long, long time. "Couldn't be better."

Amador said, "Almost done."

Emilio Legaspi, who had been standing guard outside, walked in. "Hapons. Sonsabits ona *banca* out of Nasipit. Come soon."

Amador kept tapping. "How far?"

"Three kilos. No lights," reported Legaspi.

Amador brushed long white hair from his eyes. "You better go up and look, Helen."

Turning the generator over to Wong, she dashed outside with Legaspi and followed him up the ladder to the roof. There, the thin Filipino pointed to where the moon had set. Helen squinted while her eyes adjusted. Finally she saw it and called down to the open window. "They're in a barge. No running lights. Headed straight for us. About fifteen minutes away." It was typical of the Kempetai. They were trying to hit the town by sea with everything darkened rather than clank up the coast road in their rickety trucks. Luckily for them, the Japanese had timed their raid with moonset, making the barge well silhouetted.

"Just signed off," was Amador's muffled reply.

Twenty minutes later, the radio equipment was stowed and they stood on a path half a mile into the hills. By the village's dim lights, they watched the Japanese soldiers jump off the barge's bow ramp, dash through the surf, and dart among the huts like insects.

"Now we wait," said Amador. "Wait and pray."

"Did you remember to ask for MSG?"

CHAPTER TWELVE

The thunderstorm crashed overhead as the cab pulled up before the Soviet Consulate on Divisidero Street.

"You get him," DeWitt ordered.

Lieutenant Junior Grade Oliver P. Toliver III cast an uncomplimentary salute. "Yes, Colonel. Right away, Colonel. I'll do as you say, Colonel." He dashed into the downpour, leaving the door open.

With rain thumping on the taxi's roof, DeWitt reached out and swung it shut. "Someday I'll teach that little bastard some manners."

Ingram grinned. DeWitt and Toliver had been going at it since they'd first met on Corregidor.

The taxi door opened, admitting Dezhnev and Toliver.

"Wong Lee's Café on Grant Avenue." As the cab drove off, Toliver said, "Well, Otis. Now that you're a colonel, how about a loan?"

DeWitt surveyed the three. "Henceforth, use of my first name is strictly prohibited. I demand proper respect. Especially from"—he sniffed at Toliver—"a mere lieutenant jay-gee."

"Ahh, come on, Otis. Just a little something to help me open a liquor store." Toliver, a lanky, towheaded Navy officer who had escaped from Corregidor with Ingram and DeWitt, hailed from a prominent Long Island family. His father was Conrad Toliver, a founding partner in the Manhattan Law firm of McNeil, Lawton & Toliver. Conrad Toliver had been shocked when his son entered the Navy upon graduation from Yale. Young "Ollie," as the boy was called, had been expected to continue on to law school and then enter the firm. But with the realization that a war was coming, Conrad learned to put up with his son's intransigence. Besides, he figured, having Ollie strut around someday in a Navy uniform with flashy ribbons would be good for business.

Ingram asked, "Well, then, Otis, how should we address you?"

"His Majesty, of course."

Dezhnev smiled. "Is this what you call a drenching party?"

"Wetting down," said Toliver. "It's what happens when someone is promoted."

"Or receives the Navy Cross." Dezhnev looked at Ingram. "Again, congratulations, Lieutenant."

"They pasted the Navy Cross on him two nights ago, Rita Hayworth and all."

"What?"

DeWitt picked it up. "That's true. We both have something to celebrate."

"What's this Navy Cross stuff?" asked Toliver.

Ingram looked out the window.

DeWitt glared at Ingram, then said, "Admiral Spruance told Todd he was being awarded the Navy Cross at the Chiefs of Staff conference last week." DeWitt explained.

"Congratulations, Todd. I think that's great," said Toliver, shaking Ingram's hand. "Now where's the ribbon?" He nodded to Ingram's chest.

"Tomorrow." Ingram had been uncomfortable adding the ribbon to his chest. Most recipients of the Navy Cross had received their awards posthumously.

"Since you're so tight with Admiral Spruance, could you ask him what gives with my orders?" Toliver asked.

"What orders?"

The cab pulled up to Wong Lee's. Thunder rattled as they jumped out, leaving a grumbling Toliver to pay the fare. He caught up with them inside, finding the others crowded into a small vestibule. DeWitt stood before a comely young Chinese woman with hair down to her waist and a long red skirt slit up the side. DeWitt talked, waving his hands, imploring. She shook her head. DeWitt tried again. Once again she shook her head while flinging an arm toward a full house.

DeWitt threw his hands in the air and cursed.

Toliver leaned around. "Hi, Suzy."

Suzy flashed a dazzling smile. "Ollie." She walked up and pecked Toliver on the cheek. "You're late. Hold on for a sec." Suzy hurried off to a series of curtained booths in back.

A fuming DeWitt cocked an eyebrow. "Suzy?"

Toliver shrugged.

Ingram asked again, "You were saying about orders, Ollie?"

Toliver smiled at a blonde who brushed past on her way to the powder room. "My XO heard through the rumor mill that I'm getting new orders."

"Go on." Toliver had been "parked" as gunnery officer aboard the U.S.S. *Ammen,* another destroyer under construction at the Bethlehem Steel Shipyard.

"The word is, they're scared shitless after this Savo Island business. They're scouring the fleet for people with experience."

"My news is about the same." Ingram told them what Spruance and Falkenberg had said.

"So, I thought we had a deal, Toliver said. Six months, they told us."

Ingram glanced at Dezhnev, who toyed with a book of matches and stared in the distance. He wondered, *How can we be bitching like this when Russians are dying by the tens of thousands every day?* Quoting Falkenberg, Ingram said dryly, "Probably just convoy duty or something boring. Our Corregidor days are over."

"Huh?"

Suzy returned. "Your booth is ready, Ollie." Smiling and waving menus, she turned and led them across the room.

Ingram marveled that the place was so packed on a rainy night. To their right was a bar jammed. Cigarette and cigar smoke hung over crowded tables in the main area. Most of the patrons were in uniform, although a few silver-headed civilians were scattered here and there. Curtained booths were situated around the room's periphery, most of them closed. Ingram followed Toliver to the rear. "I don't think we have a choice, Ollie."

"But they promised."

"People are dying out there."

"Don't I know it?"

They were shown into a booth decorated with Chinese bric-a-brac. Waiting for them were four place settings complete with hot tea, ready to pour. As they arranged themselves, Suzy bowed. "Anything else, let me know, Ollie."

"Thanks, honey."

Suzy withdrew, whisking the curtains closed.

DeWitt looked around. "Perfect choice, Ollie. I forgive all your previous sins. What do you think, Ed?"

"I'm in wonderland. Ummm, smell that. I could eat everything in sight."

"You'll have your chance," Toliver told him.

A spectacled waiter in his mid-fifties eased through the curtain, his pad poised. "Drinks?"

"Ginger Ale."

"Root beer."

"Soda water."

Dezhnez looked as if he'd swallowed a cow. He looked up to the waiter, who shrugged. The others laughed as Dezhnev said with an edge to his voice, "Vodka?"

"Sorry. We don't carry vodka."

"Ummmm. Do you have single-malt scotch?"

"What kind?"

Dezhnev raised his eyebrows. "Well, I do have a favorite." He told him.

All were amazed when the waiter reported that they had Dezhnev's brand of single malt scotch in stock. But with war rationing, it was very expensive. Toliver said, "It's okay. The tab's on McNeil, Lawton & Toliver. Just make sure we talk about something to make it deductible. Let's see, uhh . . . how does this sound? The 1942 Tax Reform Act?"

"What the hell is a Reform Act?" demanded DeWitt.

"Sounds deductible to me." Dezhnev grinned, then turned to the waiter. "I'll take the single-malt."

The waiter started to back away.

"Hold on," said DeWitt. "This is supposed to be a celebration. What do you say, fellows. Just one?"

Ingram growled, "You're a bad influence, Otis."

DeWitt nudged Dezhnev. "But this is in the interest of maintaining strong relations with our esteemed comrades from the Soviet Union."

Dezhnev slapped DeWitt's forearm. "*Da, tovarisch.*"

Ingram gave in. "Oh, all right. I'll take the single-malt."

Toliver sighed. "Single-malt."

"Same," DeWitt echoed.

The waiter backed out and Toliver called after him, "You might as well bring the bottle."

Five minutes later, the waiter had poured four glasses of single-malt, neat. Leaving bottle and appetizers, he took their orders and backed away, easing the curtains closed.

After two sips, Ingram smacked his lips, finding that outside of the fiery feeling in his throat, nothing much happened. He hadn't fallen out of his chair nor did Toliver or DeWitt slur or go cross-eyed.

On the other hand, Dezhnev sat calmly, knocking back his scotch and watching the three of them as if they were prey, recently flushed from the forest at the height of a winter blizzard.

"Ed," Ingram began. "This may sound strange, but we haven't had any booze for at least eight months." He explained why.

Dezhnev's eyebrows went up. "Ahhh. Don't worry. I'll take care of this." Dezhnev grabbed the bottle, poured two fingers in his glass, and rose to his feet. Widening his stance just a bit, he raised his glass with his right hand and jammed his left in the small of his back. "To the wisdom of the armed forces of the United States of America for promoting Major Otis DeWitt to lieutenant colonel." Then, with a roll of his tongue, he growled loudly, "Uhhh-rah!" It rhymed with *doo-dah*. He knocked his scotch back in one gulp.

They sat speechless and stared.

Dezhnev poured another. "And congratulations to Lieutenant Todd Ingram, hero of the United States Navy's Pacific Fleet and winner of the Navy Cross. Uhhhh-rah!" He drank.

"My God." Pouring his own two fingers, DeWitt raised his glass and stood saying, "Uhhh, this is to Joseph Stalin and Boris Tchaikovsky, the best damned Russians to walk the face of the earth. Yeee-haw!" He drank and sat, wiping his mouth.

"For a proper Soviet toast you must say, 'Uhhh-rah!' "

"But I'm a Texan."

"Uhhh-rah!" commanded Dezhnev.

"Awright, awright. Anything in the interest of maintaining good relations." He raised a fist: "Ooooo-rahhhh!" His voice resonated over scotch-lubricated vocal chords.

"Better." Dezhnev waved a finger at DeWitt and admonished, "But never forget, *tovarisch,* it's Pyotr Tchaikovsky, not Boris."

"You sure?"

Ignoring DeWitt, Dezhnev pursed his lips, poured another round, and stood.

"And now I insist we all acknowledge that most treasured son of the *Rodina,* the one soul who single-handedly led all of civilization from darkness into an enlightened twentieth century. Gentlemen, I give you Yuri Bulzuluk, inventor of the electric light bulb."

"Who?" asked DeWitt.

Ingram and Toliver stood with Dezhnev and went, "Uhhhh-rah!" They emptied their glasses.

Dezhnev poured and began to stand, but Ingram waved him down and said, "Gentlemen, we've been remiss in not acknowledging the arts. And we must realize that we are gathered here in uniform so that one day, others may follow in peace and liberty to once again create beauty on this planet."

"Hear, hear."

Ingram raised his glass. "I give you Alfred Schmidlapp, composer of that rapturous American ballet *Swan Lake.*"

In unison: "Uhhhhhh-rah!"

Ingram parted the curtain slightly and looked out to see if they'd been too loud. Apparently not. Waiters bustled about and the patrons seemed engrossed in their own tables. The ambient noise was high and a male-female duet in the bar competed with a chorus of slurring male voices three booths away.

From his seat, Dezhnev raised his glass. "To Leonid Vladimir Anichkiov, inventor of the steam engine."

Relieved that Dezhnev hadn't stood, they growled, "Uhhhh-rah!"

Toliver raised his glass. "To Ignatius Klutz, that Nobel Prize–winning author from the great state of West Virginia."

"What did he write?" demanded DeWitt.

"*War and Peace.*"

"Uhhhh-rah!"

The bottle was empty. Toliver reached for the curtains, but Dezhnev stood. "*Nyet.* Please. My turn. The Soviet Union's turn, really. Also, I must pay homage to the porcelain monster. I'll be right back." Grabbing his cane, he stumbled off.

With a shrug, they let him go. As soon as the curtains fell into place, DeWitt croaked, "I think I'm toasted."

"Where's our food?" Ingram was convinced he wouldn't be able to rise again.

DeWitt said, "Guess I can tell you, while Ed is gone. We got a message from Amador last night."

"Yes?" said Ingram.

"They're doing okay."

"Shhh. Keep it down, Otis," said Ingram.

Toliver waved a hand at Ingram. "Easy, Todd. It's not like we're talking about radar."

"That's enough of that, mister," snapped DeWitt, his voice lower. Radar, a new, top secret range-finding device, was something never mentioned in public. Ingram knew of a fellow officer who had been questioned at length by the FBI after boasting of it at a cocktail party.

DeWitt said, "Amador wasn't on the air long. Just enough to ask for ammo, clothes, medicine."

"What about Helen?" Ingram blurted through his mental fog.

"She's okay, too. Amador made sure to say that." DeWitt glanced at Toliver. They knew how Ingram felt about Helen.

"Whew."

DeWitt scratched his head. "Pablo says the Japs are converting Nasipit to a ship repair yard. And they're testing torpedoes there, too." He turned to Ingram. "Any reason why they would choose Nasipit for torpedo testing?"

Ingram shrugged. "I don't know. Can you help them? Send something in?"

"It's difficult to get supplies up there."

"What about airdrops?" asked Toliver.

"Only PBYs with long-range tanks can get in. Even at that, it's a twenty-five-hour trip. A sub got in a while back, but it's hard to get your guys to turn loose of the damned things on a regular basis." He turned to Ingram. "Our crypto guys asked me to ask you. Todd. You did graduate from the Naval Academy in 1937, didn't you?"

"Yes, why?"

DeWitt explained how Amador's checkerboard code worked and that he had used Ingram's year of graduation as top-row decoding key. He wiped his forehead. "Man, getting woozy. Time to eat." He gulped some tea, then parted the curtain and looked out. Seeing their waiter, he signaled and closed the curtain, not realizing Dezhnev stood just on the other side, a full bottle of scotch in his hand.

DeWitt continued, "I need a code for tomorrow to send on to our crypto unit in Brisbane. Something to use as a left-column key that only Amador knows about. Something simple. But something that will stump the Japs until we can set up a more secure code."

Ingram stared at their empty glasses, surprised he hadn't passed out.

"There must be something," said Toliver.

A thought hit Ingram. "Yeah, graduation dates. I'm 1937. Helen is 1939. How about that?"

DeWitt tried to focus. "Uh, 1939 what?"

"Scripps College. She graduated in 1939 and nursing school in 1940." Ingram pulled out Helen's ring and passed it over.

Toliver said, "Same year as my Packard. Can't be all that bad."

Suddenly the booze disappeared and Otis DeWitt became a lieutenant colonel. With a level voice, he turned the ring in his hand. "Where'd you get this, Todd?"

The waiter pulled the curtains and, working from a large tray, began to lay their table. Then he bowed and eased out, nearly stumbling over Dezhnev, who still hovered on the other side.

"Screw the chopsticks." Toliver forked a dripping load of almond duck into his mouth. "Ummm."

"Otis, I drove down there—"

"—in my Packard." Toliver gargled through stuffed cheeks.

"I met her folks. They needed to know she was okay."

"That's a breech of security."

Toliver turned to Ingram. "You still owe me seven dollars for gas and another buck fifty to fix the flat."

Ingram pleaded, "Otis, they got a telegram three days before I showed up. It said she was missing in action. They were beside themselves."

DeWitt shook his head.

"Her mother," Ingram said. "Her name is Kate. She looks just like Helen."

"Doesn't matter," snapped DeWitt. "You should report this to—"

"Oh, Otis. Just shut up," said Toliver. "Your left-column key is 1939. Use it and chow down before your food gets cold."

DeWitt sputtered for a moment. "I'll think about it."

Dezhnev stepped in, propped his cane in a corner, and sat, thumping a new bottle of scotch on the table. He sniffed his plate. "Ahh. I have waited such a long time for this. I, too, will forget the chopsticks." He grabbed his fork and dug in.

Ingram looked over. "Otis?" He extended his hand.

DeWitt dropped Helen's ring in Ingram's palm. "Forget it."

"Thanks."

"Forget what?" asked Dezhnev.

"Uhhhh-rah!" said Ingram.

CHAPTER THIRTEEN

27 AUGUST, 1942
SERVICE BARGE 212, NASIPIT, MINDANAO
PHILIPPINES

The sun had barely risen when the five foot eight, one-hundred-sixty-five pound Lieutenant Commander Katsumi Fujimoto rose from his bunk. Padding down the spartan passageway of the two-level barracks barge, he took a quick shower and found himself perspiring as soon as he toweled off. There was just no way to escape Mindanao's humidity. Back in his cabin, he peered out the port, watching the morning mist swirling about the little town. But every so often, tiny zephyrs parted the fog, revealing Nasipit's little twenty-room hotel, feed store, and ship's chandlery. Just across the wharf stood the Amador family lumber mill, a once-proud structure dynamited by Americans and reduced to a few pathetic sticks pointing skyward, a forlorn reminder of the Amadors' influence in northern Mindanao. Now the largest building was Rameriezes' meat locker, long abandoned for lack of pigs and cattle, and currently used as the Kempetai's headquarters and jail. Farther away stood the proud steeple of St. Mary's Catholic Church, still attended by the villagers each Sunday, even though the rector had been shot. Services were conducted by an unordained twenty-five-year-old parishioner who had lost his arm in the fighting near Davao last January.

A floating dry dock was moored aft of the barracks barge; both were gifts from the United States Navy, which had fled their Manila Bay–Cavite Naval Station in December 1941. But Corregidor, which defended the approaches to Manila Bay, didn't fall until five months later, May 1942. Thus, it wasn't until a few weeks ago that the Japanese were able to extricate barge and dry dock from Manila Bay, tow them 450 miles south into Nasipit, and secure them to the deepwater wharf.

Fujimoto turned from the port hole and began to dress, trying to forget the dream. But the dream was reality, and night and day there was no escape from the shame and embarrassment that constantly followed him. A little over three months ago, on the night of May 7, 1942, Fujimoto had been the proud skipper of the *Kurosio,* a *Hubuki* class destroyer. It was a day after Corregidor had fallen, his orders had been to patrol a sector off Luzon's west coast and capture Americans escaping by sea. That night, he swept on an east-west axis just outboard of Fortune Island when they trapped a small American boat in their searchlight. Close off their starboard bow, it looked to be no more than twelve meters long with eight or ten men huddled inside. An easy target, his men stood ready to open fire as Fujimoto ordered hard right rudder to cut off their escape.

To his surprise, the little boat shot first with a devastating fusillade of small-arms fire, shattering the *Kurosio*'s twin searchlights. In the melee, the pilot-house glass splintered, wounding two sailors, the rest of the crew screaming and dropping to the deck. Fujimoto fell with them and banged his head on the binnacle base. A warm thickness gushed over his forehead, as a frightened ensign tumbled on top of him. With the rudder still jammed hard right and men shouting and writhing on the pilothouse deck, the *Kurosio*'s graceful bow carved through a landing barge, killing three soldiers of the Imperial Japanese Fourteenth Army. Soon after, the destroyer, with Fujimoto frantically ordering all back full, ran aground on Fortune Island. With the screws fully reversed, she backed off easily enough, but the damage was done. Bottom mud, sand, and silt were sucked into the condenser inlets, clogging the system, taking the ship out of commission for two weeks.

Three weeks later, Fujimoto, his gashed forehead heavily bandaged, stood before a Naval Board of Inquiry in Manila. The proceedings took place in Malacañan Palace, evacuated by President Manuel Quezon, who fled with

General Douglas MacArthur to Australia. The board consisted of a commander, three captains, and an admiral. Fujimoto was fully convinced he would be automatically sentenced to a weather station in northern Manchuria and wondered why they wasted their time. He would have been right except for two things. First the board, consisting of frustrated shore-based officers, secretly took pity because of his bandaged forehead.

But his family background was what actually tipped the scale. From his birth on January 17, 1910, in Buenos Aires, Katsumi Fujimoto had seemed destined for prominence. His father, Hayashi Fujimoto, had been assigned as a naval attaché to the Japanese Embassy in Argentina, a plum assignment after having sailed with his classmate, Isoroku Yamamoto, in 1905 when they defeated the Imperial Russian Navy at the Battle of Tsushima Strait.

During his years at the Etajima Naval Academy, young Fujimoto made up his mind about women. He stated outright that he would remain at sea, foreswearing shore duty and vowing not to marry until, perhaps, reaching the rank of commander. Even then, he would not marry unless it became a political necessity for important assignments, promotion, and, ultimately, flag rank.

With that determined, Fujimoto chose destroyers when he graduated in 1929. He was billeted as torpedo officer on the brand-new 1,315-ton *Sikinami*. Based in Sasebo, they practiced torpedo tactics day and night in the Sea of Japan; so much so that after ten months, Fujimoto could disassemble and reassemble a torpedo in near-darkness, much like his Army friends fieldstripped a rifle blindfolded.

By the time he was promoted to *chū-l*, lieutenant junior grade, he'd become a gunnery officer on the *Wakaba,* a destroyer of 1,368 tons, built in 1924. He drilled his torpedo gang hard, until they held the fleet record for reloading a four-tube salvo in complete darkness. Their time: an incredible nine minutes and two seconds.

Soon he became visible among the upper ranks of Japan's fast-growing Navy. It was time for shore duty, and his father, now a retired rear admiral, or Shōsō, pulled strings and got his son assigned to Yamamoto's staff in 1938.

Katsumi Fujimoto was on his way.

During that time he was promoted to lieutenant or *tai-l.* Working at the super-secret naval torpedo factory in Yokosuka, Fujimoto became one of Japan's leading design and test experts for a brand-new torpedo designated Type 93. It was an amazing weapon driven by pure oxygen, giving it a unheard-of range of twelve miles at a phenomenal speed of forty-nine knots, the high speed setting. In low speed, thirty-six knots, the Type 93 traveled twenty-four miles. There was literally nothing like the Type 93 in the world's navies, and Fujimoto and his fellow officers knew it. Miraculously, Fujimoto and his brethren kept their secret, leaving everyone else, Axis *and* Allies, unaware of the Type 93's deadly capabilities. Long after the war's outbreak, the Americans were still unaware that it was specially modified Type 93 oxygen-powered torpedoes that slammed into their battleships on December 7, 1941.

In 1940, Fujimoto went back to sea, becoming executive officer of the 1,315-ton destroyer *Yuduki*. He served there for a year when, in early 1941, his career took a bizarre turn. They assigned him to intelligence work, as a naval attaché in Mexico City. There, he worked in two areas. The first was commanding a station that listened to U.S. Navy radio signals emanating from the North American continent. This also involved code-breaking, and forwarding the information to Japan. In many cases, his cryptanalysts successfully broke the relatively simple American codes, ascertained the disposition of the U.S. Navy in the Atlantic at any given time, and passed the information to the Germans down the street.

His second task was the outright black-market purchase of strategic materials. He enjoyed moderate success at this until the following September. On the docks of Vera Cruz, a drunken boom operator lost control and a drum of bronze scrap plunged from a cargo net that had been swinging aboard the *Ottawa Maru*. Crashing on the wharf, the drum split open to reveal a false bottom. Splattered about for all to see was a runny, viscous, silvery liquid, quickly identified as mercury; a substance embargoed by the Mexican and American governments. If that wasn't bad enough, authorities discovered *twelve hundred* other drums of phony scrap barrels on the docks, all consigned for the *Ottawa Maru*. Each drum contained a ninety-pound bottle of mercury Fujimoto had purchased through a Mexican general. The price of secrecy was a $100,000 pay-off to the president of Mexico. Unfortunately, the negotiations included Fujimoto's expulsion as persona non grata since he'd become so visible in the deal. ·

Fujimoto returned home a hero. He was next assigned as an aide to General Yoshitsugu Tatekawa, Japan's Ambassador to the Soviet Union. With this he was promoted to lieutenant commander, or *shōsa*. But with war's outbreak, and the increased demands on the Imperial Japanese Navy, Fujimoto gladly returned to sea duty in March 1942. It was then that he realized the dream of all naval officers—his own command. She was the destroyer *Kurosio*: *Black Tide*.

Conjecture at fleet headquarters was that nothing could stop Fujimoto's promotion to commander, then captain. Top naval personnel placed even money that Katsumi Fujimoto would become a rear admiral commanding a cruiser/destroyer squadron in the next two or three years.

Until the embarrassment at Fortune Island on the night of May 7.

Until the shame three weeks later at Malacañan Palace.

To rub his nose in it, the Board of Inquiry flaunted the name of the American Navy Lieutenant who had eluded him: Todd Ingram.

Because Fujimoto had bungled the opportunity to sink the American boat, Ingram had gone on days later to blow up the Amador lumber mill in Nasipit, killing sixty-seven Japanese soldiers. The blame lay at Fujimoto's feet.

But, he ruefully noted, the board seemed to have a convoluted sense of humor by posting Fujimoto to Nasipit; the same place where Ingram left his calling card last May. They told him they had taken into account his extensive experience at sea, and his torpedo and intelligence background. It was a good out-of-the-way place to hide him and see how things turned out. The Nasipit command consisted of a small radio intercept and ship repair post on Butuan Bay in northern Mindanao that guarded the passages to the Surigao Strait. With Fujimoto's torpedo expertise in mind, an added task was to test the American torpedoes; a number of them had been captured in various store-houses in the Philippines, Guam, Wake Island, and the Dutch East Indies. His orders were to determine what caused the failures, see if they were repairable, and then recommend if they could be used aboard Japanese ships. But to keep things in perspective for his crew, he kept a Type 93 torpedo on display. The thirty-foot monster made the American's twenty-four-foot surface-fired Mark 15s seem paltry by comparison.

Things were on schedule now. They'd had twelve test firings of American torpedoes over the last four days. Many ran erratic, but he put that down to poor maintenance. Cracking the whip over his crews, he stayed up evenings with his torpedomen, meticulously overhauling the torpedoes, checking every-thing. Now they ran with a consistent error: at least ten feet too deep

Fujimoto ground his teeth as he looked out the port at swirling fog. Al-though the torpedo research was interesting, his former classmates rapidly approached the peaks of their careers, driving destroyers, commanding whole carrier squadrons, becoming department heads of battleships and cruisers, sinking the enemy wherever they steamed.

But all Fujimoto could do was sit in this slough and look at . . . fog . . . which saturated this insignificant little village with a white hell.

Two weeks ago, he'd seen a fleet broadcast message asking for volunteer officers to participate in the new Eighth Fleet formed almost overnight to block any advance the Americans contemplated in the Solomon Islands. The man in charge was Vice Admiral Gunichi Mikawa, a longtime family friend now stationed in Rabaul. But Mikawa didn't respond to Fujimoto's desperate requests.

The Americans did land in the Solomons: on Guadalcanal on August 7. Two nights later, Mikawa counterattacked with his flagship, the heavy cruiser *Chokai*. He led four other heavy cruisers, the *Aoba, Kako, Kinugasa,* and *Furutaka;* two light cruisers, the *Tenyru* and *Yubari*; and the destroyer *Yunagi* in a high-speed column down New Georgia Sound toward Guadalcanal. A little after midnight, they caught the Americans by surprise off Savo Island. In two hours, Mikawa wiped out three American heavy cruisers, one de-stroyer, and one Australian heavy cruiser: all lost to the Type 93 torpedo that bore the stamp of Fujimoto's heart and soul. Delirious with victory, Mikawa retired to Rabaul without a scratch. In frustration, Fujimoto sent a message to his father asking him to intercede and have him reassigned to the

Solomons—even on shore, as long as it was combat. The old man sent word back that he would discuss the matter with Yamamoto.

Fujimoto sat and waited and watched the fog swirl and each morning checked the message board: nothing from his father, or from Mikawa. Just . . . nothing . . .

Yawata, an orderly dressed in spotless whites, came in and wordlessly set a tea service. Without asking, he'd also included some rice cakes. Drawing backward, he bowed and stepped out. Fujimoto sat heavily at his desk and sipped. The dream followed him. Night and day, it followed him. Today, it seemed to have a soul of its own and would follow him once again.

CHAPTER FOURTEEN

12 SEPTEMBER, 1942
SERVICE BARGE 212, NASIPIT, MINDANAO
PHILIPPINES

Fujimoto checked the calculations for the fourth time and felt a flush of glory. Wouldn't his father be proud? He checked his watch: nearly two in the morning. At this hour, it was very quiet except for screeching monkeys across the harbor. He should have been in bed, but tinkering with torpedoes was one of Fujimoto's favorite pastimes and, over the last two weeks, he had passed the late evenings pleasantly sitting on this stool, taking American torpedo components apart and reassembling them, working on the torpedo depth control problem.

And here it was. Simple. But there was no one else to share his victory except Takarabe, a leading torpedoman. Everyone was asleep except the gangway sentries. With a face full of acne, Takarabe was young, but very, very, smart. Actually, it was Takarabe who had given him the idea. Yesterday, he had asked innocently, "Wouldn't the depth sensor function better if it was in a free-flooding chamber inside the torpedo rather than being mounted on the skin?"

And now Fujimoto sipped tea and sat at a workbench, reexamining his math. He said, "You just may be right, Takarabe."

"Sir?" Takarabe bent closer under the torpedo shop's floodlight.

Fujimoto tossed a pencil on the workbench, leaned back, and said, "It goes something like this. The Mark 15 depth sensor doesn't work because it *is* skin-mounted. With the torpedo going thirty or forty-five knots, the velocity of water over the sensor gives a far different pressure reading than the actual hydrostatic pressure or real depth. The error is proportional to the square of the torpedo speed; the faster it goes, the deeper it runs.''

Takarabe's eyes lit up. ''Amazing.''

''That's why American torpedoes run so deep. Ten to fifteen feet, by our tests. The depth sensor is sending the wrong signal to the depth control engine.''

Takarabe grinned. ''And the Americans don't even know it.''

''Apparently not.'' Fujimoto's gaze swept across the torpedo machine shop. On the far bulkhead were two American Mark 15 torpedoes, all cleaned and ready for testing tomorrow. ''We'll try to jury-rig a new sensor and see what happens.''

''Yes, Sir.''

Fujimoto's eyes darted to the Type 93 torpedo mounted above the two American torpedoes. ''If only . . .''

''Sir?''

Rubbing his eyes, Fujimoto eased off the stool. ''Time for sleep. I'll have to write this up and send it on to Tokyo.''

''Good night, Sir.''

Fujimoto walked out.

The next morning, Fujimoto ambled up and down the wharf until the fog lifted. An hour later, it cleared somewhat, revealing a misty, drowsy Nasipit. To him, it was a far more pleasant view into town than what he saw to the west across the narrow, mile-long bay. One could only see shoals, a drying reef, and then the deep jungle going to sleep after another night of life-riot punctuated by the screeching of monkeys and the occasional carabao's bellow. But some evenings here were very pleasant, he admitted to himself. Especially when soft winds blew from the east, bringing some of the most interesting odors to Fujimoto. He smelled honeysuckle, which on occasion became a mixture of rose and gardenia. But with the stronger winds from across the bay, the scents turned foul with the stench of feces and rotting vegetation and decaying marine life.

He was still tired from last night, but with his American torpedo discovery, there was a spring in his step. And with the promise of the sun burning the overcast, Fujimoto felt better and returned to the barge, walking to the wardroom for an early breakfast. As expected, nobody was up on this Monday morning, except Lieutenant Ogata, who conducted torpedo drills on the foredeck. The others were still in their bunks, having suffered a night of too much eating and drinking.

The tablecloth was starched white, and six places had been set with gleaming silver service stamped USN. Yawata served a breakfast of dried fish, coconut, and two fresh eggs, a rarity in wartime. After finishing, Fujimoto was about to get up when Yawata walked in with another plate.

''What's this?''

''I made it this morning, Sir.'' Yawata placed before him a bowl of pineapples drenched with a dressing of coconut milk and muscovado sugar. "There was only enough for you." Yawata bowed. He'd taken advantage of the fact that no one else was up yet. A polite way of saying screw the others if they wanted to frolic all night.

Fujimoto looked quickly out the hatch to see that no one else approached. There really wasn't enough pineapple to split among the others. Besides, to refuse meant the dish would be thrown overboard in the next five minutes. He sighed. "Thank you."

"Sir," hissed Yawata, withdrawing.

The pineapples were excellent. He patted his lips with a starched napkin, meticulously rolled it, and inserted it into a silver napkin ring, also stamped USN. Yawata was a good find, Fujimoto mulled, as he picked up his cap and walked out at exactly seven a.m. Hailing from a Kobe restaurant family, Yawata was barely twenty years old. With the savoir faire of a young nobleman, Yawata had quick eyes and an intellect Fujimoto knew he shouldn't keep back. Perhaps he should transfer him to gunnery or maybe even the torpedo gang. But then, who would fix pineapples for him?

He made his way forward along the main deck, past the machine shop, power-generating station, optical shop, boiler repair shop, instrument overhaul station, diesel repair station, gun repair facility and finally, the torpedo shop. Most of the barge's services were for the Army garrison ashore, but with the newly arrived floating dry dock, they would soon overhaul and berth the crews of small combatants up to the size of a destroyer.

Mounted in the bow was an American triple-tube torpedo mount he'd purloined from the scrap heaps in the Cavite naval shipyard. He'd put his shipfitters and torpedomen to work, and they realigned the mount on its base ring and repaired the training, targeting, and firing mechanisms. When it worked perfectly, his crew scraped away all the rust and chipped paint, making the mount look brand-new. Now the mount kicked out American Mark 15 torpedoes into Butuan Bay for later recovery by the landing barge.

For authenticity, Fujimoto ordered daily torpedo-loading drills at the mount, just like he'd done on the *Wakaba*. And he would time his after-breakfast stroll just as they were ready to begin.

Sure enough, he walked onto the bow just as his repair officer, Lieutenant Ogata, raised his stopwatch and yelled, "Go!"

Cursing and grunting, the crew struggled with their chain-falls and torpedo skids and finished stuffing three Mark 15 torpedoes into their tubes. The watch was clicked when the last breech door was slammed shut and dogged.

With a flourish, Ogata clicked his watch off. Seeing Fujimoto's raised eyebrows, Ogata barked his report, "Twelve minutes, four seconds, Sir." Carefully, he logged the time on a clipboard.

"Yesterday?"

Ogata checked his board. "Eleven minutes and forty-three seconds."

"What happened?"

"Takarabe crushed his thumb on the spoon yesterday. Hirota is the new second loader."

"Tell them they have a week to get ready for night-loading drills. And that means nine minutes or less." Fujimoto turned to leave.

"Sir?"

"Yes?"

"Isn't that too soon? I mean, someone could lose a hand or finger."

Fujimoto smiled. "That's up to you, Lieutenant. Now tell them they have five days before night-loading exercises."

Ogata's mouth dropped open. "I thought you said a week."

"Now it's five days . . . and Ogata?"

"Sir?"

"Are those the ones we are firing today?"

"No, Sir. These are warloads."

Fujimoto chuckled to himself. The American warloads were fifty pounds heavier than the exercise warheads. The crew had done a little better than Ogata knew, but Fujimoto wasn't going to say anything just then. "Very well, Lieutenant. You have thirty minutes to unload the warhead torpedoes and reload with the exercise shots.

Ogata's jaw flinched, but he stood to attention and saluted. "Yes, Sir."

Good, thought Fujimoto. Ogata hadn't groused. Normally his technicians would have extracted the warloads and installed the exercise heads. But Ogata seemed to be a good performer. Fujimoto wanted to give him his head.

Tipping his fingers to his cap, Fujimoto walked to the companionway and took the steps two at a time for the second deck. He stopped at a door whose sign read:

RADIO SHACK
SECURITY CLEARANCE REQUIRED.

Actually it wasn't a shack. It was the most habitable space on the barge. Three rooms were crammed with radio equipment that would have sent the temperature soaring. Instead, air-conditioning was installed, maintaining a tolerable seventy-one degrees. Lieutenant Koki Jimbo stood to near-attention. He was taller than average at five feet ten inches and weighed 165 pounds. This morning he was barefoot, wore a short-sleeved shirt, nonregulation khaki cutoffs, and gold spectacles. "Morning, Sir."

Fujimoto walked past rows of radio receivers, each attended by a radioman who sat guarding a series of frequencies for unauthorized traffic. "Anything?"

"Quiet so far, Sir," said Jimbo, following, his hands behind his back.

Fujimoto picked up the daily board, finding a long, two-page message from last night. He picked it up and scanned it quickly. "Ahhh. Our first customer." A ship was en route, a destroyer, for major repairs. It would be the first ship to be overhauled using the floating dry dock.

Jimbo kept quiet as Fujimoto read further. "Whaaat?" he exclaimed.

"Exactly my words, Sir."

Fujimoto read on. It seemed the U.S. Navy had abandoned one of their destroyers, the U.S.S. *Stockwell,* in Soerabaja in the Dutch East Indies after it had been bombed in dry dock. Now the ship, an old World War I four-stack destroyer, had been refloated and was being towed to Nasipit for overhaul and, presumably, for service in the Japanese Navy.

Fujimoto sat against a table and slapped his forehead. "This is stupid."

"Guess who is towing her."

"I'm not in the mood for mysteries, Koki."

"Hisa Kunisawa."

"No!"

Jimbo grinned and showed him the order. Fujimoto couldn't believe his luck. Kunisawa, a true old man of the sea, was one of the most capable sailors in any Navy. A confirmed alcoholic, he'd once commanded merchant ships but fell out of grace because of his habit. Now he was a warrant officer in the Navy with just a tug to command. Also, Kunisawa was an acknowledged expert in dry-docking operations.

Fujimoto read the order again. "This says he's being attached to us."

"Ummm."

"What great luck." With Kunisawa about, things would get done correctly as long as he stayed sober. Keeping him sober, Fujimoto reckoned, was *his* job.

Fujimoto suspected someone in Tokyo was looking after him.

Jimbo said, "Just remember to lock up the booze. But it sounds like they're serious. Not only do we get Kunisawa, they're sending shipfitters, too. Lots of them. An overhaul packet is on its way via guardmail."

"Just what I need. Hisa Kunisawa." With a sigh, Fujimoto tossed the clipboard on the desk, wondering if things were turning around. So far, they'd had nothing to do. That's why Lieutenant Ogata was down on the first deck conducting torpedo loading exercises. Now they had a ship to repair.

"There's something else, Sir." Jimbo nodded to a clipboard labeled MOST SECRET.

With a grunt, Fujimoto picked it up and read:

MOST SECRET

TO: TWENTY-FIRST FLEET INTELLIGENCE AND REPAIR UNIT, NASIPIT, MINDANAO

VIA: FLEET INTELLIGENCE COMMAND, YOKOSUKA

RELAY FM: TATEKAWA, MOSCOW

MOSCOW EMBASSY SENDS: BE ADVISED AMADOR CODE IS CHECK-

ERBOARD. TOP LINE KEYWORD IS 1937. VERTICAL LINE INDISTIN-
GUISHABLE. ASKING MOSCOW TO RETRANSMIT. WILL ADVISE.

BY DIRECTION
ARITA

Fujimoto said, "Old Tatekawa's at it again."

"How do they get this stuff?" Jimbo asked.

"He knows how to bend a few arms. Have you tried this 1937 business yet?"

"The animals are working it." The animals, so called because fresh meat kept them productive, were three warrant officers who specialized in crypt-analysis. They had been flown from Japan in a desperate effort to crack the Amador code. "So far, nothing."

"How about Amador's previous two messages?"

Jimbo shook his head.

"Have them try those as well." Fujimoto took another look at the message board. Nothing else had arrived since he'd heard last night's traffic. For proof, he looked to Jimbo, who silently shook his head; nothing from Mikawa.

Then something hit him. He grabbed the unclassified message, the one about the American destroyer, and reread it. "Interesting. A bastard ship. Incompatible with anything we have."

"Sir?"

"This says they plan to commission it here, if possible."

"Yes, Sir."

Fujimoto slapped the clipboard on his thigh. "I wonder who they have in mind for skipper."

CHAPTER FIFTEEN

14 SEPTEMBER, 1942
SERVICE BARGE 212, NASIPIT, MINDANAO
PHILIPPINES

The visibility was only fifty feet. It was one of those frustrating morning fogs where one was enticed by the clear blue skies just thirty feet above. Some-where on the edge of town, a carabao bellowed, but nothing else stirred in the harbor or the jungle. Each day, four fishermen were allowed to work the sandbars and the mouth of the Kinabhangan River, but even they elected to stay in port, the unrelenting chalky vapor growing denser each day.

Fujimoto had taken his early breakfast and stroll on the wharf and now stood at a distance, watching the torpedo gang go through their daily loading drill. Clicking his stopwatch with Lieutenant Ogata, Fujimoto could tell they did better, much better. But he wanted to hear it from Ogata.

Fujimoto waited until they were finished, then walked by as if headed for the second-deck companionway. From the corner of his eye, he saw Ogata salute.

"Morning, Sir."

Fujimoto made a show of stopping and saluting with a tinge of annoyance. "Good morning." He paused. "Say, how are your loading drills doing?"

Ogata smiled. "Last two mornings, Sir, under nine minutes."

"Really?"

"Eight minutes and forty-one seconds this morning. Eight-fifty-five yesterday. And no broken fingers or hands." Ogata stood stiffly. And his torpedomen, all ten of them, also stood at near-attention, still breathing heavily, shirtless, sweat running down their chests and arms.

"And last night?"

"Eight-fifty-seven, Sir. They can do it in their sleep."

"Excellent." Fujimoto beckoned for Ogata to stand closer. "I'm pleased about the enthusiasm here, Ogata. That goes for all of you."

Ogata beamed.

"All of you will make good destroyermen. But haven't you forgotten something?"

"Sir?"

Fujimoto pointed. "Look at those handwheels. The brass is dull. And the zerk fittings don't have covers. The breechplates need paint, and I can see from here the spoon locking pin on tube three is bent. When was the last time you overhauled this mount?"

Ogata spread his hands. "We've only had it six weeks or so."

"Fine. But if you don't take care of it, your times are going to go up again, and then you *will* have some broken bones." Fujimoto paused. "Have your maintenance logs on my desk before noon."

"Yes, Sir."

"And while we're on the subject of cleanliness, the berthing compartments and heads look like they're inhabited by Mongolian heroin addicts. The officers' quarters, too. They're awful."

"We're very undermanned, Sir."

"Do something about it, then." Fujimoto walked to the companionway, making his way to the second deck.

A flabbergasted Ogata saluted. "Yes, Sir."

He headed for the radio shack when he heard a loud horn blast. Three more mournful blasts shattered the gloom. With the damned fog-laden air, it sounded as if a twenty-thousand-ton troop ship were speeding toward them at twenty knots, poised to cut them in half.

Fujimoto ran to the port side and leaned on the rail, only to see a white translucence.

Jimbo dashed from his radio shack. "Is that him?"

Within seconds, watertight doors thunked open, and sailors tumbled onto the barge's decks. It seemed everyone was on deck, leaning on the rail, peering into the fog.

"It has to be. Only Kunisawa would try to shove a thirteen-hundred-ton destroyer around in this mess." Nasipit wasn't that difficult to enter under normal conditions, but in the fog, tug and tow could have ended up on the reef just outside.

Hisa Kunisawa, age fifty-seven, had been licensed as a Mater Mariner since 1923. But he'd been relieved of command some time back, due to an abiding interest in alcohol. Drafted into the Navy as a senior warrant, he was assigned to the Nasipit facility as dry-docking master and tugboat skipper. Fujimoto was damned lucky to have him. A sober Kunisawa was highly skilled in everything from seamanship to rigging to downright paint-chipping. Kunisawa maintained these fundamental skills were regrettably ignored by young midshipman cadets of today: men who were more interested in standing close to the south end of their commanding officers than the business end of a spanner wrench.

The *Stockwell* had been due six days ago. But because of fog, Kunisawa radioed that he would anchor by night and in daylight hug the coast, where he could pick up navigational references as best he could, prolonging his voyage from Soerabaja to a snail's pace.

The horn bellowed again, triumphantly—almost as if saying, *At last, here is Hisa Kunisawa, who really knows his stuff.* Moving dead slow, the destroyer's bow poked out of the fog just thirty meters away. Soon her bridge hove into view, then two of her four stacks became visible. She stopped in midstream abreast of Service Barge 212. The *Stockwell*'s pilothouse door was clipped open. With the mist swirling through the hatchway, Fujimoto felt as if he were looking down the throat of a cadaver venting putrid gases. Inside, the instrument's glasswork gleamed, but the shine was long off the brass. Cables hung from the overhead, and seaweed and dead tree limbs lay about on deck. With no one to man her, and no steam to invigorate her engines and course through her veins, there was no life in her. The ship seemed to revel in the murkiness. She carried a slight list to starboard, and the lines securing a canvas cover over her number two stack had rotted, letting the cover droop down one side like a corpse dangling from a noose. Paint peeled from her superstructure in great strips. Faint light glinted off her dirt-streaked pilothouse windows, giving the old warhorse a demonic grin.

The tug was snubbed amidships for tight-quarters maneuvering and Kunisawa stood on top of the *Stockwell*'s pilothouse, hands jammed on his hips. Wearing pea coat, denim work trousers, and merchantman's cap, his posture begged the question, *Are you ready for me?*

Fortunately, they were. The keel blocks had been laid, and Ogata had flooded the dry dock two days ago, waiting for this moment.

Fujimoto ran to the top deck, grabbed a megaphone, and hailed, "One moment, Hisa." Then he looked at the crew gathered on the main deck, gawking up at the dark gray apparition. It hadn't yet hit them that their job was upon them. Putting the American destroyer back into running condition was going to challenge their skills to the ultimate. And some hoped the ship would become their sea billet, their chance to break from the living, white-hot hell of Nasipit.

Fujimoto hailed to the lieutenant on the main deck. "Ogata."

"Sir?"

"Get on the dry dock with the line-handling party at once. Make ready to receive the ship."

Fujimoto's eyes lingered once again on the *Stockwell* as Ogata scrambled and shouted at his men. She had been built at the New York Shipbuilding Company in Camden, New Jersey. Commissioned in 1920, she carried a full load displacement of 1,340 tons, was 314 feet in length, had a beam of thirty feet, and, with four boilers and two geared turbines driving twin screws, had a design speed of thirty-five knots. But now, mud, litter, and hoses looking like dead snakes lay about the *Stockwell*'s decks. All four of her four-inch single-fire guns pointed in every which direction, looking as if the one who last controlled her main battery had been a maniac. But she did have, Fujimoto noted, two tripletube torpedo tube mounts: one starboard, one port, just like the one on the barge's foredeck, and she carried a full load of U.S. Navy Mark 15 torpedoes.

Part of the Asiatic fleet that fled the Philippines in the early stages of the Pacific war, the *Stockwell* had fought a delaying action, finding herself in Soerabaja in the Dutch East Indies by March 1942. She was in dry dock to fix a leaking packing gland when Japanese bombs struck, sinking the dock and blowing the *Stockwell* on her beam ends, partially flooding her. Then the Japanese swarmed ashore. In panic, the fleeing Americans did a poor job setting the scuttling charges. Instead of breaking her back, or at least bending her propeller shafts, a useless hole had been blown in the aft magazine, which was empty for dry-docking. The charge in the forward magazine, also empty, didn't go off. When salvaged by the Japanese, she was in relatively good shape except for the hole in her bottom and dents in her hull plating where she'd fallen on her side. To put the Soerabaja dock back into use, Japanese engineers quickly patched the *Stockwell*'s hull, pumped her out, towed her free, and left her anchored in a nearby cove, forlorn and nearly forgotten. Then they decided to dump the whole mess in Fujimoto's lap.

Fujimoto had many times gone over the repair list with Ogata. Besides restoring the ship's hull integrity, her boilers needed retubing, her pumps needed overhauling, her armament needed to be refurbished and recalibrated. In addition to a thorough cleaning, inside and out, she needed a complete bottom job to bring her back to her designed thirty-five-knot capability.

Kunisawa called to Fujimoto from atop the destroyer's pilothouse. "Some fun, ehh, Katsi? Ran over three logs and a waterlogged sampan getting here. And I think half a lifeboat is jammed under the screwguard."

"Everything else intact?" asked Fujimoto, his voice echoing across the cove.

"Of course."

"We were worried you would break into the liquor cabinet."

"Damned Americans don't drink."

"Good."

"Except you should see what we found in the captain's sea cabin."

Fujimoto's heart sank.

"Scotch. Good stuff. Greek."

"They don't make scotch in Greece," shouted Fujimoto.

Deeper in the cove they heard a toot. It was a whistle on the dry dock, signifying they were ready. Just then a launch laid alongside the *Stockwell,* and ten men scrambled aboard to help with the mooring lines.

Kunisawa watched for a moment, making sure everything was in place. Then he leaned over the pilothouse rail and shouted an order down to his bo's'n waiting patiently in the tugs' pilothouse. The bo's'n gave two blasts on his horn, and water boiled under the tug's stern.

The ships moved ahead. Kunisawa shouted back to Fujimoto, "Greece. Scotland. Germany. Who cares? That stuff burned like hell when it went down."

"Did you save any?"

Kunisawa gave a deep bow. "Sorry. It went to good use."

"I'll bet it was paint thinner."

Instead of looking back, Kunisawa waved over his head, concentrating on the dry-docking's precision.

A zephyr twirled in from Butuan Bay, clearing the death haze from the *Stockwell.* They couldn't see the sun yet, but the destroyer's port quarter was visible as she eased toward the dry dock's yawning mouth.

Jimbo spoke for the first time. "What a disgusting wreck."

Smiling broadly, Fujimoto was sure his luck had changed. "She's perfect, Koki."

CHAPTER SIXTEEN

A brilliant half-moon set over the Agusan jungle, turning the night sky from a royal blue to a deep cobalt, a sharp contrast to the fog that had been hugging the coast for the past two weeks. With the moonset, the star carpet overhead became thick, yet, despite the sky's stark beauty, Helen's teeth chattered. Someone was watching her, she was sure.

Take hold.

Crouched under a tall bush, she watched the moon plunge through a grove of narra trees, where three monkeys were silhouetted as they jumped gracefully from one limb to another. Their screeching told her she was safe. At least that's what Amador had said before he marched to the runway's south end to take up his position. "Listen to the damned monkeys. And the cicadas. They'll tell you if you're alone. If you don't hear them, scram. Because the Hapons won't be far behind."

She was near the north end of a three-thousand-foot dirt runway, one of many caches set up by General MacArthur in a crash program eighteen months ago. The idea was that the emergency airstrips could take over the Philippines' defense, should the primary bases be wiped out. MacArthur's idea was good one. In one quick raid, the Japanese wiped out over half the bombers and fighters of the U.S. Army Air Corps at Clark Field on December 8, 1941. But MacArthur hadn't planned on the sell-out by Filipino fifth columnists and saboteurs, who tipped the Japanese. Thus the bombers at dirt airstrips everywhere were blasted in their camouflaged revetments within days of the war's outbreak, nullifying any serious airborne threat from MacArthur.

So now Helen stood beside a cratered runway with the wrecks of a half-dozen early-model B-17s scattered about. The jungle riot in the trees failed to calm her, her eyes snapping to every new sound. The Kempetai could play the same game and she wasn't going to be careless, especially on this, their first airdrop. If the enemy was hidden out there and she moved too quickly, she could be easily spotted by a Japanese who had been more patient than she.

"I can't stand it." Wong Lee stood next to her.

"Don't!" Her voice between a whisper and a guttural rasp.

Too late. Wong Lee flicked his Zippo.

"Damn you," she hissed.

He cupped his hands so tight that hardly a glow escaped.

"You'll kill us all."

"No Japs tonight." Wong Lee took an enormous drag, then exhaled luxuriously.

"They have noses, you idiot." Automatically, she looked to her right, upwind. They were about two hundred feet from the runway's northern end. Beyond that was a little more clear ground, then the tree line. Nothing stirred.

"Their noses are ruined. They smoke more than I do." Wong Lee lay back, putting his hands behind his head, studying the night sky.

"Pffft," she went.

Wong Lee closed his eyes and feigned sleep.

Helen's watch was barely visible in the fading light: almost ten minutes to two. *Anytime now.*

DeWitt's terse message explained the plane, a long-range amphibian, loaded with food, ammo, and medicine, would make one pass at two o'clock sharp, north to south, right over the Amparo runway at five hundred feet. They would heave out their bundles, letting them settle by parachute to the runway. Amador had placed his *guerrilleros* strategically around the field. He and Renaldo were hidden at the runway's south end, Legaspi and Carillo about midway, Helen and Wong Lee at the north. With Legaspi were two carabao hooked up to two logging skids. It would take at least an hour to drag the stuff to the main highway, where they would transfer the goods to a wagon. With any luck, the stuff would be hidden in Amparo within the hour, Buenavista the next day.

She wondered what Otis was sending. Food? Penicillin? Soap? Would Otis have thought of soap? What a luxury.

At exactly one-fifty-five, Amador was to point his flashlight to the sky and flash three shorts and a long—something from Beethoven, she remembered. Then he was to do it once again a minute later.

She squinted once again at her watch: about eight minutes to two. "Damn."

"Huh?" Wong Lee took a final drag, ground the butt out with thumb and forefinger, field-stripped it, and stuffed the remaining little wad of paper in his pocket. "What's wrong?"

She waved at the jungle around them. "You don't know who is out there. Our most vulnerable moment is when we go for the supplies."

"Why does Don Pablo say you're lucky?"

That's out of the blue. She reached inside her blouse for Ingram's ring and palmed it for a moment. "What on earth are you talking about?"

"I mean that Navy guy."

"You don't know him."

"He's one damn lucky sonofabitch."

"Shut up." *What the hell is he doing?*

"Someday I'm going to throttle that bastard for cutting in on me."

Helen could barely see his face in the gloom. "You're married. And he was there first."

"All's fair in love and war. Besides, my wife is stateside and I'm here.

And your boy is stateside and you're here. Don't you believe in providence? That you're here and I'm here?''

"Wong, you're hopeless." Helen realized her teeth had stopped chattering. *Thank you.*

He sat up slowly. "You wanna know why I smoke so damned much?"

"That's easy. You're trying to kill yourself."

"You bet. Because I don't want anything of me left over for the Japs to have."

They were back on familiar ground, having had this argument many times, yet she still played the game. "It's not working. You don't have lung cancer."

"Not yet. But I'm working on it." His tone changed. "When they get me, I'm going to have a ton of dynamite strapped to my body, and I'll light the fuse with my last cigarette."

"Poetic." *I wonder if he really does have a death wish?*

"Kaboom! Right out of Verdi."

"Shh." Her watch read one-fifty-five. Just then Amador's flashlight blinked with three short flashes and one long flash from the runway's south end. The night was still so clear and beautiful, Helen refused to believe the Japanese were ready to burst in on them. "Someday soon you'll be once again cooking roast duck with plum sauce."

"Thought you didn't like plum sauce."

"At this point I'll try anything. How about tonight after we get to Amparo?"

"Maybe. But it'll be breakfast time by then."

"I'm game to try anything by the great Wong Lee."

"My mother cooks it best."

Wong Lee's mother, Ginger, managed his restaurant in Los Angeles. His daughter, Suzy Lee, and his wife, Mary, managed Wong Lee's in San Francisco. "Is it as good in San Francisco?"

"Mary adds a bit of ginger. Makes Mom mad as hell."

"Which one's the best?"

"Mary's stuff seems to go better with beer. The business crowd likes it." Wong Lee rubbed his chin for a moment. "Helen. I want you to stay here after the plane drops the supplies."

"We'll go together." She stood slowly, making sure she remained in deepest shadow.

"No, you stay here. That way you can take some of them out."

"Not tonight, Wong." Now the roles were switched. She was trying to convince him there were no Japanese hidden in the night.

He rose and stood beside her, his hands on his hips. "You know what? I haven't tasted roast duck with plum sauce for eight months. I've not seen Mary or my mother for eight months. Okay. I can stand the snakes. I can stand the heat. I can stand the starvation. The lack of food, medicine. I can stand it all."

"I know."

"What I can't stand are the damned dreams."

She hadn't heard Wong Lee talk like this.

"I hear them. I see them. The Japs kicked the door in. Didn't give them a chance. I'd barely jumped out the window when they shot my uncle and my nephews in bed. Little kids, Tom and Jerry, we called them. They were five and seven. I heard the bullets hit; they screamed." He was talking about Malaybalay and the night he'd escaped from the Kempetai. "All we were doing was washing dishes for a little ten-table place down the street. Tom and Jerry—they helped, too. Someone snitched I was American."

"I dream, too, Wong."

"Do you have pills for it?"

Something whistled in the distance, growing louder as engines softly backfired. A shadow flicked directly overhead. For four or five seconds she heard the rush of airframe noise as the airplane glided over the runway. Then the airplane's engines roared as the pilot firewalled the throttles, clawing for altitude, heading for home. It had the same growl of the PBYs she'd seen so many times at Corregidor.

"Damn good pilot. No noise. Must have glided all the way in from high altitude." Wong watched the red glow of the plane's exhausts fade to the south.

Helen heard a thunk off to her left, near the runway. Then something smacked the grove, farther to her left.

"The Lucky Strikes are in that one over there." Wong pointed to the grove.

They started walking. "How can you tell?"

"By the sound it made when it hit the trees."

"Come on."

"That's what bothers me."

"What?" In the darkness she saw his hand point toward the sky.

"That guy. The pilot. He sleeps in clean sheets tonight, or whenever he gets home."

"Good for him."

"But don't you see? Like just a little bit of ginger in the plum sauce, the airplane is a new taste for us. Americans. Freedom. Those crates out there. Makes you almost not want to have them, for fear there's a Jap hiding behind the next bush, ready to take it all away and kill you."

They parted, heading for their respective bundles. "Wong?"

"Yes?" He stopped.

"Amador isn't going to die. He promised me."

"Oh?"

"I want your promise, too."

After a moment, his voice drifted over. "I promise."

They started walking again and Helen said, "Good. You'll stop smoking, then?"

"Never."

* * *

They reached Amparo within an hour and while Wong Lee, Amador, Renaldo, Legaspi, and Carillo unloaded the skid, Valentino Lubang called Helen into his little two-room hut to set little Emilio's arm, the five-year-old having fallen into a ravine earlier that day. The boy did his best not to cry while Helen set the limb. When it was done, Helen took him in her arms and rocked him to sleep.

Shaking Helen's hand over and over, the wafer-thin, five-foot-two Valentino praised her arrival as a godsend, especially since, his wife, Corazon, wasn't there to be with her son; months ago, she'd been dragged off by the Kempetai for duties as a comfort girl.

Amador and his *guerrilleros* had made camp outside the village. Too exhausted to join them, Helen fell asleep on a *banig,* a woven mat, in Lubang's *sala,* a little front room.

Outside, her mind barely registered a truck crunching to a stop in the gravel.

A scream. Gunfire. "What?" She rose from her *banig* and blinked as two men stormed into the little room, waving flashlights. A male voice screamed in Tagalog. Then another shouted, "Get up!"

"What?" she mumbled. Amazing. That was in English. Mentally, her system was telling her something was very wrong. But her body wouldn't respond.

Two pair of hands pulled Helen to her feet. This time the shouts were in Japanese and the soldiers reeked of tobacco and *basi,* a local wine of sugar cane and herbs.

A candle was lit and Helen was dragged across the room and shoved against the wall. One soldier pushed again, this time against her breast, for good measure; then they walked out.

Other women screamed and cried out in the village. A pig squealed. But a rifle cracked and the squealing stopped.

The soldiers shouted back and forth, some in Tagalog, some again in English.

Valentino rushed in. "Put this on, quick."

"What?" Desperately, Helen tried to blink sleep away. But her eyes seemed as if covered by sandpaper.

Valentino pressed a garment into her hands and turned his back. "A dress of Corazon's. It's the best I can do."

"What do they want?" She began taking off her overalls.

Valentino looked out the door. "They're conscripting ten of our women to clean their ship. That Hapon out there, their officer, promises to return you home in a week. With money in your pocket as well," he snorted.

"At daybreak they'll see my face, my eyes."

With a snap of his fingers, Valentino ran into the back room and returned with a long black veil. "Corazon's," he puffed, out of breath.

She squeezed his hand and took the veil. It had a lingering perfume scent.

"She wore it to church. It . . . it was her parent's wedding gift," Valentino stammered.

"Thank you." She draped the black veil over her face and looked down to see the dark floral-patterned dress extended to her ankles. "I'm no longer an Occidental."

"They're loading the truck. I'm sorry there's—"

"Quick. Do you have a piece of paper?"

"Yes, but—"

"Get it."

Valentino did so and brought it to her.

Fortunately Valentino was literate in Tagalog, so she asked him to print in bold letters:

LEPER (in remission)

Then she scribbled a name with the legend MD beside it. He'd just pinned it on her when the two soldiers stomped in, screeching in Japanese.

Valentino hung an old cracked leather musette bag over her shoulder. "A few things."

She tried to mouth *Thank you*, but they dragged her out the door to the truck. She must have been the last one, because right after they heaved her in the back, the truck started, doors slammed, and they drove off.

The truck bounced down the Agusan Valley toward Butuan. Helen lay on the floor near the back, watching the eastern horizon grow red. Two guards sat in back, both asleep, their rifles jiggling between their legs. A few whimpers ranged through the truck, but most of the women remained quiet, stoic, almost accepting their fate: convinced they would not return alive. One caught Helen's eye, an overweight mestiza, and returned a malevolent stare, as if this whole thing were Helen's fault. That this would not have happened had she and her damned *guerrilleros* not showed up at two in the morning.

She rolled on her back, watching a marvelous cloudless day develop, so unlike the recent fog-shrouded mornings. Terror coursed through her veins as the truck drove on. Despite what Valentino said, she thought she was headed back to some sort of interrogation. Occasionally, she raised her head and looked out, wondering if she could somehow scramble over the guard's legs as they crossed a bridge, leap far into space, and end it all.

Never again would she let them interrogate her. Never.

CHAPTER SEVENTEEN

The bachelor's officers quarters was a batten-board, faded yellow, two-story, utilitarian building that looked as if it were built in a hurry. Ingram's room, which he shared with Toliver, had a bed on either side, two dressers, two closets, two easy chairs, and a long desk under wooden venetian blinds. A portable radio in the corner softly played Artie Shaw.

Ingram had just finished donning his dress khakis, getting ready for dinner. Waiting for Toliver, he walked to the window and flipped open the venetians. A cold breeze stirred scrap paper outside and pulled along mist and fog. Sometimes the damned city could be so forbidding, he thought. And this evening, it well matched his mood.

A gray bus drew up and a sailor stepped off. As the bus rumbled off, the sailor buttoned his pea coat and tucked two large manila envelopes under his arm. Squaring his white hat, the young man stubbed out a cigarette and walked toward the front door.

Instinctively, Ingram knew why the sailor was here and his stomach seemed to shrivel to the size it was at Corregidor. He went to the door, propped it open, and peeked out to see steam gush from the shower over the green linoleum-covered hallway. Toliver was in there singing with the verve generated by hot water on a cold evening. His perfectly executed phrases wafted into the lobby in a beautifully pitched baritone, the r's rolled to operatic perfection:

Aye, yi, yi, yi,
In China they never serve Chili
Here comes the next verse
It's worse than the other verse
So Waltz me around again, Willy.

There once was a young lady of fashion
Who had oodles and oodles of passion
To her lover she said,
As they climbed into bed
"Here's *one* thing the government can't ration!"

He smiled as the limerick ricocheted up and down the hall for another two stanzas. He found most limericks gross and unimaginative, the themes running from adultery to the loss of one's virginity to hypocritic clergy. But some were brilliantly conceived. Marveling at their intricacy, Ingram felt sorry in a way that they had to be wasted in barracks and barrooms of the Pacific and Europe theaters. With a smirk, he went back to the desk, sat in a chair, propped his feet on the desk, and aimlessly picked up a manual labeled *MARK 15 Torpedoes, Maintenance and Overhaul. TOP SECRET.*

Outside, he heard the shower squeak off and Toliver say, "Help you, sailor?"

A voice said, "Lieutenant Ingram?"

"Right there. Room 112. He's in."

Soon there was a knock on the doorjamb.

"Come."

The sailor pushed open the door and walked in. He was a beanpole of about six-three, weighing 165 pounds, but his thin frame was well masked by regulation tailor-made dress blues. He had a long, narrow face, sharp nose, and freckled cheeks. His sandy hair was long and straight and parted in the middle. With thick, bushy eyebrows, his countenance was overly serious, almost cruel at first glance. But it was his light blue eyes that gave him away. They crinkled at the corners, letting one know he was all at once mischievous, perceptive, deeply serious, humorous, and intelligent.

"Lieutenant Ingram?"

A shadow passed over Ingram's face. "That's me." He put the torpedo manual in a drawer and closed it.

"I'm supposed to ask for ID, Sir."

"Who are you?"

"Seltzer, Sir. Leonard P. Boatswain's mate second, Sir."

Ingram stood and walked over to a bed and pulled a wallet from his blouse. As he reached, he saw Seltzer looking at his two rows of ribbons; among them was the Philippine campaign ribbon with two battle stars; another was the Navy Cross.

"Okay?" Ingram held up his ID card.

Seltzer checked his ID, then wrote down his serial number on a separate sheet. "Chief Bradshaw has this envelope for you, Sir. But you need to sign this first." Seltzer handed over a receipt form. Ingram signed, then Seltzer handed over the manila envelope.

"Orders." Ingram's eyes were vacant. "Nine copies, I'll bet." He slapped the envelope on his desk. "Is there anything else?"

Seltzer checked the other envelope. "I'm looking for a Lieutenant jay-gee Toliver."

"Here."

Seltzer spun. The limerick singer stood in the doorway, a towel wrapped around his waist. To Seltzer, he looked very thin, almost gaunt. In fact, his ribs and clavicles protruded, making him look much like magazine photographs of starving children in China.

Seltzer grinned.

"What's so funny, sailor?"

"I enjoy your singing, Sir."

"What can I do for you?"

"I need some ID, Sir."

Toliver tried to tuck in his towel. "If you don't mind waiting, I'll—"

"I'll vouch, sailor," said Ingram.

"Thank, you, Sir. Could you sign here, Mr. Toliver? And write in your serial number, too, please?"

Juggling towel and ink pen, Toliver leaned over and signed the receipt form. As he did, Seltzer noticed Toliver's blouse hanging from a coat tree on the other side of the room. He also had the Philippine campaign ribbon with two battle stars.

Ingram caught him staring. "Any questions, sailor?"

"Corregidor, huh?" said Seltzer.

"That's right."

"I was on the *Houston*." The heavy cruiser U.S.S. *Houston* had gone down during a point-blank-range slugfest with the Japanese on the night of February 28, 1942. "Shrapnel hit me in the butt. Million-dollar wound. They dumped me in Tjilatjap with some others a week before she was lost. We were among the last to be airlifted to Darwin before the Japs invaded."

"Rough." Toliver tossed his envelope on the desk and grabbed another towel.

Ingram stared at Seltzer.

Seltzer gulped. "The chief said I should wait until you opened the envelope, Sir."

"Very well." Ingram wrinkled his brow and unsealed the flap.

FROM: Commanding Officer, Bethlehem Shipbuilding Company
TO: LT. Alton C. Ingram, 638217, USN

DATE: 15 September 1942

SUBJ: Orders

INFO: Commanding Officer, Twelfth Naval District
            Commanding Officer, U.S. Naval Station, Treasure Island
            Commanding Officer, U.S.S. *Howell* (DD 482)

1. Upon receipt, you are detached as program manager, U.S.S. *Tingey* (DD 539).

2. You are ordered to proceed to port in which U.S.S. *Howell* (DD 482) may be.

3. Upon receipt, you will proceed to San Francisco and report to the Commanding Officer U.S. Naval Station, Treasure Island, for transportation.

4. Accounting data 1701453.2218 060 22/31600.110.

By Direction
P. J. Hoenig

Ingram sat back, ran his hands over his face, then looked over to Toliver, who had just opened his envelope. "Spruance was true to his word. He sent me to a can. The *Howell*."

Toliver looked in the distance, not aware his towel had dropped to the floor.

"What gives, Ollie?"

"I'll be a sonofabitch."

"What?"

"They're sending me to the *Riley*." He turned to Ingram. "I thought they'd put us on the same ship."

"I guess the *Riley* knows quality when they see it."

"Damn."

"Don't look now, but you're out of uniform, Ollie."

Slowly, Toliver picked up the towel and wrapped it around his waist.

Both looked to Seltzer as if to say, *If there's nothing else, then get your butt out of here.*

Seltzer stammered, "They are both new destroyers. *Fletcher* class."

Ingram nodded. Toliver turned to his dresser and opened a drawer.

Seltzer said, "I'm shipping out, too, Sir. Uh, the *Howell,* with you, Mr. Ingram. The chief wanted me to tell you that."

"Where is she?"

"Nouméa. Both of them." Nouméa was the major naval base for the Allies on New Caledonia, a French territory about nine hundred miles southeast of Guadalcanal in the Solomon Islands.

Toliver groaned and sat. "Nouméa. About as close to the shit as you can get without smelling it. Ow, damnit!" He'd stuck himself pinning his jg bars on a starched khaki shirt.

"Get dressed and let's go eat, Ollie."

"Right."

Looking up, Ingram asked, "What's your name again, sailor?"

"Seltzer, Sir. Bo's'n second."

"Where's home?"

"Rapid City."

Ingram laced his fingers behind his head. "The *Houston* was a damn good ship. What was your battle station?"

"Gun captain. Five-inch mount, Sir."

Not bad. "Any torpedo experience?"

"Used to be a trainer, but I like the five-inch better."

"Well, I look forward to serving with you, Seltzer."

"Thank you, Sir." After a silence, Seltzer said, "Well, I guess I better get going." He walked out.

Ingram scanned his orders again as Toliver leaned over the dresser, fussing with socks. "I'll wait outside, Ollie."

"Be there in a minute."

Grabbing his coat and combination cap, Ingram walked out and down the hall.

Hurry.

He gagged as wave after wave of nausea cascaded through his belly. Quick-stepping into the lavatory, he tossed his coat and cap on the counter and dashed into the stall. Falling to his knees, he let it go in a single, gushing burst.

It took at least two minutes to gain a semblance of control and another three to overcome the dizziness. After washing his hands and face, he patted his cheeks, trying to return color to his face.

"God." He leaned against the counter, no longer caring, letting the pictures, clear in every gruesome detail, swarm through his mind. *The hell with it.* It was as if a gigantic box had sprung open in his head, spewing image after image of the tortured and maimed men he had known, those without hope of rescue, or food or medicine, without hope of another day of life, as their own life oozed onto the merciless, hot steel decks of dying ships. It was worse for those ashore on Corregidor, where they either were ripped apart by artillery or went crazy in dust-choked tunnels.

Holding his head in his hands, Ingram marveled at how long he'd kept the images at bay, even in his sleep. *Maybe it's time to see the doc?* he wondered. At least get some pills. Maybe he should see the chaplain. Maybe—

Get hold! Ingram leaned over the sink and, once more, splashed water on his face.

"... Skipper?" Toliver's voice echoed outside.

"In a minute, Ollie."

"I'll be at the car ..." Toliver let the front door slam behind him.

Who was Spruance's aide? Falkenberg. He'd said, *Don't worry. It'll probably be convoy duty or something very boring. Your Corregidor days are over, Lieutenant.*

Bullshit, Ingram thought. *Those guys out there in the Solomons are dog meat.*

Ingram put on his blouse and buttoned up. *Here's hoping you're right, Captain Falkenberg. Here's hoping the U.S.S.* Howell *has a very, very boring cruise.*

He was astonished when his hand came out of his pocket with her ring. Turning it in his hands, he saw the inscription HZD-1939 inside the band. The ring was small, definitely a woman's size. Yet it fit neatly on his fourth finger. He was finally gaining weight and knew that in a few weeks it would hardly fit his little finger. He missed her terribly and felt guilty for not being there. And with this vomiting business he felt worse knowing he didn't want to be there, to help Helen and Pablo. Would he take a bullet for her? For Don Pablo Amador? Instinctively, he knew Amador would take one for him. He almost had last May in Nasipit.

Helen.

Hers was one of the images he had held back, especially after he'd been to Ramona and met Kate and Frank. *Damnit!* He felt like such a hypocrite. Sitting in San Francisco, slopping up chocolate ice cream, and getting fat, while Helen dodged Jap bullets.

A horn tooted lightly outside.

"On my way, old chum . . . ," he murmured.

Ingram walked out into the brisk evening, where Toliver's four-door Packard convertible waited, the engine running. He jumped in, finding the heater on. It felt good.

Toliver started out and shifted smoothly through the gears, saying, "You okay?"

"Never better."

"What sounds good tonight?"

"Actually, I'd rather—"

"Hey." They passed a sailor who had just exited the administration building. In the rearview mirror, Toliver saw him stick his thumb out. "That's our boy. What's his name?" He slowed to a stop and backed up.

"Seltzer." Ingram cranked the window down as Toliver drew to a stop.

"Give you a lift, sailor?" Toliver shouted, as Seltzer drew abreast of the car.

Wind ruffled Seltzer's pea coat. His freckled cheeks were bright red as he leaned in. "Yes, Sir. Thank you." He jumped in the back seat and sat in the middle like a reigning potentate.

Toliver started out again. "Where to?"

"EM club, Sir. Nice car, Sir. Cadillac?"

"Packard. You have your liberty pass?"

"Matter of fact, I do, Sir."

"Well, then, why don't you let us treat an old Asiatic sailor to dinner?"

After his recent bout, Ingram wasn't hungry. But he was glad Toliver had offered.

"Wow. That's keen, Sir. Thanks," said Seltzer.

"Ever tried Mexican food, Seltzer? I know this little place down in San Jose," said Toliver.

"No, I haven't, but I'll eat anything that won't crawl off the plate."

Ingram thought about the kid sitting in back. They were to be shipmates.

Perhaps for a long time. He wondered how they would get along. "Good thing you remembered your liberty pass."

"My *Houston* training, Sir." He gave a long sigh. "She was a wonderful ship, I'll tell you."

"Your first ship?" asked Ingram.

"Yessir."

Toliver examined Seltzer in the rearview mirror. "They taught you well, huh?"

"We started out with three basic rules, Sir. After that, everything was easy."

"Oh?"

They stopped for the Marine sentry at the main gate. After checking IDs, the Marine saluted. Toliver returned it and started up again. "Go ahead."

"Pardon?" said Seltzer.

"Your three basic rules."

"Uhhh, yes, Sir." Drawing a deep breath, Seltzer said, "Keep your eyes, ears, and bowels open, your mouth shut, and nine copies of your orders at all times." They'd all heard it, with Toliver joining in on the last phrase.

After the obligatory chuckle, Toliver said, "If they give you any trouble on the *Howell,* Seltzer, you just come on over to the *Riley.*"

"Yes, Sir. Thank you, Sir."

Toliver said softly, "You sure you're okay, skipper? We don't have to go out."

Their orders allowed no time for leave. Ingram and Toliver were detached from Mare Island and were ordered to report for transportation to the southwest Pacific. Period. End of stateside séance. End of rest and recreation. Tonight would be one of their last dinners in the U.S. "Never better, Ollie."

CHAPTER EIGHTEEN

22 SEPTEMBER, 1942
WONG LEE'S CAFÉ
SAN FRANCISCO, CALIFORNIA

The plates were cleared, and they sipped the remains of their second bottle of wine. It was quiet, their feigned levity running stale. Toliver had called for a cab, and Dezhnev, their host for the evening, asked, "What time is your plane, Ollie?"

"Midnight." Toliver exhaled and looked at his watch. "Two and a half hours to go." He'd been manifested on a lumbering four-engine PB2Y amphibian taking off at midnight for Pearl Harbor. Ingram was due out the next day, DeWitt the day after that, when he would accompany General Sutherland back to Brisbane.

"I hate night takeoffs." While at Corregidor, Toliver heard of PBYs water-looping at night during their takeoff run, having slammed into Manila Bay's flotsam of war.

DeWitt pointed toward the front door. "My God, Ollie. This is San Francisco Bay. You won't find any crap floating out there."

A forced smile crawled across Toliver's face. "I know." He signaled to Suzy, who came to the table. He whispered in her ear. With a nod, she walked away.

All knew what was on Toliver's mind, and it wasn't night takeoffs. He was returning to the war zone. Ingram was, too, with DeWitt not far behind. Four days ago a farewell dinner had seemed a good idea. But now, quite simply, the hour was nearly upon them and their demeanor was morose.

The booths had all been taken, so they were seated at a table in the room's center this Tuesday evening. A pall seemed to hang over the booths, anyway, and Ingram was glad to be among people. For some reason, most diners were male this evening. Most were in uniform, and it seemed there was a lot of forced cheerfulness throughout. Their conversations were somber and, instead of guzzling cocktails, they merely sipped, their brows furrowed. The bar was full, but even in there, the spontaneity of the other night was gone. That was it. There was no music. Maybe it was the piano player's night off.

Surprisingly, Ingram had finished his meal: roast duck in plum sauce, the house specialty. But he had eaten with a detached sense, almost as if he were someone else, looking over his own shoulder and watching himself chew, wondering if it tasted good. It was the belladonna, he supposed, that made him feel this way. The shipyard doctor, a white-haired man named Hawkes who played poker all night, had prescribed it for him, and it had blocked the terrible vomiting he'd had last week. He slept better at night and the nightmares weren't as bad, although he was drowsy in the daytime and had a dry mouth. Yesterday, Toliver had discovered his little bottle of belladonna tablets and gave him a great razzing. But Ingram grinned and shrugged it off.

For a moment Ingram closed his eyes and drew a deep breath, trying to lock in that universal odor common to restaurants the world over: polished wood, worn leather, ladies' fragrance, and good food. He opened his eyes, matching the aroma to the people and decor around him; an attempt to some-how center himself on this one single place on earth, to somehow freeze this crowd and create a picture he could call up at will. A picture that would carry him through whatever was to happen out in the Pacific.

Like Toliver, all he was doing now was standing around, biding his time, waiting for an Army Air Corps B-17 to take off tomorrow and fly him into the Pacific to start the whole mess over again. Knowing what awaited him, Ingram knew better than to harbor the *go gettum* attitude of the grinning, gum-chewing eighteen-year-olds boarding trains and troop ships throughout the country. Toliver and DeWitt, too. On the surface, they conversed with a detached sangfroid, well masking what actually went on in their minds. Ironically, Dezhnev, the foreigner with only a few weeks in town, had offered to line up dates for the evening. But they declined, already drawn into the same mental cocoons they had used in the hell of Corregidor. It was a mind-set that obviated everything except autonomic bodily functions: sleep, a basic level of nutrition, and satisfaction that one's back was protected were all that was required. Everything else, from women to stock portfolios to sports and clean sheets, were peripheral interests.

Suzy walked up with a tray and three small gift wrapped boxes and placed it before Toliver. "Your cab is here." She kissed him on the cheek and stepped back.

"Whoa!" Toliver groped behind his chair for Suzy, but she withdrew. He sighed and pushed his chair back. "Okay, troops, time to go yachting."

"Ollie, for crying out loud," DeWitt laughed. "We're trying to stick you with the bill. How are we going to do that if you take off?"

Dezhnev spoke up. "Tonight you are guests of the Union of Soviet Socialist Republics. I insist."

"Forget it, Ed. It's more fun screwing Toliver," said DeWitt.

Ingram coughed; Dezhnev looked under the table to pick up his napkin. The gybe had fallen flat and their eyes drew to Toliver. "I want to leave something behind. Make you guys think of me and how much fun we're going to have arguing over who gets to pay for our next dinner when the war's over. That's when we'll find out who screws who. And I'll tell you what, let's meet right here. Deal?" He held out his hand. Toliver, Ingram, and DeWitt shook. "You, too, Ed."

"*Da.*" Dezhnev smiled broadly and thrust out his hand.

Toliver passed out three little elegantly gift wrapped boxes from Gump's. DeWitt looked at his. "What the hell is this?"

"See for yourself."

They opened their boxes. DeWitt said, "My God, Ollie." He held up a glimmering pair of gold cuff links, the initials OD in enameled black. He shook again.

Dezhnev's cuff links were initialed ED. He bowed slightly. "I am indeed honored."

"Sorry, Gump's couldn't do them in Cyrillic."

Ingram held up cuff links initialed ACI. "Thanks Ollie." They shook. "See you in Nouméa."

Toliver scraped his chair back and stood. "Just make sure you don't shoot the friendlies, Todd."

"Come on."

"Nouméa?" Dezhnev gave a sly smile. "Ahhhh."

"Now, damnit! Ed. You didn't hear that," DeWitt drawled.

Dezhnev took Toliver's hand. "I heard Alaska. But wait. I can't let you go yet. Here, I want you to have this." He held out his brass-tipped mahogany cane.

Toliver ran a hand over his face. "Ed. Damnit. You need that to . . . to . . . well, get around."

"Nonsense. I have seen many in the stores here. I'm ready for a new one. Take this. Please. I insist." He held it out.

Toliver took it. They hugged and slapped backs. "You'll get it back next time we meet." He swung around. "Tell you what. Suzy!" He raised his hand and waved.

When she came over, Toliver said, "Suzy, could you keep our names and addresses and route our mail? That way, we'll figure out how to set up our reunion after the war."

"I probably won't be here," groaned Dezhnev.

"Nonsense," said DeWitt. "We'll lick the Japs in no time and be back well before they send you home."

Dezhnev looked up. "I hope. How long do you think?"

"Two years, tops," said DeWitt with a wink.

Dezhnev recalled Beria's estimate: 1948 or 1949.

"Is there any chance it will be sooner?" Suzy had spoken, surprising them.

"It depends on a lot of things, honey," said Toliver. "Why?"

"My father, an uncle, and two cousins are trapped in the Philippines."

"Your Dad? Wong Lee himself?"

She lowered her gaze. "We don't like to talk about it."

"Rough," said Ingram. "It's not easy. But we're doing our best."

"I don't mean for you to take chances," Suzy said. "I just want to . . ."

"We all want it to end, honey." Toliver wrapped an arm around her waist.

Standing on tiptoe, Suzy kissed Toliver again, a tear on her cheek. "Don't forget your cab." Then she turned and kissed each one of them on the cheek. "God bless you." She turned. "Send me your notices. Your reunion will be on us." Then she walked to the kitchen.

"My God." DeWitt's eyes blinked for a moment.

It was a wonderful kiss, Ingram had to admit. Dearly intended, it meant a lot to him.

Toliver said, "Okay, you jerks, time for me to—"

Dezhnev clapped a hand on his shoulder. "Sit for a moment, Ollie."

"What the hell?" Said Toliver. "My cab."

"Sit. There'll be another one."

Toliver sat.

Dezhnev eyed each of them, then waited. "We live in a fluid world. Right now, we don't know if we'll ever see one another again. And yet, each of you means something to me, and these cuff links are a wonderful way to bind the moment. I salute you, Ollie. Always, will I be reminded of my American friends, heroes, all of you."

"That might be going a little too far, Ed," said Ingram.

"Please, let me finish." Dezhnev turned to Toliver. "I went through this in Riga. I lost a boat, good friends. I lost a . . ." He thumped his prosthesis on the floor.

"Lucky for me my mother is fairly safe in Sochi. But my friends have lost whole families in this mess. And soon you will know people whose loved ones are killed. Already you've seen it at Corregidor and Bataan. And I know how you feel about going back to it. We're all afraid of dying, each of us. We just see it in different ways. And as we try to—ummm, how do I say, rationalize, I think you would call it—yes, rationalize your meeting with death, it is then that things become complex. This is the danger point. It becomes very, very hard to see your way through life, to plan for your future; for your vision is blocked by the next row of machine guns. It is then that some people just give up, thinking they don't have anything to live for."

Dezhnev sipped his wine for a moment. He released Toliver's hand and waved at the crowd. "Some live, some don't. Those of us who are still alive feel guilty about why we make it and why others don't. I still have the dreams, the nightmares, of the men on my patrol boat. I hear their screams . . . but that's not the point." He jabbed a finger at the table. "The worst thing is not guilt, nor trying to stay alive. The worst thing is holding on to the past, and letting these feelings from events over which you have no control drag you down. You feel you can't go on; things become jumbled, large obstacles are thrown into your path."

"If you only knew," said Ingram.

Dezhnev waited a moment. "I do know. I spent months in a hospital with my leg. There was nothing to do except listen to the moans of those around me. Twice, I almost committed suicide. But I botched it and lived. Can you believe that? I lived.

"Others were more successful. You see, people go crazy. They can't stand it. I certainly couldn't stand it until I met Viktor. He was a tanker whose head was wrapped in bandages. His T-34 was already knocked out when he jumped and ran into a phosphorus shell. He was blinded and terribly disfigured. But he said something to me."

Their eyes searched Dezhnev.

"He could barely speak, but one evening Viktor rose up from his cot and told me in a clear voice, 'Let the dead bury the dead. It's time for you to move on, Eduard.' I thought about that all night. *Let the dead bury the dead.* I was stuck to something I could not put aside, all these deaths, all this horror. Viktor was right. I was alive. It was time to move on."

Dezhnev took a breath. "The next day, I felt better and turned to thank Viktor. But during the night, something had happened. He was gone. Just like that. Dead."

He gave a slight smile. "Perhaps Viktor was trying to emphasize his point." He reached again for Toliver's hand. "At the risk of sounding very,

very melancholy, it's been my pleasure to know all of you, my American friends. Now go, Ollie. The dead will bury the dead. You have a grand life to live."

Toliver stood. "Uhhhh-rah!"

"Uhhh-rah!" they growled.

Suzy walked up. "I can't hold the taxi much longer."

"Best of luck, fellas. Thanks again for the cane, Ed." Grandly swinging Dezhnev's cane, Toliver walked away. But as he did, something fell out of his pocket, clanked on the floor, and rolled to Ingram's feet.

Ingram picked it up. "Be right back." He dashed after Toliver, catching up just as he exited the front door. "Ollie."

Toliver turned. "You can't stand to be away from me."

"You dropped these." Ingram held up a small prescription bottle. The label read: *Belladonna Extract: ¼ grain, 3–4 times daily.* "It looks half-empty, Ollie." He handed it over.

Toliver gave a sheepish grin. "Got them same day as you did, skipper. I'm just not dumb enough to admit I'm scared shitless."

"You'll do fine, Ollie."

"So will you, skipper. Stay out of Pearl City, you'll get the clap. And if you do go to Pearl City, I'm telling Helen." Toliver climbed into the cab and it drove off.

CHAPTER NINETEEN

22 SEPTEMBER, 1942
CONSULATE, U.S.S.R.
SAN FRANCISCO, CALIFORNIA

The cab drew to a stop across from the Soviet consulate at the top of Divisidero Street. A door opened and Eduard Dezhnev wobbled out into a gloomy, overcast night. "Thank you for the ride, Otis."

DeWitt's voice echoed from inside the cab, "My pleasure, Ed. And thanks again for dinner. It was wonderful."

Both turned, hearing a commotion about a half-block down the street. Four sailors walked up the hill toward them, their steps uncertain. "How the hell do you find a woman in this town?" one said, his voice magnified by the dense nighttime air.

Dezhnev turned and leaned in the door. "The next dinner will be our victory dinner. You will write?"

"Do my best. You do the same." DeWitt scribbled his address on a scrap of paper and handed it over.

"*Do svedaniia.*" Dezhnev shut the door.

DeWitt cranked the window down, his twang ripping through the night. "Ahh, pardon for asking, but can you get across the street okay?"

Dezhnev smiled. "I need the practice, believe me. I'm supposed to exercise my leg once a day without the cane."

"Hey, buddy!" yelled one of the sailors. They were closer, just two houses away.

DeWitt looked at them. "They're drunk. Ignore them. Well, so long, Ed." He slapped the back of the front seat and the cab drove off.

Dezhnev turned and headed for the consulate, but one of the sailors called out, "Can you help us?"

"What?" The street was slippery from the mist and Dezhnev found it hard to keep his footing, so he turned, walked to the curb, and leaned against a tree.

The four sailors walked up. They wore dress blues, except one was without hat and pea coat and Dezhnev caught a tinge of the odor of vomit. The hatless one was thin, prematurely bald, and had piercing ratlike eyes. Another was blond, medium build, and chewed gum rapidly. Behind them, two heavyset sailors stood in shadows, their hands jammed in their pockets. As they drew close, the vomit smell was stronger and was mixed with that of cheap liquor. "Can I help you?" asked Dezhnev.

"This town's a shithouse, man. They ain't no women. And we're out of hooch." The hatless one stood closer, belched loudly, and giggled. "As amatteraffact, we could have hooch if we had money." He examined Dezhnev's mufti with great exaggeration. "Ummm. Nice togs. San Francisco stud, huh?"

"No. Actually, I'm from—"

"Bet he's a 4-F, Ernie," slurred the blond sailor, stepping closer, his gum clicking loudly.

Dezhnev could see this was going nowhere. He turned and tried to step off the curb and walk across the street. But the two heavyset sailors blocked his way. His heart beat faster as he stepped up the curb and leaned against the tree again. He turned and looked across the street to the consulate. To keep a low profile, the consul general's policy was not to have a guard outside. But a twenty-four watch was always posted in the lobby near the front door; Georgiy Voronin was the man on duty this evening, if Dezhnev remembered correctly. But the building was dark and he couldn't tell if anyone was looking out the window.

"Jeepers! I never seen a real chickenshit 4-F before." Ernie strolled around the tree, looking Dezhnev up and down. "Nice clothes. Neat haircut. A real stud. You don't look so chickenshit to me. You chickenshit, studly? How 'bout some money, studly? We need money. Kind of help with the war effort. After that, when we go overseas, you can move in and bang our girls."

"You ain't got no girl, Ernie," said the gum-chewing blond sailor. "He'd just be bangin' sand." This seemed enormously funny to the others, for they began laughing and cackling.

"We'll see who bangs sand." Ernie chopped Dezhnev's arm away from the tree and stepped close, his eyes within six inches. He hissed, "Gimme your wallet, sucker."

"You're making a mistake," said Dezhnev.

"Ohhhh." Ernie grinned and looked at the others. "I'm making a mistake." Quickly, he pulled a switchblade out of his pocket and pressed the tip against Dezhnev's left cheek. "Gimme."

A car pulled around the corner, its headlights flashing across the sailors, everyone momentarily blinded. With a backhand, Dezhnev chopped Ernie across his Adam's apple. Ernie's eyebrows jumped to the top of his face and he gurgled horribly. Grabbing his throat, he dropped his knife and fell to his knees, gasping and wheezing. Dezhnev kicked Ernie's switchblade away, where it went spinning across the street and into the gutter.

"Shit!" The gum-chewing blond stepped in, swinging a fist. Dezhnev parried it and caught him with an uppercut squarely on the chin. "Ahhhh," the man wailed, falling to the sidewalk. Just then, Dezhnev felt a blow to the side of his head. He fell against the tree. Another blow thundered into his kidney. He sank to his knees as yet another fist smashed against his shoulder. He held his hands to his face, knowing the two large thugs were on him. Another heavy fist drove him on his back.

"Aiiiiyeeee," someone shrieked. Through the haze, Dezhnev looked up to see a wiry creature—it looked like a baboon on one of the thugs' back—clawing at the man's eyes. It was Otis DeWitt. All 165 pounds. Amazing!

"Jesus, Walt. Get this little bastard off me," the heavyset sailor howled to the other thug.

With large beefy hands, Walt ripped DeWitt off his friend's back. DeWitt swung uselessly as Walt laughed, saying, "Well, blow me. Iza damned Army colonel. Time to join the Air Corps, Colonel." He punched DeWitt twice in the face. Then he spun him around and threw him across the sidewalk, where DeWitt thudded against a low stone wall and slumped groaning into rosebushes.

Dezhnev nearly gained his feet, but his prosthesis slipped out from under him and he fell to his knee. Nevertheless, he planted a fist in the heavyset sailor's groin. It was partially deflected, and Walt yelled more out of surprise than pain.

Both sailors stood for a moment to take stock. The blonde lay still on his back, but Ernie was coming to his senses and staggered to his feet, still wheezing. "We gonna cut you up, studly," he mumbled.

Suddenly Dezhnev heard a deep guttural roar. One of the heavyset sailors fell to his face, remaining still as if nailed to the cement. Something twirled in the dark at the other sailor, hitting, choking, the man frantically stepping back, buying time. As Dezhnev struggled to his feet, he recognized the bull-like creature that tore at the sailor: Georgiy Voronin . . .

Dezhnev poured a glass of schnapps from a crystal decanter and handed it to Otis DeWitt. The U.S. Army colonel sat before a fire, wearing nothing except skivvies and a blanket. Both had showered, with Dezhnev changing into slacks and a short-sleeved shirt. In the basement, DeWitt's uniform was being cleaned and pressed; and his trousers were being mended by the consulate chauffeur who doubled as a gardener and tailor.

They were in a seldom-used anteroom off the main lobby that was decorated like a study. It seemed like the whole consulate had awakened as Georgiy Voronin victoriously clomped in with Dezhnev and DeWitt under each arm, screaming for someone to call the police. Now people buzzed back and forth, looking out the windows, murmuring in Russian.

Dezhnev poured himself a schnapps, then stepped to the window and looked out. The San Francisco police were finishing with Georgiy Voronin, the shore patrol long ago having dragged the drunken sailors off to the Treasure Island brig. He paused for another moment, thinking about what had occurred to him in the shower. It could be an opportunity to make inroads on Operation KOMET. Certainly Zenit would order him to pump the man for information. DeWitt, who was just one level removed from General Douglas MacArthur, now sat before him in the consulate, waiting for his clothes to be pressed. Dezhnev looked upon this wiry, small-boned Army colonel who had leaped screaming among the two beefy sailors like the proverbial Russian bear. DeWitt had virtually risked his life for him. There must be another way. *But what?*

"Looks like the police are about done," Dezhnev said. "What will happen to those sailors?"

A shadow crossed DeWitt's face. "Stockade, I hope. Ten years is too good for them, as far as I'm concerned."

"I see." He took a wing chair next to DeWitt and held out his glass.

DeWitt winked. "Here's to joint Soviet-American exercises."

"Uhhhrah!" They clinked.

"Wheeeou. Stronger bite than tequila."

"How do you feel?" asked Dezhnev.

"Oh, I'll get by." DeWitt extended an arm, articulating it. He'd banged it when the sailor threw him against the wall. A goose egg grew on the back of his head, and he knew a black eye was not far behind. But in a way, he felt good about it; the throbbing of the black eye reminded him of the fights he'd had as a teenager. He knew he should have applied an ice pack, but he was too embarrassed to ask for anything more; everyone had been so nice to him already.

"Do you think General Sutherland will believe your story, or would you prefer a note on our stationery, signed by the consul general?"

DeWitt laughed. "I'm fine, Ed. And I have all day tomorrow to recuperate. We don't take off until the day after."

"You'll look like hell."

DeWitt glanced at him, then took another sip. "Maybe they'll send me to the front lines. Scare the Japs to death."

"*Dobryi vecher, gospoda.*" Good evening, gentlemen. Sergei Zenit strutted in, wearing the full dress uniform of the Soviet Navy. It was almost as if he had momentarily stepped away from a state dinner. He shoes were polished to an immaculate shine, and he wore medals, none of which Dezhnev recognized except . . . he almost broke out laughing, Zenit wore Dezhnev's own medal: the Order of Lenin. The little bastard must have broken into his room.

DeWitt shot to his feet, clutching the blanket around his neck. "Sorry, Sir. I didn't know—"

"Colonel! Otis DeWitt, may I present Captain Third Rank Sergei Zenit of the Soviet Navy." To Zenit Dezhnev said, "*Kapitan Zenit, eto Polkovnik Amerikanskoi Armii Otis DeVit.*" Captain Zenit, this is Colonel Otis DeWitt of the United States Army.

Zenit clicked his heels and gave a slight bow. "*Poznakomitsa s vami bol'shaia chest' dlia menia, Polkovnik.*" I am honored to meet you, Colonel.

DeWitt must have figured that out, for he said, "A pleasure, Sir."

Zenit turned to Dezhnev, "*Tak eto on, Eduard. On ponimayet po Russki?*" So this is the one, Eduard. Does he understand Russian?

"*Nyet,*" said Dezhnev, as DeWitt stood politely off to one side.

"What a grand opportunity, you see," continued Zenit in Russian. The man actually rubbed his hands together.

DeWitt smiled nervously. "What should I say, Ed?"

Dezhnev said, "Actually, you outrank him. Tell him to go shit in his hat."

"Haw, haw, haw. I can't do that. We're friends," laughed DeWitt. "That's a good one, Ed."

Dezhnev laughed along with DeWitt.

"What is so funny?" Zenit tried to grin with them.

"Colonel DeWitt just told you to go shit in your hat," Dezhnev said in Russian.

For a moment, Zenit's nostrils flared. But then he broke into a wide grin. "Americans and their jokes. Always with their jokes. Ha, ha, ha." He bowed and extended his hand. After DeWitt shook, Zenit eyed Dezhnev, still grinning. "Isn't this the one from Texas?"

"*Da,*" said Dezhnev.

"I leave it to you to do something interesting, Lieutenant." He bowed again and began backing away.

"What was that about Texas, Ed?" asked DeWitt.

"He said he learned of a new way to get to there."

"How the hell did he know I was from Texas?"

That's a good one, thought Dezhnev. He looked at Zenit, whose eyes had narrowed a bit.

"What's going on?" said, Zenit, still in Russian.

"He's very impressed with your medals. I was telling him about them."

"Ahhh, thank you." Zenit beamed and bowed deeply, with Dezhnev wondering if he would ever get his Order of Lenin back.

DeWitt bowed in return, still clutching his blanket.

"Also, the colonel is interested in learning how you know he's from Texas."

Zenit turned pale. *"I . . . I . . ."*

DeWitt asked, "Well, how does he get to Texas?"

Dezhnev stood to his full height, fixed his eyes in the distance. "Captain Third Rank Sergei Zenit recommends that you walk east until you smell Texas; then walk south until you step in it."

It was DeWitt's turn; his eyes narrowed. But then he broke out laughing. "Step in it, huh?" He reached and slapped a nervous Zenit lightly on the shoulder.

Zenit said, "I must go, Lieutenant. Please tell Colonel DeWitt it was a pleasure meeting him. And"—he looked at Dezhnev—"don't forget why you are here." He extended his hand and shook with DeWitt. *"Do svedaniia."* Good-bye.

"Good-bye, Captain," said DeWitt.

Zenit walked out and they sat watching the fire, sipping their schnapps. With a slow nod, Dezhnev finally made his decision. But still he hesitated and sipped as the fire crackled and popped.

He really had no choice, and it was time to do it. Dezhnev leaned forward in his chair. "Otis. You would be amazed at what I heard from the consul the other night."

"Yes?"

"About a year ago, one of our operatives in Tokyo learned that . . ."

CHAPTER TWENTY

22 SEPTEMBER, 1942
SERVICE BARGE 212, NASIPIT, MINDANAO
PHILIPPINES

The single forty-watt light flicked on, waking Helen instantly. She groaned and blinked at the bulb. *Last day: six a.m.* They'd been here a week and hadn't showered, the tiny bunkroom smelling of human sweat and cleaning fluids and fear and misery.

"Uppa you bitches!" It was Carmen Lai Lai, their forty-year-old mestiza strawboss. At nearly two hundred pounds, it was a mystery how the half-Chinese, half-Filipina kept her weight, considering the paucity of food in the Islands. But that must be why the Japanese trusted Carmen. Many of the betrayals, Helen had learned, involved mestizos. Perhaps that was the Japanese philosophy: *Divide and conquer.* It must be why the Japanese had hired Carmen. It was a good arrangement for her; all she had to do was make sure the women cleaned the ship.

Carmen Lai Lai was smart. She had figured Helen by the second day. Helen had been scrubbing on the second deck next to the captain's cabin when the door banged open. The captain, with papers in hand, walked out and into the wardroom, shouting at someone. With the door gaping wide open, Helen couldn't help but look in. The room was a mess. Before her was a desk, with books and paper stacked on top. Next to that was a floor safe that stood open just five feet away, its double doors gaping wide. Books and documents spilled out of that, too. Some were loose-leaf with white covers and bold block Japanese characters stamped in red across them. Some covers had pictures and diagrams of weapons: cannons, machine guns, ammunition. One cover was dark blue with a picture of a torpedo.

Looking from side to side, Helen saw no one watching. She rose higher to see into the safe—

"Whatchu doin'?" Carmen Lai Lai stood right behind her.

Carmen bent down to within six inches of Helen's face. "Damn leper stuff don' fool me. I got you pegged, you damned *guerrillera.* One of Amador's, huh?" She wrapped her stubby fingers around Helen's throat with one hand and pointed toward the wardroom with the other. "They pay plenty to turn in a *guerrillera,* an American no less. But it's too damned late now. They think I'm part of it. So you work. Understand? Otherwise I take my chances and turn you ass in."

"Y-yes."

After that, Helen was so frightened, she'd only slept a few hours each night. But, miraculously, Carmen didn't say anything to the Japanese. Perhaps, as Carmen had said, it was too late to cash in. Carmen's head could have ended up on a stake on the Agusan Valley Road. It had happened before.

The women groaned and raised to their elbows as Carmen rattled at them in Tagalog, telling them the Japanese were planning to return them to Amparo at sunset. Then Carman barked an order. Like robots, they rolled from their bunks and put on their clothes for work. Helen's bunk was on the third tier and she had to wait for the two below her to climb out. Just then, Carmen waddled down the aisle, reached up, and slapped Helen on the rump. "Lazy bitch, offa you ass."

As Helen slid to the floor, Carmen walked to a small table and plunked an envelope down. "Here's our payment. But no money inside. Just a letter." Then she looked up, her eyebrows raised. *Anybody here read?*

At different intervals, all eyes in the cramped space flicked to Helen.

"All right," she muttered. *How ironic.* It was the first time they had asked a favor of her. Except for Rosa Augustino, the Lubangs' next-door neighbor, the others shunned her, trying to believe she really was a leper. The scars on her face and arms were convincing enough. They didn't realize they were cigarette burns given to her five months previously by the demonic Lieutenant Kiyoshi Tuga of the Kempetai. Some were still bright red, running with pus. Beyond that, most of the women held Carmen's belief that none of this would have happened had Helen and her *guerrilleros* not intruded last week. Even today, none were certain they would return home safely. For everyone knew the Japanese were very poor at keeping their word.

Helen walked to the table and opened the envelope. There was just a single page in Japanese, English, and Tagalog. A Japanese signature was scrawled at the bottom.

Helen read it and almost smiled. *Typical of the little bastards.* She looked over to Rosa Augustino. "Tell them it's a voucher."

Rosa translated, then looked back to Helen, her face as clouded as the others'.

"This voucher promises to pay five hundred pesos."

Rosa spoke again. A few smiled.

Someone knocked. A Japanese guard poked his head in, held up five fingers, then shut the door.

They looked back to Helen.

"They will pay in Japanese pesos, to be claimed at Imperial Army headquarters in Manila."

Rosa translated.

"Sheeeyatt," spat Carmen.

The others groaned and turned to their bunks for their meager ablutions.

Carmen walked among them, as she did each morning, doling out the work assignments. She spoke to Rosa, who translated for Helen. "Main deck again, honey. Bathrooms. Carmen says make sure you restock the paper this time." Carmen had stolen the two toilet paper rolls from two days ago and stowed them in her backpack.

Helen nodded and turned. She'd done the main deck latrines, three plus a small one in the torpedo shop, day before yesterday. *Oh, God, just one more day.* She pitched the veil over her head. Something thumped against her breast. Todd's ring.

Breakfast was a clear soup, a piece of dry toast, a ball of rice, and tea. It seemed to revive Helen and she didn't feel as hungry as before.

By seven a.m., she had drawn mop and bucket and, with a guard in tow, walked behind Carmen to the front of the boat. Following Carmen had its advantages, Helen learned. Carmen was so wide, sailors pressed their backs to the walls and let her by, letting Helen pass unmolested. For the past six days, Carmen had walked the decks of Service Barge 212 as if she were the queen of a Mississippi riverboat. In her wake was her squire, Helen, and a

Japanese guard, a corporal carrying a dusty rifle, impatient to find a place where he could sit and nod off.

Carmen stopped at a door. The Bakelite label on the jamb read, C-102 HEAD. She ripped it open and stepped in. A shout rang at her and she quickly backed out. "Damn lazy Hapon supposed to be at work."

Nice. Helen leaned against the rail. She had learned to sleep standing up, and like the corporal, nodded off.

Someone shouted and there was a loud chuffing noise, waking Helen. A splash quickly followed. Helen heard men muttering, then another shout and a second splash.

The door to the latrine opened and a Japanese sailor walked out, giving her a cold stare.

Curious, Helen edged forward about four feet and peeked around the deckhouse. Ten sailors were gathered at the front of the boat by what looked to Helen to be a torpedo mount. Three men sat on metal stools fixed to the mount, while the others stood aside, looking out to sea, binoculars pressed to their faces.

An officer shouted. The mount went *chuff.* Amazing! With propellers spinning, a torpedo erupted from the tube as if kicked out by a demonic monster. Airborne for two seconds, the torpedo plopped in the water and raced out the harbor, trailing a bubbly wake.

Carmen screeched. Helen grabbed her mop and bucket and ran into the latrine.

By four o'clock the temperature was in the low nineties and the nearly one hundred percent humidity made it miserable. Helen was on hands and knees, finishing the latrine near the torpedo shop. She was soaked with sweat and occasionally grew dizzy as she bent low to push the scrub brush.

Rosa walked in. "The Hapons are letting us off two hours early. Here, let me." She grabbed another brush, dropped to her hands and knees. "The rest are on their way to the truck."

"Thank God," Helen gasped. She'd been thinking about what to say to Don Amador. Except for the torpedo firings and the decrepit old ship in the floating dry dock, she'd seen nothing of interest to relay. "Where do you think they'll go next?"

Rosa whispered, "Carmen told me the Hapons hit Vitos next time. Then Esperanza and Maugahay. Then it's back to Amparo."

Just then, Carmen blasted through the door the way a halfback attacks a broken field: arm outstretched, elbow locked. "What's taking you? Damn lazy. Everybody else ready. Come on!"

Helen and Rosa scrubbed furiously as Carmen stood over them, hands on her hips. After a minute, Carmen said, "If you don't—"

A shout. Something crashed in the torpedo shop. There was a loud, sickening bump and someone screamed—terribly—a loud, ululating cry of surprise and denial and pain. Helen rushed into the small cramped space. Two men had been disassembling a torpedo. Somehow the front end, the warhead, had fallen off the workbench onto a sailor's leg, catching him as he faced the other way. The man was pinned, and spasmed horribly, trying to jerk his leg out. The other sailor stood next to him, immobile, his face white.

Helen rushed in and grabbed the injured sailor's head as he fell forward on his face and lost consciousness. He jerked involuntarily and bit though his lip. Blood ran from his mouth and he snapped at the air. She grabbed a piece of cardboard and jammed it between his teeth. The man wiggled and Helen held his head, trying to figure out what to do.

Men rushed in, shouting. Helen stroked the sailor's forehead as the others hooked a chain-fall onto the warhead and frantically began whipping chain through the blocks. After an eternity, the warhead rose. Someone jerked the sailor's leg free.

The victim's eyes opened wide. He screamed again. Helen hadn't heard such a loud shriek in months. Not since in Corregidor's Malinta Tunnel hospital, where they had run out of anesthetic for amputations. The man screamed on and on, his vocal cords ripping her ears, as Helen held desperately to his hands.

Mercifully, he lost consciousness again just as two officers pushed through the crowd. One she recognized as the ship's captain, who kneeled close to her and shouted, "Takarabe!"

The other officer had red collar tags on his tunic and opened a medical kit and reached in. *A doctor.*

Something nudged her arm. The captain had taken off his tunic and shoved it at her, his face within a foot of hers. All the man had to do was look up and discover her Occidental eyes. At this distance the veil was useless. Holding her head low, she took the dark blue tunic and shoved it gently under the sailor's head.

Get out! Helen quickly rose to her feet. The others closed in, pressing her to the edge of the crowd. Across the room, Carmen jumped up and down, waving. *Go, you bitch,* she mouthed, almost as if this accident were also Helen's fault. Behind her, Rosa waited, her face drawn with fatigue and hunger, and oddly, the same sympathy Helen felt for the young enemy sailor who squirmed on the floor.

The men crowded her against the bench, and she still couldn't move. Everyone talked at once as the doctor worked on the man's leg. A stretcher was handed in and again Carmen caught Helen's eye. She tapped her wrist and her lips moved. Every other word was *bitch.*

"Bitch you, too," Helen shouted at her, shaking her fist.

Rosa's face turned white. Carmen's mouth fell open.

Then it hit Helen what she had done. Loosing her temper, her invective was in English. She covered her mouth, her eyes darting among the Japanese before her. But they were involved with their injured comrade and didn't seem to notice. Rosa ran out the door, while Carmen stood across the room, her fists planted on her hips.

Wait it out. Helen boosted herself on the workbench and sat back, relieved to be away from the center of twenty or so sweating, shoving men. The crowd grew larger and pushed her down the bench into a corner. She looked around. The torpedo shop was crammed with machinery, open parts bins, and disassembled components. Mounted on heavy racks on the adjoining wall were two torpedoes. The labels were right beside her head: The lower torpedo had a sleek body and a yellow warhead. The label was in English:

TORPEDO, SURFACE LAUNCHED MARK 15
WINSLOW RIVER CORPORATION, 1939.

Above that was a much bigger torpedo. She had to lean out to take it all in. Yes, it was much longer and wider, she decided, the entire body and warhead a menacing deep copper color. The warhead lifting lug in the nose was shaped differently from the American torpedo beneath it. The Bakelite label beside the upper one was in Japanese. She recognized two Arabic digits on the top line: 93.

The yelling subsided somewhat as she leaned back, trying to brace a hand behind her. Something was in her way and she looked down, seeing books, manuals, and technical papers scattered about. Many were in English. One lay open beside her. It was stamped TOP SECRET on the top and bottom of both pages. In the upper left-hand corner was a legend: BUORD INST. 93-715670-T15. The facing page had several pictures of torpedoes, while the other page displayed a large schematic drawing. The caption above the page read, "Torpedo Mark 15, depth engine maintenance."

On a shelf near her head was another manual, an all-blue one. In Japanese, it had a picture of a torpedo on the cover, like the one she'd seen in the captain's cabin. She recognized the bold Arabic numbers: 93. It must be the same torpedo, she decided, and checked the lifting lug on the big torpedo above the American torpedo. *Yes. The same.*

Her gaze returned to the open American technical manual on the bench. It seemed as unremarkable as a medical manual on performing appendectomies. But what caught her eye were the Japanese characters in the margins. Lots of them. And many numbers and calculations.

My God! The page with the schematics and handwritten calculations was loose! Blood rushed to her head as she looked up at the Japanese. They were still gathered around the injured man, hands on their knees, muttering, jostling to get a better look.

DO IT! A quick prayer and she snatched the page, shoving it down her blouse. Did anyone see? She looked around. No. No one, except . . . the captain? No.

Carmen screeched from across the room, pointing to a break in the crowd. Thankfully, the Japanese's attention was still directed at the injured man. Helen pushed off the bench and ran for the door.

*   *   *

Six hours later, she walked down dusty Agusan Valley Road with Don Pablo Amador, Wong Lee, and Emilio Legaspi, hoping to reach Buenavista by sunrise. Legaspi walked thirty yards ahead, Wong Lee ten yards behind.

"Are you sure you don't want to stop?" asked Amador.

"No."

"You must be very tired. Why don't you let us make camp?"

"No." Helen shivered. She was as amazed as everyone else that she'd walked from the hands of the Japanese unscathed. "I just want to get as far from Amparo as possible."

"You'll sleep tomorrow."

"Maybe."

Amador nodded and they walked for a while.

"Pablo?"

"Yes, dear?"

"I'm thirsty."

"Again?"

"Sorry."

"Well, I shouldn't wonder. Here." Amador gave a short whistle that sounded like a monkey screech. They stepped off the road and walked into the bush for twenty yards, stepping behind a large narra tree.

It was so dark, Helen could hardly see the canteen Amador handed over. She took it and gulped and gulped.

Wong Lee walked up. "Time for a butt?"

"No," said Amador.

Helen wiped her mouth with the back of her hand and gasped, "You know, those torpedoes could mean something."

"What torpedoes?"

She told Amador about what she'd seen in the torpedo shop earlier that day. "Here. I took this page." She handed it to Amador.

Amador folded it and stuck it in his pocket. "Have to wait for daylight. But"—he patted her shoulder—"you were very brave."

"Scared, I'll tell you." She sat and leaned against the tree.

"I think we should tell Otis about this."

"That's what I was thinking."

"You ready . . . Helen? Helen?" Amador stooped to within inches of her face finding her eyes closed, her breathing steady.

"What's wrong?" asked Wong Lee.

"Tired lady." Amador unrolled his *banig,* a woven sleeping mat, then gently lifted Helen onto it. She moaned once, curled fetal, and was gone.

"What about Buenavista?"

Amador pointed to Helen. "I think you can have that cigarette now."

CHAPTER TWENTY-ONE

Takeoff was scheduled at three a.m., but with generator problems the plane was still glued to the tarmac at five a.m. Cursing mechanics stood under her number two engine as a thick fog swirled about, the visibility no more than twenty feet.

To keep Sutherland out of spitting distance, a harassed duty officer had sequestered the general and Otis DeWitt in Admiral Billings's second-floor office, where the two grunted at one another. Sutherland lay on Billings's couch, his shoes off, reading a logistics report for the third time. DeWitt was slouched in an armchair, scanning a month-old issue of *Life* magazine with a picture of General MacArthur's son on the cover, his little four-year-old face grave and forlorn.

"You sure our gear is aboard, Otis?" Sutherland looked over his report with red-rimmed eyes. It was the third time he'd asked in the last hour.

"Yessir," drawled DeWitt.

A moment passed. "You sure you don't need any ice for that thing?" For the past day and a half, Sutherland had been having fun, proudly showing off DeWitt's black eye to all who passed close by.

DeWitt patted his shirt pocket, tempted to put on his dark glasses. "No, thank you, Sir."

With another grunt, Sutherland returned to his report and turned pages aimlessly. As he did, DeWitt mulled over what Dezhnev had told him two nights ago. And Colonel Willoughby, MacArthur's intelligence chief in the Brisbane Command Center, had forwarded Amador's message this morning. It conformed what Dezhnev had said. Something about a Japanese torpedo with a secret label of Type 93. It seemed so far-fetched, he had put off telling Sutherland. Also, with all the last-minute arrangements for their return to Australia, DeWitt hadn't had any time alone with Sutherland until now. But the problem with telling him right now was that at five in the morning, without any sleep, Sutherland was as irritable as a rattlesnake in a shoe box.

Better do it. "Uh, General?"

Sutherland looked over the top of his report.

"That Russian told me something the other night I think you should know."

"Is this before or after they sent in Ivan the Terrible to keep you from wrecking all of San Francisco?"

DeWitt shook his head. "Nothing that simple, I'm afraid. I think it has to do with national security."

Sutherland lay his report on his belly and propped his hands behind his head.

"It was after the fight. We were inside the consulate. Ed poured schnapps and—"

"Who?"

"Lieutenant Dezhnev, the Russian naval attaché."

Sutherland nodded.

"It seems the Soviets inserted some spies into Tokyo about six or seven years ago. Doctor Richard Sorge and Doctor Dieter Birkenfeld were their names."

Sutherland sat up and rubbed his scalp. "Sorge. Sorge. Have I heard of him?"

"Not sure, Sir. I just learned about him two nights ago."

Sutherland nodded.

"Dezhnev says Sorge and Birkenfeld set up a network in Tokyo that ran for five or six years. They penetrated into the highest circles." DeWitt leaned forward in his chair. "Posing as German citizens, they worked right out of the German Embassy as newspaper correspondents. They had airtight credentials from here to Timbuktu.

"But they got careless. Especially Sorge. Apparently he was a drunk and a womanizer. He bedded everyone, even the German ambassador's wife. And that finally sunk their game. People talked and their whole gang was captured about a year ago."

"Go on."

"Here's the scoop, General. Birkenfeld confessed and the Japs executed him. They've kept Sorge alive as a bargaining chip. But Dezhnev told me that Sorge and Birkenfeld dug up the damnedest things."

"Like what?"

"Sorge predicted Hitler's invasion of Russia within a period of two days. And that was three months before the attack."

"Oh, come on, Otis. You mean to say Stalin just sat there and didn't do anything?"

"He didn't believe him. But with the attack on Russia as predicted, Sorge and Birkenfeld's credibility went way up. Until they were captured last October, Moscow relied on everything Sorge and Birkenfeld unearthed. A major coup for them was discovering through Prince Konoye that Japan's Imperial war plans contemplated no thrust to the West into Soviet Siberia. Konoye told them that Japan's military intentions were primarily to the south through Indochina and the Dutch East Indies and into Burma and India, where they planned to hook up with Hitler in Arabia somewhere. Without the threat of a Japanese Axis attack from the east, Stalin was able to pull 120 divisions from Manchuria, bring 'em west and stop the Nazis at Moscow's doorstep last December.''

An airplane engine coughed into life just outside the window, breaking the silence. The general ran a palm over his head and blinked. ''That it?''

''Well, a couple of other things. He said Sorge and Birkenfeld learned the Japs have the world's best torpedo.''

Sutherland lay back and waved a hand, ''Oh, bullshit, Otis. The only things the Japs have are what they copy from us. And it's all piss-poor at that.''

DeWitt persisted. ''They call it the Type 93. It has a range of twelve miles at forty-eight knots.''

''Sounds like those sailors scrambled your brains, Otis.'' Sutherland picked up his report and began reading.

''Well, Pablo Amador in Nasipit confirms it. Claims one of his people saw a Type 93 close up.''

''Oh, hell, Otis. Those hillbillies are so undernourished, they wouldn't know a torpedo from a test tube.''

Sutherland was in no mood for triviality, so DeWitt decided against telling him that Helen was the one who reported the Japanese torpedo, not that it would have mattered. He tried a different tack. ''There's something else.''

Sutherland grunted.

''Ed—Lieutenant Dezhnev—says Birkenfeld learned of Tokyo's plans to hit Pearl Harbor well over a year ago.''

Sutherland sat up again, his eyes latching on to DeWitt.

He's angry, thought DeWitt. ''This was after the German invasion of the Soviet Union, so Stalin knew Sorge and Birkenfeld weren't making this up.''

Sutherland's voice grew to a staccato. ''Let me get this right. Stalin knew of the Japs' plans to bomb Pearl Harbor?''

''Over a year ago, General, August 1941.''

''And?''

Here goes. ''And Stalin told Roosevelt. Right away. He—''

Sutherland jumped to his feet. ''Goddamnit! You're telling me that over three thousand of our boys died in a sneak attack that our commander-in-chief knew of well beforehand?''

''At least four months, Sir. They—''

''That he let them die needlessly?''

''Well, except FDR didn't realize the attack would be so serious. That the Japanese—''

''Commie bullshit!'' Sutherland slammed his fist on Billings's desk. Pencils jumped. A silver frame containing an eight-by-ten photo of Mrs. Billings toppled over.

DeWitt felt his bile rising. Why was Sutherland so defensive? He couldn't understand. ''I thought General MacArthur would want to know, Sir. With his plans to run for president next—''

"Colonel DeWitt!" Sutherland roared.

"Yessir."

"This is a Commie crock. Torpedoes, spies, Pearl Harbor. It's just horseshit. Disinformation. Time and again, people keep blaming the president for Pearl Harbor. Now it's the pinkos. Believe me, we've looked into it. There is nothing there and"—Sutherland sliced a hand away from his body—"you are to ignore it."

For some reason, a smirk broke on DeWitt's face. "Yessir. But if—"

Sutherland's voice resonated, "I order you, Colonel, to ignore it. It's Commie disinformation. You are not to repeat this to anyone. Do you understand?" Sutherland stepped close to DeWitt, his hands on his hips.

DeWitt looked up to him. Disinformation. He barely knew the word. "Sir. As your aide for intelligence, I'm merely reporting to you—"

"Disinformation, Colonel. And if you persist, against my direct order, there will be serious consequences. Is that understood?"

As a youngster, DeWitt had spent many cold, bone-chilling nights chasing cattle on his father's ranch east of El Paso. But no nighttime air had ever penetrated him so thoroughly as what General Sutherland had just said. His brow became moist and he took a deep breath, trying to decide if it was rage or fright that he felt. Also, something nagged at the back of his mind that Sutherland knew more than he let on. His reaction, although typical, was a bit too outraged.

DeWitt rose to his feet. His voice choked with, "Yessir. I'm sorry, Sir. I was only trying to help."

Sutherland studied him for moment, then, to DeWitt's surprise, held out his hand.

They shook.

Sutherland returned to his couch, lay down, and picked up his report.

Someone rapped outside. Their heads jerked up.

"Come," DeWitt barked.

A flight sergeant poked in his head, wearing fleece-lined flight gear. "Ready when you are, gentlemen," the sergeant reported.

"What was it?" demanded Sutherland.

"Generator, Sir. Took a long time to pry the Navy guys out of the sack and dig up a new one."

"Typical," Sutherland snorted.

"Yessir." The sergeant backed into the hall.

Once again Sutherland gave DeWitt a look that said, *You sure all our gear is aboard?*

DeWitt nodded automatically, held the door wide for Sutherland, then followed him down the hall, carrying his briefcase. The sergeant walked a pace behind and said in low tones, "Hope you don't mind, Colonel, but the Navy manifested three officers to ride out to Honolulu with us." When DeWitt glanced back, the sergeant shrugged as if to say, *I can't help it.*

This base belongs to these Navy jerks. Sutherland had chosen to fly out of the Alameda Naval Air Station, since it was right across the bay from San Francisco.

One way or the other, Sutherland would make the decision. If the general blew his stack, then that would be it, the Navy guys would be SOL. After all, it was MacArthur's new plane, and Sutherland was determined to ride it in glory to Australia, where he would deliver it to his commander-in-chief.

DeWitt caught up to Sutherland. "General, is it okay if three navy officers ride with us to Honolulu?"

"Just three?"

"As far as I know."

"I don't mind hauling them to Pearl, but that's it."

"Yessir." DeWitt nodded to the sergeant, who stepped ahead to get things going.

The lounge was dark and smelled of stale cigars and decayed leather. Sutherland quickly walked through, shoved the door open, and strode into the mist. DeWitt hung back and scanned the shadows, finding the three Navy officers. Apparently the sergeant had awakened two of them; both were Airedale commanders who stood and stretched. They stooped to pick up their bags and walked out. The sergeant stood over the third, who dozed in an armchair, his head braced on his fist. He looked familiar.

DeWitt walked up and nudged him. "Todd?"

Ingram looked up. "Huh? My God. Otis." He stood and rubbed his eyes.

"Looks like you're going with us. What happened?" The last DeWitt knew, Ingram was supposed to have flown out yesterday.

"Engine trouble. Two hours out and we turned around. You should have seen—Good God, Otis, what happened to you?" Ingram ran a thumb across DeWitt's cheek.

"Tripped over a barstool. Let's go."

"Some barstool. Look at that shiner. What's the other guy look like, Otis?" As Ingram leaned over to pick up his B-4 bag, something fell from his pocket and clanked on the floor.

DeWitt leaned over and picked it up. It was a little brown medicine bottle and he examined the label. *Belladonna.* He handed it back to Ingram and cocked an eyebrow.

"Had a sour hamburger the other night. Food poisoning. Stomach's still acting up."

DeWitt mulled that over for a moment. "Ollie?"

"As far as I know, he got out all right. They put us on different planes."

With a grunt, DeWitt walked out the door with Ingram in tow, lugging his bag.

The air outside was thick and moist and still. Except for a few lights, the terminal was pitch-black. After a few steps, the airplane materialized. Ingram recognized it as a four-engine bomber from the Boeing Airplane Company.

With Sutherland already aboard, they waited while the Navy commanders scrambled in. DeWitt was next, then it was Ingram's turn. But he lingered, as the number one engine cranked and fired. Working his shoes at the pavement, he realized this would be his last contact with his homeland.

DeWitt leaned out and beckoned. "Okay, Todd."

The number two engine coughed into life. Then number three began turning—the inboard engine on the right wing, which was directly in front of him. He was startled when it caught and revved for a moment, its fuel-rich exhaust belching flame and smoke under the wing, engulfing and whipping at his clothes before it dissipated into the predawn. Number four began turning and the flight sergeant poked his head out and beckoned vigorously, grimacing as he held the door against number three's prop blast.

Go!

Number four caught as Ingram climbed up the ladder, the added prop blast pushing the door even harder. The sergeant let him ease past, then let the door slam shut and pointed into the cabin. "Take any chair, Sir. And buckle up, please." The sergeant latched the door and disappeared forward.

Ingram was in a spartan, but comfortable, executive lounge with a small galley arranged against the forward bulkhead, which was decorated with a large picture of Douglas MacArthur sporting dark glasses, hat with fifty-mission crush, and corncob pipe. A chemical toilet with modesty curtain was situated aft. Sutherland was already asleep on a couch, his back to them, his shoes kicked off, scattered on the deck. Ingram sat in an armchair next to DeWitt and fastened his belt as the pilot revved the B-17's engines. The plane began rolling.

Ingram looked out a large window that once was used for the waist gun, he supposed. "Traveling in style, Otis."

DeWitt stared into space. He seemed preoccupied.

"Otis?"

"Huh?"

"Otis, damnit."

Something clicked and DeWitt focused. "Yes, this ship was custom-built for the general. She's a converted B-17E. Her armor plate's been removed and we have long-range tanks in the bomb bay. All of the machine guns have been stripped except for a thirty caliber in the nose and the twin fifties in the top turret. And that's because MacArthur wants it to look as if he's cruising around in a fighting B-17 like any other jerk." He sounded like a jaded tour guide.

Like many in MacArthur's inner circle, DeWitt referred to Douglas Mac-Arthur, the supreme commander in the Southwest Pacific Ocean Area, simply as *the general.* "It's a replacement for one that's pretty well clapped out." He flung a hand forward, toward the nose. "The radio compartment has been converted to a command center, and in here, where the ball turret and waist machine gun positions were situated, is where the powers that be conduct war plans when they're airborne."

The B-17 dipped to a halt and Ingram knew they were poised near the runway's end. The pilot locked the brakes and ran the engines up one by one, checking the magnetos, fuel and oil pressure, manifold pressure, and a hundred other things.

As the pilot cycled through his runup, Ingram's mind was flooded with dozens of reasons to yell, *Stop,* or simply unlatch the window, jump out, and dash into darkness like a terrorized rabbit. He peered out again, seeking a last glimpse of his beloved United States of America. There was nothing but swirling white vapor.

With no one close by to bid farewell, a pang of loneliness ran through him. He'd called his mother and father in Echo, Oregon, day before yesterday and said his good-byes. To them, he wasn't allowed to say anything more than that he was shipping out. For security reasons, he couldn't say where he was going, except that he would be somewhere in the Pacific. With Toliver gone, he really didn't know anyone else except DeWitt and the Russian. Maybe it was because he inadvertently snubbed others who hadn't been there. They hadn't seen what he'd seen. They hadn't heard the screams of the dying. They hadn't felt—

With a jerk, the brakes released and the B-17 bounced onto the runway and drew to a stop, its engines confidently rumbling. Ingram and DeWitt exchanged glances as they waited for what was to come: that this B-17 would carry them once again into the Pacific maelstrom.

Ingram looked out the window again, only to see the damned white vapor. *What the hell is taking so long?*

"Todd?" DeWitt's voice was low.

"Yeah?"

"Can you spare a belladonna?"

"Okay." Ingram reached in his pocket, but just then, the pilot firewalled the throttles while standing on the brakes. All at once, the four Wright R-1820-91, thousand-horsepower engines bellowed as they strained at their mounts, their three bladed propellers scything the air at full pitch. The roar was incredible, and it seemed every bolt shook, every window rattled, and each rivet vibrated as if the plane would tear itself apart.

Then the brakes popped off and the B-17 rolled, slowly at first, but soon picking up speed. Blue runway lights flicked by in the vapor as the Flying Fortress lunged into the early morning.

With escape cut off and his return to the Pacific inevitable, Ingram dug into his pocket to fish out the belladonna for DeWitt. Instead, his hand found Helen's ring. He took it out and clasped it with both hands. Tightly.

The B-17 thundered into the fog, the pilot coaxing her through a small crosswind, the mains bouncing. With a final hop, her wheels broke free, and the plane lifted through the mist toward the Golden Gate.

PART TWO

I, Alton C. Ingram, do solemnly swear that I will support and defend the Constitution of the United States against all enemies, foreign and domestic; that I will bear the true faith and allegiance to the same; that I take this obligation freely without any mental reservation or purpose of evasion and that I will well and faithfully discharge the duties of the office on which I am about to enter;
so help me God.

U.S NAVAL OFFICER'S OATH OF OFFICE

God sends you the weather, kid. What you do with it or what it does to you depends on how good a sailor you are.

NELSON DEMILLE

GOLD COAST

CHAPTER TWENTY-TWO

It was close to midnight as Ingram stood atop the pilothouse, watching the men on the bridge below. They wore helmets, and their shirts were soaked with sweat, their faces gaunt. Captain, officer of the deck, talkers, signalmen, quartermaster—all stepped silently in macabre practiced movements, bracing their elbows on the bridge bulwarks, peering through binoculars, speaking softly into sound-powered phones. Outwardly, they seemed composed, determined, but Ingram wondered if their chests felt as tight as his. At the officers' noon meal, they'd laughed and spoken with bravado. At the evening meal, with the prospect of meeting the enemy, it had been quiet. And they ate lightly: soup and sandwiches. Nobody wanted anything else.

Ingram poked at his diaphragm with his thumb. All knotted up. For the third time in the last fifteen minutes, he forced himself to think of Helen. It didn't work. All he could think of was the blood pumping through his system, feeling like ninety-weight lubricating grease.

Waiting. Every time the TBS loudspeaker crackled with a bit of static, they stopped and turned to it as if in worship to this gray-painted steel cone, mounted on the pilothouse's aft bulkhead. *Come on, come on.* The waiting, the damned waiting. *Why doesn't the commodore order commence fire?* The last radar range on the Japanese column was close: ten thousand yards. Only five miles.

The *Howell* had been at general quarters since sunset. And for the past five hours, Leo Seltzer had stood beside Ingram, fidgeting and grumbling that they hadn't made him a mount captain. Wearing sound-powered phones, Seltzer walked in aimless circles, tangling the phone cord around his feet. Ingram only hoped Seltzer wouldn't figure out how scared he was. That would pop the bubble. Spruance and his damned Navy Cross! He never wore his ribbons, and yet everyone seemed to know he had it. The medal made it twice as difficult. Ever since he'd stepped aboard the *Howell* they treated him with a quiet respect, even the skipper. Hero of Corregidor, they looked up to Todd Ingram, obviously expecting him to set some sort of courageous example in combat. Maybe even bring them luck. Yet he knew if he could find a hole in the deck, he would crawl into it.

Ingram's teeth chattered in spite of the fact that the temperature was at least seventy-five, the humidity making it feel ninety-five. But the relative wind generated by the *Howell* slicing through a calm sea at twenty-four knots made it tolerable. It was a clear and moonless night with a balmy, light breeze out of the southeast. And if Ingram chose to do so, he could have taken a deep breath and smelled the soft scent of honeysuckle drifting from Guadalcanal, just ten miles off their port bow. But he didn't. This close to action, he had great difficulty even breathing. He exhaled, realizing his respiration rate was near zero. It was a deliberate act of will to inhale. Never before had he thought so hard about anything as simple as taking a deep breath.

Newly formed under Rear Admiral Norman Scott, the force of eleven ships was designated Task Group 64.2. After sunset, they changed their formation from a bent-line screen to a column, and ran north through the Coral Sea, closing Guadalcanal. In the van were the destroyers *Farenholt, Duncan,* and *Laffey.* Next were the cruisers *San Francisco, Boise, Salt Lake City,* and *Helena.* Behind them were four more destroyers, *Buchanan* and *McCalla.* Joining up only yesterday were *Howell* and Toliver's ship, the *Riley,* new arrivals from Nouméa, tacked on to the column's end, almost as an afterthought.

They stood into the passage between the Russell Islands and Guadalcanal at about eleven that evening. Fifteen minutes later, they left Guadalcanal's northwestern tip, Cape Esperance (French for "hope") off their starboard beam. Then they swung right and dashed northeast across the New Georgia Sound (nicknamed "the Slot") toward Savo Island. As it neared midnight, they sighted the enemy on radar and reversed course. Steaming in a southwesterly direction, Scott looked to intercept the column of Japanese cruisers and destroyers heading down the Slot to once again bombard U.S. Marines on Guadalcanal. The course reversal seemed a brilliant move, with Scott trying to cross the "tee" in front of the enemy, a classic move dating from the days of Lord Horatio Nelson. Peering into the gloom, Ingram hoped Scott knew what he was doing.

Except for the main battery director, Ingram was on the highest point of the ship, yet he couldn't see a damn thing. His mouth was dry and his stomach jumped at every new sound. Pressing his binoculars to his eyes, he searched the western horizon, sweeping from south to north, seeking the enemy. *Nothing, damnit!* But, like Scott in his flagship the *Salt Lake City,* the *Howell* had also picked up the Japanese on their SG radar, the newest in electronic marvels. The distance had quickly run down to twelve thousand yards—well within range of their five-inch guns. All they needed was the order to open fire.

Commander Jeremiah T. Landa stepped out on the bridge wing, looked up, and shrugged. Landa was thirty-three, stout, weighed 195, and had dark wavy hair. A pencil-thin mustache outlined impossibly white teeth that gleamed as brightly as the phosphorescent white wake shooting down the *Howell's* sides. Throughout the fleet, Landa was known by the nickname "Boom Boom." Ingram didn't know why. He asked once if it was connected with his love of gunnery, but Landa changed the subject.

"Any closer and they'll have us for breakfast," Landa grumbled. "Why can't we see 'em?"

"Star shells should do it, Captain."

Landa nodded, as if this were the wisest thing he'd heard in 1942. "What's the range now?"

"I'll check." Jabbing his talk button, Ingram called down to the combat information center (CIC), "Combat. Gun control. What's the range, Luther?"

The microphone clicked; Ingram heard yelling in the background.

"Luther? What's going on?"

Lieutenant Luther Dutton's cultured MIT tones wafted over the line. "Radar's down." He sounded as if it were a huge encumbrance to report such a thing.

"Shit!"

Dutton's voice was testy, as if it were a major effort to talk. "It's the magnetron. Installing a new one right now. Three minutes." His inflection was as if he had added, *Dope.*

"Luther. We have Japs in our face!"

Dutton's answer was, "Yes."

"Control, aye." It took all of Ingram's willpower to keep from saying, *Step on it, you trade school jackass.* But Dutton was doing everything possible. Even now, the young lieutenant was most likely on his back, surrounded by schematic diagrams, spare parts, and innumerable tools, tweaking wires in a mysterious tributary of the radar console. A thin man with a pouting mouth, Dutton was imbued with an aggravating calm. Nevertheless, even he would be sweating profusely at this moment, something easily done in the tropics.

Ingram was all too aware of the Japanese's reputation for devastating night torpedo attacks, especially after the Savo Island debacle two months ago. He took little comfort when Landa told him that he would never see the torpedo that struck at night. Just one loud *smack* and the *Howell* would be vaporized in a gigantic conflagration of exploding magazines.

As the ship's executive officer, Ingram would normally have been stationed in CIC for general quarters. Likewise, Dutton, the gunnery officer, would be where Ingram now stood: at the gun control station on the pilothouse. But Dutton, with his electrical engineering degree from MIT, was a genius with black boxes. Landa, not bound by protocol, swapped them, the successful response to subsequent SG radar breakdowns proving his wisdom. His phone circuit was also connected to Jack Wilson in the gunfire control director. With six men inside, the tanklike cupola rotated just above him. It looked like a small gun turret except there was no gun barrel, just optics and radar equipment for directing the aim of the five, five-inch guns throughout the ship. Also on his line were the forty millimeter and twenty millimeter battery captains and main battery plot, a space two decks below the waterline manned by Chief Skala, a fire controlman. Seltzer, his talker, was connected to the captain's talker on the bridge, the ship's engineering spaces, and damage control parties.

"Todd, damnit! What's going on?" demanded Landa.

Ingram must have been daydreaming. "Radar's down, Captain. Magnetron."

"Sonofabitch!"

"Luther said we'll have it back in three minutes."

"What's the last range?"

"Ten thousand yards."

"Screw this radar stuff. Let's make sure the star shells go with—"

Inside the pilothouse, the TBS speaker screeched with, *"Gillespie, this is crabtree. Execute to follow. Dog Item. I say again, Dog Item. Stand by, execute. Out."* The squadron commander had signaled all ships: *Commence fire—begin with illumination rounds.*

Landa urged, "Go gettum, Todd."

Ingram barked into his sound-powered phone, "Director 51, gun control. Commence illumination shoot!"

Jack Wilson's voice resonated inside the main battery gun director, "Mount fifty-five commence fire—illumination!" He had ordered the after five-inch mount to fire a star shell.

Mount fifty-five's captain must have already stuffed a round in the breech, for his gun immediately erupted with an earsplitting *crack*. At a muzzle velocity of twenty-six hundred feet per second, the projectile streaked toward the western horizon, seeking out the enemy. The other ships, cruisers and destroyers, opened up as well, their star shells paralleling the *Howell's*. Five hundred yards behind the *Howell*, the *Riley's* after five-inch roared as she cranked out her own illumination rounds.

Thirteen seconds later, the incendiaries popped from their shells to ignite six miles distant, where they dangled from little parachutes about two thousand feet above the water. Lighting the western sky with a ghostly silvery-white brilliance, the flares danced on the wind, leaving a sinuous trail of ivory smoke. Swaying beneath their parachutes, the star shells slowly floated to the ocean's surface, lighting up the sea. Their journeys done, they blinked out, only to be replaced by other star shells popping open. Then still more. That was illumination mount's job. Keep pumping out the stars, fifteen rounds a minute. Turn night into day. Find the enemy. With that, it was up to your main battery to aim properly and kill him before he killed you.

Ingram jammed his binoculars to his eyes and scanned the horizon.

Nothing.

Crack! Mount fifty-five pounded the night with another star shell, the flashless powder barely illuminating the fantail.

As he watched the star shells dance on the wind, Ingram caught a glance of three destroyer-sized ships off their starboard bow steaming on a parallel course. His blood ran cold as he tightened the focus on his binoculars. *What are they doing there?*

Landa must have seen it, too, for he shouted, "Todd! Who the hell is that?"

Ingram's nostrils caught the harsh scent of cordite left by the ships ahead. "They must be ours." He hoped his voice didn't sound too plaintive.

"I hope so."

Crack! Another round streaked from mount fifty-five.

"Maybe they're Japs!" Landa walked to the bulwark, yanked a phone from its bracket, and started yelling. In a way, Ingram felt sorry that Dutton was on the receiving end, but what if those *were* Japs out there? In a short time, the *Howell* could likewise be on the receiving end of something far more unpleasant than a tongue-lashing. Except for the *McCalla's* wake, Ingram had no idea who was where. Had the Japanese, with their superior night tactics, hauled in among them? Visions of torpedoes exploding in the *Howell's* magazine coursed through his mind.

The rate of gunfire almost doubled. Tracers ripped the night, and there was a constant pounding from the heavies. And yet, the star shells dangling from their parachutes illuminated . . . nothing.

"Todd. Damnit," Landa bellowed. "Hear that? Someone up there is firing for effect. Find us a target!"

Ingram tried to think of something. But nothing came to mind as the thunderous roar deepened, the smoke growing thicker, the odor raking his lungs.

Luther Dutton grunted into his phone, "Gunboss, CIC. We just copied a message from *San Francisco.* Remember when we reversed course?"

"Yes."

"Looks like *Farenholt, Duncan,* and *Laffey* came around properly in column. But then the cruisers turned at the same time."

"All four?"

"Sounds like it. Dumb bastards turned inside. What you see out there is the *Farenholt, Duncan,* and *Laffey.* They're between us and the Japs."

"Well, how do you like that?" gasped Ingram, watching as tracers joined the other shells screeching toward the enemy. He leaned down and told Landa what had happened. This meant the formation was snafued, with nobody having any idea of who was where. And with each round fired, the cacophony grew louder. Then, to Ingram's dismay, tracers reached for him out of the west: Japanese!

A voice rasped on the circuit with, "Okay."

"Gun Control, who is this? Who is 'Okay'?" demanded Ingram.

"Sorry, Sir. It's Dutton, er, Combat. Radar's up."

Ingram imagined Luther Dutton getting off the deck and arranging himself on a padded stool. Like Superman, he had changed from electronic genius to combat information center officer, assuming command of eleven men responsible for gathering and disseminating information to properly fight the ship.

Ingram couldn't resist a bit of Dutton's sarcasm. "I'm so pleased the radar is functioning again. Now, when you're ready, tell me what you see."

"Lots of contacts. Radar screen looks like it has measles. Ranges are close. Can't tell one from the other."

"How close?"

"Three, four thousand yards."

My God, near point-blank.

Ingram leaned on the rail and relayed Dutton's information down to Landa. Landa nodded. "Keep cranking out stars."

"Yessir," said Ingram. Ingram shouted into his sound-powered phone to Jack Wilson, "Jack. Keep pumping out illumination till we say to stop. And set fuses for five thousand yards. The Japs are much closer."

Wilson's "Roger" was obliterated as mount fifty-five hammered the night with another star shell. Except Ingram couldn't see through this smoke. It became more acrid and he coughed, wishing for a drink of water. His lips were dry, his heart thumped in his chest . . .

Once again, he swept with his binoculars. Nothing. Except a fire suddenly erupted aboard one of the ships forward, then just as suddenly went out. Bent over with a racking cough, Ingram wondered if he should call for gas masks. That was it. The Japs had fired mustard gas! Jesus! "Captain!"

"Todd! We have to find a target. Train aft." Landa was shrieking now.

Not aft. He means forward, thought Ingram. He pressed his talk button. "Jack, train mount fifty-five thirty degrees forward and light up that sector."

There was a ten-second delay as mount fifty-five trained to the new bearing, then the next star shell rang out, its blast louder, as the muzzle was closer to them. As Ingram studied the blackness, his teeth chattered. He felt exposed and . . . lonely.

Wham. Another round left mount fifty-five, soon bursting among the other stars, dancing and swaying its way to the ocean, where it would expire.

"Gun Control, CIC," replied Dutton. "Something's coming at us."

"What?" said Ingram, Wilson, and Skala simultaneously.

The line was silent as muzzle blasts cascaded through the night like rolling thunder. All around them now, detonating projectiles, large and small, flashed in a brilliant kaleidoscope of hell.

Just then, there was an enormous explosion off their bow. The night became day. A gun turret spun lazily toward the sky, people tumbling, twirling alongside, sucked into the vaporous maelstrom of orange-brown smoke before they began their journey back to the ocean and darkness.

"What was that?" gasped Dutton.

"Ship. Looks like her magazines blew." Ingram's ears rang. Enormous chunks of debris smacked the water and he forced himself to sweep the horizon. Like Landa, he was desperate to find a target, as mount fifty-five faithfully pumped out star shell after star shell, one every four seconds, back breaking work.

Nothing, damnit! "Luther, where's your target?" called Ingram.

"Lost in clutter." Dutton's voice was suddenly devoid of pomp.

Ingram tried to make sense of the firefight's stroboscopic confusion that enveloped him. But he gave up, as thunderous explosions flashed everywhere, momentary fires shot high into the sky, then, inexplicably, extinguished themselves. The loudspeakers on the bridge rang with human voices, hideously distorted as they yelled and screeched.

Suddenly a loud, high-pitched voice squealed on the phone circuit. Clamping his earphone to his head, Ingram shouted, "Whoever it is, say your last."

No wonder the voice was unrecognizable. It was Dutton, shrieking, "Target! Big bastard. Right in front of us!"

CHAPTER TWENTY-THREE

12 OCTOBER, 1942
U.S.S. *HOWELL* (DD 482)
NEW GEORGIA SOUND (THE SLOT)

"Luther! For God's sake, calm down!" Ingram shouted. "Where is he?"

Dutton wheezed, "Two . . . two-eight-five, forty-five hundred yards."

In spite of the relative wind blasting his face, Ingram felt the hairs on his neck stand. *Whatever it is, it's on top of us.*

Landa croaked, "Todd!"

"What?"

Landa pointed to starboard.

Ingram looked. Suddenly—"My God!" Outlined by a star shell, an enormous pagoda-shaped superstructure loomed before them. And it *was* close. Steaming on a perpendicular course, the ship looked as if she would cut them in half. Even as he watched, the ship's forward guns loosed a thundering salvo toward the American cruisers.

Thick, cordite-laden smoke swirled around Ingram, making tears run. But he had to relay the target data to the director. He punched his talk button and rasped, "Jack! Damnit. Target. Cruiser, I'd say. Bearing two-seven-five, range four thousand. Target angle three-four-five, target speed twenty-five knots."

"On target and tracking!" said Wilson.

Ingram heaved a sigh of relief. Wilson's crew had acquired the target quickly. "Plot! Do you have a solution?"

The wind whistled in Ingram's headphones for a moment, then Chief Skala bellowed, "Plot solution. Target course one-two-zero. Target speed twenty-seven knots!"

Rapidly, Ingram did some rough math. With the alacrity of two cheetahs after the same prey, the ships closed one another at a relative speed of over forty knots.

Quickly looking fore and aft, he checked to make sure the guns didn't point at their superstructure. Then he stooped and yelled down to Landa, "Solution, Captain."

Landa, overcome by smoke, was coughing into a handkerchief. Finally, he looked up and jabbed a finger in the air. "Shoot the sonofabitch!"

"Commence fire!" barked Ingram to Wilson.

Wilson's order caromed through the director hatch, "Mounts one, two, three, four, director control. Match pointers. Stand by. Commence fire!"

The four, five-inch mounts instantly belched their fifty-four-pound common ammunition projectiles in a single salvo, their base-detonating fuses designed to explode after punching through a ship's interior. The combined muzzle blast hurled Ingram against the director. "Sonofabitch." He fumbled at a hand grip, and was surprised when Seltzer grabbed him under the armpits and pulled him up in one jerk.

"Deck's slippery," Ingram muttered.

"Your secret's safe with me, Mr. Ingram."

Ingram ignored it and watched two white-hot flashes erupt on the cruiser's upperworks. Just then, the *Riley* opened up, the multiple *cracks* from her barrels, stabbing the night like lightning bolts.

Thrusting a fist into the air, Landa shouted, "Fire for effect."

Ingram relayed the order to Wilson, who cranked out another salvo at the cruiser, which by this time was backlighted by star shells. Three rounds splattered into the cruiser's superstructure. But Ingram was astounded that the Japanese cruiser, like a four-hundred-pound sumo wrestler, seemed to shrug them off and plow on, gunfire still spitting from her main battery.

Landa yanked off his helmet and waved it in the air. "Yeeeehaw!" Then he called to the torpedo director on the aft end of the bridge. "Stand by torpedoes."

A fire broke out just forward of the cruiser's number one main gun turret. Two figures ran toward the ship's prow, their clothes afire. Within seconds, both leaped overboard. The smoke cleared; the outline of destroyer *McCalla* was barely visible as she blasted out a salvo. Beyond her was the rumble of a full nine-barrel salvo from *Helena*'s six-inch guns.

Another *Howell* salvo ripped into the Japanese ship. The fire on her main deck lighted her upperworks, her lifeless deadlights looking like skeleton's eyes.

All but one of the stars shells had gone out. But it was enough to see that the cruiser heeled to starboard. "Looks like she's turning, Captain."

"Stick it to the bastards!" shouted Landa.

Ingram's heart thumped. The cruiser's two forward turrets had trained forward, their six barrels pointed right at him. He hoped that at this range the guns couldn't depress low enough. He keyed his mike, but fell into a racking cough as gunsmoke once again swept around him. Finally, he wheezed, "Captain. They're going to—"

Landa yelled in the pilothouse, "I have the conn. Evasion course. Right five degrees rudder!" Then, "Rudder amidships!"

The star shells went out. Ingram couldn't see a damn thing, and yet the *Howell*'s guns still fired. *At what?* He was thinking of calling a cease-fire when one of mount fifty-five's star shells burst on the horizon, once again illuminating the cruiser.

"Jeez." The cruiser was closer, but still turning to port. Soon they would pass on reciprocal courses.

Ingram found his voice and ordered the ship's forty millimeter cannons to commence fire. They let go instantly, the guns pumping with a deliberate, methodical cadence.

"Todd," Landa yelled up to him. Red lights inside the pilothouse cast a soft glow on his face, and his pupils glistened as Wilson fired another four-round salvo. Landa's lips twisted into a grin. "Give the sonofabitch everything we got."

So Ingram ordered the twenty millimeter cannons to commence fire. Soon the *Howell* was engulfed in a world of hammering, thudding gunfire, smoke and flame spitting from muzzles of all calibers.

"Ingram!"

"Sir?"

"I said everything, damnit." Even in the dark, Ingram could see Landa's fist shaking at him.

"I don't understand."

"Take mount fifty-five off illumination. Switch 'em to common ammunition."

"What about—"

"Do it, damnit!"

"Yes, Sir." Ingram keyed his mike and relayed the order to Wilson.

"How the hell do we see the target?" yelled Wilson.

"Captain's orders."

"Director fifty-one, aye," Wilson said dryly.

With three stars still up, Ingram could see white smoke pour from the cruiser's superstructure. And at twenty-seven knots, she heeled so far, it seemed her pagoda-shaped upperworks would topple right into Ingram's lap. Sliding past at a dizzying speed, her forward gun turrets belched a soft orange flame.

Before Ingram knew it, projectiles ripped overhead, sounding like express trains. Without thinking, he was on the deck, his fingers frantically scratching for something like a foxhole surrounded by a three-foot-thick belt of armor. He looked up to see Seltzer lying beside him, his arms over his head. They looked at one another with stupid grins, then regained their feet.

"I swear that one had my street address on it." Seltzer's teeth chattered.

Expelling a long breath, Ingram wondered how long he had been holding it. "Take me six months to clean my underwear after that one," he agreed.

Landa yelled. "Mount one. Fire torpedoes!"

At two-second intervals, five bursts of black-powder charges kicked the five Mark 15 torpedoes from their tubes. Ingram looked for their wakes, but they were lost in the darkness.

"What the hell?" It was Dutton.

"What?" shouted Ingram, just as Wilson fired another five-gun salvo.

Dutton had found some composure, for his voice was again coated with frost. "Looks like the *Riley* is out of column. In fact, hold on—let's watch the next sweep—yes, she's pulled out. To starboard."

Ingram looked aft, but the *Riley* wasn't visible. To port, he couldn't see Savo Island anymore. Just smoke.

"You sure, Luther?"

"Absolutely. They're about a thousand yards off our starboard quarter now. The interval between the cruiser and her is now about fifteen hundred yards. And I think she's increased speed."

"Ollie," Ingram mouthed.

The TBS receiver crackled in the pilothouse. *"Little Joe, Little Joe. This is Crabtree. Interrogative your intentions."* Little Joe was the *Riley*; Crabtree was Destroyer Squadron Twelve's commodore.

The response from the *Riley* was garbled, ". . . big dope . . . mine . . ."

"What do you think the *Riley* is doing?" Landa yelled up to Ingram.

Wilson loosed yet another salvo, all five mounts firing common ammunition. "I wish I knew. Do you suppose—"

"Quiet." Landa leaned in the pilothouse and cocked an ear to the TBS loudspeaker. "Looks like she's reversing course."

The voice on the TBS was desperate, *"Little Joe. This is Crabtree. Return to formation. I say again. Return to formation."*

". . . Have . . . Tojo for lunch . . ."

The last two of mount fifty-five's star shells descended to the western horizon, the cruiser still visible. It was obvious now that she turned rapidly, heading back the way she came. Ingram swept aft with his binoculars but couldn't spot Toliver's ship. Nothing. Something lingered. Then the flares dropped into the ocean, the cruiser lost again to the night.

"Jack," Ingram called to the gun director. "You have visual on the cruiser?"

"Barely."

Ingram hung on the grab rail as Wilson squeezed off another five rounds from his guns. Then he keyed his mike. "Luther, what's damned *Riley* doing?"

"Going faster 'n hell, in fact—Todd! Jesus!"

Ingram figured it out at the same time. The *Riley* was steaming in between the *Howell* and the Japanese cruiser. "Cease fire! All batteries," he shrieked, punching the rail-mounted cease-fire lever. Had everyone heard? Sometimes, when men were in a rhythm, their heads down, giving it their all, they ignored the cease-fire alarm; they didn't want to hear it, didn't want to stop shooting.

He listened. In mount fifty-two, the five-inch mount just forward of the bridge, projectile and shell dropped in the gun's tray with a *clang-clang*. Then the ramming motor hummed as the spade shoved the round in the barrel and the breech clicked shut. Then . . .

Nothing.

Mercifully, the *Howell*'s guns fell silent.

Landa, his voice hoarse from the smoke, yelled, "Ingram! Who told you to cease fire?"

Ingram's reply was obliterated as three rounds cascaded from the Japanese cruiser's after turret. Involuntarily, Ingram ducked, holding his breath as the projectiles screeched past. He looked up. Amazing. He was still alive.

"Right five degrees rudder!" Landa was sending *Howell* into an evasion routine. "Ingram! Resume fire, you stupid sonofabitch."

"The *Riley* is—" Ingram clutched a stanchion as the cruiser fired a round. It smacked the ocean a hundred yards abeam of the *Howell* and skipped over her with a shrill *wheeeeee*.

Ingram pointed abeam. "She's right there!"

Spittle flew as Landa yelled, "What the hell are you—"

"The *Riley*! Between us and the Jap."

"Oh."

The man on the TBS almost sobbed. *"Little Joe. Little Joe. Imperative you—"*

Crack! The *Howell* lurched sideways, as if ambushed by an overweight thug in a dark alley.

Ingram looked around. *What the hell am I doing on the deck?* He shook his head, but he couldn't hear. Next to him, Seltzer was on hands and knees, spitting over the side of the pilothouse.

Ingram ripped off his headphones and pressed his fists to his head, a vain attempt to staunch the high-pitched ringing in his ears. After a moment, he grabbed a stanchion and pulled himself to his feet.

Seltzer looked up to him, his face stark white, his lips moving.

Landa was talking, too. Shouting, maybe, but Ingram still couldn't hear. In the light's red glow, the captain's eyes searched and darted from Ingram to the ocean, his face an orange-red, his uvula wiggling a macabre dance in the back of his mouth.

Then the ringing receded and Ingram could once again hear, as if someone had just flipped a master switch in his skull.

". . . Ingraaaam, damnit!"

"Huh?"

"Listen to meeee."

"Sir?"

"Are you okay?" Landa had swung the *Howell* to port, heading almost due south.

Ingram shook his head. "Yeah, yes, sir." Then he looked up, seeing Jack Wilson lean out of his hatch, raising his eyebrows.

Ingram gave a thumbs up and mouthed, ''You?''

Wilson's lips moved with, ''We're okay.'' But with his hands he panto-mimed the numerals five-three, pointed aft, and drew a finger across his throat.

Ingram checked aft. In the darkness, everything seemed jumbled; he couldn't tell what was going on. ''How about mounts fifty-four and fifty-five?'' Ingram mouthed to Wilson.

''Okay,'' Wilson answered.

Seltzer, still on hands and knees, looked up and said, ''No word from the aft torpedo mount or mount fifty-three.''

''Anything from the damage control party?'' asked Ingram.

''Not yet.''

Ingram wiggled on his headphones and keyed his mike. ''Luther, what's with the Japs?''

''Gone. Headed back up the Slot.''

''What about the *Riley*?''

''DIW,'' reported Dutton. Dead in the water.

Ingram knelt. ''Captain, do you suppose the *Riley* is in trouble?''

At least six men swarmed around Landa, all wanting something. He held a palm toward Ingram. ''Wait.''

After a few moments, Dutton announced, ''*Riley* is gone.''

''What do you mean, 'gone'?'' demanded Ingram.

''I mean there's no blip.''

CHAPTER TWENTY-FOUR

12 OCTOBER, 1942
U.S.S. *HOWELL* (DD 482)
NEW GEORGIA SOUND (THE SLOT)

A vacant coldness swept through Ingram. Without thinking, he reached in his pocket to fumble at Helen's ring. ''Are you sure?''

''Yes, Sir. The *Riley*—uh, the blip is gone.''

Landa was alone for a moment, so Ingram called down, ''Captain, can we ask for permission to assist the *Riley*?''

''Lieutenant, if she's in trouble, the commodore will take care of it.'' Landa wiped his brow. ''We have enough trouble right here.''

''Captain, I—''

''Listen to me, damnit. This business back aft doesn't sound good. Damage control reports are sporadic. Sick bay is off the line. So is the aft torpedo mount. We had a fire in the after deckhouse, but it's out. Do you have contact with mount fifty-three?''

Ingram shook his head. "Nor the aft torpedo mount. Uh, Captain?''

"What?''

"What about the Japs?''

"We're disengaged. Looks like Admiral Scott's given them enough for one evening.''

"Well, then. You sure we can't help the *Riley*?''

"No, damnit.'' Landa's voice became hard. "Turn gun control over to Wilson. Go aft. Assess damage. Figure out what's happening, then get back here on the double. Don't hang around; come right back.''

"Yessir.'' He stood and took off his headphones.

Seltzer groaned and heaved himself to a sitting position.

"You okay?''

"Think so.'' The second-class bo's'n rubbed his head, blood running down his face.

"Ingram?'' Landa said.

Ingram straightened. "On the way, Sir. But I think Seltzer needs a corpsman.''

"We'll send one up.''

Ingram gave a thumbs up to Wilson, told him to take over, then quickly ran down two ladders to the 01 deck, making his way aft. He passed the number one torpedo mount, the bare-chested crew silently watching, their faces running with sweat, their gaunt eyes reptilian under their helmets. But with satisfaction, Ingram noted the tubes were empty. "Looks bad back there, Sir,'' one said.

He passed the aft stack and sucked in his breath. The water-tank-shaped blast shield on the aft torpedo mount looked as if a cosmic scythe had hacked it open. Bodies, once young living beings, lay about in bloody disarray.

Slowly, Ingram walked farther aft, finding dark shadows staggering around mount fifty-three. He recognized Lavrey, a shipfitter first class, who was in charge of the repair party. He'd been the poker king aboard the *Howell*. But the day before Ingram reported, Lavrey was busted from chief for running high-stakes games in the after engine room. "What's happened?''

Lavrey's helmet was off, his face ran with sweat, and his eyes were open wide as if propped with matchsticks. His Adam's apple bounced. "Took a round head-on through the mount, Sir. Didn't blow up and the sonofabitch exited out the back.'' Lavrey gulped. "But shit. It looks like a hamburger grinder in there. They're all dead.''

"No.''

"Yessir. Monaghan's in there now, just to make sure.''

Just then, a short, dark-haired sailor with a pug-nose climbed out of the hatch, dropped to the deck, and leaned against the gun mount. His face was white and he was obviously trying to hold it in. He was the ship's leading medical technician, the closest they had to a doctor. Lavrey walked over, put his hand on the sailor's shoulder. "What's the matter, Bucky, too much pink for you?"

The man whipped around, his fist chopping away Lavrey's hand. "I can't help them," he yelled. "They're . . . they're like . . ." His lip quivered.

Lavrey drew a face. "Oh, gee, Doctor. We're sorry to take you from the comfort of a stateside hospital. And we thought you was full of miracles."

"Shut up."

Ingram stepped over. "Leave him, Lavrey. You sure, Monaghan?"

"Like butchered cattle."

"Okay. Go forward to the torpedo mount. See what you can do there."

"Yes, Sir." With a cold stare at Lavrey, Monaghan disappeared into the gloom.

My God. Eight men gone, just like that, Ingram thought. *Another five killed on the torpedo mount.* He looked up, seeing mount fifty-three's four-thousand-pound gun barrel bent almost straight up. Beside it, an enormous hole, eight or so inches in diameter, had been punched through the turret's face. The rest of the mount was filled with puncture holes, some the size of baseballs.

"How about the handling room?" Ingram referred to a space just below the gun mount where ammunition was received from the magazine, deep below the waterline.

"One dead. The rest are okay. They had a fire and put it out before we got there."

"Lucky."

"I'll tell ya. One of them powder cases goes up, and *whump.*" Lavrey's hands wiggled out an explosion. Then he yelled, "Hopkins, Thomas! Get in there and make sure the mount is secure."

Two men climbed a ladder from the main deck, hauling a large toolbox.

"Lavrey, the captain needs a status report," Ingram said. "Find a place to plug in and tell the bridge what's happening."

"Yes, Sir." Lavrey turned to look for a sound-powered phone outlet.

Ingram walked a few paces forward, but then stopped. His mind raged, *You must go back there and look inside mount fifty-three. You owe it to them.* Then a wave of nausea swept over him as he thought about Monaghan: *I can't. I just can't.*

He leaned against a stanchion, listening to the ship around him, the whine of air whistling through her uptakes like breath on the wind, the hiss of water foaming alongside, the luminescence casting a soft glow. Right now, he was alive, the ship, the sea making him feel whole, almost giddy. And the *Howell* felt alive, too, as she rolled through moderate waves. The sky was clear now and he looked up trying to pick out Southern Cross; but he couldn't find it among all the sky's shimmering brilliance.

He took a deep breath, relishing that the *Howell* was a living being, her engines breathing oxygen, her hydraulics coursing, as it were, with blood, her crew giving her spirit and character and purpose.

Except, he knew as he leaned on the lifelines and looked aft toward mount fifty-three, that he had to go back there. To force himself to look inside the gun mount to pay his respects to those lifeless lumps of flesh and blood; those poor souls who were, until a few minutes ago, talking, laughing men, most of whom had yet to shed their boy's bodies. Would Landa look in there? Probably. Anyone else? Did it matter?

Okay.

He walked aft to the hatch, but had to wait as Thomas and Hopkins scrambled in, shoving in a toolbox. Thomas clicked on a battle lantern. "Wheeeow."

Ingram looked in, knowing the image would stay locked in his mind for the rest of his life. It was as if someone had spun furiously inside, like an ice skater, spewing a bucket of thick red paint, letting it splatter everywhere. Bodies, parts of bodies, chunks of flesh were heaped on the deck, or hung from fittings and hydraulic lines. Thomas and Hopkins slipped on the bloody deck and, seeking footholds, booted the carcasses aside. Hopkins yelled, "Holy shit!"

Ingram leaned in farther.

"Here, goddamnit. Uh, sorry, Sir." Hopkins grimly handed a five-inch projectile out the hatch, committing it to Ingram as if it were the devil's own Hope Diamond.

Ingram sucked in his breath. No time for protocol. He took the fifty-four-pound projectile, grunted, and passed it to Lavrey.

With a mighty growl, Lavrey heaved it into space. It cleared the main deck by five feet and plopped into the ocean.

"Sonofabitch," Ingram said.

Lavrey shrugged, then nodded at mount fifty-three's hatch.

Hopkins stood there with a blood-streaked brass powder case: only twenty-seven pounds this time. Ingram passed that to Lavrey, who once again gave a great heave, sending it to the bottom of the New Georgia Sound.

Ingram called inside, "That it?"

Hopkins was retching. It took a minute, then his voice echoed weakly, "Breech open, all clear, Sir."

"You okay?" Ingram asked.

"We'll be fine, Sir."

Ingram turned to Lavrey. "Good toss." The lateral distance to the outboard side of the main deck was at least ten feet.

"High school shotputter, Sir."

"Get a gunner in there to make sure the electrical circuits are secure."

"Yes, Sir."

Ingram turned and walked forward. Just then the ship wallowed in a swell, and he steadied himself on the outboard torpedo tube. A shirtless man was slumped over the tube, a large Chinese dragon tattooed on his bare right shoulder. Ingram knew it belonged to Ketchum, a torpedoman second class who had served in the Asiatic Fleet before war broke out. A real

China sailor, Ketchum boasted of all the whores he knew from Shanghai to Singapore.

"Ketchum?" Gently, Ingram reached up and poked at the torpedoman's shoulder.

Ketchum rolled over and fell backward atop the tube, his chest ripped open from navel to neck, lifeless eyes staring at the sky. Ingram quickly turned, grappled for the lifeline, and vomited with an urgency he hadn't known possible.

CHAPTER TWENTY-FIVE

13 OCTOBER, 1942
U.S.S. *ZEILIN* (APA 3)
TULAGI HARBOR, SOLOMON ISLANDS

Ingram jumped off the whale boat and onto the *Zeilin*'s gangway. Standing under a searing noon sun, he looked back to Seltzer, perched in the stern sheets, tiller between his legs, a grin on his face.

"I'll be about an hour," Ingram said. "Make the PT boat dock, pick up our mail, and come right back."

"Aye, aye, Sir. Okay if we look into town? Maybe get some chow?"

Ingram shrugged. "Don't see why not. Just be back here in an hour. And no booze." A rumor had reached him that a working still was aboard the *Howell*. The chief master at arms was trying to put the finger on Seltzer.

"One hour, Sir. Thank you, Sir." Seltzer checked his wristwatch. "Right here at 1330, Sir. Let's hope we get some mail this time." The *Howell* hadn't had a letter since they'd left Nouméa two weeks ago.

Seltzer rang the bell. Dudley, a stocky engineer sitting amidships, fed in throttle, while Travillion, standing on the foredeck, pushed away the bow. Soon the twenty-six-foot motor whale boat ambled toward a ramshackle pier that extended into the bay. Seltzer didn't have to go far. The *Howell* lay anchored five hundred yards offshore, licking her wounds amid a yellow, humid haze.

A figure-eight-shaped island, Tulagi lay fifteen miles north of Guadalcanal, with a fine anchorage jammed with craft of all sorts, from destroyers to cargo and attack transports, oilers, and other supply vessels. All maintained a head of steam for a quick exit, in case the Japanese sprung another one of their frequent air raids.

The 12,700-ton *Zeilin,* once the luxury liner *President Jackson* of the American President Line had been converted to an attack transport and had just landed Marines on Guadalcanal and Tulagi. Painted in dappled greens and grays, she swung at anchor, off-loading her cargo and caring for wounded Marines shot up from intense fighting ashore.

Ingram's shirt, clean and dry when he had boarded at the bottom of the gangway, was drenched with sweat when he reached the top. He saluted the fantail and the officer of the deck. "Permission to come aboard?"

A redheaded ensign replied, "Granted." When Ingram stepped aboard, the ensign asked, "May I help you, Sir?"

Moving under the welcome shade of a canvas awning, Ingram inquired, "Survivors from the *Riley*? I understand you have some here."

The ensign's chin was covered with stubble and his shirt looked worse than Ingram's, almost as if he'd just jumped in the water. His shoes had the green tinge of jungle rot. He ran a hand over his jaw, his voice an odd baritone. "Don't know, Sir. I know we took some people aboard last night. You're welcome to check in sick bay."

"How do I get there?"

He pointed with a scrawny arm. "Take that companionway down to the second deck. It's forward, on the starboard side."

Ingram scrambled down the ladder, edging past tired-looking Marines and ship's personnel. The interior was drab, much of the metal surfaces bare, including the decks. This was in response to a recent ALNAV ordering ships to strip interior flammables, which included wood trim and paneling, paint, and deck coverings such as teak or linoleum. The Navy had learned the hard way: Pearl Harbor, Coral Sea, Midway, and recently Savo Island. Niceties cost lives and ships.

As he reached the second deck, the combined odors of alcohol and Lysol leaped into his nostrils. He followed his nose, eventually stepping through a large hatchway, finding a compartment painted in a dazzling white, with decks of polished green linoleum, almost in defiance of the ALNAV. It was as if the doctors had said, *Damn your restrictions, this is a hospital and we're keeping our paint and linoleum.*

It was hot and stuffy even with the vent and exhaust fans roaring at full speed in a frantic effort to exchange the air. But other odors lingered that Ingram recognized from his days in Corregidor's tunnels: that of human sweat, putrefying flesh, and the stark odor of fear and resignation. He stopped before a man in tee shirt and white trousers seated at a small metal desk. He had thin sandy hair and J. PRENTICE was stamped on a Bakelite nameplate. Prentice was one of the pharmacist's mates, dubbed "shanker mechanics" because of their ruthless treatment of crabs, gonorrhea, and other venereal diseases. "Help you, Sir?"

God, it's hot. "Looking for a survivor off the *Riley*. Toliver, Lieutenant jay-gee. Is he here?" Ingram loosened two buttons off his front shirt and checked the overhead for the nearest vent blower. It figured. Prentice was seated right beneath the duct, which blew so hard it ruffled papers on his desk.

"Ummm. Oliver. Oliver." Prentice ran his fingers down a list. "Sorry, Sir. We—"

"Toliver with a 'T.'" Ingram yearned to stand under that duct. But Prentice was comfortably seated directly under it. Immovable.

"Yes, Sir. Toliver. Ah, yeah." He jabbed a thumb over his shoulder. "Aisle thirty-one, bunk one-oh-five, starboard side."

"Thanks."

"Excuse me, Sir. But are you a doctor?"

"Friend."

"What ship, Sir?"

"Howell."

Prentice pursed his lips for a moment. *"Howell, Howell."* He snapped his fingers and grinned. "Bucky Monaghan's ship?"

"That's it."

Prentice laughed.

"What?"

"I'm sorry, Sir. It's just that..." He returned to the medical chart, still chuckling.

Curiosity got the better of Ingram. "Come on, sailor."

"How long you been on the *Howell*, Sir?"

"About ten days."

"Ahh." Prentice looked both ways. "Well, Sir. This guy Monaghan is supposed to be a real lady-killer. A shanker mechanic's shanker mechanic, you know what I mean?"

"Frankly, no."

"He was a third-year medical student at the University of Chicago. They kicked him out when he knocked up a doctor's daughter. Turned into a drunk. I heard he ended up on the *Howell*."

Ingram leaned on the desk with his fists. "Well, what about him?"

"A real screw-off. I heard..." Prentice found a chart and examined it, flipping pages. "I dunno, Sir. This says visitors are restricted."

"What's that mean?"

"Well..."

Another man, wearing white surgeon's scrubs, stepped up, dropped his mask. "Prentice. Can you help us pull the Marine out of post-op and get him into a bunk?" He drew a handkerchief and dabbed sweat from his brow, then effortlessly pushed Prentice's chair, easing him from under the vent blower.

Prentice struggled with his composure. "Yes, Doctor. Uhh, this officer here wants to visit a patient." He pointed to a list.

The doctor whipped his cap and gown off and stood under the vent. With a smile, he luxuriated in the air blast for a full ten seconds, then grinned. "Ahhh. Best thing in the South Pacific. Now, if they can only figure out a way to cure crotch itch." The doctor was stocky, large-boned, with a broad face and clear blue eyes. A name tag read W. M. GOBBELL, MD, LT, USN (MC).

Ingram seconded that. He'd only been in the tropics for a few days and already was scratching constantly, his groin and armpits broken out with a rash. And his socks and underwear were turning a putrid green, just like that ensign's shoes topside.

The doctor glanced at Prentice. "You have a chart?"

Prentice reached in a metal tub, withdrew a clipboard, and handed it over.

The doctor dabbed more sweat. "Yeah, I remember this guy." He gave Ingram a cold stare.

"Is it serious?"

With a nod, the doctor said, "It's what we call an intertrochanteric fracture. Also he's got—"

"A what?"

The doctor leveled his eyes to Ingram's. "Let's get one thing straight, sailor."

"Yes, Sir?"

"Doctors speak in words of at least ten syllables so you can't tell how screwed up they are."

Prentice gave a short laugh. Ingram smiled, too.

The doctor lay down the clipboard. "If things are really bad, we resort to Latin."

"Well, then, Ollie's going to be okay?"

"No, he's not."

"But, I thought—"

"Who are you?"

"Close friends. I was his CO on his last ship. We escaped from Corregidor together."

"Ahhh. You might be just what I ordered." The physician eased to the edge of Prentice's desk and parked a cheek, his dark brown hair lightly ruffled by the blower. "Here it is, Mr. Ingram. Toliver has a broken hip. That's what 'intertrochanteric fracture' means. Also, he's suffered first- and second-degree burns on his face. Burning fuel oil on the water, I suppose, after his ship went down. It's painful, but I don't think he'll need skin grafts."

"Will he . . . I mean—"

"No, no. He's out of danger. Barring infection, he'll live. The best part is that we're shipping him to Stanford-Lane Hospital in San Francisco. He needs an orthopedic surgeon to nail his hip back together. Out here, it's too dangerous to try; the most qualified people to do it are back home."

"Oh."

"But he's on the restricted list because he's in pain. He's in traction, and that's uncomfortable as hell. And we don't have enough morphine for everybody. There are far more serious cases here who couldn't make it without the stuff." He waved a hand around the compartment. "Plus, we had to bandage the poor bastard's head damn near to his mouth. So he wakes up all the time thinking he's blind."

"He can see?"

"Perfectly."

"Okay."

The doctor stared at him.

There was something else, Ingram realized. "Okay, Doc. What is it?"

"In a word, your Mr. Toliver is despondent—dejected. You know what I mean? There's only so much you can do for a man. After that, it's up to him. And I think he's ready to give up."

"Doc, he's a combat veteran. A real hero. We fought Japs for six months."

"Sounds to me like he's had enough. Do you think you can help?"

Ingram rubbed his chin, mulling over what he and Toliver had been through in the Philippines. By comparison, Ingram had been afraid of the dark since returning to the States. He had trouble sleeping. At times, like two nights ago, he was consumed with an urge to run. Except on board ship, there was no place to run, he thought ruefully. *The doc wants me to help. But,* he thought, *if I'm as screwed up as Ollie, maybe someone else should step in.* A shrink, perhaps. Someone who was skilled with a solid clinical approach. Otherwise, he could botch it up with Toliver more than he could help him.

He looked up, to find the doctor hadn't blinked.

Ingram's mind raged over what to do. He surprised himself when he said, "I'll try."

"Okay. He's all yours. Five minutes. Good luck.

"Prentice. Let's get that Marine out of post-op." The doctor and the pharmacist's mate walked off.

Ingram walked aft among a sea of bunks filled with men ripped up by the fighting. Many were asleep; some stared as he walked by. One or two cried softly. In a bizarre way, he was thankful for the ones who were dressed with head bandages. That way he didn't have to look them in the eyes.

It was impossible to miss Toliver's bunk. The weights suspended around him looked as if he were poised to be catapulted over a castle wall. A bandage covered the upper part of his face and nose. But his mouth was clear. He was covered with a light blanket to his waist, and his arms and chest were bare and looked unharmed.

"Ollie."

Toliver's head jerked slightly.

Ingram grabbed Toliver's hand. "Ollie, for crying out loud."

Toliver shifted his head away.

"Ollie, what happened?"

"I pissed my pants. That's what happened." Toliver's voice was surprisingly strong. And he obviously knew to whom he was speaking.

"Can I get you anything?"

Toliver grabbed at Ingram with both hands and held tightly. "Something to knock me out. Morphine, maybe. Hurts like hell."

"You'll be fine, Ollie."

"Please. Please." He squeezed Ingram's hand.

"I'll see what I can do." Ingram reached for a stainless steel pitcher and paper cup. "How 'bout some water?"

"No!"

"Huh?"

"They put stuff in there to screw you up. Saltpeter, for sure. Other stuff, too."

"Ollie. Come on."

Toliver grasped Ingram's hand and tried to raise to his elbows. "Todd."

"Yeah?"

"We took hits. Five-inch."

"I imagine." Ingram visualized the *Riley* pulling out of formation and being mauled by the Japanese cruiser. But wouldn't a bigger ship like that have larger-caliber guns? "Just five-inch?"

Toliver's laugh came out a shallow gargle. "The hits were on the port side."

"What?" The *Riley*'s port side was the side away from the Japanese cruiser. The side toward the American column.

"Two hits. Both dye-loaded. One took out the wardroom; the other hit us in the aft engine room." American warships inserted a colored dye in their ammunition so they could distinguish their shots from other ships shooting at the same time. It turned the water splash to a distinct color, so they could adjust their aim accordingly. As far as anyone knew, the Japanese didn't dye-load their ammunition.

"Jesus." Ingram nearly bit his tongue. He was almost afraid to ask. "Do you know what color?"

"Yeah. Damage control team got in the wardroom. Everybody dead, all sprayed with yellow dye like . . . like a bunch of Easter eggs." Toliver gargled again. He turned his bandaged face to Ingram and released his hand. "Tell me, Mr. Ingram, what color is the *Howell*?"

Ingram sighed. "Green."

"Who's yellow?"

"Don't know."

"Well, if I ever get on my feet, I'm going to find the gunboss on the ship with yellow dye-load and rip out the sonofabitch's guts with a bayonet."

"Ollie, I'm sorry."

Toliver started breathing in short gasps. "Actually, that wasn't what did it. We could have survived. Weigh was coming off, and we had our rudder over to left full, trying to get the hell out. Then a torpedo smacked us. Right under mount fifty-two." Toliver released Ingram's hand and mimed an explosion.

"How do you know it was a torpedo?"

"Lifted the ship up in the air. Blew off the damn bow. The biggest explosion . . . shit. Bigger than any torpedo I've ever seen or heard of. Threw me off the pilothouse like a rag doll. Landed aft somewhere on the bridge, I think. Then we capsized. I dunno . . . next, I was in the water; fire all around . . . I reached for a guy. All scalded. His face was a big red mass, like a beet with a mouth and . . . teeth . . . God." Toliver pressed both hands to his head. His lips quivered.

"Ollie."

"Water."

Ingram poured and eased the cup to Toliver's mouth.

He slurped, letting water dribble down his face. "Feels good."

Ingram checked his watch. He'd been here almost eight minutes. "Gotta go, Ollie."

"No!" He reached and took Ingram's hand.

"The doc said I couldn't stay more than five minutes."

"Screw the doc. Don't leave me."

"All right." Ingram found a stool and sat.

Toliver gave a long exhale. "Tell me, how'd you come out?"

"Just fine. We were lucky." Ingram couldn't tell him about the grisly carnage in mount fifty-three. Tomorrow morning, the *Howell* was due to head to Nouméa, about nine hundred miles to the south, where she would receive a new barrel for mount fifty-three. Along the way, they would bury the fourteen souls who had died in mount fifty-three and on the torpedo mount. This afternoon, Ingram was to plan the ceremony; he wasn't looking forward to it. Besides the men who died, it turned out the barrel was just about the only thing wrecked. Trunnion, base ring, hydraulics, even the optics were in good shape.

They would need a new crew for the mount. A detail was in there now, scrubbing away the blood, getting it ready. Ingram planned to recommend Seltzer as mount captain. He had experience and good leadership qualities. Seltzer would take it, even jump at the chance. Others would hesitate, wondering if mount fifty-three was jinxed. Already they were calling it the shooting coffin.

". . . Todd? You there?" Toliver's hands waved in space.

"Yeah."

"I said, 'What happened to the Japs? Did we lick 'em?' "

"Admiral Scott says we sunk a bunch of Jap ships. Nobody knows for sure. But we did keep the Marines on Guadalcanal from being bombarded. Now they love us."

"Eacchhh!" He reached for Ingram.

"What?" Ingram took his hand.

"Get the doc. I need something!"

"Ollie, damnit. Hold on."

Toliver squeezed for a moment, then let go. He gasped, "I really did piss my pants. Todd, I was so scared. Worse than on the Rock. I don't know why. Maybe it was the night. The darkness. I couldn't see. Everything happening at once."

"It's all right."

"And those guys laughed at me. Called me chickenshit."

"What?"

" 'Cause I pissed my pants."

"Ollie. It was dark as hell out there. How could they tell you pissed in your pants?"

"I dunno. The captain, all those guys on the bridge. They were yelling," Toliver sobbed, "I let 'em down."

"No, you didn't, Ollie. Hell, the same thing happened to me." Ingram looked up to see the doctor, Prentice, and another pharmacist's mate gently ease their Marine onto a bunk. Still asleep, the Marine's mouth was open wide, his arm and chest wrapped in an enormous cast.

"Now they're dead," Toliver wailed.

The doctor watched Ingram for a moment, then nodded to Prentice. The pharmacist's mate had a little steel tray with two small white pills. With an open palm, the doctor drew a hand over his eyes, then mouthed, *Time.*

"Ollie. The doc's here. So's the shanker mechanic. Gotta go. And you're a lucky bastard. The doc tells me you're going stateside. San Francisco. Think of the girls."

"Todd, please don't go," Toliver sniffed.

Ingram drew close. "Ollie. It's okay. They have something to make you feel better. I'll come back tomorrow." The lie came easily. By this time tomorrow, the *Howell* would be on her way to Nouméa.

Toliver took a deep, shaky breath and tried to wipe his nose. "Okay, sure."

"Take care, pal." Ingram stood.

"I need light. Are there any lights?" Toliver said.

Ingram clicked on the reading light over Toliver's bunk. "You see that?"

Toliver waved his hands in front of it. "Yeah, actually, I do. Just a little."

"Good." Ingram grabbed Toliver's hand, showing him how to switch the light on and off. "Okay, Ollie. Don't forget to wax that damned Packard."

"Okay." Toliver scratched at his crotch. "Burns. Feels like ants crawling around."

The doctor said, "Could be worse. Like two ants on the toilet seat."

Toliver barely moved his head. "What's wrong with that?"

"One got pissed off."

"Awww . . . shiiiit." A corner of Toliver's mouth curled up.

The doctor gave an exaggerated nod and mouthed, *Okay*, to Ingram.

Ingram shook the doctor's hand and looked down. "See ya, Ollie."

"Todd."

"What?"

"What about Helen?"

Ingram felt as if Toliver had thrown a spear through him, and he didn't know why. He was powerless to do anything. And yet, in a strange way, he felt closer to her out here. Not just physically, but . . . closer. He'd dreamt about her last night after the battle. "How did you know, Ollie?"

"Do something."

Ingram raised his hands and let them flop to his sides. "Tell me. What can I do?"

"I don't know. But if it were me that she loved, I'd sure do something."

My God. Who is helping who?

"Hell, talk to Otis. He's on the radio with her all the time. Didn't he set up a code based on her graduation date?"

"Shhhh. That's supposed to be a military secret. Besides, he's in Brisbane."

Toliver lowered his voice. "She graduated in 1937?"

"No. That's me. She's 1939."

"You still have the ring?"

Ingram stuck his hand in his pocket, making sure it was there. "Yeah. Now be quiet."

"Find a way to get to Otis."

"Ahem." The doctor cleared his throat.

"Take your pills, Ollie."

"Thanks for coming, Todd."

They fumbled hands and shook.

"And Todd."

"Yeah?"

"Do something. Talk to Otis."

CHAPTER TWENTY-SIX

13 OCTOBER, 1942
TULAGI HARBOR
SOLOMON ISLANDS

Seltzer stood smartly at the motor whale boat's tiller, shirt tucked in, hat cocked over his eyebrows. Ingram jumped aboard, finding the mail had caught up. Five large bags had been tossed in the passenger compartment, and he had to shove them aside to make room. Travillion pushed away the bow and they wove their way through anchored ships to the *Howell*. Ingram leaned back and yelled over the diesel's clamor, "Anything in town?"

"Not much, really, just a bunch of GIs running around."

"Yeah?"

Seltzer grinned. "The PT boat skipper who gave us the mail. Not a bad guy except he kept bumming cigarettes. Told me about a SEABEE who found a bunch of pipe lying around and ran it up to a stream. Now they have fresh water twenty-four hours a day. He showed us the place. Guys from all over lined up for showers.

Ingram thought about that one and decided it was why Seltzer looked so snazzy. Dudley and Travillion, too. "Did you take one?"

Seltzer's smile was broad.

Ingram grumbled to himself that he hadn't bathed in fresh water for ten days. Just as bad, his underwear was becoming a rich shade of green, taking on its own foul form of organic personality. In the tropics, the *Howell*'s evaporators couldn't provide the fresh water needed to feed the ship's boilers or cook or launder clothes or bathe. Thus, the boilers rated the highest priority, with officers and men taking saltwater showers and washing their clothes with saltwater soap.

Seltzer stood at his tiller, shirt rippling in the breeze, clean, comfortable, while Ingram smelled like a goat. His mind lingered on fresh water gurgling over him, cleansing the fumes and grit of battle. All he had to do was tell Seltzer to turn around. He checked his watch. No. Too late. He would lose at least an hour, and he didn't have that much time. He had to prepare for a tomorrow nobody wanted to see.

"Sir?"

"What?"

Seltzer pointed. "The PT skipper said the flyboys sunk a Jap destroyer over there. Want to take a look?"

"Sure."

Seltzer swung his tiller. Soon they cruised to the spot where he backed the engine and stopped. Bracing their hands on the gunwale, they peered down. Tulagi and Guadalcanal were volcanic in origin, with steep beaches quickly dropping off to deep water. Without the sediment, one could easily see a hundred feet in any direction. Directly below, in perhaps forty feet of water, a Japanese destroyer lay on her side, the detritus of war scattered about. Sporting a graceful clipper bow and raked superstructure, she looked to be perhaps four hundred feet long and was dark gray on top, her bottom a dull anti-foulant red. With no signs of human life, she had obviously died a hard, violent death. Her hull was riddled with holes and gashes, her stern mauled, one propeller gone, the shaft dangling at an obscene angle. One of her raked stacks was shredded, as if hit by a giant claw. The other stack had fallen off and lay nearby in white dazzling sand, where schools of brightly colored fish swam in one end and out the other. As if still hemorrhaging, large oval globs of fuel oil lazed from ruptured tanks and climbed to the surface to spread into large blossoms of glistening brown scum.

Seltzer found his voice. "Blew the shit out of her."

"Lookit them tarpeders," Travillion whispered.

Several torpedoes, having fallen off when the ship capsized, were scattered on the bottom.

Ingram sat back, shocked, completely disbelieving what he'd seen. Again, he leaned over the gunwale to stare. The Japanese torpedoes were enormous, far bigger than the *Howell*'s torpedoes. For a moment a shaft of sunlight bounced off one, highlighting its copper color, almost like dried blood.

They drifted two or three minutes, staring at the wreck, the only sounds those of the boat's idling engine and a gull squawking overhead as it flew in lazy circles.

Those torpedoes. They were what got the *Riley,* he realized, a cold wave running through his veins. What had Ollie said? *The blast lifted the ship out of the water.*

Dudley whistled. "Can you believe all the junk down there? I betcha a brass dealer would make a mint."

After another minute of gawking, Ingram nodded to Seltzer. "We better scram."

Seltzer rang up full speed. "We got torpedoes like that, Mr. Ingram?"

Ingram didn't know what to say. "Wish I knew."

Early the next morning, the *Howell* weighed anchor, pulled alongside an oiler, topped off with fuel, and cleared Tulagi Harbor by nine a.m. With sixty thousand horsepower at his command, Commander Jeremiah "Boom Boom" Landa ordered all four boilers and two generators on the line and told his officer of the deck to ring up all ahead full and make turns for twenty-five knots. There was no wind, and a late morning haze hung on the eastern horizon as the sleek destroyer stood into the Sealark Channel. Flying fish led their way, soaring inches above the flat, glossy sea as the *Howell* steamed easterly, dragging a smoldering white wake. At 1122, Marapa Island, at Guadalcanal's east end, lay off their starboard beam. Landa ordered his OOD to increase speed to twenty-seven knots and to come right to head south into the Coral Sea. Steering a zigzag course around a base leg of one-five-eight true, Landa planned to arrive in Nouméa late the next evening.

Rich seafaring traditions have been handed down through the centuries, the passage of time often blotting the original intent. Many of these traditions descend from Greek and Roman mythology, and today are universal to sailors of all languages and cultures. For example, the Roman practice of placing a coin in the mouth of a corpse just before burial was for payment to Charon, the ancient boatman, who transported the newly departed across the River Styx to Hades, the land of the dead. For seafarers, a logical follow-on was placing a coin of the realm face-up under the butt of a mast when it was first stepped into position on the ship. This ensured that Charon would be paid for transporting all hands across the River Styx in case their ship met with disaster and went down at sea.

Another tradition is for the sailmaker to take the last stitch through the nose of the deceased when closing a canvas shroud around the body.

Yet another tradition handed down is firing a volley of three shots just before the deceased is to be interred. This stems from ancient Rome's belief that the numeral three had magic qualities. At funerals, Romans cast earth into the sepulcher three times. Three times, relatives and friends called out the name of the dead as they departed the tomb for forever. Three times they mourned in their native Latin, *"Vale, vale, vale."* Farewell, farewell, farewell.

In medieval days, the three volleys became a superstitious custom, the gunfire's noise intended to drive away the evil spirits as they made a panicked escaped from the hearts of the dead . . .

Landa and Ingram felt as strongly about tradition as the crew, but not at the compromise of a proper service. Ingram pulled out a copy of Navy regs, then he assembled a burial detail. He was surprised during the meeting when Franklin, a first-class bo's'n's mate, said that he thought it was proper to run the final stitch through each corpse's nose. As a boy, he'd heard many stories sitting at his uncle's knee. The man was a sailmaker in the Royal Navy who had done the same thing with their dead after the Battle of Jutland. No, Ingram told them, no stitch through the nose; these brave men had been mutilated enough. And no coin in the mouth, either. But a fifty-four-pound, five-inch projectile was to be secured inside each shroud to ensure it sank. And yes, there would be a firing squad that would shoot three rounds just before a body was tipped into the ocean.

Boom Boom Landa's worst fear was being torpedoed by a Japanese submarine while the *Howell* was hove to, pitching bodies into the ocean. So he wanted Ingram, his most experienced officer, on the bridge, while Landa conducted services aft on the fantail. Also, he refused to slow to less than eight knots, and only when they tipped the dead over the side.

Let the dead bury the dead, Dezhnev had quoted. That crazy Russian wouldn't have slowed at all. Well, today, Ingram reflected, the crew would do their best to ensure the dead were properly honored for their sacrifice to their country. Then they could crank up the turbines and return to the grim business of living.

The next morning, Ingram cleared paperwork, then had lunch, and at 1325 climbed to the bridge and relieved Luther Dutton as OOD so he could stand with his division.

Ingram walked to the aft to the signal bridge and took a huge breath, glad to be away from Tulagi's oppressive heat, reveling in the ship's cool, twenty-seven knots of relative wind. The sea was still flat, the ship hardly rolling. There wasn't a cloud in the sky, and the deep blue horizon merged with water so turquoise and so clear, one could see down almost a hundred feet. The air rushing through the uptakes whistled a tune of radiant life while the *Howell*'s broad wake streamed from the fantail, where her twin screws furiously spun, churning the water into a brilliant white, leaving a long foaming carpet hundreds of yards behind. With satisfaction, Ingram noted the wake was straight, meaning the helmsman in the pilothouse was paying attention, keeping the ship on course.

Beside the wind and the whistling uptakes, there was another sound.

Ingram looked up to see the flag of the United States, its thirteen stripes and forty-eight stars, flying from the yardarm, snapping in the breeze. He remembered now that he'd heard that sound two nights ago, during the battle, not realizing until now how much it meant to him.

From here, thirty-five feet above the water, he could see the after two-thirds of the *Howell* in fine detail. Her twin stacks, her dappled gray-green topsides, her gun mounts, and torpedo tubes.

And her fantail.

He turned away and took another deep breath, realizing he felt guilty. Guilty that he was so alive and that fourteen others weren't. *Damnit.* It was a nice day to be buried. The chart in the pilothouse said the bottom was at a little over two thousand fathoms, twelve thousand feet, over two miles, a long, cold journey to eternity.

It was about time. He checked his watch: 1330. Yes. Ingram turned and nodded to Miranda.

The short, barrel-chested coxswain flipped on the 1MC, his metallic tones echoing throughout the ship. "Now hear this. Now hear this. All hands not on watch, lay aft to the fantail for burial detail."

On the fantail, the crew lined up in ranks facing port, hats off, hair blowing in the breeze, as light brown stack gas whipped over their heads. The portside lifelines were undone, and neatly lined at the deck's edge were fourteen white canvas shrouds. Blood seeped through two or three of the shrouds, running in a crimson stream to the scuppers and then over the side. The shroud farthest forward lay on a greased plank, ready to go.

Standing on a crate, Landa began his recitation, while the ship, so alive now, seemed to go faster, her bow wave sizzling down her sides. Ingram watched Landa talk, his white teeth gleaming in the sun. Then Ingram gazed at the sky, realizing that the doctor on the *Zeilin* was right about Ollie. He'd simply had too much. Ingram wondered when his own time would come to go nuts. He felt as if he'd earned the right.

No.

Looking aft at the canvas shrouds, he realized it was a right he could never exercise. Those men back there had been shoved into the abyss, giving him and the rest of the *Howell*'s crew, a right to stand here and breath God's clean air. He owed it to them.

Landa waved from his perch.

It was the signal. Ingram turned and ordered quietly, "All engines ahead two-thirds. Make turns for eight knots."

Wilson relayed the order to the lee helmsman in the pilothouse. The man cranked his engine-room telegraph, its little bell ringing. Aft, a corresponding *clang, clang* echoed through an open hatch on the main deck that led to the forward engine room. Far below, the machinist's mate spun his fourteen-inch throttle valve, reducing steam to the turbine. The ship slowed, the uptakes' urgent whistle faded, and the loss of blessed speed brought a rise in temperature, making the sailors sweat for the first time that day.

Ingram turned to the six lookouts he had posted atop the pilothouse and yelled, "Okay, watch for periscopes, torpedo wakes, airplanes, anything. We don't want to get caught napping out here. If it looks like an airplane, report it. I don't mind a plane turning into a bird. But I do mind what you think is a seagull turning into a Jap bomber. So if you're not sure, say something. And keep your eyes off the fantail, look in your sectors only. Okay?''

They gulped, mumbled, "Yessir," and pressed their binoculars to their eyes.

Looking aft, he knew Landa was at the part of the ceremony that went:

Unto Almighty God we commend the souls of our brothers departed, and we commit their bodies to the deep; in sure and certain hope of the Resurrection unto eternal life, through our Lord, Jesus Christ; at whose coming in glorious majesty to judge the world, the sea shall give up her dead; and the corruptible bodies of those who sleep in him shall be changed, and like unto his glorious body; according to the mighty working whereby he is able to subdue all things unto himself. Amen.

Ingram handed Briley, the thin quartermaster of the watch, a neatly typed necrology of fourteen names to be entered in the deck log. It was a list of those who were leaving the ship for the last time. Then he turned and looked aft as the first three-round volley sounded. Two men held a United States flag over the first shroud, while two others, at Landa's nod, raised the plank. The weighted shroud slipped into the sea without a sound:

. . . Hamer, F. P., (Jr.), 121 49 61, SN1, USN.

Quickly, a seaman regreased the plank with a paintbrush. Four men gently hoisted the second shroud on the plank, then held the flag over it. Landa nodded to the firing squad.

Bam. Bam. Bam. *Vale. Vale. Vale.*

They lifted the plank and the shroud plunged over the side, Ingram imagining a splash this time.

. . . Springer, W. W., 362 74 31, GM2 USN.

Vale. Vale. Vale.

. . . Ketchum, R. M., 316 37 89, TM2, USN.

Vale. Vale. Vale.

And thus were buried the fallen men of mount fifty-three and torpedo mount two—men unknown to Ingram, except that they had fought valiantly. His chest heaved and his eyes became moist. Around him, the men on watch cast a glance his way and he realized he didn't care. He thrust his hand into his pocket, searching for a handkerchief, instead finding Helen's ring.

Briley stood beside him, the list still clutched in his hand, tears running down his cheeks.

Wiping his own tears with the back of his hand, Ingram marveled that after all he'd gone through at Corregidor, he still had a shred of emotion. And it made him realize the fourteen sailors who now marched on their last noble journey had, in their quiet dignity, given the men of the *Howell* a reason to live, to fight, to look to the future.

The last plank was tipped. Men on the fantail blew their noses and wiped their eyes as Landa uttered his closing words. Then he waved from his crate and stepped down among his men.

Ingram walked to the pilothouse. "All engines ahead full. Make two hundred seventy turns for twenty-seven knots."

The *Howell*'s uptakes whistled, feeding air to her four hungry boilers. Her screws dug in, making her fantail squat low in the water. The new breeze generated by her speed swept across the destroyer's decks, drying their sweat . . . and their tears.

Vale. Vale. Vale.

CHAPTER TWENTY-SEVEN

14 OCTOBER, 1942
11° 07.2' S; 162° 34.2' E
CORAL SEA, EN ROUTE NOUMÉA

Ingram walked into his stateroom and drew the curtain closed. Flipping off the light, he sat at his desk in near-darkness, his head in his hands. The burial services over, they had set a condition three watch, allowing one-half of the crew to turn in for the afternoon, a Friday. They were beat, with plenty of work facing them when they arrived in Nouméa. Even the tireless Boom Boom Landa was asleep in his sea cabin. Besides a new gun barrel for mount fifty-three, and blast shield for torpedo two, a hundred other things had popped up.

Ingram rubbed his nose with thumb and forefinger. Landa had the right idea. As he stepped toward his bunk, his elbow knocked something on the deck. He flicked on the desk light. It was an envelope with a typewritten note from his yeoman clipped to it:

Lt. Ingram,
Please excuse me for not delivering this yesterday. I mis-routed it. I'm very sorry.

Sincerely
W. F. Justice, YN3

The return address was Echo, Oregon: his mother. Strange, there had been two letters in yesterday's mail bag. Now this. Tearing it open, he found another envelope inside. His heart skipped a beat when he saw it was postmarked Ramona, California, addressed to Lieutenant Todd Ingram, c/o General Delivery, Echo, Oregon.

He sat back and opened it, finding three pages of onionskin written on both sides in a graceful cursive handwriting. It was dated three days after his visit to Ramona.

August 24, 1942
Dear Todd,

I want to thank you for driving all the way down here last Friday. And I don't want you to think Frank and I took it for granted. It was a major effort for you, especially after all that you have been through. We really enjoyed meeting you and appreciate very much the risks you took. Frank showed me the War Department telegram yesterday. After your visit, my mind is a lot more at ease now than it has been for a long time. It sort of confirms things.

What I mean is, there is something you should know. I have this way. Let me give you an example. One day, about ten years ago Frank was out on Lightning, his horse, checking the groves, pulling out deadwood.

Suddenly, I got a feeling. Things were not right. Then and there, I grabbed Tom and Helen and ran into the grove. We found Lightning but no Frank. I was scared. Ten minutes later, Helen found him. Lightning had bolted at a rattlesnake and pitched Frank into a ditch. He was out like a light. Some water on his face woke him but he was woozy. Tom got Lightning and it took all three of us to prop him in the saddle and keep him there. Later, I gave him ten stitches. He didn't peep. You know Marines. It must be why they call them jarheads.

Last May I sat straight up in bed. It was Helen. Something was not right. After that, things seemed to smooth out. That's how I knew she was alive when you drove up.

I feel stupid saying all this. I don't have any claims on clairvoyance. These things only happen where my family is concerned.

Speaking of feelings, we had word from Tom yesterday. He's finished all his pilot training and is shipping out to England, flying B-17s. So far, my feelings about him are good. This damn war. A daughter in the Pacific, a son in Europe. What more can we give?

How is your new ship coming along? I hope things are going well for you in San Francisco; it's a beautiful City, a nice place to get over what you've been through. I didn't have your exact address, so forgive me for sending it to Echo. Come again any time, next time we'll roast a pig. Bring a pal if you wish.

Frank sends his best. We pray for Helen and Tom, constantly. You too. Please write.

Sincerely
Kate Durand

He read the letter three times before he realized it had taken seven weeks to catch up. Guilt swept over him; he should have written, even called them. *But what the hell do I say?*

He pulled a writing pad from his desk.

Dear Kate and Frank,

Thanks for your kind letter. Best to keep that pig in the pen for a little while longer because I've shipped out. I can't tell you where we are but I've been assigned to a great ship as executive officer and . . .

Nouméa, a large port in New Caledonia, a French province, was jammed with ships of all sizes. Had the *Howell* been told to anchor, they would have had to use bow and stern anchors, lest she swing on the tide and foul one of the eighty or so nameless cargo ships sitting out there, waiting to off-load precious war matériel.

Luck was with them. A berth had been reserved alongside the *Vestal*, an 8,100-ton former collier converted to an oil-fired repair ship. At 2316 that night, Boom Boom Landa, the hot-rod destroyer driver, pulled in and moored starboard side to the *Vestal*. Flashing his phosphorescent grin, Landa rang only one backing bell, expertly positioning *Howell*'s mount fifty-three precisely under the *Vestal*'s portside crane. Even before the mooring lines were doubled up, the *Vestal*'s crane operator lowered his line to be secured to mount fifty-three's pretzeled barrel, soon to be pulled straight up like a ruptured tooth. By the time the engineering plant was secure and shifted to "cold iron," welders were at work, patching the holes in mount fifty-three's splinter shield. Likewise, the welders began their stroboscopic cutting and reshaping of torpedo two's blast-shield. Guardmail sacks gushed their official paperwork and Ingram didn't turn in until two-fifteen in the morning, putting in a wake-up call for seven.

After a quick breakfast the next morning, he stepped into a dreary overcast and walked to the quarterdeck, where he was amazed to see mount fifty-three's new barrel in place, canvas bloomers and all. Now the gunners worked on the dicey part: realignment.

It was loud on the quarterdeck. An incessant pounding echoed from the *Vestal* next door, as someone worked a steel forge deep inside her bowels. Electric grinders and pneumatic chipping hammers clacked around the decks of the *Howell*. Welders, with bug-eyed dark goggles, looked like monsters from Flash Gordon and created their own form of urgent cacophony, their torches buzzing, blue ionized smoke drifting up to rake one's nostrils. The urgent sounds of war were multiplied by two more destroyers moored outboard of the *Howell* with their own clanking and grinding.

The ship's twelve officers stood at officer's call, waiting for Ingram in two loose ranks of six each. Another ancient seafaring tradition, the purpose of morning quarters was to make sure no one had been lost overboard during the night. Each day at 0800, officers and men fell into quarters, each division assembling on a certain part of the ship's main deck. Noses were counted and reports generated by the division chief as to who was present and who was absent, for whatever reason, whether it be sick call, or if in port, AWOL or business off the ship. During this time, the exec briefed the ship's officers. The officers would then return to their divisions, receive the muster reports, then brief their men on upcoming events and work requirements.

Ingram took a moment to flip through the radio message board and found one ordering the *Howell* to cast off from the *Vestal* and anchor out in the bay no later than 1000. As far as the *Vestal* was concerned, her heavy repair work was done with the replacement of mount fifty-three's barrel. She was now ready to wean the *Howell* and kick her out of the slip, where the destroyer could swing at anchor and serve her problems by shore boat just like all the *Vestal*'s other hard-bitten customers.

He found another message and decided to talk about this one first. He spoke in a loud voice, "Listen up. Admiral Scott sends his congratulations to the cruisers and tin cans of Task Group 64.2 who shot it out at Cape Esperance. He says we sank fourteen Jap ships!"

"Fourteen. Wow." They grinned and shook hands. It was good to see them like this, especially after yesterday. Scott's victory message had given them a needed boost.

"It says also that, because we licked the Japs, the Army was able to land the next day their entire 164th Infantry Regiment from the Americal Division."

"So the Marines don't hate us anymore?" Asked Dutton.

"Everything's swell."

"*Semper fi,* Mac."

"Right."

Wilson asked, "Is it okay to tell our troops?"

"Absolutely. Next. This morning we shift berths. Sea detail is at—"

ZZZZZSHHHHHHHHHHHHHHTTTT!

A large cloud of steam blasted from a four-inch pipe attached to the rear of the aft stack. Ingram waited while the others shook their heads in disgust. Ghoulish engineers in the after fireroom had chosen this moment to calibrate the safety valve on number four boiler. It involved running up the pressure on the boiler, then checking to see if a safety valve automatically opened to relieve the pressure. The only warning was a slight whistling in the uptakes, the blowers feeding air to the boiler as it built pressure, then the earsplitting roar, easily heard a quarter mile away.

It stopped. Ingram tried again. "Okay. Sea detail is at—"

ZZZZZSHHHHHHHHHHHHHHTTTT!

Seagulls squawked and scattered, their sleep interrupted. Junior officers in the rear rank, looked at one another and grinned. In front, three department heads, all lieutenants, turned and glared at Hank Kelly, the chief engineer. Their hard stares accused Kelly of letting his snipes in the after fireroom give the officers the finger.

Kelly, a Purdue graduate with sandy hair and clear blue eyes, stood redolent in his oil-stained engineer's coveralls. Supposed to be at parade rest, he actually teetered at a near-insubordinate stance, his face mirroring the traditional destroyer engineer's countenance of you guys ain't going nowhere without my boilers and turbines. Kelly's mouth grew into a lopsided grin. "Sorry, fellas. But you have to realize that—"

ZZZZZSHHHHHHHHHHHHHHTTTT!

It was a game they played that was as old as the first steam-driven ship. Engineers versus everyone else topside: deckforce, gunners, torpedomen, storekeepers, signalmen, the rest of the ship. Ingram had seen it many times and didn't pay attention as Kelly made his excuses. He took his time flipping through the rest of the messages. Most had to do with supply items or ship movements. But one interested him. A conference for all destroyer captains and executive officers was scheduled at 1500 that afternoon.

"XO?" Lieutenant Dutton, standing in the first rank, raised his hand.

"Yes, Luther."

"Can't we ask Mister Kelly to knock off the crap, so we can get some real work done around here?"

Kelly piped up, "Oh, I'm so sorry for making the ship safe for you, Luther. Next time I'll just let the safety clog, so the boiler will blow. Then you'll see shit fly, while seven-hundred-degree steam carves a hole in your ass."

Uncharacteristically, Dutton spouted, "Shit fly? Shit fly? I've got a five-inch gun mount and a torpedo mount to repair and you're slinging shit?"

Dutton was from Massachusetts, Kelly from Alabama. The two were as opposite socially as they could get. Yet they were good friends. Half the time, Ingram couldn't tell if they were arguing or kidding. He began, "Come on, you two. We don't have time for—"

ZZZZZSHHHHHHHHHHHHHHTTTT!

Kelly said, "Yeah, I'm slinging shit all over your face, Luther."

Dutton turned and stuck out his chin. "Who says?"

"Me! But come to think of it, you're so ugly, I wouldn't use your face for a shield in a shit-fight."

"That's enough, damnit," said Ingram, turning to Kelly. "Who do you think you are to—"

The quarterdeck phone buzzed. The messenger of the watch answered it, leaned over to Ingram, and said in a low voice, "It's for you, Sir."

"Take a message."

"Sir," said the messenger, "It's the captain."

"Oh." Ingram jammed the phone to his ear. "XO."

"Knock that shit off! Goddamnit." It was Landa, screaming.

On the way to quarters this morning, Ingram noticed Landa's cabin door was closed. And he hadn't shown up for breakfast. Deservedly, the captain was sleeping in. At sea, skippers don't get much time for rest, especially in a war zone.

"Who the hell authorized—"

ZZZZZSHHHHHHHHHHHHHHTTTT!

As the steam blasted, he checked the faces of the officers standing before him. All of them rested, eyes gleaming; kids again, after war's somber business. They were happy to be alive, and happy to be part of the victory at Cape Esperance.

The safety valve reseated. A world of ugly, wrenching shipyard stridency became a relative atmosphere of peace and tranquillity.

"—those bastards to set safeties without my—"

Ingram handed the phone to Kelly. "It's for you, Hank."

CHAPTER TWENTY-EIGHT

16 OCTOBER, 1942
U.S.S. *ARGONNE* (AG 31)
NOUMÉA, NEW CALEDONIA

Moored to the downtown dock in Nouméa's sweltering heat, the *Argonne* was headquarters for Admiral Robert L. Ghormley, Commander South Pacific Area and South Pacific Force (SoPac). She was built in 1921, displaced 11,100 tons, and had twin turbines powered by a six-thousand-horsepower plant that could drive her at fifteen and a half knots. But the *Argonne*'s crew muttered that she wasn't going anywhere. They called her the "Agony Maru," and to all within earshot claimed she was high and dry on coffee grounds, glued to the damned dock. What the old girl needed was a week at sea to exercise her machinery and to let the sharp sea air cleanse the tropics' moldy stench from her compartments and passageways.

But Admiral Ghormley was not in a mood to cruise anywhere. The man was a workaholic, wrestling with the terrible responsibility for the First Marine and Americal Divisions, now locked in deadly combat with the Japanese on Guadalcanal, 950 miles to the north. Ghormley, also responsible for the naval forces in the Solomons, was outnumbered and outgunned by his opponent's Navy, and thus worked twice as hard to maintain a semblance of support for the beleaguered Marines at Guadalcanal. SoPac staff and the *Argonne*'s crew dared not smile, lest they be seen by the admiral, lest they be accused of slacking off. Ghormley, a classmate of Admiral Chester Nimitz, was not going to slack off. His men were locked in a death struggle, and with the Japanese beating the U.S. Navy to every punch, there was simply nothing to laugh about.

* * *

At 1512, Landa and Ingram stepped up the *Argonne*'s gangway, saluted the quarterdeck and OOD, and walked quickly forward, looking for the wardroom, sweating and puffing as they went. They were late for the skippers' conference.

"Whew!" said Landa. "I haven't been in an air-conditioned space since I left the States. Ahhh." They found a large door, pulled it open, and walked down a passageway to a set of double wooden doors. A small Bakelite tag announced, WARDROOM. A Marine corporal stood guard, dressed in helmet and clean, crisp battle fatigues, a Thompson submachine gun hanging over his shoulder by its strap. "Finally." At the Marine's demanding glance, Landa said, "Landa and Ingram, U.S.S. *Howell*."

"Yes, Sir. Of course, Sir." The corporal turned and opened the door for them.

They stepped in, finding a large compartment. A pantry was situated forward and six long tables were set up in a U shape and covered with the traditional green baize tablecloths. There were perhaps twenty-five to thirty officers gathered on either side of the U, with ten or so at the head table. In spite of the open ports, it was hot and stuffy; all perspired freely and fanned themselves. "Damn, no A/C," Landa muttered.

Everyone looked as they stepped in, the room becoming silent. Obviously, the meeting was in progress.

"Good evening, gentlemen. So nice of you to join us." The speaker sat at the head table. His nameplate read, CAPTAIN ROBERT A. JESSUP. He had brown wavy hair, dark eyes, and the largest set of canines Ingram had ever seen. It reminded him of a saber-toothed tiger. Seated to Jessup's left was an older man, heavily jowled, with thinning hair. Dark circles ran under his eyes, making him look as if he hadn't slept for a week. His nameplate announced, VICE ADMIRAL ROBERT L. GHORMLEY, and he shuffled through an enormous stack of papers, slowly shaking his head from time to time, almost oblivious to the others gathered in the compartment. A clean-shaven lieutenant in pressed work khakis stood directly behind Ghormley, handing papers over the admiral's shoulder, retrieving them after Ghormley scrawled his signature. Other officers were seated to Ghormley's right. One Ingram recognized as the totally bald, stocky, red-faced Captain Theodore Myszynski, the division commodore of Destroyer Squadron Twelve, who sat chewing a cigar and puffing blue smoke. Ingram hadn't yet met Myszynski, but he and Landa complemented one another, both quick-tempered. Myszynski, with an impeccable career in the surface Navy, was nicknamed Rocko and called the "Mad Pole" behind his back. Seated to Jessup's right was—

"I'll be damned," Ingram muttered. It was General Sutherland, MacArthur's aide. Otis DeWitt sat to his right. Ingram smiled and waved.

DeWitt returned the greetings with a barely perceptible nod, which Ingram recognized as his servile, brown-nosing facade, a dark habit that DeWitt had so richly cultivated in the peacetime Army.

Landa slipped into a chair. "Sorry, Sir. The launch ran out of gas."

"Perhaps you should plan better, Commander," said Jessup.

Ingram caught a glance from DeWitt, who rolled his eyes, his face saying, *Don't screw with that guy.*

Landa grinned. "Sorry, Sir. Won't happen again."

Jessup leaned forward. "What ship, Commander?"

Landa stood and swept his gaze across the room at large, his best white-toothed smile flashing, "I'm Jerry Landa, skipper of the *Howell,* DD 482." He waved at Ingram. "My XO, Todd Ingram."

Jessup asked, "Do you make it practice of being late?

Landa sat slowly and looked around. "Sir?"

"Isn't it true that you were late also when forming up with Task Group 64.2 on its way to Cape Esperance?" snapped Jessup.

Eyes in the room fell on Landa and Ingram. Landa said, "Ordered to Espiritu Santo, Sir, to pick up my new exec, er, Todd Ingram here. You see, Al Stoner, my old exec, got appendicitis, and we were without him for three weeks while—"

"Very well. I suppose that's a good enough excuse."

Landa sat straight up, dark blotches forming under his eyes. He muttered to Ingram, "Shore-based, backwater sonofabitch."

Ingram had become used to Landa's hair-trigger temper and knew when the man was close to the edge. He wondered sometimes if Landa would ever be selected for captain. "Easy, Skipper," he muttered softly. He patted Landa's arm and glanced at Ghormley. The vice admiral seemed oblivious to what was going on around him as he studied a thick report, slowly rubbing his chin. At the other end, Sutherland smirked and DeWitt's head was in his hands, his face tactfully masked.

"Now that we're *all* here, gentlemen"—Jessup looked at Landa—"the purpose of this segment is to discuss—"

"Sir?" Landa stood, shaking off Ingram's hand.

"Xnay, Skipper," said Ingram quietly.

"What is it this time, Commander? By the way, is it true they call you 'Boom Boom'?"

" 'Boom Boom.' Yes, Sir. Every bit of it, Sir. It started in my sophomore year at the University of Michigan. You see, I could fart louder than anybody else."

"What?" Jessup sat back, his mouth open.

Ghormley looked up. Sutherland's smirk turned to a grin, while DeWitt's head remained in his hands, slowly shaking.

"Nobody better. You see, we had contests. I was always the loudest. And the most precise, I might add. Then my pals gave me the great honor of placing me in charge of a term project where we researched and recommended a fart classification system. We did a white paper and submitted it to the *Atlantic Monthly* under the title of *The Social Impact of Flatus in the Common*

Man and Its Emancipatory Challenges. In it, we hypothesized ten nondistress categories of—"

Jessup found his voice. "Commander, this is not the time to—"

Landa's gaze leveled on Jessup like a five-inch gun. "As far as Al Stoner goes, his appendix burst six days after we reported it. We were at sea on convoy duty and he almost died because some gold-brick right here on the *Argonne* delayed permission for us to bring him in."

The room was silent, four fans, one in each corner, buzzed back and forth, ruffling papers. The ports were all open but the day was still without wind. The men fanned themselves fervently as it grew warmer.

"As far as the launch running out of gas, it was the *Argonne*'s damned launch that picked us up, not mine. We always make sure the *Howell*'s launch is topped off with fuel at all times."

Ghormley looked up and tapped his pencil. "I'm sorry, son. We're all a little on edge, here. Please sit down, Commander."

"Yes, Sir." Landa sat, glaring at Jessup.

The door opened and an ensign wearing a holstered .45 pistol stepped in, his face deeply furrowed. He walked up to Ghormley, handed him a radio flimsy, and stood at a semblance of parade rest, his eyes fixed in the distance.

Ghormley sat back, read the message, then ran a hand down his face. "Oh, my God. What are we going to do about this?" He closed his eyes for a moment, then nodded to the ensign. "No reply."

"Yes, Sir." The ensign turned and left.

Ghormley looked up as if seeing everyone for the first time. "Please, continue, Captain."

Jessup eyed his audience and cleared his throat. "We're here to examine our failure at Cape Esperance, which includes a review of night tactics, radio procedure, and"—he paused—"gunnery and torpedo tactics."

Their was a roar among the skippers. One shouted, "What the hell? How can you call sinking fourteen Jap ships a failure?"

Myszynski, the bald division commodore, barked, "Enough."

After they quieted, Jessup said, "Your gunnery wasn't quite that good. With aerial reconnaissance and coast watcher's reports, we now have a more accurate picture of what happened. The results are, gentlemen, we sank just two ships. Not fourteen."

"Two?" they yelled.

"A heavy cruiser, the *Furutaka* and a destroyer, the *Hubuki*. As you know, we lost the *Duncan* and the *Riley*."

They sat back, unable to find words.

"You were eleven ships: two heavy cruisers, two light cruisers, and seven destroyers against only five Japanese ships: three heavy cruisers and two destroyers." He folded his hands on the baize and looked around. "You had radar, gentlemen, they didn't. You had numerical superiority and the advantage of surprise. They didn't."

The room was silent. Jessup continued, "We're very concerned. The Japs outsmart us at every turn. We're losing capital ships faster than we can replace them, and we're down to just one carrier, with another, hopefully, soon to rejoin us. Whether you know it or not, the Japs own the seas at night and are replenishing their Guadalcanal garrison, where they will soon achieve parity to our ground troops by''—he held up a document, running a finger down a column—''November first. It just doesn't look good.'' He glanced at Sutherland.

Sutherland confirmed it with a somber nod. ''I'm sorry to say we don't believe Guadalcanal can be held.''

Ingram sat back, dumbstruck. Sutherland's use of the royal ''we'' meant that it was General MacArthur's belief that the Solomons couldn't be held.

Myszynski gasped, ''Why the hell did Admiral Scott tell us fourteen ships?''

Ghormley blinked, laid down a sheaf of papers, and looked up. ''It was a mistake. He had bad dope. But then, don't get us wrong. You accomplished one of the primary missions: that of turning away the Japs who were there to bombard the Marines. As you know, they've had it pretty rough the last few weeks . . . and the Army was able to land their troops.''

''The worst thing is''—Jessup's voice was a whisper—''that we were hit by some of our own ships. Can I see a show of hands of those who were hit by one of us?''

Three skippers raised their hands.

''Any of them dye-loaded?''

Here it comes, Ingram thought. Toliver had mentioned a yellow dye-load that crashed through the *Riley*'s wardroom. Ingram had to admit he was curious as anyone else as to who was shooting with yellow dye-load.

Jessup was saying, ''I hear the *Riley,* before she went down, was hit by shell with—''

''Don't answer that!'' shouted Myszynski. ''Identifying dye-loads is counterproductive; I'm not about to tie a can to someone's tail. This is not the time. I think you all performed remarkably. Yes, we lost two ships, but we bloodied the Japs' nose. Let's take it from there.''

''What if I order you to tell me?'' said Jessup.

''Bullshit!'' said Myszynski, sitting straight and interlacing his fingers. Nobody looked at him, their eyes fixed on the tablecloth. Each of them knew that one look at the DESRONTWELVES's Squadron Doctrine would tell them which dye-load colors were assigned to what ship.

The thought must have occurred to Jessup, because he smiled. ''I'm sure we can take a look at your—''

Ghormley said, ''I agree with Rocko. I don't want to lay blame, either. So just leave it be. That won't do any good. But I do want to adjust our night tactics so we're not doing the Japs' work for them.''

Jessup didn't give up and turned to Ghormley. ''I realize that, Admiral. But if it hadn't been for friendly fire, the *Riley* would be here among us. We lost a brand-new ship and three hundred American boys.''

Ghormley shrugged. ''I don't know. Pointing the finger isn't going to—''

The door opened, announcing the return of the duty ensign from radio central. All fell silent as he walked up to Admiral Ghormley and handed him another message.

Ghormley signed for it, then sat back to read it. Soon he let out a sigh, "Oh, my God."

"Sir?" The ensign stood at attention, his eyes fixed in the distance.

"No. No." Ghormley's voice was faint. He shook his head as he stared at the flimsy. At length, he waved the back of his hand to the ensign. "Go."

The ensign walked out, closing the door softly.

Jessup looked at Ghormley, then at the assembled officers. "Well, I agree dwelling on the culprit isn't going to accomplish anything. I only wanted to underscore that the *Riley* would be here if—"

Ingram stood. All eyes focused on him.

Jessup eyed him warily. "Well, Lieutenant, ahhh . . ."

"Ingram, Captain." He took a deep breath, realizing he could well be jumping in the same boat with Landa, committing career suicide. A holdover from the peacetime Navy psyche was that one never argued with a superior in the presence of others, no matter how wrong the superior was. But Jessup had led with his chin today. There would be a time, Ingram knew, that Jessup could whisper in the right ear at the right selection committee, leaving Ingram frozen at lieutenant for the rest of his life. Or worse. *Screw it.*

"Actually, the *Riley* was hit by a Jap torpedo," Ingram said.

"We're not sure of that, Lieutenant," said Jessup.

"Well, I am. I talked to her gunnery officer."

"How could you? He's missing."

"No, Sir. He's a friend. I found him on the *Zeilin* in Tulagi, in her sick bay with a broken hip."

"We have no reports of that."

"They plan to air-ship him stateside, Sir. To have his hip fixed by a specialist. He's probably gone by now."

"I see. How can he be so sure?"

"Well, Sir. I know Toliver. We were together at Corregidor. He was my gunboss on the *Pelican,* a minesweeper, and is well qualified to tell what hit him. He said a torpedo smacked them so hard it lifted the ship out of the water and threw him in the air, tossing him down onto the pilothouse."

"Thank you, Lieutenant." Ghormley gave a thin smile.

"One more thing, Sir."

"Yes."

"I think I've seen one of the damned things. They're far bigger than anything we've got."

"What the hell?" said Jessup and Ghormley at the same time.

"Just a few days ago. From a sunken Jap destroyer in Tulagi. Torpedoes all over the bottom. Big bastards. Far bigger than ours."

From the corner of his eye, Ingram noticed DeWitt and Sutherland were both focused on him. Intensely.

"Jap torpedoes aren't worth a damn, Lieutenant," countered Jessup.

Landa stood. "I concur with Lieutenant Ingram, Sir." From the corner of his mouth, he whispered, "Todd, this guy's dangerous; he's fifth-generation Navy."

"The hell with him," Ingram shot back through gritted teeth. He turned to Jessup. "I'd say *our* torpedoes are the ones that aren't worth anything, Captain. We launched a salvo of five Mark 15 torpedoes into that Jap cruiser at point-blank range. Not one went off."

Jessup sighed. "If it's not too much trouble, I'd like to see your maintenance records."

Myszynski shot to his feet. "Over my dead body."

Another destroyer skipper stood. "I had duds, too."

Then another. "Me, too."

Doing his best to wave down the clamor, Jessup said, "Gentlemen. I assure you, the Winslow River Corporation has verified that—"

The men started shouting. Jessup stood and pounded his fist for quiet. They still shouted, ignoring him.

"Quiet! All of you!" It was Ghormley, his voice an earsplitting resonance. He leaned toward Jessup. "Captain, may I suggest a fifteen-minute coffee break?"

"Yes, Sir. Reconvene in fifteen minutes, gentlemen." Jessup got up and left quickly. Ghormley followed, his flag lieutenant handing him papers as he went. As Ghormley passed, a large report fell from under his right arm and plopped at Ingram's feet.

Ingram bent to pick it up. TOP SECRET was stamped in red on all four corners and he couldn't help but notice the title, *Joint Evacuation Plan for Guadalcanal.* He handed it to Ghormley, who mumbled a distant, "Thank you, son," and kept walking, his flag lieutenant close behind, glaring at Ingram.

For the second time that morning, dark splotches grew under Landa's eyes. He'd seen the report, too. Quickly standing, he muttered in a cold rage, "Jesus! Can you believe these goldbricking sonsabitches? We lay it on the line and these behind-the-lines crybabies are ready to give up." Shaking his head, Landa stood and nodded to a coffee service in the far corner. "Let's go hit the slop chute." He walked off.

Ingram went to follow, but something stopped him. He turned to see General Sutherland staring. And Otis DeWitt beckoned with a hand.

Ingram furrowed his brow.

Sutherland stood, DeWitt just behind, walking for the doors and motioning for Ingram to follow.

The two Army officers stood in the shade of a companionway. Sutherland ran a highly polished toe over the *Argonne*'s hot deck. "This is getting interesting, Otis."

"Sir?"

"This torpedo business—ah, here he is."

Ingram walked up and Sutherland shook his hand warmly. "How are you, Lieutenant? I haven't seen you since . . . since . . ."

"San Francisco, General."

"Damn, that's right! You're the Navy Cross guy. Rita Hayworth gave you a big smackeroo right on the mouth."

Ingram rubbed his chin. "Haven't washed since, General."

DeWitt piped up, "She kissed me, too."

"That's right." Jabbing a thumb at DeWitt, Sutherland made an aside to Ingram. "You know what, Lieutenant? Otis hasn't washed, either, and he smells like it."

They smiled for a moment, then DeWitt said, "Todd, could you repeat for the general what you saw up there in Tulagi?"

Ingram repeated his story about the torpedoes at the bottom of Tulagi Harbor. While Sutherland mulled this, Landa stuck his head out from the passageway. "They're getting ready to fire up the griddle, gentlemen."

Sutherland said, "Thank you, Commander. We'll be along in a moment." Sutherland extended a hand to Ingram. "And thanks to you, Lieutenant, for the recap. I hope to see you again soon." He waved at Ingram as if he were King Herod dismissing an exhausted messenger.

Watching Ingram walk away, DeWitt patiently waited for Sutherland to speak.

"Otis?"

"Yes, Sir?"

"I think I owe you an apology."

"I don't understand, Sir." *Yes, I do, damnit.*

"This torpedo business. It tends to validate what the Commie . . . what's his name?"

"Lieutenant Dezhnev."

"Yeah. What Dezhnev told you that night in 'Frisco. So maybe it is true about what Dezhnev is saying about FDR. My God, think of it. Think of what General MacArthur could say in the 1944 election campaign—that FDR knew about Pearl Harbor well in advance and got us sucked into this war. They'd roast him alive. Damn! We'd be a shoe-in." He snapped his fingers.

Sutherland had never been so candid about MacArthur's political plans. All DeWitt knew were the rumors. "He's really going to run, then?"

"Damn right." Sutherland patted DeWitt on the shoulder. "Look, Otis, go up to the radio room and give Willoughby the following instructions." Colonel Charles Willoughby was MacArthur's German-born intelligence chief in Australia. "Tell him to get some people into Tulagi and salvage a couple of those torpedoes and see what we have here. And tell him to get the Navy involved. It's really their show, you know."

DeWitt pulled out his pad and scribbled. "Yes, Sir. Shall we info Admiral Ghormley?"

Sutherland scratched his head. "Yeah. Next, I need more stuff off that Jap barge. Have Willoughby ask Amador in his next message to get whoever it was . . . ?"

"Lieutenant Durand."

"The nurse?"

"Yes, Sir."

"I want Lieutenant Durand to try again for anything on that Type 93. If she can't do it, fine. The page she has now with the notes sounds very helpful. But if she can get some Jap torpedo stuff, so much the better."

"Got it."

"And then tell Don Pablo we're pulling her out of there by submarine by, let's see, October twenty-fourth. That should give her enough time. I'm anxious for her personal commentary."

What? "How can we do that, Sir?"

Sutherland laughed. "Otis. You haven't been on my staff long enough." He turned and walked toward the wardroom.

I don't understand any of this. DeWitt stopped at the companionway leading up to the radio room on the 03 deck.

Sutherland stopped at the wardroom door, his voice echoing in the passageway. "Douglas MacArthur owns this part of the world, Otis. That's how we get a submarine in there."

CHAPTER TWENTY-NINE

17 OCTOBER, 1942
BUENAVISTA, MINDANAO
PHILIPPINES

TO: DPA
FM: GMD

1. *REQUIRE MORE DATA TYPE 93 ASAP.*
2. *SAME ON MK 15 IF POSSIBLE*
3. *ALSO, SEEK DATA: MK. 14 OR MK. 13 TORPEDO IF POSSIBLE.*
4. *IMPERATIVE EXTRACT HZD+DPA WHETHER DATA ABOVE (1)(2) (3) OBTAINED OR NOT. ORIGINAL MK 15 SINGLE PAGE DATA REQUIRED URGENTLY.*
5. *RENDEZVOUS SUBMARINE NEEDLEFISH ONE MILE SOUTH CABADBARAN 10240200.*
6. *SIGNAL PDT. COUNTER ZDQ.*

Amador reread the radio message. "Helen, do you realize what this means?"

Helen sat back, astounded. "I think so."

Wong Lee sat at his generator, sweat pouring off his face, an unlit cigarette dangling from his lips. "We really going home?"

Helen nodded slowly. "Home."

"Should I put the stuff away, or do you have a reply?" Wong Lee's voice was a whisper.

Amador shook his head. "Stow the gear, Wong." He turned to Helen. "They must be desperate. It sounds like you lit a powder keg."

Helen bit her lip. "Otis wants me to go back to . . . cleaning toilets."

Amador growled. "Those generals and staff lackeys in Australia eat steak and play golf every afternoon. They have no idea what you had to do to get one piece of paper. If they did, they would be sending you a medal instead of—" he slapped the message with the back of his hand.

Using a sturdy line, Wong Lee began easing the transmitter into the pit. "You don't have to go back there. Tell 'em to stick it. All we have to do is make that submarine rendezvous the night of the twenty-fourth. California, here I come! Wheeou." He shot a fist in the air. "Ahhh." The line burned through his other hand and the transmitter fell free for three feet and crashed atop of a crate of Springfield rifles.

"Wong!" Helen grabbed his right hand, finding two blisters across his palm. "Let me get some—"

"Hold on." Wong Lee scurried into the pit. "Gimme a light."

Helen handed one to him.

"Well." Amador stepped over to peer down with her.

Wong looked up. "Shit. Couple of tubes busted."

"We have replacements?" asked Helen.

"I think so. You want me to bring it up so we can test it?"

Amador turned to see Legaspi walk through the door, the copper antenna wire coiled over his shoulder. "Plug in the tubes. We'll test it next time. I want to clear out soon just in case Buenavista is on the Hapons' schedule."

"Okay. Sorry."

While Wong Lee worked, Helen asked Amador, "What if it's broken?"

Amador rubbed his chin. "We're fortunate in that I don't think it matters at this point. We meet the submarine in seven days and we'll be out of here. If not, we'll have to steal something."

As she listened, Wong Lee grumbled at the bottom of the pit. "It sounds like they really need that book."

Amador patted her arm. "I don't think Otis gave it any thought."

She stood and stared out the window. The early hours—it was one-thirty in the morning—were her favorite time in Buenavista, especially when the moon was out. Little waves lapped at the beach and it was almost serene. "Maybe."

Amador knew what she was thinking. "No."

"Don Pablo, the Kempetai next strike where?"

"I said no!"

"Pablo. We at least have to talk about it."

"No!" he roared. "I won't let you go back aboard that barge. What if you're captured again? They'll torture you. You don't want that. We hear your nightmares."

"But—"

Amador waved her off. "All right. Look at it this way. They can make anybody talk. They will make you talk. They could make you tell about . . . about . . ." He swept an arm around the bungalow. "All this. Anything. Anybody."

"Pablo. That's going to happen if any one of us is captured. It a risk we take."

"I don't care, damnit. I'm not throwing you to the Japs because of some stupid whim from Otis DeWitt."

Wong Lee crawled out of the pit, replaced the trap, and swept dirt over it. Then he sat back, lit a cigarette, and puffed mightily. "Here's my advice, honey. That message is your ticket to freedom. Take it. The sub surfaces off Cabadbaran in a week. There's no reason you should jeopardize that. You've done enough fighting for ten people. That's it. Adios. Amen. Why don't we hide up in the hills until the sub comes?"

"For once I agree with you, Wong," Amador said.

"Here's what we can do," said Helen opening a small bag and pulling out a tube of burn salve. "What if—"

"I said no!" Amador shouted.

"Shut up!" She took a step toward him, her fists balled.

They stood speechless. Amador said, "Dear, dear Helen. It's . . . we don't want anything to . . . happen . . ."

"I don't like it, either, Pablo. But I think there's a way. And we have to try. It must be important. Otherwise Otis wouldn't have asked."

Amador walked over and hugged Helen. "I won't let them do this to you." He looked down at her with moist eyes. "Wong Lee is right. We'll hide for seven days and wait for the submarine."

"There's a way."

"Please. Don't make me."

"Just tell me where the next Kempetai strike will be."

"Maugahay." Even as he said it, Amador felt as if he'd issued her death sentence. He held her tighter. "But you're not going to Maugahay. By this time tomorrow, we're going to be up in the mountains. I know a little place where the water runs clear and there are no leeches. There are deep pools were you can swim, and rocks were you wash your clothes and dry them in the sun. Pineapples grow wild and you can . . ."

* * *

Maugahay was a little village ten miles east of Buenavista. It was a Saturday night and by ten o'clock the ancient power system had decided it had done enough work for the day and tripped out by itself. It was quiet, and no lights shone save the glow of a few candles in nipa huts here and there. One of those lighted windows was Madero's Cantina, a local joint that had prospered from the interisland trade. With a thirty-foot bar, ten tables, and four bedrooms upstairs for the *putas,* the whores, Rafael Madero had everything a retired copper miner could want. Then the war came. Now his business was just a trickle of poor local customers. To them, he could only offer *tuba,* a home-brewed coconut beer, and *basi,* sugar cane wine, if he had time to make it.

Felipe Estaque, one of Amador's *guerrilleros,* sat with Don Pablo and Helen at a corner table. Emilio Legaspi and Wong Lee stood guard at either edge of the village.

Felipe, an ex-scout for the Philippine Army, wore his light blue denim uniform blouse in defiance of a Japanese edict. He was an inch taller than Helen and had attended Santo Tomas University for two years, where he had studied economics, just like Don Pablo Amador. Also, he spoke most of the Islands' popular tongues, along with English. Working loosely under Amador, Estaque had his own band of *guerrilleros* in this section of the province. He wore a sergeant's chevrons on his sleeves, carried a .45 in a holster, and an immaculately clean Thompson submachine gun was slung over his shoulder. Estaque waited until Rafael walked away, then sipped his *tuba.* His eyes flashed at Amador's question. "Yes. The Hapons dropped Carmen Lai Lai right here, late this afternoon."

"Why not just bring her in for the raid?"

"Looks like they're trying to improve their game. They want her to study the place beforehand. Point out the best conscripts."

Amador scratched his white hair. "You would think people would figure this out and melt into the countryside."

Estaque shrugged.

"How can we get her to do what we want?" asked Helen.

"There's just one rule about Carmen," said Estaque.

"What's that?" said Amador.

"Carmen Lai Lai is only for Carmen Lai Lai. When she started working for the Japs, the people of Amparo burned her little shop where she worked as a seamstress. Now they won't let her return. So she works now for the highest bidder: the Hapons."

Amador asked, "Where does she live now?"

"Amparo."

"But I thought you said—"

"She fingered the mayor of Amparo. The Japs came in and took off his head. Now she lives where she chooses: Amparo."

"For the time being," said Helen.

*　　*　　*

Carmen was lodged in a single-room common hut on the outskirts. It was not yet moonrise as Legaspi crept in. Estaque followed, trailed by a nervous Wong Lee.

Outside, Helen squinted at the hut, imagining a squad of Japanese soldiers was creeping right at her. "Maybe she heard us coming and got out."

Amador patted her arm. "Patience. Felipe is usually—"

A shot rang out. There was a high-pitched scream. Wong Lee charged out and dashed passed Helen and Amador into a coconut grove, bushes rattling as he went. "Hold on," said Amador, unholstering his revolver.

A few moments passed, then a figure stepped out and waved.

"It's Felipe." Amador put away his pistol and walked to the hut. With a glance at the coconut grove, Helen followed.

At the door, Estaque held up his hand. Blood!

"What happened?" gasped Amador.

"Sonofabitch bit me," said Estaque. "She's a tough customer, I'll tell you. Had a Nambu eight-shot under her mat. And a knife strapped to her leg."

Amador turned to Helen. "You sure you want to do this?"

"We have to try."

Amador sighed, then waved toward the hut.

With Estaque in the lead, they ducked inside the one-room hut. Legaspi sat picking his teeth in the far corner, keeping watch over the hog-tied, gagged bulk of Carmen Lai Lai, a candle burning near her head. She looked just the same as when Helen worked for her three weeks ago. Except blood ran from Carmen's mouth. Her eyes grew wide and darted, as she sensed others had just entered the hut.

Legaspi held up a canvas pouch. "Shhhht." He dumped the contents into the sand. "By damn. Candy bars the Hapons pay her." Scattered at his feet were assorted candy bars, two tubes of toothpaste, several rolls of toilet paper, and a bottle of aspirin.

Estaque leaned over her. "Carmen. Do you remember me?"

Carmen squirmed violently against her bindings. A look of hatred sprang from her eyes as she growled from behind her gag.

"Ummm." Estaque grabbed something from his belt.

"What?" said Amador.

A bayonet flashed in Estaque's hand. "Carmen. You must remember my mother, then? Vitos, two weeks ago. You worked her so hard, she got over-heated and had a stroke. She can't walk or talk, Carmen." He raised the bayonet.

Estaque's parents had died in an earthquake five years ago. "What are you doing?" Demanded Amador.

Estaque said in a matter-of-fact voice, "I'm going to take off her ear. Then pop out an eye. Maybe both."

"No!" Helen moved close. "When they see her, the Japs will come after us."

"They don't care. Happens all the time," said Estaque. "One of us works for them. Sooner or later, his body ends up on the Hapons' doorstep without a head. They just find someone else.''

Amador laid a casual hand on the bayonet's hilt and leaned over her. ''Carmen? Carmen? Do you know who I am?''

Carmen focused on Amador, then shook her head.

Amador said, ''I am Don Pablo Amador. And the Hapons have a price on my head. But that doesn't bother me because they have taken my country and everything I owned in it. I don't mind killing them and I wouldn't mind letting Felipe kill you right now.'' He let that sink in, then said, ''How about her? Do you know her?'' He tapped Helen's cheek near one of her burn scars.

It took a moment, but Carmen nodded.

''We have to talk to you. If we take off your gag, you'll be quiet?''

Another nod.

''Take it off.''

''Pablo, let me first cut off her ear.'' Estaque flipped the bayonet in the air and caught it after two full revolutions.

''Maybe later.'' He nodded to Legaspi, who reached down and untied the gag.

Carmen gasped for breath as saliva ran from her mouth.

Helen felt sorry and wanted to wipe the blood off Carmen's chin in spite of the cruel things she'd done.

Estaque held the bayonet's tip to Carmen's cheek. ''I know where your father is.''

''You do?'' she sputtered.

Estaque smiled. ''He was a good tailor. With a shop in Del Monte. Before the war he made uniforms for the Americans. A nice business. Now he makes uniforms for the Hapons.''

Carmen worked her mouth for a moment. ''What would you do if you were him?''

''Good question.'' Estaque pressed the bayonet tip, producing a tiny trickle of blood. ''Nothing wrong with the uniform business. But one wonders why he suddenly needs fifteen slave laborers to work there when it was just him before. How much are the Hapons paying him? And how does he get to drive around in a Buick?''

Carmen's eyes darted around the room.

''Like father, like daughter. Hmmm, Carmen?'' said Estaque. ''Do you get the gist of things?''

She met his cold stare with one of her own.

''What I mean is that you will receive your father's ear in the mail someday soon. Then his fingers, toes, and so forth. And when we run out of his parts, I'm going to do the same thing with you. Send pieces of you to the Hapons. To their generals. Maybe your head in a box, Carmen? Maybe your head in their Sunday stew pot. How's that sound?''

Carmen's eyes grew to slits. ''What do you want?''

Carmen speaks English far better than she lets on, Helen noted.

Amador leaned close. "Helen will be joining your group tomorrow. Except that you will let her be on her own. Let her go anywhere she wants. You will treat her kindly and not turn her over to the Hapons. Understand?"

"How much you pay me?"

Estaque's arm flexed as he made to shove the bayonet.

Amador grabbed Estaque's hand. "Hold on, Felipe. What do you want, Carmen? More toothpaste? Candy? Just tell me."

"Soap. Chewing gum."

Estaque and Amador exchanged glances. Carmen was running a black market business. Just to make sure, Amador said, "Okay. Cigarettes, too?"

"Yes, please." She smiled her toothless grin and tried to sit up.

Helen said, "Ask her if she can get me back into the captain's cabin."

"Anywhere you wanna go, bitch."

Estaque cocked his hand to backhand Carmen, but Helen caught it. "That's okay, Felipe. That's the way she talks." To Carmen: "Well?"

"Yeah, sure. Captain's cabin."

"First thing?"

"Sure."

Estaque rubbed his chin for a moment, then said, "Okay. Let's make sure of one thing. Carmen, you must return Helen to us, safe and sound, no later than the twenty-third—before that, if possible. Because if you don't . . ." He leaned close and whispered in her ear.

Carmen's eyes grew wide as he spoke. She began moaning. "No!" she gasped. Estaque kept talking and she moaned louder and louder. Finally, she wailed loudly and Estaque shoved the gag in her mouth.

After she quieted, Amador pulled the gag. "Carmen, when do the Hapons come?"

She drooled for a minute, then whimpered, "Ten tomorrow morning."

"What?" Amador said. "Isn't it to be a predawn raid?"

Carmen took a deep, shaky breath. "Everybody ready for that. They try something new."

"What?"

"Church. They raid the church tomorrow during services. Plenty of women."

"Good Lord." Amador exchanged glances with the others.

"I can't think of a better place to start," said Helen.

CHAPTER THIRTY

At an altitude of ten thousand feet, the PB2Y-3 Coronado flying boat lumbered along at 140 knots. She was a four-engine brute, capable of flying well over three thousand miles nonstop. This version was a "flagship" model, assigned for the use of Admiral Nimitz and his staff. She carried a crew of eight, with accommodations for eighteen high-ranking passengers who rode in better-than-solid comfort, especially when compared to the PB2Y-3R version, an amphibian cattle car that hauled thirty-four passengers.

Skirting just beneath a 10/10 overcast, the Coronado's pilot and copilot kept their gaze out of the cockpit, vigilant, ready to yank back on the yoke and leap up into the clouds if jumped by enemy aircraft. But for the most part, it had been a boring ride from Fiji. With just a few patches of turbulence, their world consisted of the overcast and the South Pacific far below, a smooth, milky gray, here and there punctuated by whitecaps.

In the Coronado's midships galley, Rear Admiral Raymond A. Spruance glanced out the small port as he brewed coffee. A hobby he'd cultivated over the years. Another hobby was growing tomatoes; yet another, raising pet schnauzers. As with work or play, Spruance did everything by the book, examining all possibilities before taking action. With coffee, he'd received praise using a bean raised in Kona nearby on the big island of Hawaii. When he could, Spruance also brewed with a bean from Espiritu Santo, in the New Hebrides, where the U.S. Navy maintained a forward base four hundred miles from Guadalcanal. On his upcoming inspection tour, he hoped to pick up a few pounds of the bean on Espiritu Santo and perhaps ship some back to his wife, Margaret, living in a three bedroom rental in Monrovia, California, a suburb northeast of Los Angeles.

Spruance checked the burner on his little portable electric coffeemaker, ensuring the element heated properly, then looked out the port again. This leg, the last of a forty-two-hundred-mile trek from Pearl Harbor, wasn't as long as the others; he didn't feel as tired. They'd left Hawaii three days ago, overnighting at Johnston Island, then Canton Island, and last night at Fiji. This morning, they'd taken off at eleven o'clock local time, and with a slight tailwind, anticipated landing in Nouméa about three p.m. So far, it had been a smooth flight. No headwinds. Just the ever-present overcast.

Strange: Until two nights ago, their destination was Guadalcanal for an inspection tour. But then Admiral Nimitz had radioed from his Makalapa headquarters in Pearl Harbor, ordering them to proceed directly to Nouméa; why, Spruance didn't know, and he felt a tinge of frustration, since he was Nimitz's chief of staff and therefore should know everything.

Vice Admiral William F. Halsey, Jr., wandered up in stocking feet, working khaki uniform rumpled, his eyes puffy from a two-hour nap. He leaned over the coffeemaker and made a show of sniffing at steam rising from the spout. "How much longer, Ray?"

Spruance knelt to look in the brewer's sight glass. "Two minutes."

Halsey grabbed a mug off a rack. "Better hurry up before someone else picks up the scent."

"Who won last night?" On Fiji, Spruance had gone to bed early, with Halsey staying up to play cribbage with Captain Falkenberg, an expert.

"Sonofabitch killed me. He's a damned ringer. That the way you always do business, Ray? With ringers?"

Spruance allowed a little smile.

Halsey leaned over to sniff again. "What kind is it?"

"Kona."

"Ummm. The best." Halsey wiggled his cup.

Just then, the Coronado shuddered in turbulence, Halsey spreading his feet, adapting his fighting cock stance to keep his balance. Putting on a scowl, he knitted his beetle brows, stuck out his barrel chest, and braced a hand to a bulkhead as the plane pitched and bucked. Spruance knew Halsey too well to be alarmed at his fierce expression. The way you gauged Halsey's temper was to check the wrinkles around his eyes. Those tiny little gullies belied a marvelous sense of humor. But without the gullies, one was in trouble.

Halsey had led the carrier group that launched the B-25 raid on Tokyo last April. Then, in May, he contracted a severe case of dermatitis and was hospitalized. From his bed, he recommended to Nimitz that Spruance take his place to face the Japanese at Midway. Nimitz followed the recommendation and put Spruance in charge, where he sank four Japanese top-line carriers while only losing one of his three carriers.

That summer, Halsey recuperated on the mainland, then returned to Pearl Harbor to wait for reassignment. One day, Nimitz invited him as a guest for a medal award ceremony aboard the carrier *Saratoga,* which had just limped in—the victim of a Japanese torpedo. With all hands lined up in ranks at attention on the flight deck, Nimitz stepped up to the microphone. His voice echoed throughout the ship as he said, "Boys, I've got a surprise for you. Bill Halsey's back!" The entire ship's company broke into cheers.

Spruance was there that day, standing two paces behind Nimitz. He could have sworn tears welled in Halsey's eyes while the sailors roared and yelled and threw their hats in the air.

And now, Halsey and Spruance were headed into the South Pacific on an inspection tour. Halsey was slated to take command of Task Force 16, where he would fly his flag in the U.S.S. *Enterprise,* another carrier completing battle-damage repairs in Pearl Harbor. Also aboard the Coronado was Captain Miles Browning, Halsey's chief of staff, a highly capable administrator and *Robert's Rules of Order* wizard, the perfect counterbalance to the flamboyant vice admiral. Also aboard was Major Julian Brown, Halsey's intelligence officer completed the entourage.

The coffee brewer gave a final gurgle and Spruance leaned over to check the sight glass. "Okay." He poured, and Halsey nodded thanks, just as the Coronado jiggled again. But they kept their balance, with not a drop lost. They leaned against the bulkhead and sipped for a moment, lost in thought, two admirals at the opposite end of the personality spectrum. Spruance, a rank junior to Halsey, brilliant, introspective, extremely deep with a piercing, intimidating gaze. Halsey, the archetypical gravel-voiced sailor man, descended from a long lineage of sailor men, some he claimed were pirates. He was a cigarette-smoking man's man with a joke a minute, who immediately imbued one with a feeling of confidence, accomplishment, and dedication.

Halsey sipped and smacked his lips. "Ahhh. Perfect."

"Thanks."

After a moment, Halsey said, "What's been after you, Ray?" The turbulence gone, Halsey took another sip and leaned against the bulkhead.

Spruance checked the passenger compartment. It was still forty-five minutes to Nouméa. The others were just beginning to yawn and stretch. "It shows?"

Halsey shrugged. "To me it does. Maybe I know you too well."

Spruance rarely shared his feelings with anyone except Margaret. Again, he looked both ways. Falkenberg and Rear Admiral William L. Calhoun, Nimitz's service force commander, were awake now and looking out the window, but, perhaps out of respect for the two senior admirals engaged in their impromptu tête-à-tête, had decided not to approach, the coffee's delicious odor notwithstanding. "It's Midway."

"What about it?"

"The rumor mill works overtime. I've heard that people say I wasn't bold. That I should have chased the Japs after we sunk the carriers. That I missed a bet and could have wiped out the whole fleet."

"What?" Halsey was incredulous.

"That's it. Now, does someone know something I don't?"

"Oh, bullshit, Ray." Halsey dropped his voice. "Keep a secret?"

Spruance pulled a face.

"Layton told me the night before we took off that they had just broken the rest of the Jap radio traffic from April and May. It turns out that if you had sailed west, you would have stumbled into the main body of the Jap surface force." Commander Edward Layton was Nimitz's intelligence expert. "It would have been a buzz saw, Ray. They had at least one light carrier attached to that group with fresh fighters just itching to shoot down your bombers, many of which were pretty tired by that time. Right?"

"Right."

"Besides that, there would have been plenty of AA with all their cruisers and destroyers. And then they could have come after you and taken a bite out of your ass. No." Halsey shook his head "It doesn't make sense. Don't you think?"

"That's what went through my mind."

"I wish whoever started that crap would knock it off. I think they're flat jealous of your success." He looked up at Spruance. "So forget it. Right? You did your job. Your orders were to stop the Japs at Midway and that's exactly what you did. And you sank four carriers to boot. What the hell? I put you in the job. It couldn't have turned out any other way."

The stone-faced Spruance allowed one more smile. He admitted to himself it felt good to learn this, especially from Halsey. He made a mental note to ask Layton on his return for details. "Thanks, Bill."

Both looked out the little port, unable to generate small talk. After four days, they were dry. Eventually, Halsey said, "I wonder why Chester wants me in Nouméa instead of Guadalcanal. You can't find out a damn thing by sitting on your ass in Nouméa." He searched Spruance's face.

Spruance held his hands apart, a mock form of surrender. "I have no idea what's on Chester's mind, Bill." He checked his watch. Two-thirty. Another half-hour or so to Nouméa.

The tiny wrinkles crept around Halsey's eyes and he waved his empty coffee mug.

Spruance poured.

CHAPTER THIRTY-ONE

18 OCTOBER, 1942
SERVICE BARGE 212, NASIPIT, MINDANAO
PHILIPPINES

Lieutenant Commander Katsumi Fujimoto and his graying father, Rear Admiral Hayashi Fujimoto, stepped from the officers' mess into a muggy day and strolled on the aft promenade, a deck on the second level reserved for officers. They had just enjoyed a breakfast of eggs, fresh pineapple, and coconut milk. Rich coffee, canned in America, had been served. It had been produced by Warrant Officer Kunisawa, who had been sniffing around the *Stockwell* one day, finding a case in her larder.

Katsumi's father had flown from Del Monte late yesterday afternoon on an inspection tour, having just been reactivated as a rear admiral, or Shōsō. The accoutrements of his office included a twin-engine (Type 99) high-wing Nakajima flying boat, which bobbed at anchor in the middle of the harbor. Its crew had the cowling off the port engine and were doing a routine change of spark plugs.

The humidity, and its threat of rain later on, created a somber tone. Father and son stood silently for a moment, the elder Fujimoto taking in the surrounding mountains and extinct volcanoes, whose rich ash had given birth over millions of years to the lush forests surrounding the little town. It was especially verdant on the harbor's western side, where jungle tumbled down to the water's edge and branches laden with red and orange bougainvillea flowers trailed on the tide.

"Not a bad place to retire." The Shōsō took a deep breath, separating the mixed scent of food frying in coconut oil from charcoal smoke, feces, animals, flowers, dust, urine, chickens, and wet leaves.

"Some have tried." Katsumi pointed east. "Six or so kilometers that way is a pleasant little fishing village called Buenavista. Clear blue water laps within meters of your door—no, excuse me—doorway. Doors aren't necessary. The little wavelets lull you to sleep at night. Coconuts fall on the ground and all you have to do is walk outside and gather them for breakfast.

"A rich gambler, a Portuguese from Macao, settled there, they tell me. He had two concubines."

"Ahhh."

"Eurasians."

The Shōsō allowed his son a smile.

"But then the Moros got him in a raid. Beheaded him."

He took in his father's plain dress blues. Compared to Katsumi's loose working tropical uniform, his father's uniform looked hot and stifling, especially in this sultry weather. But then a Shōsō was a Shōsō. He must look the part. "Today, you are going back to . . . ?"

"Manila. Conference tonight." The Shōsō seemed to be mulling something in his mind. Then he straightened and put his hands behind his back. He nodded and raised his eyebrows to the American destroyer in the floating dry dock just behind them. "When can you flood? They need that back in Manila."

"Five days, no more. I'm shorthanded, but we're just about ready for the bottom painting. And the holes are repaired."

"The plant?"

"Ready to light off. But there is still a lot of topside cleanup and repair. Another two to three weeks, then we'll be ready for sea trials. What I want to do is—"

A canvas-covered truck screeched to a stop. Six soldiers jumped from the back and stood, their rifles poised. An officer climbed from the cab, strode around, shouted into the back, unlocked the tailgate, and stood aside. A heavy-set woman alighted, stretched her arms to the sky, then yelled into the back of the truck.

Unaccountably, the Nasipit docks, usually awash in shipyard sounds, grew silent. On the Service Barge 212, Katsumi and his father heard soft moaning. Soon a figure climbed out. Nine or ten others followed.

The Shōsō nodded. "Women. What the hell, Katsi? Too lazy to go into town and find your own stuff?"

"No. I'm not that bad off. I have a policy. My men use only the cathouses in Butuan. I don't want to stir up the people of Nasipit." He pointed toward Amador's burned-out lumber mill. "Enough has happened here. The truth is, I have so many men working on the destroyer that we don't have enough labor to keep our own quarters clean. So the Kempetai make a little sweep for us once or twice each week. It keeps them entertained and helps us out at the same time. This batch came from Maugahay. Next week, Cabadbaran. The supply is nearly inexhaustible as long as we keep moving from town to town."

"Who's the fat one?"

"Carmen something or other. A mestiza. Knows how to make them work. Scares them more than the Kempetai, so we put her on the payroll."

The Shōsō chuckled as guards prodded the scattered group up the gangway. "You think of having an auction? Of course you could have the pick of the crop."

"Not these dregs."

"Look. There is one down there, slender, taller than the rest. Hot stuff."

"Hmmm."

"How long do you keep them?"

"A few days, maybe a week. Then we send them home with pay and collect a fresh batch."

"You pay in script?"

Katsumi shook his head. "We tried that. It didn't work. Now we pay in food."

Just then, the Shōsō flag lieutenant stepped up and bowed. "The engine is done, Sir. We're ready to take off when you are."

Father and son looked at the sleek Nakajima flying boat. Indeed, its engine cowl was back in place, the crew pulling the anchor to short stay.

"Thank you, Tomo. I'll be just a minute. Please ready the shore boat."

"Sir." Tomo bowed and walked off.

Katsumi was surprised when his father took him gently by the elbow; it had been years since he'd done that. They walked to a corner of the deck, out of earshot.

The Shōsō said in a low voice, "We're trying to assign you to the Solomons. But it's political; Gunichi Mikawa is ambivalent. Since he made vice admiral, he's had an eye on Isoroku's job."

The fact that Mikawa wanted the impossible made Katsumi smile. Isoroku Yamamoto was a *tai-sho*, or admiral of the fleet; and, as the top admiral of the Imperial Japanese Navy, had the added title of Rengo Kantai.

The Shōsō continued, "Mikawa makes a big point of blaming Isoroku for the Midway disaster. Now, if Isoroku fails in the Solomons, Mikawa might be able to do some damage. Maybe even take over. Since I served with Isoroku, they look upon me, and you, with''—he tilted his hand back and forth—''all three of us, really, as, you know, opponents. Doesn't that sound stupid?''

"Frankly, yes. All I want to do is serve my country and fight the enemy. I've trained for this for years."

"And you shall, but we must move carefully. All you have to do is get this ship ready. It's a gift from the Americans. I can assure you that you will have orders as her skipper. Then it's only a matter of where you are assigned." The Shōsō looked at the *Stockwell* and drew an expression of disgust. "Bastard ship and all."

Katsumi felt his chest swell, as if he were floating off the deck. *Vindicated.* His own command again. He actually had to fight for control for a moment. "Thank you, Sir." He almost said *Father.*

The Shōsō gave a short nod and continued. "Ambassador Tatekawa continues to receive good intelligence from the Soviets. Apparently they have a man now in San Francisco who really knows his stuff. I have a packet for you with statistics on their new *Fletcher* class destroyer, just entering the fleet. Apparently, they're not as fast as our destroyers. Designed for thirty-seven knots, they overloaded them, and now all they can do is thirty-two. Even this tub''—he made another face and pointed at the *Stockwell*—"can do . . .'' He raised his eyebrows.

"Thirty-five knots."

"Yes. And our Soviet friend tells us the reliability of their torpedoes is horrible."

"He's right about that."

The Shōsō's eyebrows went up.

"We've been testing them here. At least the Mark 15s, their surface-launched torpedo. The depth-control sensing device is all wrong. It generates a signal that makes the torpedo run three meters deeper than it should."

"Three meters?"

"At least."

"Amazing. It would almost be laughable if we weren't doing our best to kill each other."

Katsumi thought that one over and decided he hadn't lived long enough to properly appreciate the remark. "Yes, Sir."

"Well, by the time your ship is ready, I'll have this political nonsense with Mikawa straightened out. I think that's why Isoroku yanked me out of retirement. To act as a buffer between him and these younger fellows."

"Guess what else the Soviets sent."

"Yes?"

"It came directly from Moscow. Tatekawa to you, so to speak. Isn't it nice to have friends in high places, Katsi?"

Katsumi pursed his lips. This was not the time to talk.

The admiral handed over a pouch. "There's a picture in here from the *San Francisco Chronicle* that shows ships at the Bethlehem Shipbuilding Company. They forgot to censor it. Cruisers, destroyers—all with radar antennae."

"Oh."

"This makes them dangerous. So don't think our torpedoes can do everything."

"Yes, Sir. How long before we get radar?"

"Six months, maybe a year. They're trying an experimental set now on the *Yamato*." The *Yamato* was one of Japan's two super-battle ships of forty-six thousand tons.

The Shōsō rubbed his chin for a moment. "There is something else."

"Yessir?"

"I think you can handle this, for experience has taught me that rage and love make immature people blind. In this regard, I think you are mature."

"What?" Katsumi struggled to keep from sounding impertinent.

"Tatekawa had your best interests in mind when he sent a copy of another article from the *San Francisco Chronicle*. It's a picture of Todd Ingram receiving a medal, the Navy Cross, I believe. Apparently it's the highest honor one can receive in the U.S. Navy. Admiral Spruance is pinning it on him."

Katsumi stiffened. His father was right; rage could make him blind. And for a moment, he wrestled to keep it in check. Later, he would get blind drunk with Kunisawa and wreck something. Maybe a cathouse somewhere, not here. There was one in Davao City that had treated him shabbily; perhaps that's where they would go. "Thank you . . . and thank General Tatekawa for me as well. Please give him my regards." Katsumi bowed.

"Of course." The Shōsō regarded his son for a moment. "Have you thought of a name for your ship?"

"Actually, yes."

"Well, what is it?" It wasn't an order. It was a polite request, as if from a friend.

"Namikaze." Wind on the Waves.

Admiral Hayashi Fujimoto mulled that for a moment. "Good. I like it. *Namikaze.*

"Well"—he took a step back—"watch out for Kunisawa. He drinks like a fish."

"I know. I think I have him under control." Katsumi wasn't about to tell his father about his plans to visit the bordello in Davao City with Kunisawa.

"A good sailor, though."

"The best."

The Shōsō became silent and clasped his hands behind his back.

Since his very youngest days, Fujimoto knew it meant, *We're done for now.* He drew to attention and saluted his father.

While the Shōsō return his son's salute, Lieutenant Tomo whistled to the crew aboard the Nakajima and pumped his fist up and down.

The amphibian's starboard engine began turning and soon coughed into life, belching blue smoke.

Katsumi escorted his father down a companionway to the main deck, where eight side boys, dressed in whites, stood at attention. After another round of salutes, Tomo went first, stepping aboard the shore boat. The Shōsō turned and nodded to his son, "Good day, Captain." Then he stepped down the little ladder and into the shore boat. They cast off and headed for the Nakajima, her anchor up, both engines now comfortably idling.

It had been months since Katsumi felt so good. Back on track! At last! And his father had addressed him as captain in front of his crew. He and Kunisawa would have more than a few glasses of saki tonight.

He headed for the stairway to his quarters. One of his sailors, a leading seaman, shouted in Japanese, "Make way for the captain." Lieutenant Commander Katsumi Fujimoto barely noticed four women, mops and buckets in hand, pressing their backs to the rusty bulkhead as he passed by. His mind hardly registered the one his father had picked out. A black scarf was drawn across her nose and she wore dark wire-framed glasses.

He walked into the wardroom, poured a cup of tea, then strode across the passageway to his stateroom. There he opened the pouch his father had given him. Inside was a large manila envelope, stamped MOST SECRET. Sitting at a small conference table, he ripped it open, letting several documents and photographs tumble out.

A note from his father read, *Dear Katsi. For your eyes only. Keep this in a safe; burn it if necessary.*

With a grunt, Katsumi reached behind and opened the safe beside his desk. It was crammed with books and documents. Some fell out, scattering on the floor, as had happened since he'd been here. Someday, he vowed, he would organize it. In fact, his stateroom looked much like his safe. Books all over the place. Soiled laundry thrown in the corner. Claiming he knew where everything was, Katsumi forbade his orderly, Yawata, from touching the place.

Sipping his tea, he found the specification sheet on the *Fletcher* class destroyer on top. One picture was a glossy eight-by-ten black and white photograph of a *Fletcher* moored to a dock. Sailors scurried over her gangway and around her weatherdecks, carrying boxes and crates that looked like foodstuffs. A bedspring antenna was mounted atop her mast. Amazing, mast tops in other pictures he'd seen had been airbrushed out, showing a mast sticking ridiculously in the air, supporting nothing. He grabbed a loupe from his desk and bent over to study the picture in minute detail. "Mmmm. Graceful, yet compact, utilitarian. She doesn't look that heavy," he mused, sitting back for a moment, taking in the whole ship. He decided he liked her lines.

Someone knocked. "Commander?" It was Yawata.

Katsumi Fujimoto moved the loupe around the picture and settled on the torpedo tubes. Quintuplets, a bank of five. Hmmm. "Come," he muttered.

Yawata walked in, a stout woman just behind, looking over his shoulder.

"Sir, the cleaning woman. Is it all right if she comes in now to tidy up and collect your laundry?"

"All right." Fujimoto leaned back to the safe and drew the manual on Mark 15 torpedo maintenance. Then he looked through his loupe again at the *Fletcher* class destroyer. There were two quintuplet banks of torpedoes. Not just one. He shook his head. Too bad the Americans' torpedoes were so lousy. Too bad. And he couldn't find any provision for reload.

He found something else. There was another bedspring device atop the main battery fire-control director. That meant they could direct five-inch gunfire onto a target with great accuracy. Even at night!

A roar of the Nakajima's engines announced the Shōsō's takeoff. For some reason, the sound made him feel good. Secure. His father would be in Manila for a while, close by if he needed him, yet far enough away not to cause trouble.

The engines faded to the north and another noise filled the room. A bucket clanked and water slopped back and forth. Fujimoto turned, finding Yawata gone. Across the room was the tall woman his father had noticed. She was making his bed, her back turned to him. Not bad. Her figure showed well through her dirty clothes, damp now from the humidity. A black scarf was pulled over her head and her dress was an ankle-length floral pattern that had been washed far too many times. She wore those strange glasses and a card was pinned to the front of her shawl.

"Yawata?" he snapped.

The door opened and his orderly stepped in. "Sir?"

Fujimoto gestured to the woman with the back of his hand. "This woman. She's odd. And the glasses. What is this?"

"She should be all right, Sir."

"What do you mean, all right?"

"She's a leper. Minor case. In remission, they say. Her face is scarred."

Fujimoto stood quickly. "What? Is she contagious?"

"No, Sir. Shall I get another woman?"

Fujimoto rubbed his chin. "No, no. I'll get out and move to the wardroom, so she can finish in peace."

"Very good, Sir."

The heavyset woman stood in the doorway. Yawata muttered at her, pushed her back, and closed the door.

Fujimoto began to gather the pictures. As he did, he found something else: another *San Francisco Chronicle* article and photograph. A little note was clipped to it from his father. *Katsi. Something else the Soviets sent along. After much hesitation, I give this to you. You are entitled to see this.*

Fujimoto studied it for a moment then moaned, "Aaaaiiiiyah!" He stood and slammed his fist on the table.

"Aaaaiiiiyah!" Fujimoto screamed again. His breath came in great gulps, and he hardly noticed the woman pressed against the wall, her hand over her mouth, her eyebrows above her glasses.

"Aaaaiiiiyah!" Fujimoto yelled again, slamming a fist and then throwing the papers across the room. ·

Yawata burst in the room. "Sir? What—?"

Kunisawa surged in right behind. "Katsi. Are you all right?"

Fujimoto stood breathing heavily for a moment, then stiffly walked from his room out on deck, grasping the railing. Yawata and Kunisawa followed.

"Katsi," Kunisawa pleaded, "what the hell is it?"

Helen's heart thumped loudly in her chest. Their voices faded as that crazy Jap commander walked down the deck, still moaning. She stood on tiptoes, pressing herself into the wooden bulkhead, desperately trying to become part of it.

Carmen dashed in. "What the hell did you do?"

Helen could only shake her head and spread her hands.

"Work, damn you!"

Helen nodded and bent to make the bed, a pilot berth style with high sideboard. Carmen watched for a moment, then walked out. Books and papers were piled at the bed's foot and she picked them up and put them on the side table.

What happened? What made him so crazy?

She looked around, seeing the room in disarray. There. The safe was open. Papers spilling on the floor. Papers scattered on the table, too. She looked around, realizing what had just fallen in her lap. *My God. I've only been aboard five minutes.* That open safe, all the secret stuff lying around. But what? She walked over to the safe and looked at what was on floor. *They're all in Japanese.* She leaned over for a closer look.

Bingo! There it was. The manual she'd seen in the torpedo shop. Written in Japanese with the Arabic character: 93. The one Otis wanted. She picked it up. *How do I get it out of here?* She tried to stuff it in her dress, but it looked too bulky. The bucket! She could wrap it in wax paper and drop it in the bucket. No. She didn't have wax paper.

There! In the safe was a waterproof pouch. Quickly, she unzipped it and stuffed the manual inside. Her hands shook as she rezipped it. As she walked toward the bucket, something caught her eye on the table. Pictures. An article from the *San Francisco Chronicle.*

"My God!" It escaped her lips in English and she didn't even realize it. Quickly she looked around. The Japanese were still outside. Her eyes snapped back to what was in her hand—the clipping was dated last August. Two men were in the picture. The caption identified one as Admiral Raymond A. Spruance as he pinned the Navy Cross on the chest of Lieutenant Todd Ingram, his name underlined in red.

He looks wonderful.

Carmen walked in, seeing the clipping in Helen's hands. "Put away, bitch." She pointed. "Hapons ona way back."

Carmen was right. The voices grew louder as they returned, the captain now laughing, sounding nonchalant.

Carmen raged, "Hurry!"

Helen gritted her teeth. "Do something. Delay them!" She dropped the article on the table and rushed toward the other side of the room before she could be seen.

Even as Helen spoke, a Japanese's shadow fell through the doorway and across the floor. With perspiration beading on her brow, Carmen backed into the doorway, effectively blocking it, and began shouting at Helen in Tagalog.

The bucket! The damned bucket was right next to the man's shadow, which meant he would see her if she dropped the waterproof pouch in it.

Her heart beat faster as her gaze swept around the room in panic. *Do something. Here I am with a top secret document in hand and some Jap gunsel standing just outside the room.*

She stepped close to the bed as the voices drew close, all laughing.

Carmen interrupted her inner tirade. "Damn, you!" she hissed.

Someone barked at her in pidgin Tagalog. She turned to Helen and said under her breath, "They want us otta here, honey."

Quickly, Helen lifted a corner of the mattress, threw the waterproof pouch underneath, and then dropped it into place. She was smoothing the pillow as the three Japanese clomped in, ignoring her. Then she bowed and backed out of the room.

CHAPTER THIRTY-TWO

18 OCTOBER, 1942
U.S.S. *HOWELL* (DD 482)
NOUMÉA, NEW CALEDONIA

DeWitt held out his cup and saucer.

Ingram poured.

"For Navy coffee, this stuff isn't bad." DeWitt stirred in sugar, condensed milk, and slurped. They had just returned to the *Howell*'s wardroom after a tour, where Ingram had shown DeWitt the nearly repaired mount fifty-three and its quilt of welding patches over fragment holes.

Ingram peeked out the porthole. "Looks like the overcast has burned off. Let's go outside and grab some fresh air. We can watch for your boss." General Sutherland was once again aboard the *Argonne*, conferring with Admiral Ghormley. He was due any moment to pick up DeWitt, then go on to meet Rear Admiral Kelly Turner aboard his flagship the *McCawley,* anchored just two hundred yards away.

Ingram opened the hatch and they walked out onto the main deck, to find the wind had shifted from southwest to northwest. Sipping their coffee in the shadow of mount fifty-two, they watched the myriad of cruisers, destroyers, attack transports, ammunition ships, cargo ships, tankers, repair ships, all swinging at anchor in the overstuffed harbor. The *Howell* was jammed among anchored ammunition ships, the *McCawley,* and a long waterway lined with buoys used for seaplane takeoffs and landings. As they watched, a matte-black PBY lunged into her takeoff run, engines growling, white vaporous mist spewing under her wing and horizontal tail. She bounced as she climbed on the step, poised for the moment when she could work herself free.

The PBY rose off the water and eventually shrunk to a dot.

DeWitt pulled out one of his Lucky Strikes, lit it, and took a long puff. "There's news." He squinted in the distance, bracing a foot on a bit, ever the crag-faced Texas Ranger, the Lucky hanging from the corner of his mouth.

Ingram was still tracking the PBY. "Um."

"I shouldn't be telling you this, but Helen's coming home."

"Damn!" Ingram jiggled his cup and saucer. He quickly stepped back just before two drops splattered where his shoes had been.

DeWitt offered an uncharacteristic grin. "We ordered in a submarine, the *Needlefish,* to pick her up next week. They're also bringing out a party of Fil-American women and children."

Ingram looked at DeWitt for a long moment. Then he ran a hand over his face. God! If he could only call Helen's folks. No matter. But wouldn't they be surprised? To make sure, he looked at the deck to check that he wasn't floating two feet above.

"Todd?"

"When do they arrive?"

DeWitt shrugged. "If all goes well, Brisbane around the end of the month."

Ingram turned away. "How is Amador? Did he say anything else?"

"No. It sounded like he was in a hurry. The Japs have a D/F truck running around, so his transmissions are sparse."

Amador, the old man with his mane of silver hair and his legends of Corregidor. He wished he could see him and thank him for taking care of Helen.

"Todd? Todd? How do you feel?"

Like I'm alive, you stupid jackass. Like a block of cement has been lifted from my chest. Like I'm home. Like I have something to live for.

"Todd?"

"I'm fine, Otis."

DeWitt took another drag and clapped him on the shoulder. "You're one lucky sonofabitch. You know that?"

"Yes, I know that."

"Not a word to anybody."

"Okay."

"If General Sutherland knew I told you, he'd crucify me."

"Not a word."

"And remember. Some of these rendezvous don't go as scheduled. There may be changes, so keep that in mind."

"Okay."

"But I wanted you to know."

"Okay."

They watched the harbor in silence for a few moments until DeWitt nodded toward an admiral's barge. It ducked around a tanker and headed right at them. Unlike a barge or a scow, this forty-foot launch had handsome lines, a square transom, and two gleaming brass stars mounted at her bow. Her freeboard was a dark blue and she had two white deckhouses, a large one forward and a smaller, more intimate one aft. Freshly shined brass, chrome, and stainless steel glittered throughout. Two crew stood at parade rest behind the coxswain, all three wearing freshly starched whites. "Here comes my boss."

They stepped into the wardroom, put down their coffee cups, and grabbed their hats. Returning to the main deck, they walked aft, then to the quarterdeck. Just then, a PB2Y Coronado flew over at five hundred feet on a downwind leg. With a wing up, she turned onto her final approach. Moments later, she glided past, her four R-1830 engines softly backfiring as her pilot cut the throttles and eased her to the water. At first her wake spewed delicately when she touched, almost as if a feather had glazed the water. Soon she settled, spray and foam announcing her arrival. The giant seaplane slowed, then turned and taxied to a buoy two hundred yards abeam of the *Howell*.

DeWitt said, "Do me a favor?"

"Sure." Ingram nodded.

"I want you to clam up. Don't say anything more about the torpedoes just now."

"Otis, the damn things are at the bottom of Tulagi Harbor for anyone to see."

"Consider it a favor to me."

The admiral's barge swooped in, her coxswain backing down with a flourish and stopping precisely beneath a metal ladder hanging over the *Howell*'s side. Sutherland stepped out of the little cabin and looked up to Ingram, his hands on his hips. "Could you join us for a moment, Lieutenant?"

What the hell did I do? "Yes, Sir." He turned to Jack Wilson, OOD on the afternoon watch. "I'll be off the ship for a few minutes." After salutes, he turned and climbed down to the barge, with DeWitt following. Ingram saluted again. "Good afternoon, General."

"So nice to see you again, Lieutenant." Sutherland shook Ingram's hand, then waved to a padded velvet seat. At the same time he nodded to the coxswain. The engine roared and the barge shoved off. Sutherland gave a bit of a smile. "Don't worry, Lieutenant. I'm just borrowing you for a moment. Besides, you'll be able to say hello to your mentor."

Ingram looked at a shrugging DeWitt, then back to Sutherland.

Sutherland said, "Admiral Spruance is aboard that plane. This is Kelly Turner's barge and we're taking him over to the *McCawley*. I need a moment alone with him before we get there.

"I see," said Ingram, who didn't understand anything at all.

The Coronado's engines wheezed to a stop as her crew snagged a buoy from the forward hatch and rigged a diprope. Just then, another brightly adorned admiral's barge, this one with three stars at her bow, roared up and fell in behind, bouncing in their stern wake.

"Looks like a parade," Sutherland grunted, then sat back and folded his arms. "Tell us again, Lieutenant, what you saw in Tulagi Harbor."

DeWitt sat beside Ingram to hear better over the engine's growl.

Taking a deep breath, Ingram described the sunken Japanese destroyer, the torpedoes on the bottom, and his visit with Toliver aboard the *Zeilin*.

As he spoke, Sutherland and DeWitt exchanged glances. When Ingram finished, Sutherland sat back and stroked his chin. "Lieutenant. Do you realize that this is very sensitive information?"

"Well, Sir, Otis . . . Colonel DeWitt just told me not to say anything to anyone about it."

At DeWitt's nod, Sutherland said, "Good. Very good. Now. Otis, is Lieutenant Ingram aware of what the Commie told you?"

DeWitt turned to Ingram. "Todd. Have you ever been with that Soviet naval attaché Eduard Dezhnev at any time when I wasn't there?"

The staccato manner in which DeWitt phrased the question meant he once again suffered from his brown-nose syndrome. But Ingram wasn't going to call him *Sir* after dragging him two thousand miles though the Philippine Archipelago. "No."

"Did Ollie have any contact?" DeWitt asked.

"Not that I know of."

Once again Sutherland and DeWitt exchanged glances. DeWitt said, "What about—"

Suddenly the admiral's barge following them swung out to port and, with a roar of its engine, passed by, leaving Sutherland's barge to bounce in a choppy wake and exhaust fumes.

"What the—" Sutherland sputtered as they hit a wavelet, water spraying over the boat. "Just a damned ensign in there. I am going to have his ass." He stood and bellowed, "Driver. Pull in alongside that boat."

But the other barge got to the Coronado first and had stopped under the flying boat's aft hatch by the time Sutherland's boat caught up.

Sutherland, Ingram, and DeWitt stood as the coxswain slowed to ease alongside the other barge. Soon, mooring lines were secured and the engine was turned off. The only sound was of thumping inside the Coronado, and little wavelets slapping the amphibian's hull.

"Ensign," Sutherland called.

The ensign turned to Sutherland, his voice plaintive. "One moment, Sir, please. I'm under orders." It was the same young officer that kept delivering messages to Ghormley last Friday at the conference. He wore a .45 and under his arm was a small leather briefcase. Then he turned his back on Sutherland and hailed someone in the Coronado.

"Ensign, look at me goddamnit!" sputtered Sutherland. "Get away from there before I throw you in the stockade."

The ensign gave Sutherland a nervous look. "Sorry, Sir. I'm under orders from Vice Admiral Ghormley."

"What?" yelled Sutherland. "Get that—"

Just then, a large, olive-drab B-4 bag flew out of the hatch and fell into the boat. Then another; each bag had three gold stars stenciled on both sides. Quickly following was a short, stocky admiral who had one of the most familiar faces in the Pacific Fleet. "Bill," exclaimed Sutherland, "what the hell are you doing out here?"

Several other men jumped in the boat. Ingram recognized Admiral Spruance and Captain Falkenberg among them. In fact, Spruance caught his eye and gave a quick nod.

Halsey looked to Sutherland and held up a hand. "Hi, Dick, be right with you." He turned to the ensign. "Okay, son. What's so important that I have to read right here?"

The ensign reached in his leather briefcase and drew an envelope. "My orders are to deliver this personally to you, Sir."

"All right. Thank you." Halsey took the envelope, then, with a look at the officers around him, ripped it open and sat against the gunwale to read.

For a moment it was quiet as the boats bucked gently together, in the mid-afternoon wind waves. Halsey's eyes popped wide open. His jaw fell, and he braced a hand on the boat. "Jesus Christ and General Jackson. This is the hottest potato they ever handed me." Halsey paced for a moment, then put a palm to his forehead. "Ray?"

Spruance moved close.

Halsey handed Spruance the message. "You know anything about this?

Spruance read it then handed it back. "I'm in the dark, Bill."

"Okay." Halsey turned. There were no little gullies around Halsey's eyes as he called across to Sutherland in the other boat. "Dick, is that Kelly Turner's barge?"

"Yes, Sir."

Ingram didn't miss the *Sir.*

"Very well. Ray, you and Bill and Maynard head over to the *Wacky Mac* and get settled with Kelly. I better head over to the *Argonne* to see Bob and get all this straightened out. My God. Can you believe it?"

Spruance extended a hand. "Congratulations." They shook.

"Here." Halsey passed the message around. After reading it, Browning and Brown broke into broad smiles. "Congratulations, Admiral."

Spruance's, Calhoun's and Falkenberg's gear was tossed in Sutherland's barge, and all three stepped aboard. Sutherland moved up and shook Spruance's hand. "Good to see you again, Ray. What the hell happened?"

"I'm not sure if I can—"

Halsey shouted from his boat, "You might as well see this, too, Dick." He handed the message across to Sutherland.

Like Halsey, Sutherland leaned against the gunwale to read. "My God." He read it again, then handed it to DeWitt.

Ingram leaned over DeWitt's shoulder to see a radio flimsy marked:

TOP SECRET:

IMMEDIATELY UPON YOUR ARRIVAL AT NOUMEA, YOU WILL RELIEVE VICE ADMIRAL ROBERT L. GHORMLEY FOR THE DUTIES OF COMMANDER SOUTH PACIFIC AND SOUTH PACIFIC FORCE.

NIMITZ

Sutherland shook his head for a moment, then sighed. "I guess he's as good at running a withdrawal as anybody else."

"Dick, Bill's middle initial is 'F,'" Spruance said. That means full speed ahead."

CHAPTER THIRTY-THREE

20 OCTOBER, 1942
U.S.S. *HOWELL* (DD 482)
NOUMÉA, NEW CALEDONIA

"Uh." Ingram sat up in bed, startled by his own voice. For a moment his mind whirled with images of explosions and torn bodies fading in and out. Fumbling, he clicked on his reading light. The little wind-up alarm clock read two-thirty-five. It was hot, humid, and, in spite of the fan's buzzing, he sweated, his top sheet in a rumpled heap on the deck. He ran a hand through his hair, finding his scalp drenched in sweat as well as his tee shirt and shorts. Leaning back for a moment, he was thankful that, as executive officer, he rated his own stateroom where no roommate would hear his moans.

He needed sleep, yet here he was, staring at the deck. They were getting under way tomorrow to join Task Force 61 under Rear Admiral Thomas C. Kinkaid. No more convoy duty. No more chasing the Japanese up the Slot. This time they would be screening the carrier *Enterprise*. It would be hard steaming, day and night, dashing among other destroyers at thirty knots, where sometimes the relative speeds achieved sixty knots, the tactical situation changing with mind-numbing rapidity.

"Damn." Ingram stood and walked to the small stainless steel basin, drew water, and rinsed his face and scalp. Now he remembered what had made him awaken. Before the explosions, he'd been dreaming of avocados and . . . Helen. Yes. She seemed so vivid, he even heard her voice . . . or was it her mother's voice? No. It was Helen. He could almost touch her smooth, fine, ebony hair; look into her quick brown eyes that missed nothing; see her smile when she laughed at everything, with everyone.

He wished he'd had a picture; he'd almost asked her parents when he'd visited last August. On the living room bookcase, he'd seen a picture of Helen and another of her brother, a B-17 jockey outfitted in Army Air Corps uniform, his peaked hat with the fifty-mission crush. Helen looked as beautiful as her brother looked proud. Yet there was something more in her photograph: confidence, her lovely face looking to the future, smiling.

All he had to do was close his eyes and there she was, the same as the picture, looking as good as she did that last night in Nasipit. He'd held her in his arms; he'd kissed her for the first time, an enormous release after the horror of Corregidor, where they'd been too afraid, too hungry, too tired to reach for one another. But that last night, the night they blew up Amador's lumber mill, they'd held one another, giving themselves all they had.

Avocados, hell. They were pineapples; he'd been dreaming of the Philippines. Helen in the Philippines. Helen, Damnit. He'd been so afraid to think of her. Until now. My God, safe in Brisbane. He looked at his desk calendar; she'd be there by a week from Saturday. *How the hell can I get to Brisbane? No. No. She won't be there long. Like me, they'll feed her, clothe her, and send her stateside.* He closed his eyes and opened them again, but they were moist and he blinked it away. *Helen.*

"Okay." He stood, slipped on a pair of trousers and sandals, walked out of his stateroom, and took the companionway ladder up to the main deck and the wardroom. The red, darken-ship lights were on, giving everything a ghostly cast. But the stewards had left coffee on the burner. Yawning, he reached for a cup and saucer and poured.

"Todd."

He turned, finding Landa sitting alone at the table's head, the place where the ship's captain always sat. Like himself, Landa wore a tee shirt, khaki trousers, and sandals.

"Evening, Skipper." Ingram took his cup and sat to Landa's right, the place where the executive officer sat during meals. *When worried or scared,* he realized, *we reach for the familiar, the accepted. We rub our rabbit's feet or hang our lucky charm around our neck or take our assigned places at the table. If not, the chain will be broken, decorum interrupted, causing that sonofabitch in the black robe to swing his scythe and send you into blackness.*

"Couldn't sleep, huh?" said Landa.

"No." Landa's breath nearly knocked Ingram over. They'd been ashore at the officer's club, the old Hotel Pacifique, with Landa slugging down beers after dinner with Rocko and two other destroyer skippers. He'd had a snootful and now, he looked strange in the red darken-ship lights. His eyes were black pencil points, his white teeth crimson-washed and large and straight, looking as if he'd just ripped the living flesh off a fallen zebra.

A shadow appeared at the doorway and knocked twice.

Landa's eyes crossed for a moment. "Come."

It was Monaghan, the dark, curly-haired pharmacist's mate. He walked in and pulled off his hat. "You called, Sir?"

Landa sat straight up. "What do you have to make a man sleep around here?"

Monaghan stared at Landa's coffee cup. "Uh, well, Sir, I could recommend—"

"How 'bout something for a straight hangover?"

"I'd say you're doing fine, Sir." Monaghan ran the rim of his hat through his hands.

"On second thought, I need something for sleep."

"Yes, Sir. Well, we have—"

"Never mind. Just go get it." Landa waved the back of his hand.

"Yes, Sir." Monaghan turned and walked out.

Ingram sat back and stared.

"What's wrong?"

"I'd ask the same of you. Why did you jump on him?" Asked Ingram.

"Have you looked at his record?"

"Yes."

"Rumors all over the fleet. He's a playboy. A Don Juan. Doesn't know his ass from a tongue depressor."

"He's only been aboard three weeks."

"Well, you tell me. Is it true he was kicked out of medical school?"

"Looks like it."

"Get rid of him."

"What?"

"We should have a doctor on board, an MD. Instead we have a drunken playboy who runs around knocking up professors' daughters. Get rid of the sonofabitch." Landa's gaze was steady. "Our luck can't hold out too long. Someday we're going to really get mauled by the Japs and I want the best in sick bay, damnit. Not some screw-off artist who thinks with his pecker."

"Jerry. He was a third-year medical student who made a stupid mistake. We haven't even—"

"Get rid of him."

Ingram sipped his coffee.

"First chance you have, get rid of him."

"Yes, Sir."

Landa looked at his cup and stirred for a moment. "You know your trouble, Todd?"

Booze or no booze, Landa was in one of his moods. Ingram stirred his coffee and raised his eyebrows.

"You're too serious. And this isn't the bottle talking. I mean this as a friend." Landa gave a short smile.

"Skipper, you don't—"

"No. I know you had a shitty time at Corregidor. But life isn't fair. Some go free while others get stuck. And you got stuck. From what I hear, you earned your Navy Cross a hundred times over."

"I was just doing a job."

Landa leaned back in his chair and grinned. "Ah-ha! My brother-in-law, Jake, is a psychiatrist. You know what he would call that?"

"I don't follow you."

"What you just said. 'I was just doing a job.' Jake would say that's deflecting a compliment. It makes the other person, who offered the compliment, feel like a pile of shit. Instead, why don't you just say thanks? Then that takes you off the detached higher plane of being the all-encompassing horseshit hero of Corregidor."

"I sound like that?"

Landa slurped coffee.

Ingram looked around the wardroom, usually so full of life and purpose. Now everyone was asleep below or at least tossing and turning. He ran a hand over his face, then checked in the passageway to make sure no one was there. "Skipper, I don't know how to tell you this, but I didn't want that damned Navy Cross. Spruance insisted."

Landa looked up, listening.

"He wants combat veterans on the line and is dumping people who, for one reason or another cave in under fire. And apparently there have been a lot of those, especially senior officers.

"Sooo"—Ingram steepled his fingers—"instead of the six months stateside they promised, they shipped me back here."

"Todd, I know—"

"Please let me finish."

"Okay."

"I have to tell you, I'm so damned scared. My stomach is tied in a knot half the time and I feel like puking. Sometimes I do. I dream, and the worst part is the damn dreams are coming true."

"We're all scared, Todd."

"I know, I know. And we deal with it in different ways. A doc gave me a bunch of belladonna."

"And?"

"It helps, and I sleep better. But I dream . . . and that . . ."

"I wish I knew how to help. I guess we all have our private piece of hell.

Yeah, you're right. When we got the word you were Al Stoner's replacement, we cheered. Al was a good exec, but you were billed as a hotshot hero to us; the greatest thing since Fibber McGee and Molly. We couldn't wait to have you aboard.''

"Sorry."

"No. I have no complaints. You're doing fine. I just hope that the belladonna won't turn you into a cross-eyed idiot."

"I'm trying to get off the stuff."

"Good. Now let me give it to you straight. I just signed your fitness report, and I recommended you for advancement to command."

"Thanks, Skipper."

Landa raised a hand. "I imagine you'll be tapped to command your own destroyer in the next six months. They're cranking out these ships like tenpins, and they'll need hotshots like you to jockey them.

"So here's how to be a good skipper. Landa's psycho service, free of charge." Landa gave a soft belch, then continued, "Rule one: Be accessible. Your door is always open."

"Right."

"Rule two: Always remember, the captain's job is the loneliest in the world."

"Okay."

"Rule three. Give of yourself, Captain. For if you don't, you'll have a bunch of prima donnas running around, usurping your authority, screwing things up."

"Okay."

"Remember, on your ship, there's only one prima donna, and that's you." Landa stood, refilled his cup, and sat again. "However, when you achieve your own command and step into the roll of 'Boom Boom Ingram,' you must not allow others to believe that you are my protégé, that you are cast in my mold."

" 'Boom Boom' Ingram." He tried the phrase experimentally.

"I hope you like it better than I do."

Ingram looked up, surprised. "Uh, I thought you sort of liked that name."

"Not really."

"Well, then, how'd you get it?"

"I don't really know. People just started calling me that." Landa spread his hands in supplication.

"I'll be damned. Well, I'll pass the word for people not to refer to you as 'Boom Boom' anymore."

"Thanks. Just like Bull Halsey." It was well known that the vice admiral did not like to be addressed as "Bull," even in jest.

"Yes, Sir." Ingram took a deep breath. "You said something about me being your protégé?"

"Actually, a serious miscalculation. Let me put it to you this way. How can a hot-rod destroyer captain attain senior rank and follow a glorious future in this man's Navy when he boasts in an open meeting before his immediate supervisor, the squadron commander, along with various and sundry peers and flag-ranked officers, that he won a farting contest in college?''

Ingram chuckled. "On the *Argonne*? That was great.''

"That's the ship, all right." Landa waved an index finger in the air. "That marvelous ship, which is irrevocably stuck high and dry on coffee grounds, while her staff sits on their dead asses nine hundred miles behind enemy lines wringing their hands and figuring out ingenuous ways to load us out with faulty torpedoes to fight against an enemy that outnumbers us two to one.

"I thought the farting contest was funny. Others thought so, too, even Rocko. It broke the ice.''

"I know. Rocko slapped me on the back and let it slide." Landa shook his head. "We're opposites. I'm too loose, out of control sometimes. But I'll tell you. I can't stand pretense. Arrogance, either.'' He threw his hands in the air. "I'm sorry. I just lose patience. And you can't to fight a war with people like that. Especially when it's all wrapped up into one person''—Landa jabbed a thumb toward the *Argonne*—"like that bastard Jessup. That makes me boil. I'll tell you. Life is too short, as we discovered at Cape Esperance.''

"I know.''

"Yeah, I guess you do. But when that goldbricking Jessup started giving me crap about being late, I saw red.''

"I tried to stop you.''

"I know. I know. And I shot my mouth off. That guy's part of the establishment. And when he's ready, he'll drop me like a hot turd.''

"I don't know, Skipper. It's a big Navy, now. Guys like him get swallowed up. Especially now that Halsey's here.'' From shooting pistols in the air to firing pack-howitzers, GIs from Espiritu Santo to Guadalcanal celebrated for hours when it was announced Halsey was in command.

Landa squeezed his eyes closed for a moment. "Yeah, except guess where Jessup is going now that Ghormley has been relieved?''

"Home?''

Landa looked in the distance for a moment, then stifled another belch with a clenched fist. "I take it back. I have had too much to drink. Have to be a good boy for tomorrow.'' He raised his cup and drained his coffee. "Did you know that Jessup's not Ghormley's chief of staff?''

"No. I didn't.''

"Rocko says he's on Ernie King's staff. They sent him out on a fact-finding mission. But really, he was a CinC spy who is now going back to Washington, D.C., where he can resume duties counting rings in the Pentagon.''

"Wonderful.''

"I pissed off the wrong man, Todd. I embarrassed Jessup in front of a three-star admiral. So Jessup will never forget what I did.'' After a pause, Landa said, "The irony is, I never won a farting contest. I just wanted to shut that arrogant sonofabitch up.''

Ingram looked up. "You're kidding.''

"It's true. I just wanted to say something bizarre. And now"—he sighed and flicked his coffee cup with the back of his hand—"I've probably blown my career."

"Does Rocko know?"

"Yeah. And so does Jessup."

"Oh-oh."

"So I'm going to need you as backup when they fire me."

"Never happen."

"Thanks for your vote of confidence." Landa exhaled loudly. "Tired," he muttered. "Now. To return to your fitness for command. All you need is to be promoted to lieutenant commander. I wonder why you haven't made it. Have you followed in my footsteps and crapped on somebody's doorstep lately?"

"Just Tojo's."

That drew a smile from Landa. He stood. "Corregidor is over, Todd. So is Esperance. Forget the past and get on with the living. Smile. Talk to people. Okay?" He stuck out his hand.

They shook. "Thanks, Skipper."

"How's that girl of yours, Audrey?"

"That's Luther's fiancée."

"Damnit . . ."

"Helen is her name."

"Oh."

"Actually, I've had a stroke of luck. She was on the run from the Japs on Mindanao. But Otis just told me the *Needlefish* will pick her up with some others. She's due in Brisbane in a week to ten days."

"My God. I didn't know."

"Yeah, but it's a secret. Otis would kill me if he knew I told you."

"Don't worry. Mum's the word. Met her at Corregidor? That's fantastic."

"Yeah." Ingram grinned.

Landa yawned, his breath less offensive. "I'm glad. Okay. Off to the sack. You, too. Big day tomorrow playing hot rod."

"I'm going to take a turn on deck for a moment."

"Right. Good night." Landa yawned and looked back. "You know?"

"Sir?"

"You look like Spruance. I've met him a couple of times."

"So I've discovered."

"You look like him. And you're just about as intense. Take it easy. Or you'll never make lieutenant commander." Landa walked out.

"Yes, Sir."

Fifteen minutes later, Ingram was back in his stateroom. It had been crystal clear outside, the Southern Cross so bright, one could reach out and grab it. From habit, he snapped on his desk lamp and started to empty his pockets.

Something was on his desk. He picked it up, finding an ALNAV radio message, a long one.

Ingram was thirty-sixth on a list. The entry said, *for promotion to lieutenant commander, approved, effective this date: Ingram, Alton C., 638217, USN.*

It had been date/time-stamped in the *Howell*'s radio room a little over two hours ago, then routed directly to the captain. Yes, Landa had scribbled his initials in the little box, and that meant he knew of the promotion before their talk tonight. And then Landa must have brought it down when Ingram was on deck.

He smiled. Sneaky. That's called getting chewed out at the same time you're being patted on the head.

A handwritten note was attached:

Todd

Congratulations, these were mine, my cleanest pair. The others are all green. Now that you have a pay raise, you owe me a few beers. And soon you'll be ready for your own command. Who knows? Some day, maybe someone will call you "Boom Boom" Ingram. God, I hate that name. Good luck.

Jerry

A little felt-covered box sat off to one side of his desk. He snapped it open, finding a pair of gold oak-leaf devices of a lieutenant commander gleaming in the pale light. He pinned them on his khaki collar, in a way feeling sad that Rita Hayworth wasn't around to do it for him. But as he lay on his bunk and clicked off his light, he remembered what Rita had asked him that night in the Pope Suite: "Got a sweetheart?"

You bet, Rita.

CHAPTER THIRTY-FOUR

20 OCTOBER, 1942
SERVICE BARGE 212, NASIPIT, MINDANAO
PHILIPPINES

Helen rose in her bunk, hearing steady rain thump on the roof. A few snored, the rest slept the stone-frozen sleep of the dead; except Mercado Colombo, a young mother of four, who whimpered in her sleep, as she had every night. Helen eased to the floor. Enough light leaked through the portholes to guide her across the bunkroom where Carmen Lai Lai slept in a tentlike arrangement, complete with double mattress, blankets, sheets, pillows, and bedside table.

The tent flap barely rustled as Helen crawled in and knelt by Carmen's bed. Helen opened her mouth to whisper. Instead, she was shocked with the cold muzzle of a Nambu resting against her temple. "Whatchu doin', honey?"

Helen tried to speak, but she couldn't; her heart detonated in her chest.

Carmen sat up and whispered, "Spit it out or I give you to the Hapons and take my chances with Felipe later."

Helen found some breath to push over her vocal chords. "I . . . have . . ."

"What?" The muzzle pressed harder.

"I have to get back into the captain's cabin."

Carmen shook her head in the dark. "The captain no like you disease, honey. You go home."

"What?"

"Last night. Yawata told me."

Yawata. The captain's orderly. The young boy had leered at her as she scrubbed the captain's stateroom and bathroom. Once, while she was on the foredeck waiting for torpedo practice to finish, he had brushed against her.

It hit her. Home! If they sent her home, there would be no chance to get the pouch. Helen bowed her head for a moment, desperately thinking.

"Outta here, bitch." The muzzle tapped her on the nose.

Only one trump card now. She had to play it. "I . . . I heard the Japs killed your father."

"Bastard!" Carmen smacked the pistol across Helen's temple.

"What?" Helen blinked her eyes. It took a moment to realize she was on the floor. And on her back. Carmen sat on her chest, shoving the pistol barrel in Helen's mouth.

"Where you hear?"

Helen gurgled.

Carmen pulled the pistol from Helen's mouth and backhanded her. "Where?"

Unaccountably, Helen realized there was no snoring. They were all awake now. And listening. "The Japs!" she yelled, wiping a trickle of blood from the corner of her mouth. "That lieutenant. Jimbo. He brags about it. I thought you knew." It was true. Helen and some of the other women had seen Jimbo making great sword-chopping motions each time Carmen walked nearby. And he would mutter in pidgin English, "How can we trust her? Better off dead like her father." After a while, Helen pieced together that Carmen's father had been blowing up bridges at night while custom-tailoring uniforms for the Japanese by day.

Carmen slapped her again. "He's lying!"

Young Mercado Colombo wept openly now, her chest heaving with great, racking sobs. Then another joined in. Then another.

With amazing alacrity, Carmen jumped to her feet. Waving the pistol in the air, she yelled into the room, "Alla you. Shut up!" She repeated it in Tagalog.

The door creaked open. In the shadows a guard popped his head in as Carmen crouched behind her tent flap. Then another looked in. The room became silent as they peered inside. One laughed and spoke to the other, their thoughts obvious as they closed the door.

Carmen went to her bed and sat. Giving a long sigh, she said, "Go to sleep."

"I have to get in there."

"What for? That damned bag?" Carmen shoved the Nambu under the pillow and leaned close. Her eyes were slits and her tongue flicked over her lips. "Look. I get it for you. How much you pay me?"

"It has to be me. I know what I'm looking for."

"Let me help you out, honey." Carmen laid a hand on Helen's forearm, her voice changing from a one hundred to a six hundred grit.

"Please. I'm the one who has to get in there. I'll see that you're well paid."

Carmen lay back and pulled the blanket over her. With her hands under her head, she said, "Can't. Captain no want your diseases in his room."

"But—"

"Truck at noon. I done my bargain. We go to Maugahay; trade you in." Carmen seemed pleased with that, for she chuckled.

"Please." Helen grabbed the blanket.

Something rustled. Suddenly the Nambu was under her chin. "Go," Carmen hissed. "You wanna do business, think of what I said. You have till noon." She pushed the Nambu hard. "Hapons don' care if this thing goes off. They just throw your carcass to the sharks. And no more you say anything about my pop."

Helen backed out and crawled to her bunk. By the time she was under her blanket, it had stopped raining. But she didn't sleep.

By the next morning, the clouds had disappeared. The sky was a clear, brilliant blue, washed clean by last night's rain. At eleven o'clock an olive-drab sedan drew before the barge and Fujimoto, Kunisawa, and Jimbo walked down the gangway. A sailor snapped open the doors for them and they drove off. Helen, on hands and knees, scrubbed the second deck, watching them go. With puddles gleaming here and there, her work was easy, but her mind turned frantically.

The captain was gone. His stateroom door was just ten feet away, but she was guarded by a decrepit army corporal of at least fifty years, who sat dozing in the shadows of a lifeboat, his rifle balanced across his lap. If only—

A match struck; a trace of cigarette smoke curled into her nostrils. Turning her head slightly, she saw a pair of starched white trousers and polished black shoes standing only four feet away.

Yawata.

She looked up, seeing him blow smoke nonchalantly, watching the dust trail left by the captain's sedan.

She bent over the deck and scrubbed hard.

A foot scraped. He'd stepped closer, she knew. Cigarette smoke engulfed her. She looked up, her face as much a mask to Yawata as Carmen's was to Helen last night. Helen's dark glasses and scarf had been Amador's idea, to throw off anyone who might have recognized her from the time before. And the rig covered her scars. But in a quick glimpse, she saw that it fired Yawata's imagination. Or maybe it was the thin dress, drenched with sweat, sticking to her hips and thighs, that got him worked up.

Quickly, she looked from side to side. *No one else around.* Carmen had assigned her to work out here, where she would be easily visible when the truck drove up.

This time she heard him exhale. Another blue cloud swirled around her head. Helen shuddered. She bent as low as she could and scrubbed hard.

A perfect smoke ring drifted by. And he grunted, his feet within twelve inches of her head.

All right, you son of a bitch.

Helen looked up and ever so slightly arched her right eyebrow. Then she turned and sat, letting her skirt fall off her knee, exposing her leg.

His youth betrayed him and Yawata looked away, startled.

Helen went back to her scrubbing.

Another smoke ring.

When she looked up this time, Yawata's gaze met hers. A thin smile unfolded across his lips. He called in Japanese over his shoulder.

With a grunt, the corporal rose and shuffled down the gangway to the first deck.

As soon as the corporal's head disappeared below the main deck, Yawata's hand was under her elbow, pulling her up. Helen rose and shook herself free, and it became clear he hadn't thought that far ahead about how to accomplish his conquest.

Good. Helen arched her eyebrow again, then turned and slowly walked away, her mind racing. *How am I going to do this?*

Yawata called after her and began to catch up just as she turned the handle to the captain's stateroom. It was unlocked.

She walked in, leaving the door ajar for him. The place was as messy as before, books and papers stacked everywhere. But the safe was closed. Quickly her eyes darted over the desk, finding a letter opener. *It'll have to do.* She grabbed it and held it behind her back as Yawata rounded the corner, pushed the door wide open, and leaned against the doorjamb.

Helen backed toward the captain's pilot berth. From the corner of her eye she saw someone had made it up this morning.

Yawata watched for a moment, taking a long last drag on his cigarette. With thumb and middle finger, he flicked it away, then walked in and closed the door.

She smiled at him and sat on Fujimoto's berth, clutching the letter opener tightly. One chance, she figured. Jam it into his throat and twist like hell. Then grab the pouch, run off the barge and take her chances. *Closer, you little bastard.*

Yawata stood in the middle of the stateroom, gripping a floor-to-ceiling brass stanchion, unsure.

Helen kicked off her sandals and braced a foot on the side of the pilot berth, her dress falling off her knee, exposing her leg. For full effect, she leaned back on one hand, the other ready with the letter opener.

Yawata gasped, then started to pull his jumper over his head.

The door crashed open. "Damn truck here, bitch."

Yawata spun, his mouth gaping open.

Carmen covered her mouth with her hand.

Yawata's lips trembled.

"Aiiieeeyahhhh!" Carmen's scream was as caustic as any Helen had ever heard.

Helen jumped to her feet and screamed with Carmen.

With all of her bulk, Carmen jumped nimbly aside as Yawata dashed out.

Helen stood speechless as Carmen stepped to the door and looked after Yawata. "Hurry up with that bag, bitch. Hapons come."

Helen lifted the mattress. It was far heavier than she remembered and she had to strain hard to lift it up. *Where is the damned thing? Maybe the captain found it. Maybe that's why the safe is locked.* Feet thumped outside.

"Hurry!" Carmen hissed.

There! The pouch! She grabbed it and stuffed it down her blouse, quickly pulling the scarf over her bosom.

She'd no sooner dropped the mattress than an officer in dress whites dashed in, followed by an Army corporal.

Ignoring Helen, they shouted at Carmen in pidgin Tagalog. Carmen shouted back.

Turning sideways, Helen eased her way behind Carmen and outside, where she waited while they squabbled. She glanced at the dock. Carmen was right. A truck was parked at the gangway, a soldier behind the wheel.

Soon, all three walked out, still shouting, the officer banging the door shut. Then the officer walked to the wardroom and the guard stepped behind them.

Carmen yelled at Helen, "Ona truck, bitch. Whatchu waitin' for?"

Threatening to fall to the ground the pouch slid to Helen's belly. With all of her might she held it to her side with her right elbow. It seemed the longest walk of her life as she gained the main deck, stepped down the gangway, and climbed over the truck's tailgate.

Thank you, Carmen. Thank you.

CHAPTER THIRTY-FIVE

Tokyo Rose's throaty voice drifted through the wardroom, ". . . and our greetings and congratulations go to Vice Admiral Bull Halsey, who arrived in Nouméa just two days ago, to take command of all Allied Forces in the South Pacific. To Admiral Halsey, we plead with you to reconsider what you are doing to your men on Guadalcanal, sending them to be slaughtered by the Imperial Forces of His Emperor's glorious Army. Admiral Halsey. Please. Give up before it is too late. Before there is nothing left of your men but shattered bodies to send home . . . And now"—Rose's voice became a seductive whisper—"in honor of Bull Halsey, we play that timeless favorite, 'I Surrender Dear.' "

"Damned Japs are full of bull," muttered Halsey, realizing Tokyo Rose knew no one called him "Bull" to his face. He walked to the pantry window, drew a cup of coffee, and said to Browning, "I've had enough of this Tokyo Rose crap. I'm going outside for a moment."

"Yes, Sir. I'll call when we're ready," said Browning, as the stewards cleared the breakfast dishes.

Halsey grabbed his garrison cap and stepped out on the 02 deck, coffee cup and saucer in hand, and ambled forward. The sky was overcast, leaden, the ocean a similar iron-gray color. He spotted whitecaps outside the breakwater, his seaman's eye telling him the wind speed in the open ocean was about twenty to twenty-five knots: good for launching planes off the decks of aircraft carriers.

That was the question: Could he get by with just two aircraft carriers? He really didn't have a choice, since two were all that was available right now. In fact, there were only two operational carriers in the entire Pacific, the rest undergoing repairs or . . . sunk, like the *Wasp* last month at Guadalcanal, or the *Yorktown* at Midway and *Lexington* in the Coral Sea. The *Hornet,* commissioned just a year ago, was in a battle group now on patrol east of the Santa Cruz Islands. In two to three days, she would be joined by the carrier *Enterprise,* now racing from Pearl Harbor. Patched up from a torpedo hit last August, Rear Admiral Thomas C. Kinkaid was aboard as Commander, Task Force 61. When formed, Kinkaid's force would include the two carriers, the battleship *South Dakota,* six cruisers, and fourteen destroyers. Halsey lit a cigarette and exhaled nervously. *Is that enough?*

Hornet and *Enterprise,* back together again. Halsey ran a hand over his neck, trying not to scratch, remembering the dark days last April. He'd been aboard the *Enterprise,* leading the *Hornet* with her load of sixteen B-25s. They steamed to within 620 miles of Japan's coast, the twin engine bombers forced to launch early after being spotted by a Japanese picket boat. As soon as Jimmy Doolittle and his B-25s safely took off into the teeth of a near-gale, Halsey reversed course and made tracks for Pearl Harbor. The B-25s carried out their bombing assignments, but, short of fuel, were not able to reach their airfields in China, the crews forced to ditch or parachute along the way. One B-25 diverted north after its bombing assignment and landed in Vladivostok, where the Soviets, strictly neutral and playing by the book, impounded the airplane, interning the crew for the war's duration.

Halsey sipped and braced a foot on a railing. That had scared the hell out of the Japs. Now they knew they were vulnerable. Even better, their leaders were embarrassed before the people. There was no way around it. Men would be moved, equipment sacrificed to defend the homeland. That alone was worth it. Moreover, the morale lift in the U.S. was priceless. Immediately after the attack, President Roosevelt had gone on radio nationwide, announcing a victory sorely needed by one hundred fifty million Americans.

Checking his watch, Halsey saw it was about time to begin his conference and turned to start back. Just then, Vice Admiral Ghormley stepped out, wearing dress khakis. He walked up. "Plane's ready, so I'll be shoving off, Bill. I hope—"

The 1MC squawked, a whistle blew, and the boatswain mate of the watch called in a tinny voice, "On deck. Attention to colors."

Halsey set his coffee cup aside, and the two admirals automatically drew to attention, faced aft, and saluted the national ensign as it was raised at the stern rail. Officers and men on every Navy ship followed suit, while a Marine band played the national anthem on the *Argonne*'s quarterdeck. When it was done, the boatswain on the 1MC called "Ready—to!"

Halsey turned. "I'm sorry about all this, Bob. I'm sure Chester will take good care of you."

"I'm sure he will." Ghormley took a deep breath and looked around Nouméa Harbor. Just then the destroyer *Porter* sounded a strident prolonged blast of her horn and began to back clear of a nest of destroyers alongside the repair ship *Vestal.* Within seconds, the *Porter* gave another three short blasts as she gained sternway toward a turning basin. Ghormley's voice was barely a whisper. "God, I love that sound."

Another destroyer, the *Shaw,* blew her own prolonged blast, and began backing clear of the *Vestal.* Water foamed beneath her screwguards as she, too, cranked out three short blasts. Soon, both destroyers twisted on their engines, then began moving ahead, forming a column, the *Porter* in the lead, as they shaped course for the harbor entrance.

Ghormley asked, "You sending them north?"

"Giving Kinkaid everything we got. There's a hell of a fight going on now." Having surrounded Guadalcanal's Henderson Field to within mortar range, Major General Kiyotake Kawaguchi's troops were locked in a bloody battle, attempting to retake the airbase. In support, Vice Admiral Nobutake Kondo was the officer in tactical command of two large naval forces. One was the Imperial Second Fleet, an advance force consisting of one attack carrier, the *Junyo,* where Kondo flew his flag, and was supported by twenty-one warships. The Imperial Third Fleet, the striking force, was commanded by Vice Admiral Chuchi Nagumo, and consisted of nineteen capital ships supporting three attack carriers: *Shokaku, Zuikaku,* and *Zuiho.* Kondo's Second and Third Fleets had been steaming north of the Stewart Islands for the past two weeks, waiting for the moment to pounce. The idea was for Kondo to launch all his fighters and bombers just as soon as Kawaguchi's troops retook Henderson Field. The planes were to fly into the airbase and, turning the table on the U.S. Marines, use it to bomb the Americans off Guadalcanal and Tulagi.

Ghormley nodded, and for a moment watched as a destroyer nearby weighed anchor, men standing on her fo'c'sle, hosing mud off the anchor chain as it clanked up through the hawsepipe.

Halsey said, "I like the lines of those new *Fletcher* class cans. Which one is she?"

"Howell."

For a moment, they watched as the *Howell* gathered way and took the number three position behind *Porter* and *Shaw,* nearing the harbor entrance.

Halsey grinned. "Yeah, the *Howell.* Who is that crazy sonofabitch for her captain?"

"Jerry Landa."

Halsey snapped his fingers. "Yeah. 'Boom Boom' Landa. Heard him do the funniest gig on farting in the Guantanamo O club one night. Damn good man."

"That's him. You should have seen what he did to Bob Jessup." Ghormley explained what happened at the skippers' conference. "Landa told those farting stories when he was a junior officer. Everyone called him 'Boom Boom.' It stuck and now that he's grown up, so to speak, he hates the name."

"Hell, I'll trade him 'Boom Boom' for 'Bull.' "

Ghormley's eyes twinkled. "I'm afraid you're stuck with that one, Bill."

"Afraid so." Halsey pawed at the deck for a moment with his toe. "About Bob Jessup. I don't think I have a spot for him out here."

Ghormley nodded. "I figured that. So I've manifested him on the plane with me. And when we land in Pearl, I'm going to stick him on the next ship for Washington, D.C."

"A slow one. Send it around Cape Horn."

"Consider it done." At length Ghormley said, "This is a tough job they've given you, Bill."

"I damn well know it. Anything I can do for you?"

Ghormley extended a hand, shaking with his successor. "No, thanks. Take off in thirty minutes. We'll be in Pearl in three days. Anything you want me to tell Chester?''

"I'm fine, Bob." Halsey smiled, hoping that he didn't show he felt awkward.

Ghormley took a last look around Nouméa. He chuckled. "Too bad those cans make so much noise."

Halsey looked at Ghormley, his heavy eyebrows knitted together.

"Wake up the Frogs. You know, they have a spy network here. Tell the Japs everything. Half the time, I would hear about ship movements from Tokyo Rose before the report landed on my desk." Ghormley explained that since Nouméa was French, she was supposedly under rule by the Vichy government, the puppet government of the Nazis who were Axis partners with the Japanese and Italians. But the Free French government, under Charles De Gaulle in London, also claimed sovereignty over Nouméa. That had made it convenient for the Allies to occupy the town, using it as a major staging and repair area. But to curry favor, the Vichy supporters in Nouméa blatantly radioed Allied ship movements to the Japanese.

Halsey grinned and they shook again. "We'll clean 'em out. Good luck, Bob."

"You, too, Bill."

The two admirals parted: Halsey heading for a staff meeting on how to thwart Yamamoto's plans to reconquer Guadalcanal, Ghormley walking to the shiny gig that would take him to Nimitz's four-engine Coronado, and Hawaii, and blessed relief from a mind-numbing job.

On Guadalcanal, the United States Marines hung on, throwing back banzai charge after bloody banzai charge—well past October 22, a day originally designated as ''Y'' Day, when General Kawaguchi had promised to retake Henderson Field.

Close to noon on October 25, a PBY Catalina out of Espiritu Santo spotted two carriers of the Imperial Japanese Navy about 120 miles north of the Stewart Islands, the ships steaming on a southerly course. Kinkaid in *Enterprise,* having joined *Hornet,* launched a search as soon as he received the report, but found nothing, unaware Kondo had turned north after being spotted. That night, Kondo, impatient and low on fuel after two weeks of waiting for General Kawaguchi's past due ''Y'' Day, once again reversed course and ran south.

At eleven minutes after midnight, on the twenty-sixth of October, another PBY sighted Nagumo's Third Fleet, also near Steward Island. The ''Dumbo,'' as the PBYs were called, reported a force of three carriers, two battleships, five cruisers, and fifteen destroyers. After sending her contact report, the Dumbo, low on fuel, turned for its base at Espiritu Santo. Unfortunately, the plane missed Kondo's group hidden nearby in a rain squall, the Imperial

Japanese Second Fleet consisting of yet another carrier, two battleships, five cruisers, and fourteen destroyers.

At 0310 another PBY, having been vectored to datum, found a group of ships and sent another contact report. But that PBY had only found Nagumo and his Third Fleet of three carriers; Kondo in the *Junyo,* and his Second Fleet, were again missed.

". . . Admiral, can you hear me?"

"Huh?" Instantly, Halsey's eyes flipped open. He sat up and switched on the little reading light beside his bed. A look at his clock told him it was 0325. "Miles?"

Captain Miles Browning said, "Yes, Sir. Sorry to wake you. We've got a Dumbo report."

"Okay." Halsey extended a hand and read the PBY sighting. "Damn." He rose and sat on the edge of his bed to get his bearings, rubbing sleep from his eyes. Then he read the 0310 contact report again while Browning took a seat.

There was a soft knock at the door and Major Julian Brown, the staff intelligence officer, padded in, wearing slippers and robe.

Halsey stroked his chin while pondering the message. Then he looked at Brown. "Better order coffee, Julian. This may take a while."

While they waited, Halsey put on a robe, flipped off the lights, and walked over to the porthole. Drawing the little blackout curtains aside, he looked out. Nouméa's blacked-out Petite Rade Harbor was, as usual, crammed with ships. The town was also blacked out, obscuring white stuccoed buildings splayed over low hills. Atop the ridge stood a massive cathedral, its twin towers silhouetted in half-moonlight, giving Nouméa a European look. He thought about Vichy French spies somewhere on the hill; maybe even now one was tapping his telegraph key, sending coded messages to the Japanese. He rubbed his chin. "You think the Frogs gave them the last destroyer movements?"

Browning said, "Without a doubt, Bill. But I don't think Kondo knows the *Enterprise* is back."

"Yeah, maybe not." Halsey closed the port and swished the blackout curtains shut. "I think you're right." He flipped on a desk light, lit a cigarette, and exhaled, blue smoke swirling around the bulb. "Yamamoto and Kondo will be betting on our having just one carrier, not two." Admiral Isoroku Yamamoto, commander of the combined fleet, was based in Truk, where he directed all offensive operations against Guadalcanal, including Kondo's ships and Kawaguchi's troops, still locked in hand-to-hand fighting around Henderson Field.

"I wonder if Kinkaid has figured this out," Halsey muttered, more to himself than to the others who sat before him. Kinkaid was under strict radio silence lest his position be discovered by the Japanese.

There was a soft knock and a steward's mate walked in with a silver coffee service. Halsey, Browning, and Brown waited while he set up their cups, poured, then retired silently, closing the door behind him.

"Ummmm." Halsey sipped coffee, took a drag, then pointed to the PBY contact report. "Have you plotted this?"

Browning pulled out a chart and showed him. "Due north of the Stewarts. Two hundred fifty miles northwest of Kinkaid."

Visions of Midway flew through Halsey's mind. "Jesus. Striking distance. We can have those Jap carriers for breakfast."

"I'm not sure." Browning handed over a two-page document. "A suggested draft of a message to Admiral Kinkaid. Fueling intervals, flight dispositions, screen deployments, everything."

Halsey read as Browning continued, "But I suggest we exercise prudence and wait to better determine Kondo's intentions. Otherwise"—he waved a hand in the air—"it could be a Midway in reverse."

Halsey bent over his desk and studied the chart. Then he sat back and drummed his fingers. "Why?"

"Intelligence tells us at least one carrier, two battleships, and several destroyers left Truk two and a half weeks ago. They're unaccounted for. And if they're with this force, we could be outnumbered two to one." Browning sat back and ran a hand over his brow.

"And right now we have parity in ships?"

"Yes, Sir. Except they have one more carrier and one more battleship."

"All right, what do you think we should do, Miles?"

There was another knock at the door, and the rest of Halsey's inner circle slipped in and, with no place to sit, leaned against the bulkhead. Among them were Bromfield Nichol, Leonard Dow, Douglas Moulton, and William Ashford. Most were in nightclothes, and stood in darkness. All one could see were the whites of their eyes.

Halsey looked up to them. "It seems things are coming to a head. There is a recommendation on the table to wait. What do you think?"

After a silence, Browning said, "Admiral. I would send an expeditionary force. Say two AA cruisers, perhaps the *San Juan* and the *Juneau,* and six or so destroyers here." He unfolded the chart and marked a spot halfway between the Stewart Islands and Guadalcanal. "That will draw them out. Then we can measure their full number and act accordingly."

"Exercise caution."

"Exactly."

"What if we go for them now?"

Major Brown cleared his throat. "We risk a chance of taking heavy casualties, Sir. Especially if there is another battle group out there."

Halsey sipped coffee and then blew a perfect smoke ring around his desk lamp bulb. "Okay. But don't forget I promised Archie everything." Three days previously, Halsey had met with Major General A. Archer Vandergrift, who commanded the Marines on Guadalcanal. Learning of the Marines' desperate situation there, Halsey promised Vandergrift "everything I've got."

"We could be slaughtered." Browning pointed toward the north. "Those destroyers, the last ones we saw getting under way. The . . . the . . ."

"*Porter, Shaw,* and *Howell,*" said Moulton.

"Yes, thank you, Doug. The *Porter, Shaw,* and *Howell,*" said Browning. "All three could be wiped out. *Hornet, Enterprise.* We could lose them all. I don't think we have the right to commit them without knowing what we're up against."

Halsey blew more smoke. *That's what Ghormley would have done: exercise caution, wait, send detailed instructions. No that's not what they're paying me to do.* "I don't think so, Miles. Tom's out there. He's the commander on the scene. He has the best dope. Let him make the decisions."

"Sir," Browning said, his voice a bit strident. "He's not in a position to."

Halsey locked eyes with everyone in the room, then looked away. "It's hot, damnit."

Brown reached over and turned on a bulkhead-mounted fan. It whirred, blowing stagnant smoke-laden air over them, providing little relief.

Halsey lit another cigarette. "Miles, let me play devil's advocate. Do you know what the essence of command is?"

"Sir?"

"Command. Leading people. What is its essence?" Halsey raised his eyebrows and again looked at them. "Anyone. Julian?"

Brown shook his head. Others shook their heads.

Rather robotlike, Browning cleared his throat and said, "well, I'll take a crack at it. The essence of command is the formal exercise of authority by properly delivering lawful orders to one's subordinates."

Halsey looked in the distance and pursed his lips. "Ummm. That may give one a top score in the classroom. But not here. Out here, in the trenches, where people are shooting at you, the essence of command is ordering men to die.

"You look your men in the eye and send them out there to do a job, knowing that some won't come back. Some will die. And that's what Archie Vandergrift is doing right now up on Guadalcanal. This very moment he's ordering some young captain or second john to go out there and die, to keep the Japs from taking Henderson Field. Now, I ask you, are we any different?"

They shook their heads.

Halsey puffed and exhaled, nearly obscuring the other faces in his compartment. "You're right, Miles. We could lose those tin cans. The *Enterprise,* maybe even the *Hornet.* But if we don't try, then Vandergrift will lose far more and we'll—you and I—be shoved back to Australia, holding hands with Doug MacArthur and his bunch.

"For my money, I'd rather start licking the Japs from right here, and then go on to Tokyo." He tapped Browning's map with his forefinger. "I promised Archie that I would deliver, and damnit, I'm going to do it. And I trust Kinkaid to do his job and figure things out."

He looked up. "Okay?"

Browning reached over and withdrew the draft off Halsey's desk while, in the darkness, the others nodded.

"All right. Here's what I want to do." Halsey grabbed a message pad and scribbled. Ripping it off the pad, he handed it to Brown. "Send that to Tom."

Both leaned over to read the message:

TO: KINKAID
FM: HALSEY
ATTACK—REPEAT—ATTACK
BT

CHAPTER THIRTY-SIX

26 OCTOBER, 1942
U.S.S. *HOWELL* (DD 482)
120 MILES NORTH OF THE SANTA CRUZ ISLANDS
8° 48.2' S; 166° 12.2' E

Like snorting black stallions, the darkened ships galloped through the night at twenty-seven knots. It was moonless and overcast, and with radio silence, Ingram felt as if he were locked in a dark room with eleven, three-hundred-pound deaf-mutes. He stood on the bridge watching *Enterprise*'s signal lantern stab the night, the rest of her 809-foot length hidden in gloom. The *Hornet* was a phantom pinpoint of light ten miles to the south, winking in response.

He had been on the bridge since early evening, when they took fuel oil from the carrier. Unable to sleep, he stayed up to watch the destroyers dash one by one to the *Enterprise* and refuel. It wasn't easy in total darkness. Using radar for their approach, the destroyers steamed to within sixty feet of the *Enterprise*'s starboard side. Holding their speed to twelve knots, the narrow 376-foot ships bucked and rolled as the carrier's sailors high-lined fuel hoses over, one forward, one aft. Topping off took about twenty minutes, then the tin cans sent the hoses back. Ringing up all ahead full, they dug in their screws to charge off at twenty-five knots, resuming station on the three-thousand-yard circle around the *Enterprise*.

Inside the destroyer screen, on the two-thousand-yard circle, the heavy cruiser *Portland* kept station on *Enterprise*'s port side, the light antiaircraft cruiser *San Juan* to starboard. Steaming just one thousand yards aft of the *Enterprise* was the new thirty-five-thousand-ton battleship *South Dakota*.

Carrying a crew of twenty-five hundred, the dreadnought had nine, sixteen-inch guns in three turrets, ten twin five-inch dual purpose mounts, and sixty-eight brand-new Bofors forty millimeter guns. Untested in combat, the Bofors were carefully placed around the 680-foot battleship in seventeen quad mounts.

To the south, the *Hornet* had refueled her own protective AA ring consisting of two heavy cruisers, two light antiaircraft cruisers, and six destroyers.

The refueling done, Ingram spent the rest of the night on the signal bridge drinking coffee with Landa, watching the *Enterprise* incessantly blink flashing light messages to the ships around her. Rocko Myszynski, the screen commander riding in *Porter,* must be nervous, too, Ingram figured. For every hour or so, they would reorient the screen, changing the destroyer's distance to the *Enterprise* from three thousand to four thousand to five thousand yards, then back to three thousand yards again.

Every once in a while, Rocko would spear one of his destroyers with his own flashing light message when they drifted too far off their assigned position. It would read something like:

TO: TEXAS RANGER.
FM: CRABTREE.
STATION!
BT

Between the lines, one could clearly see Rocko chomping a cigar and shouting, *Goddamnit, get back where you belong.* But such a reprimand was not received aboard the *Howell.* Landa lurked over the OOD's shoulder, in this case the chief engineer, Hank Kelly, watching everything, making sure Kelly paid attention.

With each new screen change, the ship's throttles were cracked all the way, the stacks belching smoke as they blasted to new stations at full speed. The relative speeds were close to sixty knots, a death ride when running against traffic. Conversely, it was a snail's pace when taking a new station in front of the formation, crawling at a frustrating four or five knots relative speed.

Around four in the morning, Ingram and Landa stood frozen in horror as the black mass of a nameless destroyer cut across their bow, kicked in left rudder at the last possible moment, and roared down their port side, her uptakes squealing their sirenlike song, the ship's heat enveloping them like a demonic blanket. By the time they saw the phantom ship, it was far too late for evasive action.

Even so, Landa yelled at Kelly, who yelled at the lookouts.

Later, Landa gasped to Ingram, "God, I can't wait for the Japs. Then at least we can shoot back."

They set up a bent-line anti-submarine screen at 0430, with all ships calling battle stations. At 0500, Rocko reoriented back to a circular AA screen, this time to run into the wind, so the *Enterprise* could launch her first strike of sixteen SBD dive-bombers against the Japanese. The planes got away safely, and at 0523 the eastern horizon glowed a pale red through low cumulus clouds, announcing an anemic sunrise. Eventually, the day dawned with a soft eight-knot breeze from the southeast, barely rippling a mild, rolling ocean.

At 0705, a signalman brought Landa a message board. With a frown, he scribbled his initials and read to Ingram, "First strike of SBDs found the Jap force. Three carriers at least. Jesus. Fifteen destroyers and two battleships. A couple of cruisers. About two hundred miles northwest." He turned to Ingram. "My bet is that we can expect an attack in one and a half to two hours."

Ingram had the same feeling, his bowels churning like a washing machine. He twirled Helen's ring in his pocket, knowing the Japanese weren't going to stand quietly while Kinkaid's planes worked them over. Like everyone else, he had a dreaded feeling that something was on its way. He cleared his throat. "Makes sense to me." *God that sounded stupid.*

Fifteen minutes later, a signalman watching the flag hoists on the *Porter* shouted, "Signals. Stand by to execute, Corpen, one-two-zero." It was a course change into the wind.

Landa glanced at Ingram. "Launching more planes. Our boys are playing for keeps."

"Frustrating."

"I know. The hell with this air war crap. Give me something to shoot at."

Once settled on the new course, they watched the *Hornet* launch a strike of fifteen SBDs, six TBF torpedo bombers, and eight F4F Wildcat fighters. Orbiting the *Hornet* until all were airborne, they headed northwest, their engines droning into the distance. As he watched them go, Ingram's mouth was as stale as an empty paint can. He was thinking of heading below to brush his teeth and shave when Kinkaid sent off a second *Enterprise* strike of three SBDs, eight TBFs, and eight more Wildcats.

For Ingram, it was hard to realize those brave flyers up there were going after an enemy unseen over the horizon, outnumbered by them, if the earlier report was accurate.

Landa headed toward the companionway. "How 'bout it, Todd? You ready for something to eat? I got a feeling it's going to be a long, long day."

"Think I'll stick around for a while."

"Okay. Tell Hank to set condition three for chow. And have them hustle. I want to get back to GQ as soon as possible." Landa's head bobbed down the companionway.

Ingram walked forward and stuck his head in the pilothouse, finding Hank Kelly standing at a porthole, binoculars jammed to his eyes. He walked up and said, "Skipper's off the bridge."

"Thank God."

Ingram couldn't help but smile. Kelly had had a hair-raising night. "I thought Luther had the forenoon watch. Why are you still up here?"

"Not hungry. I told Luther to eat, then come up and relieve me."

"Okay, Hank. Set condition three and pass the word to hustle chow." Kelly said, "All right," his voice tight.

Stepping from the pilothouse to head below, Ingram felt a tug at his sleeve. He turned. It was Kelly. "Yeah, Hank?"

Kelly looked over his shoulder, making sure he wasn't overhead. He whispered, "Todd. What's going to happen?"

They moved out of earshot and leaned on the bulwarks, watching the *Howell* slice the seas, rolling easily, her bow biting into the troughs, dark gray ocean turning to brilliant white foam as it gushed over her fo'c'sle, washing past mount fifty-one, then cascading over the side.

"I think we'll see some action today."

"Planes?" Sweat beaded on Kelly's upper lip.

"Yeah." Ingram laid a hand on Kelly's forearm. "Hank. You'll be fine. Just keep your turbines grinding."

"I gotta tell you. I didn't sleep a wink last night. God, I feel shitty. How do you do it, Todd? Nothing affects you. You're a damned iceman."

Now, that was a surprise. Someone else telling him he was an iceman. Except . . . Landa had just about said as much a few days ago. Ingram thought about his little bottle of belladonna tablets hidden in his shaving kit. He hadn't taken one last night and now he was paying for it. It felt like that washing machine was solidly lodged in his belly, churning a full load. Besides, his mouth was dry, and with no sleep, his eyelids felt as if lead weights hung on them. "Keep a secret?"

Kelly nodded as they watched the *Hornet*'s second strike claw its way into the air: nine SBDs, nine TBFs, and seven Wildcats. As they droned overhead, Ingram said, "I'm so damned scared, I can't eat. I know I'll puke if I see a bowl of mush. Yet I have to go below and sit at the right hand of Boom Boom Landa and act like I'm content as hell. I'd rather crawl into one of your evaporators and have you bolt the inspection plate over me."

Kelly looked at Ingram, obviously having trouble taking him seriously. Finally, he ran his hand over his chin. "No. I'd turn on the steam and fry your ass."

"That's me. Chicken à la king."

It didn't seem funny to Ingram, but for some reason, Kelly started giggling and stepped back into the pilothouse, laughing as he went, the crew shaking their heads as the chief engineer walked past.

Hank thought I was kidding.

On the opposite bridge wing, Kelly busied himself peering through his pelorus, making sure the *Howell* was on station.

Ingram took a deep breath and looked up, watching the yardarm sweep slowly across the overcast, the ship's motion easy, enticing. They could have been on a pleasure cruise abroad the *Luriline*. Padding down the gangway, he thought about his new talker, a fair-haired, stocky third-class yeoman named Justice. He was a replacement for Seltzer, who had been given his wish and placed in charge of mount fifty-two, the five-inch gun mount just forward of the bridge. Justice and Seltzer: both in new jobs. As things were shaping up, Ingram hoped they could handle it.

Ingram sat at the wardroom table, silent, stirring coffee, unable to eat more than two pieces of dry toast. Ten other officers were there picking at their food, staring in the distance, one or two talking in monosyllables.

Landa slopped up a bowl of mush, then pushed his chair back. "We have a job to do?"

They turned and nodded dully.

"I can't hear you." Landa cupped a hand to his ear.

One or two grinned.

"Luther, smile, damnit," said Landa.

Dutton's smile looked like a jagged slash mark across a smeared chalk-board.

"Todd?"

"Yes, Sir." Ingram raised his forefingers and drew the corners of his mouth far apart.

That got them. Even Dutton laughed.

"That's not what I wanted, damnit. Now look." Landa checked his watch. "Eight-forty-five. Japs will be here, soon. Are we ready?" Again, he cupped a hand to his ear.

"Yes, Sir," they said.

"Now, come on. I don't think you guys know how to really—"

A buzzer sounded. Landa reached under the table and snatched the handset. "Captain."

It was obvious that Hank Kelly was on the other end. Landa nodded. "Right. Sound general quarters. As soon as you're relieved, hightail it down here and grab some chow before you head down the hole."

Landa shoved the phone in the bracket. "Radar reports bogeys at fifty miles. Time to go to work."

CHAPTER THIRTY-SEVEN

Where the hell are they? Ingram's teeth chattered as he looked up to the overcast. The Japanese were up there; he heard their high-pitched engines milling about.

A desperate Kinkaid had found a squall. It was a nice one with blessed rain coming down in light sheets, enveloping them, mercifully cooling Ingram's body and washing away the grime and filth of three days hard steaming, making the ship look slick, like it had just been painted. Ingram whipped off his helmet and held his face up, the pure water running down his cheeks, his neck, his back, soaking his shirt and trousers.

Dutton called from CIC, "Japs directly overhead, F4Fs chewing them up."

Beside Ingram stood Justice, his new talker, without his helmet, a stupid grin on his face. Justice was a tall, blondish bean pole with the largest set of keys clipped to his belt Ingram had ever seen. Every time Justice took a step, his keys jingled. Ingram figured there were fifty at least, and made a mental note to ask sometime where they all belonged.

"Ingram!" Landa shouted.

"Yes, Sir?"

"What the hell. You a damned Clabber Girl? Put the helmet back on. We got a war to fight."

Ingram sighed. Only Jerry "Boom Boom" Landa could get away with talking to his executive officer like that. "Yes, Sir." He donned his helmet and jabbed Justice in the ribs to do the same.

Soon they heard rumblings to the south. The *Hornet* group was under attack, Dutton reported. Some of the firing Ingram recognized as the *crumff* of five-inch guns along with the *pom-pom* of forty millimeter cannons.

"Jesus!" said Dutton.

"What?"

"Hold on." Radio silence had been broken and a loudspeaker squawked loudly in the background. At length Dutton said, "Gun Control and Bridge, this is Combat."

"Go ahead," said Landa

"Overheard on TACT TWO from the *Anderson*." The U.S.S. *Anderson* was a destroyer assigned to the *Hornet*'s protective screen, the formation steaming on a parallel course ten miles south. "No squall for the *Hornet* to hide in. The Japs planted a bomb on her flight deck aft, two more amidships. They also stuck two torpedoes in her engineering spaces. Another Jap did a hari-kari into the hangar deck, with two bombs exploding among airplanes. Said she's burning from stem to stern, is dead in the water and listing ten degrees."

"Good God," gasped Landa. Just then they heard another loud *whump* from the south.

Ingram signed off, unable to believe that the graceful ship they had been steaming with the past few days, the one who winked her light so mysteriously last night, was now in mortal danger. *Who's next?*

Landa looked up at Ingram. "Squall won't last forever. Shoot straight, Todd."

Five minutes later, the rain stopped. Ten minutes after that, the clouds burned off, giving way to a bright midmorning. To the south, a tall, two-thousand-foot column of angry black smoke marked the spot where the *Hornet* lay dead in the water. Little specs darted overhead, spitting death, some falling in flames from the pockmarked sky.

"Luther, what's the latest on the *Hornet*?" Ingram asked.

Speakers blared in CIC, some with panicky voices. Dutton's voice was loaded with line static. "She's still in deep trouble, but the fires are under control. They think they can relight the boilers. *Northampton* is rigging a line to tow her. Now they—Oops!"

"What?"

Dutton's voice was sharp. "Air search. Bogeys on the way. Bearing three-three-zero, range thirty thousand. ETA about ten minutes."

"Gun Control, aye." Ingram turned to Justice. "Tell all stations to expect an air attack from the northwest in ten minutes."

The Aichi D3A1 Navy (Type 99) carrier dive-bombers droned in at ten thousand feet. Designated "Val" by the Allied forces, the low-wing monoplanes were powered by a 1,070-horsepower Kensei radial engine. They had a fixed landing gear, thus only flew at about 150 knots. But the fixed landing gear helped slow them in dives, increasing their bombing accuracy. The Val carried a crew of two and a bomb load of one 551-pound bomb under the fuselage and a 132-pound bomb under each wing. They approached in their standard pattern of three-plane vees, three vees to a nine-plane cluster. This morning they tried to work their way east to dive out of the sun. But the F4F Wildcat fighters, flying combat air patrol overhead, drove them to the north, the little black specs well outlined against the sky. Some fell in flames as the American fighters wove in among them.

Ingram looked up to the Mark 37 director, seeing just the top of Wilson's battle helmet. "You have them, Jack?"

"On target and tracking, Range fourteen thousand yards."

"Plan on opening fire at twelve thousand."

"Roger."

The hum of Japanese engines grew to a roar as the dive-bombers approached.

Justice's keys jingled as he pushed his helmet back and counted, ". . . nine, twelve, fifteen, aw, shiiit, there's only two planes in the last group. We was shortchanged."

You'll be okay, Justice.

Just then the lead pushed over for his dive, his two wingmen following.

An enormous explosion rocked the battle group. Ingram jerked around to see the cruiser *San Juan* completely enveloped in a dark, roiling cloud. *Bomb? Torpedo?*

"My God, she's blown up!" said Landa.

The *San Juan*'s prow nosed out of the cloud. She had simultaneously fired her 12 five-inch guns, 56 forty millimeter and innumerable twenty millimeter cannons. She was soon joined by the *South Dakota, Portland,* and *Enterprise.*

At a nod from Landa, Ingram shouted, "Commence fire!"

Within two seconds all five of the *Howell*'s five-inch guns sent their salvos to the sky with a rippling *crack,* her forty and twenty millimeter guns soon joining in.

The *Howell*'s guns were pointed to port, their barrels cranked up to eighty degrees elevation, as they fired at the Japanese airplanes. A standard five-inch thirty-eight-caliber gun has a muzzle velocity of twenty-six hundred feet per second. Shooting at a rate of twelve to fifteen rounds a minute, the gun fires with a vicious *crack* that is so strong, so piercing, that one standing near the muzzle risks a broken eardrum and possible loss of hearing. Its concussion feels as if an out-of-control freight train has just raced by, all one hundred cars at once. The muzzle of Leo Seltzer's mount was within forty feet of where Ingram stood. That damned muzzle blast could shatter the half-inch-thick glass in the pilothouse portholes if the quartermasters didn't undog them and trice them up. Stuffing cotton in his ears didn't help much. Nor did clamping on the sound-powered phones. It was worse with the other ships firing around him, a powerful anti-rhythmic concussive force, the projectiles soaring skyward, pockmarking the sky, bursting among the enemy bombers locked in their death plunges.

"Left standard rudder!" shouted Landa.

A bomb burst off the *Howell*'s starboard bow, a tall column of water hissing skyward as they raced past.

Landa shouted again as he pointed to three Japanese Val dive-bombers trailing smoke. One was on fire and coming straight down. The other two were spinning, pieces ripping off the planes as they twirled in the sky.

The *crumff crumff crumff* of Task Force 16's guns banged methodically. The destroyers of the outer ring kept a mad pace with the *San Juan* and *South*

Dakota, all pouring lead into the sky like fire hoses, dark puffs littering the atmosphere from horizon to horizon, the ships twisting in desperate serpentine movements, evading bombs. Three more Vals pushed over into their dives, two exploding in midair, flaming pieces twirling about. Just then, six Vals in two groups of three came at them from straight ahead, poised to plunge straight down.

"Ingram!" Landa shouted, his face bright red.

"Sir?"

"Take those planes under fire, damnit!" Even as he shrieked, a bomb exploded in a loud *whack* on the *Enterprise*'s forward flight deck, then another hit amidships, smoke erupting as a third bomb fell in the water alongside, sending up an enormous plume of cascading mist.

"Sir!"

It wasn't easy to shift targets. The forties and twenties were firing independently. And Wilson's five gun mounts were in local control, concentrating on a Val that had just finished its dive, leaving twin plumes of water along the *South Dakota*'s starboard side. Chased by two F4Fs, it swooped directly overhead, its engine shrieking, staying low in a mad dash to escape. Mount fifty-two erupted, blasting off the Val's left wing only five hundred yards away. The brown-green plane spun furiously on its axis for a moment, then hit the water, disintegrating in flames.

"Jack! Tell Seltzer to shift targets to the meatballs off the bow," Ingram shouted.

As if clairvoyant, Seltzer twirled his mount and acquired the planes in four seconds, then commenced fire. Down they screamed, seven thousand, five thousand, three thousand feet. Suddenly the lead Val blew up. The one to starboard lost part of its tail assembly, but kept diving, shedding parts until it flipped into a furious spin, spewing pieces through a sky already littered with the puffs of thousands of exploding projectiles.

The third Val plunged through one thousand feet. Seltzer's mount bellowed, its five-inch projectile bursting directly before the dive-bomber's nose now. The Val shuddered, its bombs prematurely released, falling harmlessly into the sea.

A cheer forming in Ingram's throat turned to a gasp of horror. The plane, its pilot most likely dying, shifted its course slightly from the *Enterprise,* a target he knew he would never reach.

With a slight wiggle of the stick, it headed directly for the *Howell.*

Mount fifty-two roared again. Mount fifty-one shifted and acquired the Val, spewing out its own stream of antiaircraft projectiles. Soon the forward forty millimeters blasted at the dive-bomber.

As it bore in closer, Ingram saw the pilot hunched over his stick, his head below the instrument panel, most likely dead.

"Left full rudder," Landa shouted.

"Eiiiyahhhh," Ingram screamed.

Somehow, the Japanese pilot raised his head at the last moment. He looked Ingram in the eyes, his Val headed straight for the bridge. But he must have shoved the stick at the last instant, possibly in pain. For his dive-bomber suddenly pitched down and smacked onto the foredeck, caroming into mount fifty-one and erupting into flames.

CHAPTER THIRTY-EIGHT

26 OCTOBER, 1942
U.S.S. *HOWELL* (DD 482)
120 MILES NORTH OF THE SANTA CRUZ ISLANDS
8° 44.1' S; 166° 29.6' E

Flames. Searing, white-hot heat. Burning gasoline and lung-rasping smoke. Men coughing and screaming. Ingram found himself behind director fifty-one, shoved against a stanchion, a leg dangling over the side of the pilothouse. Two or three red-hot nickel-sized pieces of metal were embedded in his khaki shirt, the garment blackened and tattered. And he had no idea how he had lost his helmet.

Steaming pieces of wreckage littered the bridge. Just below, a man was on fire, twirling and shrieking, as another tried to beat out the flames. The fiery wraith screamed horribly and clambered on the aft bulwark, leaving a trail of soot and blood as he frantically grabbed at air. He stood and something jingled a half-second before he jumped far into space, his body a blazing torch before it smacked the water.

"Jesus!" Ingram wobbled to his feet and grabbed a stanchion. "What the—?"

Fanned by the wind, the gasoline-fed flames leaped at him, searing his skin and eyebrows, making him throw his hands to his face.

Justice was gone.

Their phone sets lay scattered across the deck as if ripped from their heads by Frankenstein's monster. The deck heeled drunkenly to starboard as the *Howell* leaned into the left turn just ordered by Landa.

Landa! The captain!

A long, deep whistle blast sounded among the gunfire as the *Howell* rose and fell on waves heeling crazily to starboard. Jammed in her turn, the destroyer was halfway through a circle that would hurl her nose-to-nose with the *Enterprise,* the carrier's bow boiling toward them like an enormous meat cleaver, white sheets of water peeling off both sides.

"Oh, no," Ingram gasped. Then he leaned down and shouted, "Captain!"

No response. Smoke poured from the pilothouse; wreckage and bodies were splayed across the deck, some bleeding profusely, others jerking spasmodically. One or two were on their feet, holding their heads, stumbling about.

Jack Wilson leaned out of director fifty-one, his mouth open in horror.

Ingram glanced up. "You okay?"

All Wilson could do was jerk his head up and down.

"Keep shooting." Ingram pointed to another group of dive-bombers charging toward the *Enterprise*. "Go to local control if you have to."

"Right." Wilson spun his director, relieved to resume fighting with the guns aft, leaving the mess up forward to others.

Ingram scurried down the ladder to the bridge deck and rushed to the pilothouse hatch. Smoke and fire billowed off the fo'c'sle, singeing his hair and eyebrows. Coughing spasmodically, he grabbed a coat off the deck, held it over his head, and dashed into the relative safety of the pilothouse. A dozen or so fist-sized puncture holes in the forward bulkhead explained what had happened. Twisted bodies lay in the pilothouse, some groaning, some not moving at all. Through the starboard hatchway, he saw Fred Robertson, the OOD, and Lucien O'Donnell, the JOOD. Both lay on the deck in crumpled heaps.

The *Enterprise*'s horn bellowed again—closer.

No time to check.

He ran to the ship's wheel and twirled the rudder to hard right. *Nothing*. It didn't answer. He reached to the aft bulkhead and flipped the steering motor handle through its positions. *Nothing*. Then he eased the sound-powered phones away from the dead lee helmsman and held up the mouthpiece. "After Steering, Conn. After Steering, Conn."

"Captain?"

To his left was a noise like a rapidly draining bathtub. He rushed out on the port bridge wing, finding Landa, his head rested against the bulwark, his hands laying palms-up on the deck. "Jerry, you okay?"

Landa gasped, and trying to rise, wheezed horribly, his face turning ashen. Blood from a scalp wound poured over his head. But it was Landa's breathing that worried Ingram most; he almost looked blue. Landa looked at Ingram for a moment, his lips moving, but then his eyes closed and his chin fell to his shoulder, where just below—

"Jerry, for crying out loud," Ingram mouthed, looking at a golf-ball-sized chink of ragged-edged shrapnel protruding from Landa's chest. Wisps of steam rose from it.

The carrier's whistle sounded again, strident, closer. Ingram stood. *"Nooooo."*

The *Enterprise* hurtled at the *Howell* like an avalanche. Even if he could move the rudder, it wouldn't have mattered, it was far too late. The carrier's horn bellowed five times, the danger signal. Contact was imminent, the

25,500-ton carrier and the 2,100-ton destroyer rushing at each other at a relative speed of sixty knots, the result like five hundred head-on train wrecks on the same track.

But . . . she tilted to starboard.

It was hard to believe, but the carrier really was leaning into a turn to port. Ingram felt a surge of joy. Then she leaned harder, poised to snap around as was the ship's characteristic.

"Oh, thank you," was all he could think of saying as the ponderous carrier heeled more sharply, skidding into a hard left turn. Ingram dashed back in the pilothouse to the lee helm, its brass pedestal still gleaming from the polishing it had been given this morning. He rang up back full on the starboard engine, an attempt to twist the *Howell*'s stern clockwise.

The little pointers on the engine room telegraph went *clink, clink* in response. *Thank God!* At least something was working. But even if the *Howell* sideswiped the giant ship, the destroyer's hull would still be smashed like an oversized pomegranate.

The *Howell*'s engineers managed to reverse the starboard shaft, the ship vibrating as her screw bit the water in the opposite direction. Then Ingram dashed outside in time to see the overhang of the *Enterprise*'s flight deck swoop close overhead, barely missing the mast as it hurtled by. Men on the *Enterprise*'s catwalks merely glanced down at the *Howell*, and went on loading and firing their forty and twenty millimeter cannons without interruption, casually oblivious to the burning destroyer just beneath while flames roared on her own flight deck.

The ships passed beam to beam, the distance less than fifty feet. Perhaps in defiance, the *Howell*'s starboard quarter glanced off the aircraft carrier. The destroyer shuddered, her screwguard ripping away as if it were a piece of spaghetti.

With the *Enterprise* gone, Ingram ran back in the pilothouse and rang up *ahead full* again on the starboard engine, then *back two-thirds* on the port engine, an attempt to neutralize the jammed rudder, having no idea if it would work. Then he stepped outside to check on Landa as five men from a repair party surged though, herding wounded below, pitching smoking wreckage over the side.

One of them, a young redhead with pimples, stepped over. His eyes were wide as he asked, "You okay, Sir?"

"Yes. What's your name?"

"uhh . . . W-W-W-Wilcox, Sir, shipfitter third."

"Well, Wilcox. You're now lee helmsman. Go in and man that engine room telegraph and do what I tell you."

Wilcox stepped back in surprise. "But, Sir. I'm not sure if I—"

"Go!" Ingram spun Wilcox around, slapped him on the rump, and shoved him into the pilothouse.

The *Howell*'s combined after-battery roared at the dive-bombers as the destroyer boiled in her death circle at twenty-seven knots. But there weren't many Vals, perhaps six or so, and those were being worked over by the F4Fs.

Now the *Howell* spun toward the *San Juan*, whose guns still blazed into the sky. Following the *Enterprise*'s cue, the *San Juan* neatly swerved to avoid the *Howell,* as if she were a maniacal wraith lurching in uncontrolled rage among friend and foe.

Ingram pounded his fist on the forward bulwark. *Damnit. I need steering.*

The fo'c'sle was still a blazing mess, airplane wreckage littered about the main deck, 01 level, and bridge. The damage-control party shot the flames with hissing bottles of fire retardant, as other men dashed about, heaving flaming pieces over the side, pulling away wounded. On the main deck, mount fifty-one's barrel pointed in the air at an obscene angle, the rest of its quarter-inch, steel-plated gun shield smashed to pieces by the Japanese dive-bomber. Mount fifty-two on the deck above was engulfed in high-octane flames.

Just below, on the 01 deck, a man clutching a five-inch projectile to his chest staggered to the port side and heaved it into the ocean. His hair was singed black, dark smears covered his face, and his blue dungaree shirt smoked and hung to his back in tatters.

Impossible. It was Seltzer.

One look at the flaming mount fifty-two had made Ingram assume they were all dead.

"Leo!"

Seltzer turned and then headed back for the mount fifty-two's hatch.

"Seltzer. Up here."

Seltzer turned and looked up, shading his eyes. "Sir?"

"You all right?"

"Like a french fry."

"What?"

"I'm fine, Sir."

"How about your crew?"

"Three dead, two wounded, the rest working the fire party."

"I need you in secondary conn."

"What?"

"We have no helm up here. Grab a pair of phones and get to secondary conn. Now!" Behind a curved windbreak, secondary conn was an emergency steering station on the 01 deck just forward of the aft stack. It was equipped with a small ship's wheel, binnacle, and engine room telegraph.

"Yes, Sir." Seltzer dashed off.

Two corpsmen wearing helmets with red crosses painted on the sides had climbed onto the bridge and were kneeling by Landa. One was Monaghan, who quickly opened a kit, took out a stethoscope, ripped open Landa's shirt.

Ingram tapped him on the shoulder. "How is he?"

Monaghan kept working. "Dunno, Sir. He's lost a lot of blood. Looks like a sucking chest wound."

Gently, Monaghan eased the shrapnel out of Landa's chest and tossed it aside. The sucking sound became much louder, with Landa unconscious and very pale.

"How about Mr. Robertson and Mr. O'Donnell?"

Monaghan turned, his eyes like dark brown saucers. "Both dead, I'm afraid. Sorry, Sir."

Ingram knelt close. "What do we do?"

Monaghan rubbed a hand over his face. "Not sure."

Landa gave another loud gasp, turning a whiter shade of blue-white.

"What do you mean, 'not sure'?"

"Damn pulse is a thousand miles an hour."

"Well, what?"

"Sir," Monaghan said. "He needs a chest tube right now. And somebody has to gross stitch his puncture wound."

"What's that?"

"Er, close the damned thing. Fast. Forget the cosmetics."

"Well, take him below and do it."

"No time. Has to be done right here."

"Go ahead."

"Sir, I only did it once. I'm not a doctor. You need an X-ray machine, and I have to have—"

Ingram grabbed Monaghan's forearm. "Sailor, our captain will die if you don't do something."

Monaghan sank back on his knees and shook his head. "I just don't . . ." Something clicked in Monaghan's eyes. Looking at his assistant, a third class named Hopkins, he asked, "Tom?"

"Huh?"

"Tom, help me roll him on his right side and hold his arm up, away from the wound."

Hopkins rolled Landa, who gave another long gasp. Monaghan dug in his kit. "Jesus, where is it?" With a sob, he pulled out a thick tube, a quart-sized bottle, a peon, and several hemostats.

"Do your best, Monaghan." Ingram rose and patted the corpsman on the shoulder.

"Yes, sir." Monaghan began stringing a silk suture into a needle.

"Todd." It was Dutton up from CIC, his face turning to ashen white when he looked at Landa. His mouth opened and he swallowed several times, trying to absorb the carnage around him. "Ohhh, shit."

"Come on, Luther."

"Where is everybody?"

"Dead or wounded."

Dutton's Adam's apple bounced up and down as he tried to speak. Finally he looked at Monaghan making three quick stitches in Landa's chest. "You're not letting Romeo work on him."

"Any better ideas?"

"What's wrong?"

"Punctured lung." Ingram drew Dutton away from the corpsmen and their patient.

"Look. Our main problem is trying to regain steering. Got any ideas?"

"Get someone into after-steering or secondary conn."

"After-steering is out for now. It may be phone lines. I have Seltzer going for secondary conn."

"That should do it."

"Right. So why don't you grab some phones and take over gun control?"

"Where's Justice?"

"No idea."

"Okay." Dutton headed for the top of the pilothouse.

Ingram picked up a set of phones from where Landa lay, plugged in, and frantically twisted the barrel switch, looking for Seltzer. Clicking through the circuits, he heard some talkers speaking in dry, bored tones, giving status reports as if it were Sunday afternoon in Moline, Illinois. Other talkers yelled in panic, demanding help, demanding shoring, CO_2 bottles, more men, corpsmen. Ingram leaned outboard to see if Seltzer had reached secondary conn.

Seltzer was there, phones on, flipping through circuits. He looked up and waved, pointing to his earphones.

Frantically, Ingram rotated the barrel selector switch: . . . 9JZ, 3JZ, 4JZ. Static! "Seltzer? That you?"

"Yes, Sir."

"Do you have power?"

"Yes, Sir. Just came up. The rudder is answering."

"Rudder amidships!"

"Rudder amidships, aye."

The *Howell* eased from her turn and mercifully stood up straight, her course roughly parallel to the formation. For the first time in the last terror-stricken minutes, Ingram felt a surge of relief. He took a deep breath. It felt good and he luxuriated in telling himself, *We're gonna be all right.*

"Hold on a second, Seltzer." Ingram scrambled up the ladder, joining Dutton atop the pilothouse, where he had a much better view of secondary conn and the surrounding ships. But the flames were hotter up here and thick black smoke poured off the fo'c'sle. They had to stand behind the gun director to shield themselves.

"Sir, I can't hold her steady." Seltzer's voice barely found its way among the groans of the dying, shouts of the living, screaming loudspeakers, and cannon fire.

"Bridge, aye." He'd forgotten about the engines and leaned over and shouted to the pilothouse. "Wilcox. All engines ahead full. Make turns for twenty-seven knots."

Wilcox's voice echoed up, "How do I do that?"

"Shove the handles forward to the position just before flank. Then spin the dials on the pedestal to two hundred seventy."

"Yes, Sir." Wilcox shoved the brass handles, the engine room answering with *clink, clink.*

Ingram pressed the talk button. "Leo, how's that?"

Seltzer's static-ridden reply came back, "Feels fine, Sir."

"Bridge, aye."

"Todd." It was Dutton, his voice shaky. "Major problem in the forward magazine."

"Shit!" Ingram's gut tightened again. Just the mention of the word 'magazine' made him want to run. He looked over the side into the clear cool waters of the Pacific Ocean, wondering if he should just get the hell out and jump, letting everybody blow up with the ship. "What?"

"Aviation gas ran down the ammunition hoist. The fire is working its way into the handling room. It's much too hot for the repair party to get in there."

"Tell 'em to flood."

Dutton nearly shrieked. "Hatch won't shut and it's too hot to get against it. And live ammo is rolling around. We gotta get the fires out!"

Ingram looked off to port. The *South Dakota* steamed on a parallel course about a thousand yards off their quarter. *That's it!*

"Luther. Get word to the fire party off the foredeck."

"What?" Dutton gasped.

"Do it!"

"Yes, Sir."

Ingram yelled into the mike, "Leo, come left ten degrees."

"Yes, Sir. Coming left to one-one-zero," answered Seltzer.

Ingram shouted, "Wilcox. Ring up all ahead flank. Indicate three hundred turns."

"Three hundred turns . . . yes, Sir . . ."

Clink. Clink.

The distance to the *South Dakota* closed to about six hundred yards.

Neat.

With the ominous black smoke and flames roiling on the *Howell*'s foredeck, the *South Dakota*'s captain, like the captain of the *Enterprise,* leaned on his whistle. Five blasts: *Don't come near me, you crazy bastard.*

"Bridge, Secondary Conn. Mind if I ask what we're doing, Sir?" asked a nervous Seltzer.

Ingram shouted, "You're doing fine, Leo. Wilcox! Ring up all ahead full and two hundred fifty turns.

"Yes, Sir. Engine room answers, Sir."

"Good, Wilcox." As the *Howell* slowed, Ingram realized he should have called Hank Kelly in main control and told him what was going on. Kelly and his snipes must be scared out of their pants. *Soon, Hank, soon.*

"Todd," Dutton screeched. "That damned handling room bulkhead is turning red-hot."

"Another minute, Luther." The *South Dakota,* her guns still roaring, boiled along just a hundred yards off their port bow, now pulling ahead. Her horn still raged in short blasts.

Ingram keyed his mike. "Leo. I want you to stick our nose behind the *South Dakota* and keep her there. Right in her wake."

"Now?"

"Right now."

Seltzer eased in left rudder, gently nosing the *Howell* into the *South Dakota*'s furious twenty-seven knot wake. The destroyer's bow rose on the battleship's massive quarter-wave and smashed down, water spewing violently, as if she were in an Atlantic storm. With the ship rolling heavily, Ingram leaned over and again shouted, "Wilcox. Increase speed on both engines to two hundred seventy turns."

"Sir."

Seltzer steadied the *Howell* directly behind the *South Dakota,* the destroyer rising and pitching like a bronco in the Pendleton Roundup, throwing water in all directions. At times her prow went under, then rose, lifting tons of white roiling water to cascade down the deck, shoving hissing, steaming wreckage over the side.

Several times her nose was buried, the flames dwindling to a patch just forward of mount fifty-two. Suddenly the flames hissed out. And it was quiet: the world devoid of gunfire, of men screaming and shrieking, radial engines plummeting from ten thousand feet.

The air attack was over, and except for black smoke puffs, the sky was a crystalline blue, the Japanese gone. With no targets, Dutton had given the *cease fire.*

"Luther, how's the forward magazine?"

Dutton, his hands shaking, pressed them to his ears. "Fire's out. They're handing up loose rounds."

Again, Ingram's stomach unknotted. *Okay, breathe.*

It felt good. He did it once more.

"Okay. Give 'em a 'well done.' " Dutton's hands shook. And his face was smeared completely black with smoke. "Luther, you look like Al Jolson doing some stupid vaudeville act." Then he looked at his own hands. They shook so hard, he couldn't have buttoned a shirt or picked up a fork. And then he ran a hand over his cheek and brought it away to see it smeared thick with oily black smoke. He realized his face was as black as Dutton's.

He caught Dutton looking. Suddenly both giggled as if they had just tipped over an outhouse on a dark Friday night, the outraged schoolmaster trapped inside, screaming at the top of his lungs.

Ingram had to key his mike button with a fist. "Seltzer. Come right to one-three-zero."

"One-three-zero, aye," called Seltzer.

He told Wilcox to ring up flank speed and they drew from the *South Da-*

kota's wake, dashing ahead to resume station on the three-thousand-yard circle.

On the deck below, Monaghan and Hopkins gently eased Landa on the stokes litter. Ingram nudged Dutton with an elbow. "Look at that."

Landa's color was back. His eyes were open and he gave a faint smile.

Ingram and Dutton grinned back and saluted.

Landa raised an arm and tipped two fingers to his forehead. His lips moved, but just then someone shouted and Ingram couldn't hear what it was.

"I'll be damned." Dutton called down, "Hey, Romeo, what the hell did you do?"

Monaghan, looking as surprised as everyone else, returned his instruments to his kit. "Pinked up pretty good, didn't he, Sir?"

"Where did you learn how to do that?" shouted Dutton.

"Three-week course on the back of a matchbook cover, Sir. Only cost twenty bucks."

"Well done, Monaghan," Ingram said. "Take him to his day cabin and make him comfortable."

"We also do lobotomies, Mr. Dutton. That costs a little more, thirty bucks. But for you there is no charge. And easy credit terms for your mother-in-law. Please let me know if I can—"

"Get moving, Monaghan."

Gently, Monaghan picked up the stretcher's head, Hopkins the tail end. "Yes, Sir. Captain to his day cabin, Sir."

CHAPTER THIRTY-NINE

26 OCTOBER, 1942
U.S.S. *HOWELL* (DD 482)
120 MILES NORTH OF THE SANTA CRUZ ISLANDS
8° 32.3' S; 165° 19.3' E

The American strike staggered in from the northwest: Dauntlesses, Avengers, and Wildcats; tired, shot up, low on fuel, struggling to land on the *Enterprise*. Even as they approached, the carrier's shipfitters frantically worked to fix the flight deck bomb damage. And her forward elevator was frozen in the up position, making it nearly impossible to strike aircraft below to the hangar deck. Thus, the more seriously damaged aircraft were pushed over the side. On top of that, the *Hornet*'s planes returning from their strike found their ship a hopelessly burning derelict. They crowded into the *Enterprise*'s landing pattern and, once down, were simply pushed over the side to make room for the rest.

Shortly after ten, Ingram was on the bridge, stepping around wreckage, junk, toolboxes, and fire hoses, when he heard an enormous *crack* off to starboard. Everyone stopped in midstride, their mouths open in disbelief as a tall water column hissed high in the air alongside the *Porter*. A Japanese submarine had torpedoed her when she stopped to recover a pilot and gunner from an SBD that overshot the *Enterprise* and ran out of fuel before it could go around. Immediately, the *Shaw* reported sonar contact and dumped pattern after pattern of depth charges, chewing up the sea, as the rest of Task Force 16 ran for cover.

With the *Porter*'s back broken, the *Shaw* took the *Porter*'s crew aboard, including a livid Rocko Myszynski. Then, with a liberal dose of five-inch gunfire from the *Shaw*, the *Porter* rolled over and sank with eleven dead entombed in her mangled forward fire room. *Vale. Vale. Vale.*

By midafternoon, the *Hornet,* a white-hot burning hulk, had long been abandoned and lay dead in the water, listing twenty degrees to starboard. Thick black smoke poured from every door, hatch, and elevator shaft, as thundering explosions continued to savage her length, tearing her guts out. Sailors on ships nearby, like mourners on Abraham Lincoln's front porch, knew the *Hornet* was mortally wounded, that it was just a matter of time.

From Nouméa, Halsey ordered her sunk, lest the Japanese, now approaching with a numerically superior force, douse the fires and take her in tow.

Rather than risk a highline transfer to *Enterprise*'s overflowing sick bay, Monaghan recommended that Landa and the other wounded remain aboard. So at 1535 that afternoon, the *Howell,* her foredeck and bridge blackened as if Vulcan himself had exhaled his rage on her, was ordered to Espiritu Santo, three hundred miles to the south. There, her wounded would be transferred to the hospital ship U.S.S. *Haven* (AH 7), the ETA early next morning.

The seas had a moderate chop and they rode with occasional spray breaking over the bow, soaking the men who were cleaning the rest of the junk off the forecastle, welding holes in the main deck to make the ship seaworthy. The weather report was favorable. The wounded were in the wardroom, which had been converted to a temporary sick bay, where Monaghan assured Ingram that the burn victims had a comfortable ride.

But fifteen minutes later, the *Enterprise*'s signal light, barely visible on the northeastern horizon, blinked another message to the *Howell* as she ran south. Briley, the signalman, clacked out the acknowledgment, then handed it to Ingram. Luther Dutton, who had the afternoon watch as OOD, walked up and read over his shoulder.

Just then Hank Kelly, wearing his engineer coveralls, climbed up, his face beet-red from the forward engine room's 110-degree heat. Like a dog sticking his head out of a car's passenger window, he stood at the starboard bridge wing, letting the twenty-five-knot relative breeze cool his face. After a while, he stepped over. "What have they cooked up now?"

Ingram rubbed his chin. "We're to join the *Anderson* and *Mustin*, who are trying to sink the *Hornet*. They want us to use torpedoes. They've already launched their own without effect, the message says." He nodded to a tall column of smoke to the west—the *Hornet*'s funeral pyre—and turned to Dutton. "Better head over there, Luther, and go to battle stations torpedo."

Dutton gave the order as Kelly mopped his brow with a handkerchief. "God. You'd think they could tow her."

Ingram scratched his head. "She must be in terrible shape. Says here that if torpedoes don't do it, they'll sink her with five-inch." Ingram checked the compass repeater. Hopkins, the helmsman, was steering from inside the pilothouse, the damage controlmen having fixed the helm.

Kelly glanced at the gun director, blackened by smoke. "Lucky you weren't toasted."

Ingram's stomach churned with the thought. "I remember . . . that Jap sat up and looked right at me, eye to eye. Then . . . just as he hit, I ducked behind the director—Justice!"

"What?" said Kelly.

"Justice. He's missing."

"Right," said Dutton.

"He was the one that was on fire."

"You're nuts," said Kelly.

"I tell you, that was Justice. He must have been splattered with burning gasoline. The poor bastard was a human torch standing on the bulwark. I remember his keys jingled just before he jumped."

Kelly said. "Jesus. Maybe someone picked him up." They looked aft for a moment, the long foaming wake trailing behind them. The realization swarmed over them that if Justice had been rescued by another ship, they would have known by now.

Dutton looked down, studying their wake. "I've heard of guys on fire jumping over the side. Haven't heard of anyone being picked up."

Jack Wilson interrupted their thoughts. "Getting close, Sir. Ten thousand yards." He stood at the torpedo director, substituting for the chief torpedoman, who had been wounded by the suicide plane.

The *Anderson* and *Mustin* circled the *Hornet* like sheep dogs yipping at the cow who refused to come home, letting *Howell* through the gate to do their dirty work. Just then, an explosion raged in the carrier's hangar deck, spewing white-hot chunks of metal hundreds of feet into the sky, slowly twirling as they fell back to the ocean in great splashes.

"What's the range now?" asked Ingram.

"Eight thousand."

"Shoot at six."

"Yessir. What depth?"

Ingram shrugged and looked at the others. "What's she draw?"

"I'd say twenty feet," Dutton guessed.

"Okay, Jack. Let's try ten feet."

"Yes, Sir." Wilson checked a stopwatch. "We fire in three minutes."

"Very well. Luther, do we have confirmation from the *Anderson* to carry out the attack?"

"Affirmative."

"Old girl," Kelly muttered. "She was a damned good ship, only a year old. I rode her for three months after she was commissioned. It's just not right . . ."

Wilson pressed his head to the eyepiece. "Thirty seconds. Permission to shoot, Skipper?"

"Call me XO. The skipper's gonna be okay."

"Yessir."

"Shoot when ready, Jack."

Moments later, Wilson squeezed his hand trigger. The black-powder charges on the forward torpedo mount coughed one by one. Five torpedoes leaped from their tubes, one every two seconds, smacking the water with a gentle splash, streaking toward the stricken aircraft carrier at forty-five knots. "What's the run time?"

"Four minutes."

Ingram studied his watch. One minute passed. Two minutes. Three. At four fifteen, the carrier shuddered, water burbling amidships. "What the hell?" cried Dutton.

"Jack?" demanded Ingram. "Is that all we get? One hit and four duds?"

Wilson moaned, "Dudley told me the setup was perfect. The fish all seemed to run normal. He has no idea what happened." Dudley was their first-class torpedoman on the mount.

Briley, the quartermaster, called, "Signal from the *Anderson,* Sir. 'Interrogative remaining torpedoes?' "

"Affirmative, Briley. Ask them if they want us to make another run."

"Yes, Sir." The signalman clacked his flashing light. Soon the *Anderson* winked back with Briley reading, " 'Go ahead,' Sir."

Ingram bunched his fists for a moment. "Okay, Mr. Wilson. Let's try again. Set depth at four feet this time." The *Howell* circled and once again launched from the aft mount at six thousand yards as Ingram, Dutton, and Kelly watched with binoculars. A wave of disgust swept over Ingram as number three torpedo turned ninety degrees to port and raced harmlessly into the distance.

"Look at number two!" shouted Kelly. They watched the gleaming torpedo leap in the air, its counter-rotating propellers spinning furiously, spewing spray, then smacking into the water, porpoising on the surface, eventually bouncing off course and passing astern of the *Hornet.*

"Sonofabitch," exclaimed an incredulous Kelly, his hands on his hips. "You mean we can't even hit the broadside of an eight-hundred-foot-shithouse? Piss-poor maintenance, I'd say."

"Hank, damnit." Dutton whipped off his binoculars, his face flushed. "The torpedo gang lives with their equipment day and night. They baby those damned torpedoes. There's nothing they don't know about them."

Kelly smirked. "Of course, now when the chips are down they—"

"That's enough," snapped Ingram, checking his watch. The torpedo run times were well past four minutes. There were no explosions.

As the *Howell* shot past, the *Mustin* and *Anderson* moved in, pumping five-inch rounds into the *Hornet*.

Dutton, Kelly, and Wilson argued, while Ingram called the quartermaster. "Briley?"

"Yessir."

"Ask *Anderson* if they need assistance."

"Sir." Briley stood on his little platform, clacking his shutter. He squinted as the *Anderson* began winking back. "Anderson acknowledges, Sir." Then Briley read aloud, "New message, Sir. 'To: Howell, many thanks. But OTC reports strong Jap surface force approaching three CA, five DD now forty miles away: ETA under two hours. We must leave if *Hornet* not sunk by then. Regarding your wounded suggest you proceed with haste on duty assigned. BT.'"

"Tell them thank you, Briley." Ingram drummed his fingers for a moment. "And add we're sorry our torpedoes were duds."

"Yessir." Briley started clacking his shutter. After a moment, he said, "From *Anderson,* Sir. 'So were ours. We have to talk about this.'"

"Okay. Luther, let's scram before Tojo shows up. Make turns for thirty knots and set a zigzag course for Espiritu Santo."

Kelly watched. "What if the Japs tow her off?"

"Let's hope those two put her down first."

They watched as the burning *Hornet* faded in the distance. The two destroyers, like mad terriers, cranked salvo after salvo into her at point-blank range, the proud carrier sitting there, taking it like a drunken ex–heavyweight boxer.

"Tough cookie," Wilson said reverently.

"Okay, Luther. Set a condition three watch and pass the word for the officers to take their chow with the crew on the mess decks." Ingram looked at his watch. "And let's sound general quarters at a half-hour before sunset."

"Will do."

"Hank?"

"Yes, Sir."

"How's the foredeck?"

"Secure. Holes are patched. They're cutting away the last of the wreckage."

"Okay, tell 'em no welding torches on the weatherdecks after sunset. I don't want to be a damned beacon to Jap submarines out here."

"Okay."

They looked back a moment, the *Hornet* once again erupting in an enormous, Vesuvius-sized explosion. After the smoke cleared, she looked no different, the *Anderson* and *Mustin* still pounding away, their five-inch, thirty-eight caliber cannons sounding like popguns compared to *Hornet*'s gut-wrenching detonations. Ingram watched as yet another blast shook the *Hornet*, large pieces twirling in the air, trailing smoke. "I'm going down to check on the skipper."

Landa's day cabin was dim. The only light was from a small desk, where Monaghan sat fussing over paperwork, occasionally glancing at the skipper. The rest of his patients were in the wardroom, just on the other side of the bulkhead. Across the passageway, in CIC, a radio receiver squealed. Then Tokyo Rose announced, ". . . and now we hear an all-time favorite, 'Now Is the Hour.' "

As Bing Crosby crooned, Ingram sat on the edge of Landa's bunk. Except for the grotesque tube running into his chest and a bandage on the side of his head, the captain looked alert, and his color was good.

"How you doing?"

"Fine. How 'bout you?" Landa's voice was surprisingly strong.

Ingram forced a smile. "Scared shitless."

"Keep a secret?"

"Sure."

"After my breakfast pep talk . . ."

"You were great."

"I went right in there"—he pointed to a curtained shower stall and toilet—"and puked my guts out."

"You're kidding."

They fell into silence for a moment. Then Monaghan tapped Ingram on the shoulder. "Only a couple of minutes, Sir. Then you gotta scram. The skipper has to rest."

"Okay."

"I'll be a minute. Have to check my guys in the wardroom."

Ingram nodded as Monaghan walked out and closed the door.

"Did Monaghan patch me up?" asked Landa.

"Yeah. I don't think a regular shanker mechanic could have done it."

"I misjudged him. Terribly. How's he doing with the rest of the wounded?"

"Swell."

"Don't fire him."

"No."

"Okay. How's our ship? Give it to me straight."

Ingram took a deep breath. "We lost nine men in mount fifty-one, killed, we think on impact. Their bodies were washed over the side when we pulled behind the *South Dakota*. We lost another three in mount fifty-two. Five more were killed on the bridge, including Fred and Lucien."

Landa's lips pressed white and his eyes became watery. Forcing his gaze to a spot on the overhead, he rasped, "Go on."

"ETA at Espiritu Santo 1000 tomorrow morning. We've been cleared to go alongside the *Haven*, where you and the others will be transferred. They'll take our dead, too."

Landa's Adam's apple bounced up and down. "No ceremonies?"

"Not at sea."

"What else? How's the ship?"

"The whole forward battery is gone. Forties, twenties. Except for the barrel, mount fifty-one is gone. Mount fifty-two is repairable. The anchor windlass is gone, along with the starboard anchor. The port held, for some reason. Shrapnel holes all over the place. And we have to dewater the forward magazine and dry it out. But it's awful in there. Has to be rebuilt entirely. And we could use a new paint job topside."

"The plant?" Landa referred to the engineering plant with its two fire rooms and two engine rooms.

"Fine."

"Mmmmm. Well, there you are, stateside repair job, maybe. San Francisco? L.A.? Go see your honey. What's her name?"

"Helen." It sounded sweet as he said it.

"Well? What do you think of that?"

"Yeah . . . yeah, just maybe."

They were silent for a moment, each lost in his thoughts. Ingram looked over, seeing Landa's breathing seemed a bit labored and his color was whiter. "Monaghan says you should have a full recovery."

Landa wheezed, "I'll recommend that you take her back."

"What about—"

The door opened silently; Monaghan stepped in. "The captain needs rest."

"Okay." Ingram stood. "Take care, Boom Boom."

Landa's voice was distant. "Up yours, too . . ." His eyes fluttered closed, and he fell asleep.

Ingram made his way to the mess decks, two levels down. He stood in line with the men, some boisterous, shouting, euphoric over their escape. More than one asked, "Hey, Mister Ingram, is the scuttlebutt true? We going to Frisco for repairs?"

Smiling and doing his best to banter back, Ingram ladled up a tray of macaroni and cheese, lima beans, and rolls, then stepped forward into the crew's dining area, a space perhaps thirty feet by thirty-nine feet, the latter dimension the beam of the ship. The officers had commandeered a table in the far corner on the port side. Ingram sat on the end beside Kelly.

He reached for the water pitcher, but looked up seeing all their faces turned toward him. "Skipper's doing fine."

With a collective sigh of relief, they resumed their meals and talked among themselves, their tones melding with the jubilant ones from the crew around them.

"Biscuits?" Dutton passed a tray.

"Sure." Ingram took one as one of the men reached up and clicked on the radio receiver.

They pricked up their ears when Tokyo Rose purred, ". . . and to the men of Task Force 61 under Admiral Thomas Kinkaid. We are so sorry for the loss of your carrier *Hornet*. And we understand the *Enterprise* is not long for this world, either."

"How the hell does she know all this?" asked Kelly. "Pass the marmalade, please."

"Too bad the destroyers *Porter* and *Howell* were sunk . . ."

They whooped and whistled at that. "Half-right, Toots. Soooo sorry," someone jeered.

". . . such gallant crews. Now at the ocean's bottom. It's just not worth it. Think hard, men of the American Navy. It's useless. You never know when it hits you. From your blind side. Our power is complete and overwhelming and unpredictable . . ."

"Turn it off," growled Dutton.

Foster, a tall second-class gunner's mate, reached for the receiver as Tokyo Rose said, ". . . think also of the predicament of the submarine U.S.S. *Needlefish* as she returned from patrol . . ."

Foster started to flip the switch.

Ingram stood. "Leave it!" he shouted.

The men at Ingram's table stared at him, forks poised in midair.

". . . sunk with all hands from one of your own mines as she tried to enter Brisbane Harbor at night without an escort. Such a stupid captain. Such a stupid sacrifice of eighty fine men, just because the *Needlefish*'s captain failed to . . ."

Dutton asked, "Todd, what the hell's the matter?"

Ingram's fists bunched. Then he stood stiffly and lurched out of the mess room, his shoulder bouncing off the hatch frame as he exited.

At the next table, Wilcox munched lima beans and spread strawberry jam on a slab of bread. "What's with the XO?"

PART THREE

But Jesus said unto him;
Follow me; and let the dead bury their dead.

*We are much simpler mechanisms than we think, preserving life and
seeking what meaning we can find in it. The dead must bury the dead
because no one else pauses long enough to do so. Guilt is inevitable,
but the real danger, I quickly found, was in feeling that you cannot
move on away from what you cannot endure, letting deep emotions get
too tangled and blocked.*

ALVIN KERNAN

CROSSING THE LINE

CHAPTER FORTY

San Francisco, it seemed, was done with its Indian summer, a warm and balmy span of weather Eduard Dezhnev had grown to love, something never seen in his adopted homeland of Georgia. Now it was cold, blustery, and his leg hurt as he walked up the hill to the consulate. It had become a half-hour constitutional he took each day after the heavy Soviet lunches.

He paused for a moment, looking back at San Francisco Bay. It was jammed with anchored cruisers, destroyers, oilers, cargo ships, attack transports. Even a battleship, an old *New Mexico* class, swung out there with them. Little boats dashed among them, servicing the fleet with furious intent. The waterfront, San Francisco's old Barbary Coast, was as alive as she ever would be, but not as a mercantile center. Now she was a major focal point for carrying the war to the Japanese. Ships were moored stem to stern at her piers, where long, clanking trains pulled right alongside to deliver their deadly cargoes. Boxcars, flatcars, tank cars, and passenger cars were drawn from all over the nation by the great steam engines, their chuffing and moaning whistles echoing over the city. Added to the peninsula's cacophony was that of the building yards around the San Francisco Bay region. From Mare Island to Hunter's Point, capital and cargo ships were mass-produced at an amazing rate.

As Dezhnev watched, three destroyers led a heavy cruiser, a new *Baltimore* class, under the Golden Gate Bridge, where they were met by the cold, gray Pacific—the four ships looking sinister in their dazzle-pattern camouflage. He stood for a moment longer, the wind tugging at his overcoat, as he thought about the game the Americans were playing. To many, they looked like buffoons, getting smeared right and left in the Solomons by the Japanese. But Dezhnev had studied the figures. Yes, the Americans had, so far, lost four heavy carriers, but they still had enough to continue their delaying tactics. Dezhnev's information was that Admiral Spruance was soon to be put in charge of Nimitz's campaign to drive across the central Pacific. All he needed were the carriers. And plenty were on the way. Scheduled for commissioning next month was the thirty-three-thousand-ton *Essex* attack carrier. Capable of carrying eighty planes, she was the lead ship of thirteen more carriers on the way or already launched. And last August, Congress had ordered eleven more *Essex* class carriers. And last week, at a late afternoon cocktail party at the Alameda Naval Air Station, a loudmouthed staff captain blabbed about the new *Midway* class carrier that was being ordered: three behemoths of fifty-five thousand tons with a hundred-plane capacity.

Besides the heavy carriers, there were another eighty or so light or escort carriers, launched or on the way, each capable of carrying twenty to thirty planes.

The math wasn't difficult. *Twenty-seven* attack aircraft carriers plus *eighty* light aircraft carriers was an astonishing capability. And hundreds of support ships were also on the way, a fraction of which stood anchored before him. Poor Yamamoto. Did the man really know what he was in for? If he did, the admiral must be scared out of his trousers. No wonder the Japanese messages via Moscow were becoming more and more strident, demanding information of all kinds. So much so that Dezhnev had been ordered to shift from his KOMET activities to gathering straight tactical information for the Japanese.

Dezhnev rested on his cane for a moment, watching the four-ship formation steam toward a heavy mist. The wind kicked up another five knots, reminding him of springtime in Sochi on the Black Sea. The waves were furiously whitecapped and, sadly, the destroyers disappeared into the gloom. Soon the cruiser, a curious wisp of light brown smoke curling from her after stack, was lost also to view. Eduard Dezhnev tightened his collar and his grip on his cane, and walked the last half-block to the Soviet Consulate.

Zenit was in uniform. Always, something was up when Zenit wore his uniform. But this time, he was without Dezhnev's medals. Quietly, just before a consulate party two weeks ago, Dezhnev had trapped Zenit in a vestibule, pressing a forearm to the *zampolit*'s throat while he unpinned his medals. Perspiration broke out on Zenit's lip as he mumbled, "I'm sorry, comrade, I forgot."

They sat in a third-floor meeting room down the hall from the radio room, its powerful receivers squealing.

"Sit, please, Eduard."

Zenit's tone was cordial; too cordial.

As Dezhnev sat, Zenit stood. "I have great news for you, Eduard." He opened a folder and read from a sheet of paper. "Your promotion to captain third rank has been approved. Commissar Beria himself has endorsed it. Congratulations, comrade." Zenit reached out, pumped Dezhnev's hand once, then let go.

"Approved? I didn't realize it had been recommended."

Stiffly, Zenit handed over the page. "Here. Read it yourself."

It was a dispatch from naval headquarters routed via Beria. "It's dated two weeks ago."

"Transmission was garbled. It took a while to clear up the mess."

Pure shit. That telegraphist, the guitar-playing Yuri Moskvitin, who ran the radio gang down the hall, was top-notch. It wouldn't take him two weeks to ungarble a message from Moscow. Even so . . . captain third rank. Dezhnev sat back and decided to try it on for size. "So. We're the same rank, eh,

Sergei?'' Until now, he hadn't called Zenit by his first name and he rolled it off his tongue theatrically.

Zenit bristled.

His eyes are crossed. This is killing him.

"Something else has come up."

"Yes . . . *Sergei.*" Stupid to keep calling him by his first name, but it was fun to watch Zenit squirm.

Zenit cleared his throat. "Commissar Beria specifically asked for you to supervise the West Coast activities of Operation VOSTOK."

Dezhnev drummed his fingers. "Which is what?"

Zenit pulled a packet of papers from another folder and passed them over. "As your control, I've been authorized to review these, even participate in the project. But you have been selected because of your excellent English and''—Zenit bit his lip—"your ability to act."

"Act? What the hell does this war have to do with stage play?"

"You'll have to ask Commissar Beria about that." Zenit tapped the packet with the back of his hand and dropped his voice to a whisper. "It seems the Americans are involved in some sort of superbomb project, you see."

"Superbomb?"

"A bomb that can destroy a whole city block, maybe two."

"We have that capability now." Dezhnev's eyes bored into Zenit, the *zampolit,* the politician who didn't know a hand grenade from a Molotov cocktail.

"All right. Five city blocks, perhaps. All I know is that their code name is Project Manhattan. There is a section here that explains the technical parts, you see. Apparently, the project is in the development stage and still requires a lot of pure science. So much so that we have noticed that many physicists in the San Francisco area, in Southern California, and in the state of Washington''—he pointed north—"are disappearing. We don't know where. Whole families. It's bizarre. Here today, teaching undergraduate physics students at the University of California, then gone tomorrow without a trace. We need you to find them. Possibly to identify those who have not yet disappeared.

"You say Southern California?"

"Yes. From Cal Tech, primarily."

"I can go there and see movie stars?"

"Cal Tech is not in Hollywood. It's several kilometers away in a city called Pasadena. Besides, you don't have clearance to go to Southern California. But we're working on that. The Americans have declared the West Coast a war zone, but they only enforce it against people like us. For the time being, you will identify and trace physicists who have disappeared from the University of California at Berkeley and from Stanford University."

Dezhnev took the packet and thumbed its pages. "Thank you . . . *Sergei.*"

Zenit gave a curt nod.

"What about KOMET? Do we continue or what?"

Zenit stood and walked to a window, watching dark clouds roll over the bay. It looked like rain. "I think so. Tatekawa keeps asking about operations in the Philippines, Mindanao specifically. He's apparently doing a favor for a friend, an admiral."

"What difference is this to us?"

"Using the Birkenfeld business as a lever, they bark, we jump. Beria has ordered us to keep doing all we can."

"I see."

"We need more information on guerrilla operations there. Anything. Big or small. Beria wants it all. Apparently, the resistance is giving them fits, tying down troops who are supposed to be fighting the Marines on Guadalcanal."

It took all Dezhnev's composure to keep from sounding sarcastic. "What can I do?"

Zenit stood so close to the window that his breath steamed it up. "We've discovered your friend is back."

"Who?"

"Toliver. Your destroyer comrade. Gunnery officer, wasn't he? His ship was sunk and he was wounded, you see. They flew him back here, where he had surgery at the Stanford Lane Hospital. Now he's recuperating."

"You're joking." Dezhnev ran a thumb and forefinger over the solid gold cuff link on his shirtsleeve. They bore his initials, ED, in English. They were a gift from Toliver, who had purchase them at Gump's.

Zenit's lip curled. "The man must be very wealthy. Instead of staying in a military hospital, he recuperates in a suite in the St. Francis Hotel."

CHAPTER FORTY-ONE

Dezhnev watched rain pelt the window of Room 1220 (The St. Francis preferred to call them parlors) located on the hotel's top floor. Across the street, Union Square was obscured by the storm that had rumbled in three hours ago. The suite was exquisitely furnished, with a bedroom off to each side. Thoughtfully, a giant log crackled in the fireplace. Lucky, he mused. After his meeting with Zenit, Dezhnev called over and was immediately connected with Toliver. Rather than jubilant, Toliver sounded distracted, his voice faint. It took a lot to convince him to have dinner this evening.

Toliver hobbled in on crutches, wearing his blue uniform and heavy overcoat, his face the color of chalk. "Seems like every time we go out, it's raining. You ready?"

Dezhnev, also in uniform, wiggled into his greatcoat. Ever since Dezhnev's encounter with the Navy thugs, Zenit had insisted he wear his uniform when going out. "Where would you like to go?"

"Wait a minute."

"Yes?" Dezhnev's eyebrows went up.

Toliver raised his hand and brushed at Dezhnev's shiny new insignia. "Something new?"

Dezhnev gave a slight smile. "Promotion. I'm now captain third rank."

"Well, congratulations, Ed. Does that mean you make more money?"

Dezhnev shrugged. "A few rubles. Now . . . about dinner."

Toliver snatched his cap off the desk. "You know, I've been thinking about Wong Lee's ever since I've been back. Would you mind?"

"Excellent. Should we call a cab?"

Toliver shook his head. "No. We'll take my car. Except there's one problem."

"Yes?" Dezhnev opened the front door and they walked to the elevator and pushed the button.

"The doctors won't let me drive yet. Too much strain with the clutch, brake, and all that nonsense. How about it? Would you mind driving my car?"

"Of course not."

They descended into the garage, where the valet delivered Toliver's Packard, the engine running. Toliver got in the passenger's seat. Dezhnev stepped into the driver's side. "Ummmm." He released the hand brake, then pulled the gearshift, making a loud racket.

"Hey! Jeez, Ed, what the hell you doing?"

The valet stood off to one side scratching his head as Dezhnev pushed in the clutch. "It's been a while." He eased the clutch out then pulled hard on the gearshift lever. Once again the transmission made a terrible grinding noise.

Toliver reached over and switched off the engine. "Ed, how long you been driving?"

With the slightest of smiles, Dezhnev turned. "Actually, about a minute and a half."

Toliver's mouth curled.

Dezhnev giggled.

Toliver's laugh grew to a roar and he whacked Dezhnev on the arm. "You sonofabitch. Come on. We'll take a taxi."

Suzy, the comely Chinese-American waitress, recognized them immediately. With a broad smile, she gave each a kiss. "Booth number thirty-nine for you. The most exclusive in Wong Lee's Café."

With Dezhnev on Toliver's left, Suzy took the other side and began leading them into the main dinning room. What happened to you?'' she asked Toliver, helping him down some steps.

"I'm screwed together with a Neufeld blade plate.''

"You're what?''

"It's my hip.'' Toliver explained quickly. "Look, Suzy, could we sit there?'' He pointed to an empty table in the middle of the dining area.

Suzy looked to Dezhnev, who shrugged. "If that's what you want, then it's yours.''

Toliver grinned sheepishly. "I'd just like to be with people. Thanks.''

While Dezhnev helped Toliver in his chair, Suzy said, "Don't worry about ordering. Tonight, it's the house specialty for you.''

"Which is?''

With exaggeration, she fluttered her eyes. "Don't you know there are some things you don't ask a girl?''

"Oh, my God. Bring it on.'' Toliver lowered his voice. "Do you still have scotch?''

"Let me check.'' With a wink, Suzy picked up his crutches, stood them in a corner, then bustled off.

Dezhnev leaned on his elbows. "You are about to make a touchdown with her.''

"Wish I could. But I'm so full of codeine, I'm just . . . uhhhh.'' Toliver let his tongue hang over his lip.

"What will the booze do to you?''

"I'm sure going to find out.''

A waiter walked up and placed their drinks before them.

Toliver sniffed at it and smiled. "Ahhh, Suzy, you're a sweetheart. I'm sorry, Ed. You want vodka?''

Dezhnev gave a quick bow and raised up his glass. "They don't have vodka. Remember?''

Toliver slapped his forehead. "I hope we can remain friends.''

Dezhnev ignored the jibe. "So this is fine. Now—'' he raised his glass— "welcome back. And to your quick recovery. Uhhh-rah!''

"Uhhh-rah!'' grunted Toliver. "And congratulations on your promotion. Uhhh-rah!''

"Uhhh-rah!'' replied Dezhnev, noticing people glancing their way

After they clinked glasses and tossed back their scotch, Toliver dabbed his napkin at his mouth, then burped. "Ahhh. Man, oh, man, that is good. I'll tell you, Ed. There was a time a few weeks back when I thought I would never be able to do this again.''

Dezhnev leaned in again. "So can you talk about it?''

"We're on the same side, aren't we?''

"You know what I mean. You're angry, aren't you?''

Toliver's mouth opened in surprise.

"Angry that you let down your shipmates. Especially the dead ones.''

Toliver drank again.

"Remember what I said, Ollie?"

" 'Let the dead bury the dead.' Flying back on the plane, pumped full of morphine, that ran over and over in my head. I heard it again when I was coming out of surgery. Yeah, I remember. But I have to tell you, it's easier said than done."

"How did this happen?"

Toliver gulped scotch. "I don't want to talk about it."

"Better you should. I've been through it, too. Remember? Tell me. What happened?"

Toliver drained his glass, beckoned a passing waiter. "I'll take another, please. How 'bout you, Ed?"

Dezhnev quickly finished and thumped down his glass. *"Da."*

The waiter's eyebrows furrowed.

"He's a Commie. That means, 'Yes.' "

The waiter nodded and walked away.

"Come, now. Give."

Toliver gave a long sigh. "All right." He told Dezhnev the same story he'd told Ingram aboard the *Zeilin*. He finished with, "and now the *Riley* is at the bottom of the New Georgia Sound. And listen to this. They call it 'Iron Bottom Sound' because of all the sunken ships."

"You say just one torpedo hit you?"

Toliver nodded, his hands wiggling out an explosion. "Boom! Whap! Blew me in the air; actually the whole ship jumped. I was *catapulted* in the air and fell to the deck below. That's how—"

The waiter returned with the drinks and said, "Miss Lee say you should eat soon. She say you look awful and need good food."

"Bring it on." As the waiter walked off, Toliver put a hand to his head. "Damn. This scotch has a kick to it."

"You all right?"

"Sure, sure." Toliver leaned aside as the waiter placed a bowl before him. "What's this?"

"Hot and sour soup." The waiter set down a spice bowl. "Here is more stuff, if you need it."

Toliver leaned over the bowl and smiled. "Ummm. Smells good." He picked up his spoon and gulped. Within seconds, his face turned red and he made a show of gasping. Reaching for his glass, he gulped, letting water dribble down his chin.

Dezhnev chuckled and spooned with panache. Smacking his lips appreciatively, he said, "Ahh. Good choice, Suzy. Very good."

"Damn," Toliver gasped. "Poisoned on my first night out."

They sipped for a moment, Dezhnev mulling what he'd learned so far. From what Toliver said, it confirmed reports that the Japanese had the upper hand with their night tactics and their Type 93 torpedoes. In fact, if Toliver was any example, it sounded as if the Americans had no idea what they were up against. Also, he wondered if Otis DeWitt had had any success about telling the Type 93 torpedo secrets to General Sutherland. Casually, he asked, "So how is Todd? Did he come out all right?"

Toliver reached for a soup spoon and missed. His second try was successful, except that it was a teaspoon. No matter. He dipped it in the hot and sour soup and slurped loudly. "Tanned, windblown. Ingram looks like Charles Atlas. The tropics agree with him. Ahhh, Suzy." She walked by and he reached out, and coiled his arm around her. "Great soup."

She picked up his scotch glass and set it on the tray of a passing waiter. "You eat lots. The main course will arrive soon."

Toliver plunged his head into his hands and went into a falsetto. "Oh, my God. I can't stand it. Please, please. I gotta have a drink." He wracked his body with fake sobs.

Suzy ran a hand through his hair and grinned at Dezhnev.

Dezhnev looked up at her. "How long have you been here?"

"We opened this in 1935."

Toliver slurped soup. "You have more than one?"

"My grandmother runs our Los Angeles restaurant, which we opened three years ago."

Dezhnev dabbed a napkin to his lips. "And you run this?"

Suzy bowed gracefully. "My mother is manager here."

"Well, let's see her."

"She's off tonight."

"Oh."

"You've had good success, it looks like?" asked Dezhnev.

"It's gone very well, thank you."

Toliver grasped her hand and kissed it, saying, "Heard anything from your pop?"

Suzy shook her head.

"I'm sorry, hon." Toliver grabbed her waist again.

She nodded. "We pray."

The waiter arrived with a tray loaded with steaming bowls.

"Ummmm. Ollie. I'd forgotten how good this was."

"Mindanao," slurred Toliver, picking up a fried shrimp and popping it in his mouth. "Wouldn't that be something if they ran into each other."

"Who?" said Suzy. "It's a big island."

Dezhnev did his best to look casual.

"Maybe not. You know. Todd's girlfriend is with the resistance on . . . shhhh . . ." Toliver lowered his voice to a hoarse whisper and looked around the room. ". . . Mindanao. She's with Pablo Amador, the king of Nasipit. If anybody knows about your uncle, it would be him."

Suzy bent to her knees and looked up into Toliver's face, her eyes searching. "You mean someone could find out?"

"You remember Otis?"

"Yes. Yes."

Toliver grinned conspiratorially. "Well, Otis talks to them all the time. Radio messages. Secret stuff, except it doesn't mean a hill of beans 'cause there's a million Japs around them. But Pablo sure has them bamboozled, I'll tell you. Let me talk to Otis. See if he can do something."

"Oh." Suzy beamed. "Oh." She leaned over and kissed Toliver on the mouth. "Thank you. I can't wait till—"

Toliver waved a finger under her nose. "No telling anybody, honey. Okay? This is a military secret. You have to promise."

Suzy stood, seeing new customers in the little waiting area. "I promise. Oh, thank you, Ollie. Look, I'll be back in a minute." She dashed off.

Dezhnev thought about that. Mindanao. And Wong Lee. He hadn't mentioned Wong Lee when he'd first heard about him. It had seemed so insignificant. Maybe now. A tidbit for Moscow.

Dezhnev took a bite. "Ummm. The roast duck is excellent."

Toliver enjoyed his own food. "Ummmfff."

"You made Suzy very happy. Can you really do that?"

Toliver's eyes focused for a moment. "Actually, yes. A buddy of mine is a courier for ComSowesPac. I saw him a couple of days ago. Said he leaves for Brisbane in two days. I'll get a letter off to Otis. Should take a week to find out."

"What a wonderful thing for you to do." Dezhnev patted Toliver's back and drank. "Uhhh-rah!"

"Uhhh-rah!" Toliver took a long swig of Dezhnev's scotch. "Suzy's such a nice kid." Then he thumped down the glass and fumbled for a moment with chopsticks. He grinned at a surprised Dezhnev as he expertly articulated the chopsticks and dug into mu shu pork. "Fantastic."

"Ummm," agreed Dezhnev. He'd given up the challenge of the chopsticks and switched to a fork.

As he chewed, Toliver's mind swirled through a fog. A voice told him, *Let the dead bury the dead.* "You're right, Ed."

"*Da.*"

Toliver felt the glow within. For the first time in months, he felt relaxed and he sensed that maybe in this world there was a place for him after this terrible war. Maybe it would be just a simple task. He hoped it would be something where he could make at least a small difference. "Glad you called, Ed."

"*Da.*"

Last night, Toliver had thought about jumping out the window and hadn't fallen asleep until sunrise. When Dezhnev called, he was close to tears, wondering how he could survive another night seeing and hearing the ghosts of his dead comrades entombed in the U.S.S. *Riley.*

Let the dead bury the dead. Tonight, he would sleep well. Very well.

It had been quiet at Wong Lee's, so Suzy joined Dezhnev and Toliver around ten and they moved to the bar and drank themselves silly. She taught them phrases of Chinese and Dezhnev taught them Russian. After a while they sang Russian drinking songs, Dezhnev later coating the air with the melodious, mournful tones of Russian folk music. They closed the evening with a horrendous rendition of "Volga Boatman," Toliver grunting "Uhhh!" after each "yo, ho, heave, ho." After that, Suzy called a cab and Dezhnev dumped a wobbly Toliver into the arms of the St. Francis's doorman.

Fifteen minutes later, when Dezhnev walked in the consulate's door, Zenit was waiting in the lobby. "Well?"

A woozy Dezhnev told him everything.

Zenit stood. "You must inform Beria at once. I expect to see a copy on my desk by nine o'clock tomorrow morning."

Dezhnev stood with Zenit and belched loudly.

Zenit ignored him. "There is something else from when you dined with Toliver, DeWitt, and Ingram."

Dezhnev tried to belch again, couldn't bring one up. "Yes?"

"Colonel DeWitt's authenticator code in the Philippines. What was it?"

"Which column? Vertical or horizontal?"

Zenit scratched his head. "I believe General Tatekawa wants the vertical column authenticator."

Dezhnev weaved for a moment. "Mmmmm. How much will you pay me for this information?"

Zenit stood as straight as he could. "Lieutenant Dezhnev. This is no time for levity—"

"It's Captain Third Rank Dezhnev."

"Yes. Yes. Now, please, no games. Tell me."

They hadn't told Dezhnev anything. He'd overheard it outside the booth at Wong Lee's last August, the night they were drinking hard, toasting the world and everything in it, and growling, 'Uhhh-rah!' "It's 1939."

"Send that, too. Apparently it has been garbled somewhere along the line." Then Zenit stalked off to bed.

Sitting at the desk, Dezhnev stared at the wall for two hours, desperately trying to find a way out, a way to keep from cheating on his friend Toliver, a man he'd grown to love.

Finally, he shook his head, gave a long sigh, and wrote his message. At five in the morning, he shuffled up the back steps to the third floor, where he handed it to the on-duty telegraphist. "Send that at once. And give Comrade Zenit a copy."

Then Eduard Dezhnev stumbled back to his room and collapsed onto his bed, fully clothed.

While Dezhnev sank into unconsciousness, the telegraphist encrypted the message and sent it to Moscow Central.

MOST SECRET

TO: BERIA
FM: DEZHNEV
SUBJ: KOMET

FOLLOWING SUGGESTED FOR FORWARDING TO TATEKAWA.

1. ON THE AMERICAN NAVY IN THE SOLOMONS:
    A. INTERVIEW WITH OFFICER/SURVIVOR OF CAPE ESPERANCE BATTLE SUGGESTS AMERICAN NAVY STILL COMPLETELY UNAWARE JAPANESE TORPEDO CAPABILITY.
    B. AMERICAN TORPEDOES CONTINUE TO BE INEFFECTIVE AND SUFFERING HIGH FAILURE RATES.
    C. AMERICAN NAVY NIGHT TACTICS IN SOLOMONS NOT WELL COORDINATED AND INEFFECTIVE DESPITE ADVANTAGE OF RADAR.
2. ON YOUR REQUIREMENTS FOR INFORMATION ON MINDANAO
    A. LEADER OF NORTHEAST MINDANAO (NASIPIT) IS PABLO AMADOR, LAND BARON AND ONCE DEPUTY MINISTER OF FINANCE TO PRESIDENT MANUEL QUEZON.
    B. ASSISTING HIM IS AMERICAN NURSE (EX CORREGIDOR) HELEN DURAND, FIRST LIEUTENANT, U.S. ARMY.
    C. CHINESE-AMERICAN WONG LEE OF SAN FRANCISCO APPARENTLY TRAPPED ON MINDANAO AFTER JAPANESE INVASION. IF STILL ALIVE, COULD HAVE JOINED A RESISTANCE GROUP.
    D. VERTICAL AUTHENTICATOR, CHECKERBOARD CODE = 1939.

MESSAGE ENDS

CHAPTER FORTY-TWO

Lightning flashed and thunder rumbled as Wong Lee carefully lowered the radio into the underground vault. Rain pounded as he looked over to Amador. "Damn thing work okay?"

"Good enough." Amador leaned over his message pad, decoding. "Here." He gave a section to Felipe Estaque, who sat beside him.

While the two worked, Legaspi snorted and gave Wong Lee a fierce look.

Refusing to meet Legaspi's eyes, Wong Lee scrambled down the ladder to arrange the equipment in the pit. The *guerrillero* was still angry with him and watched every move. It was Wong Lee's fault the transmitter had been broken. With a lot of tinkering, it took nearly two weeks to fix, after the night Wong let the rope slip through his hands, the transmitter crashing into the pit.

And it was Wong Lee's fault they missed the *Needlefish*. On the road to Cabadbaran that Saturday night, they hid in a grove when a Japanese patrol surprised them, dashing up from the rear. But Legaspi hid them in a swampy backwater. After an hour or so, the Japanese became confused and started yelling at each other. Giving up, they headed back to the road. A truck pulled up and they began to board.

But then Wong stepped on something that slithered. He screamed, loudly.

The Japanese sergeant shouted. Soldiers poured from the truck as a powerful spotlight snapped on and began sweeping. Soon it outlined a skirmish line two hundred yards long.

Legaspi cursed and heaved a grenade, shoving everyone farther into the overgrowth. With the explosion, he deftly led them through the pitch-black swamp, while the Japanese fired flares and set up a machine gun. With the machine gun thumping away, Legaspi maneuvered them to higher country and away from the eager hands of the Kempetai.

And away from Cabadbaran and the *Needlefish* rendezvous. Soldiers searched the rest of the night and all the next day. So much so that Amador commented, "If I didn't know any better, I'd think they were tipped off."

With a cigarette dangling from his lips, Wong Lee quickly climbed up the ladder, closed the trapdoor, and kicked dirt over the top. Still avoiding Legaspi's eyes, he brushed the floor with a *sawali,* a piece of split bamboo used for thatching. Then he stood aside, waiting for Amador to finish decoding the message.

Wong Lee took a last drag and was poised to flick the butt out the window when Legaspi waved a finger. "Jackass."

Wong Lee looked at the night. "It's raining."

"Hapons pick it up, we dead." Legaspi glared again, making Wong Lee feel as if the Filipino had thrust his dagger right through him.

"Okay." Wong Lee squeezed out the ember between thumb and forefinger, field-stripped the cigarette, and stuffed the wadded paper in his pocket. He turned to Amador. "What's the dope?"

"Ummm." Amador held up a match and lit a piece of foolscap he'd used for a worksheet; then he dropped it into a metal ashtray.

Wong said, "Looks like everybody's burning tonight."

Ignoring him, Amador shouted at the door, "You done yet?"

Helen Durand's voice drifted in. "In a second."

"We'll wait. You should hear this."

Something in Amador's tone drew Wong Lee's attention.

Another bolt of lightning lit the night. Thunder crashed as Helen walked in, a large coil of bare copper antenna wire looped over her shoulder. "Anything exciting?" she asked, rain dripping off her floppy planter's hat.

"Just you." Wong pointed to the wire. "Another bolt like the last one and you become Mrs. Frankenstein."

Amador nodded. "You really should be careful, dear."

"I should be so lucky." She finished coiling the wire and handed it to Wong Lee, who climbed up to a rafter and hid it among the nipa palm.

Amador leaned against an empty crate and read, "All right. Here it is. Otis is sending another submarine." He slapped the message with the back of his hand. "It's the U.S.S. *Turbot* and she's bringing in five tons of equipment, including"—he looked at Wong Lee—"a new radio. They're giving us new M-1 carbines, it says; ammunition, grenades, food, and medicine . . . Umm, let's see, they're due on the seventeenth, next Tuesday. Good, there should be no moon. And listen to this. They're going to airdrop in a naval officer as a beachmaster to coordinate the landing. We pick him up at the Amparo emergency airstrip early Tuesday morning."

Wong Lee offered, "I hope the weather clears."

"What else did Otis have to say?" Helen murmured.

Running a hand through his long white hair, Amador smiled. "Colonel DeWitt sends his congratulations on getting the Japanese torpedo book. He has ordered you out, as before."

"Me, too?" asked Wong Lee.

"As long as you don't step on any snakes."

Wong Lee pulled a face.

Helen put an arm around Wong's shoulder. "They're just being mean, Wong. Don't worry."

Amador's brow furrowed. "Actually, it was a most fortunately missed rendezvous."

"Yes?"

Amador reread the message. "The *Needlefish* was lost with all hands a day out of Brisbane."

Helen sat on a crate, her hand to her mouth. "Oh, my God."

"Apparently she hit a floating mine."

Wong Lee lit another cigarette, forgetting the one he'd balanced on the end of an empty oil drum. He looked at Legaspi. "Damn snake was my good-luck charm."

Legaspi growled, "Too bad you weren't on it."

Conversation stopped as thunder rattled outside.

Wong rose to his feet and took a step. "I've had enough of your shit."

Felipe Estaque got up and stood between them. "Let's cool off."

Amador stepped over and crushed out Wong's old cigarette and stripped it. "He doesn't mean it, Wong. Life goes on. You get to go home."

"You bet I'm going home. I'm a civilian. I'm tired of fighting this jerk's wars for him." Wong Lee thrust his chin toward Legaspi. "You can take your bug-infested country and stuff it, Mac."

Legaspi lunged at Wong Lee, but Estaque and Amador held them apart.

Amador said, "Grow up, you two. Let's not do the Hapons' work for them."

Wong Lee took a seat across the room and crossed his arms.

Helen sat next to him and patted his back. "What's wrong with you?"

Wong shook his head. "Jitters, I guess. Too much of this. Going stir crazy, you know what I mean?"

"I do."

Amador turned to Estaque and Legaspi. "The submarine will be vulnerable during off-loading. So we must have lots of *barrotos,* Emilio."

With a final eye toward Wong Lee, Legaspi exhaled and nodded. "*Sí.* All the *barrotos* not sunk by the Hapons." Shortly after the occupation, the Japanese swarmed into Buenavista, seizing food and fishing equipment. Then, for good measure, they machine-gunned the Filipinos' boats.

Amador asked, "How many do you think you can get?"

"Oh, lots of them."

"How many, I asked."

"Plenty, no worry."

An exasperated Estaque held out his hands. "From where?"

"All over."

While they bickered, Helen recounted the past few days. She'd been lucky. Very lucky. The Japanese hadn't seen through her leper ruse, Yawata hadn't gotten his way, she'd recovered the torpedo manual, and, the big one, she'd missed the *Needlefish.* God had well blessed her. *Please, Lord, just five more days.*

Lightning flashed across Wong Lee's face. "What's the matter?" she asked.

Wong shook his head slowly, "Nothing's getting in my way this time. Snakes or no snakes, I'm catching that pigboat."

"Can you believe it? Your snake saved us."

Wong shook his head. "All I know is that I've had enough of this crap. One way or another, I'm going to get on that sub and go home."

"What if she hits a mine?"

"Then I'll get out and push."

The storm settled to a steady downpour, pelting the storehouse. For a moment Helen watched the ceiling, amazed at the nipas' durability. There were no leaks. "Some people are never satisfied."

"You have to reach for it, honey."

"Yes, but then you go home and they'll probably draft you," she said, satisfied his eyes began to twinkle.

"Not this kid. I'm too old for the draft."

"Old enough to breath, old enough to serve."

Wong Lee grunted. "They'll need a whole battalion to yank me from my restaurant."

"They'll do it anyway. And after they capture you, you're back in the Army."

"I'll make a great cook."

"Just before they send you overseas, they give you lots of shots."

"Ouch."

"And then they send you right back here. So why bother to leave at all?"

"Not a chance, honey. Wong Lee is critical to the war effort. They need me home to make fortune cookies."

Helen smiled.

"I love it when you do that. I bet he does, too."

"Who?"

"Your Mr. Todd. Where's his ring?"

She grabbed Todd's ring, then let it drop. "I told him I would keep it safe for him."

"He's a lucky sonofabitch."

Her face grew dark and she looked outside. "Don't count on it."

"Helen? I'm sorry."

She whipped around. "How can anybody know in this mess? Maybe he's dead. Maybe he has a girlfriend in . . ."—she pointed east—"in San Francisco. Maybe they sent him to Europe. Why should I care? He's there and I . . . we're here."

"But we're soon going to be there," Wong Lee shouted over booming thunder.

She shouted back in the relative quiet, "But he doesn't care. Why should he? San Francisco is soft and cushy. Women on every street corner."

"My God, Helen, what started this? I said I was sorry." Wong reached for her.

She stepped back and rasped, "Well, if he doesn't care, then I don't care, either." She tugged at the ring, trying to rip it from her neck. But the lanyard was too strong. "Ohhhh. It doesn't matter. Really it doesn't. We've had so little time together. I hardly know him." Jamming her hat over her eyes, she dashed out of the hut and disappeared into the rain.

Legaspi, Estaque and Amador watched her go. "What on earth?" asked Amador.

Wong Lee scratched his head. "You know, Pablo? She really does love that guy. Heaven forbid if he crosses her. And if he does, I kill the sonofabitch myself."

CHAPTER FORTY-THREE

14 NOVEMBER, 1942
U.S.S. *PEMBROKE* (DD 248)
MORETON BAY, QUEENSLAND, AUSTRALIA

Built in 1918, the *Pembroke,* named after Commodore Thomas C. Pembroke, a naval engineer of the previous century, was a four-stack destroyer of 1,340 tons and a once-proud member of the U.S. Asiatic Fleet based in Manila. In early 1942, she escaped the horrors of the Japanese attacks on naval bases in Manila Bay, Cebu, and Mindanao. Eventually she made her way south to Australia, just ahead of Japan's invasion forces roaring through East Asia, on their way to occupy the Dutch East Indies. Now the creaky destroyer limped about on convoy duty, from Brisbane to Nouméa to Fiji, as far east as American Samoa, then back again. Rarely using more than two of her four boilers, the *Pembroke* could still make twenty-two knots, ducking among her brood of merchantmen, who doggedly plowed in their columns at a frustrating ten knots. It was a comfortable assignment for the old greyhound, which was one of the few four-stackers that hadn't been eviscerated for conversion to a high-speed troop transport, nor a minesweeper, minelayer, or seaplane tender. Indeed, she had her original engineering layout of four boilers and twin turbines, her four ancient four-inch cannons, and two triple-mount torpedo tubes. Last month, her low, thin silhouette was barely altered with the addition of a new surface search radar. In December, she was scheduled to be fitted with a modern scanning sonar, which would make her far more capable of sniffing out enemy submarines along her routes.

But the *Pembroke* had been shifted from convoy duty to a strange task.

For the past three days, she'd been assigned to firing torpedoes into a net hanging off a barge anchored three miles northwest of Mooloolaba Harbor. No longer wallowing over moonlit, azure seas at ten knots, her crew grumbled as they stood at battle stations, their ship dashing past the barge at speeds varying from five to thirty knots, shooting Mark 15 torpedoes. Two sixty-foot torpedo retrievers stood by, recovering the torpedoes, then delivering them back to the *Pembroke* for the next day's firing. This meant the crew, primarily the *Pembroke*'s torpedo gang, worked through the night, preparing their "tin fish," as they called them, for the next day's tests.

By late Saturday afternoon, the *Pembroke* had finished her week's work and steamed southeasterly for Brisbane via the Northwest Passage and Moreton Bay. It was a six-hour trip of fifty miles, through a sinuous channel with mudflats, breaking reefs, and shallow waters to port: the eastern Queensland coast two miles to starboard. The *Pembroke*'s skipper was anxious to negotiate the hardest part before nightfall, when they would loose all their navigational aides, the entire Australian coastline plunged into strict blackout.

Todd Ingram walked out on the main deck, coffee mug in hand, and propped a foot on a chock, watching the Queensland coast slide by. The Australian summer was fast approaching, the air a balmy seventy-four degrees. On a hillside he picked out two bicyclists bumping their way down a path, scattering a flock of sheep. Well astern now was the stately Caloundra Head lighthouse, its light comatose in wartime. Through the midships passageway, he picked out Cape Moreton ten miles to port, which told him there was at least three and a half hours to go. This meant they would not make their mooring by nightfall; and for the skipper's sake, he hoped the radar worked as well tonight as it had over the last three days.

Ingram sipped, then took a deep breath, watching the sheep scatter. The scene was so pastoral, he desperately tried to take it in, make it part of him, so perhaps it could help uncoil what was inside. But it was impossible. Ever since he'd learned of the *Needlefish*'s loss, that Helen wasn't coming back, he'd driven himself, totally giving in to work, doing something every waking moment, sometimes getting only three or four hours of sleep.

After a week in a Brisbane shipyard, Dutton had walked up and told him, quite frankly, the *Howell*'s officers were complaining. Yes, Ingram had been appointed acting captain, but he was too remote, too standoffish, too inclined to fly off the handle at the slightest provocation. With a scowl, Ingram silently dismissed Dutton, even though he knew it was true; and that it wasn't his officer's fault the *Needlefish* had hit a mine. However, no one knew for sure if it was a mine. Perhaps she'd been torpedoed by a Japanese submarine. Perhaps she had suffered a battery explosion. The only trace was an oil slick that had burbled to the surface ten miles off the coast. And Helen was out there, at the bottom of the ocean. So close. At times, he wondered if he should join her.

He dreaded that Kate and Frank Durand were in for another telegram. But that would take several months, and a debate raged in his mind on whether or not to let them know, try and make things easier. A quick letter would do it; he'd had plenty of practice writing letters to the *Pelican*'s crewmember's families after his escape from Corregidor. But he didn't do it, knowing he had to abide by security measures. Unlike the time when he first met them, when Helen was alive. But there was no way to soften this blow. And if he didn't write the letter, there would come a time when the postman would drive up to the Durand ranch, get out of his truck, and hand over the War Department telegram. Who would be there to accept it? Kate? He hoped not. It would destroy her. It had to be Frank who broke the news.

Helen.

Rocko Myszynski had appointed him as temporary commanding officer to take the *Howell* from Espiritu Santo to Brisbane for repairs. On their second night in port, he'd silently slipped ashore, bought a quart of bootleg scotch, and found a cheap waterfront hotel. He holed up there in a five-by-seven cheese box and drank the bottle sitting on the bed. Unfazed, he listened to prostitutes and their johns grunting and moaning through thin walls. All he could do was stare dry-eyed out the scum-covered window into the blackout, eventually watching the sun rise while a furniture factory came to life next door. Then he lurched the four and a half miles back to the *Howell,* ate breakfast, and fell asleep for seventeen hours.

He'd wanted to cry in that hotel. In fact, he tried very hard. But he couldn't. Why, he didn't know. All he knew was that it was out of him . . . for the time being. Would he ever forget her? Maybe not. Right now, he felt . . . nothing.

Helen.

Except, his cheek itched. Strange.

Actually, it was sort of a throb as if it were mending again, after having been ripped open by a piece of shrapnel last April off Corregidor. Helen had sewn it up in the Malinta Tunnel hospital last April. But the stitches opened, and it leaked pus when he was on the run through the Philippines. The doctors in San Francisco resewed it and treated it with an antibiotic ointment and it finally healed. But now it itched, and he raised his hand absently, scratching the faint scar tissue.

Helen.

Ingram and Luther Dutton had been assigned temporarily to Rocko Myszynski's staff while Hank Kelly supervised what was to become a long and arduous repair period. Ingram's main job was to conn the *Pembroke* during the torpedo firings, ensuring the precision needed for accurate tests. Over the past three days they'd fired twelve torpedoes. Six ran deep, two porpoised, one ran circular; the other three hit the target as intended. And now, while Ingram sipped coffee, George Atwell was in the wardroom with three of his Winslow River Corporation sycophants, arguing with a cigar-chomping Commodore Myszynski and his staff. Myszynski ran the meeting, shouting and pointing his thick index finger at torpedo tracks on crinkling DRT paper, smashing his fists on data tables, his voice resonating throughout the small wardroom. With that, Ingram escaped to the main deck, away from their strident tones and haranguing. Fortunately, he wasn't needed anymore; he'd just been the bus driver.

The western sky was an orange-red and he leaned heavily on the bulwark, watching the reflections on the flat calm of Moreton Bay. It was almost the texture of glass as seagulls bobbed in the ship's wake. Others rose and winged over to the mudflats, where an ebbing tide exposed their evening meal at the tide's meander line.

A shoe scraped and Ingram turned to see George Atwell walking up, coffee cup in hand. Tonight, Atwell was without his legendary grin, and the yellowish orange streaks in his hair were beginning to fade, making Ingram wonder if he'd run out of his bleach; maybe he couldn't buy the stuff in the war zone. Atwell wore khaki trousers, and a sturdy khaki shirt with shoulder epaulets and cartridge holders large enough to accommodate fifty-caliber machine gun rounds. The entire rig made Ingram wonder if the man planned on going elephant hunting. Atwell sighed, "Rocco is tough,"

When Ingram didn't respond, Atwell offered, "You like a round of golf tomorrow?"

"I don't play golf."

Atwell guffawed and punched Ingram on the arm. "Maynard told me you're a scratch golfer." He referred to Captain Maynard Falkenberg, Admiral Spruance's intelligence specialist.

Ingram sipped. "George, I've got to go over to the *Howell* and check on her repairs." He didn't add that Landa had been detached as the *Howell's* commanding officer and sent back to the U.S. for recuperation. A new commanding officer had yet to be appointed.

"I see."

Ingram started to move off.

"You don't like me very much, do you?"

Ingram stopped. "What?"

"This golf bullshit. I've heard from several guys that you were the fleet champion at Manila before the war. And now you—"

"George. I haven't played golf since the war broke out. I just don't feel like it. There's too much going on."

"You blame me for what's happened." Unaccountably, Atwell's voice was soft, so unlike him.

"What are you talking about?"

"Did you know we tested Mark 14s in Frenchman's Bay last June?" Frenchman's Bay was near the west end of the Great Australian Bight. The submarine-fired Mark 14 torpedoes were four feet shorter than the destroyer-mounted Mark 15s.

"No, I didn't."

"I haven't told those guys inside yet, but the same thing happened. Damned torpedoes ran too deep."

"Why?"

"Damned if I know. Look, Todd. This is embarrassing to us at Winslow River. We're trying like hell to fix it, but we don't know what to fix yet. Did you know the Germans and Brits are having the same problem?"

"Did you know the Japs are blowing our ships from here to the next planet? Look. I don't care about the Germans and the Brits. I saw what happened to the *Riley* and—"

"But that was at night."

"—and I saw what happened to the *Porter*, in the daytime. Don't forget Rocko was aboard her, too. Eleven men died. And he's lost other ships. That's why he's so worked up."

"The sonofabitch has made it abundantly clear."

Ingram gripped the bulwark. "And that was just one torpedo that hit the *Porter*. The same day, the Japs chased us and the *Anderson* and *Mustin* away and sank the *Hornet* with just *four*." Ingram held up four fingers. "*Four* of their torpedoes.

"That was after we fired ten of your torpedoes from the *Howell* with zero effect. Same thing with the *Anderson* and *Mustin*. Now tell me, George. How do you figure that? And I have to say, no stupid golf game is going to give us answers."

Atwell's shoulders sagged. "I know. We have depth-control problems."

Ingram looked up, surprised. "What?"

"I said I'm ready to concede we have torpedo depth-control problems."

"Well, that's a step."

"But I need someone to run interference for me with Myszynski. The man is merciless. Would you mind? I think he respects you."

"Is that what you really want?"

"Well, yes."

"How about candor?" Ingram had acquired Jerry Landa's aversion to pretense and arrogance. Until tonight, Atwell had been brimming with it. Now he was almost . . . humble.

"What?"

"For years, Winslow River has been the only shop in town. The only manufacturers of torpedoes to the fleet. You've been shoving them down our throats even when the chips were down. Finally you admit you have a problem?"

Atwell pressed his lips together and turned to watch the sun set, darkness claiming the land.

Luther Dutton walked out and coughed politely. "Mr. Atwell?"

"Yes?"

Dutton's accent was deeply flavored with MIT, meaning he was nervous. "The commodore would like to know if you're coming back."

Atwell looked at Ingram.

"Candor."

Atwell sniffed at the wind.

"Okay. I'll help."

Atwell whispered, "Thank you, Todd." He took Ingram's hand in both of his and shook, then went inside.

Ingram picked up his coffee cup and moved to follow.

"About time, Skipper," Dutton said hoarsely.

Ingram spun, ready to chew on Dutton. But then a tiny voice wafted through his mind, *Give of yourself, Captain.*

Dutton stepped back, spread his hands, and forced a tight grin. "Atwell is baring his soul. Rocko will kill him in there, no matter what he says. If you help maybe some good can come out of this."

"What makes you go sure?"

"Look at him. He's broken."

Ingram sighed. "He just told me he's ready to concede their torpedoes have faulty depth-control mechanisms."

"That's swell."

Ingram slapped Dutton's shoulder. "Okay, Luther, let's go back in there and see what sort of sense we can make out of this mess."

Ingram was surprised they didn't tie up to their usual spot: a nest of destroyers moored alongside the destroyer tender *Whitney*, which was anchored five hundred yards off Fisherman Island. Instead, they steamed closer to town; to the darkened British Petroleum Terminal at Luggage Point and moored just aft of a large tanker. In a short time, the lines were doubled up, the brow shoved into place, and the liberty party lined up to go ashore, thankful for the hour saved by not having to take a shore boat. Ingram stood with them in dress khakis, waiting, as custom dictated, for the senior officers to depart by rank, Rocko Myszynski at the head of the column.

But there was a commotion in the gloom, the line held up for several moments as someone boarded. Men groused, then a slim shadow stood before Ingram. Just behind was the unmistakable bulk of Rocko Myszynski, cigar smoke swirling around his head.

"Evening, sailor."

Ingram knew that voice. "Otis! What the hell are you doing here?" He shook hands with Otis DeWitt.

"Congratulations." DeWitt patted Ingram's new lieutenant commander shoulder boards. "Looks like you're catching up to me."

The other officers stepped around them, mounted the gangway, and left the ship. Ingram and Myszynski moved inboard with DeWitt, saying, "How long you been in town?"

"I don't know. Two, three weeks."

DeWitt growled in his twang, "Well, why the hell didn't you look me up?"

Ingram was trying to think of something to say when Myszynski saved him with, "We better go to the wardroom."

"What?" Asked Ingram.

Walking forward, Myszynski called over his shoulder, "Follow me, sailor."

DeWitt had to repeat it three times. "She's alive, Todd." He waved a hand in front of Ingram's face. "Todd? Hey, Commander Ingram!"

Ingram took off his hat and sat on a small settee. "My God."

"She's alive, I said." DeWitt pulled up a chair opposite.

"Can you be more specific, Colonel?" said Myszynski.

DeWitt ignored Myszynski. "She's alive and—"

"I knew it."

"What?"

Ingram looked in the distance. "Somehow, I knew she was alive."

"What are you talking about? How?" demanded DeWitt.

Ingram looked at DeWitt, feeling stupid. "My cheek itched." It slipped out and he hadn't intended to say it. God, he felt good, like soaring. Helen! Helen! He wondered if they saw his grin. As a young ensign, he'd ridden the Roller Coaster at the Long Beach Pike. He loved it so much, he rode it five times that night. And now, he felt as if he were on it again, soaring, feeling the sheer power as it spun in its turns, pinned him to his seat, leaving his stomach at the top of the first plunging grade. Helen!

DeWitt's voice rose an octave. "Commander. I order you to tell me of any back channels you are using."

Ingram grinned openly. "Kate Durand. It's all her fault."

"What do you mean? What's this about your cheek?" DeWitt nearly yelled.

Rocko Myszynski sat and lit a cigar, watching the entertainment.

With great effort, Ingram focused. "Oh, Otis. Shut up and tell me what you want."

DeWitt's mouth dropped.

Ingram said to Myszynski, "Don't worry, Commodore. Otis and I go back a long way."

"I hope so." Myszynski stood. "Lots to do. Do you need me anymore, Colonel?"

DeWitt stood and they shook. "No, Sir. Thanks for letting us borrow him. We promise to return him fresh as a daisy in three weeks."

Myszynski snorted and rubbed his chin. "Fair enough. The *Howell* should be ready about then. Just tell Dick Sutherland he owes me one." He turned to leave but then snapped his thick fingers. "Oh, by the way, Todd. I bring you greetings from Boom Boom."

"How is he?" asked Ingram.

"Recovering nicely at the Oak Knoll Naval Hospital. They're going to release him in another three or four weeks, so we're giving the *Howell* back to him."

"I think that's great, Sir."

"Yes, and you'll stay on as exec. We're done with the tests here, so I'm going to cut you loose. I must say that I agree with Boom Boom. I've endorsed his recommendation for your own command."

"Thank you, Sir." Ingram shook Myszynski's hand.

"Okay. See you, Todd." Myszynski shook with DeWitt and walked out, trailing a cloud of blue smoke.

It all swirled around Ingram and he sat heavily. Finally, he looked up to see DeWitt staring at him, pushing over a cup of coffee. "Otis. You're not here on a social visit, are you?"

DeWitt shook his head.

"How long have you known about Helen?"

DeWitt stirred in two lumps of sugar. He looked like he'd gained most of his weight back.

"Tell me, damnit."

"Keep your shirt on, mister. The U.S. Army doesn't happen to be your personal cupid service." DeWitt said rather peevishly, "If you must know, we received a message two weeks ago that she'd missed the sub."

Ingram looked down, finding his fists clenched. With effort, he exhaled loudly. "Sorry."

"You would have found out sooner or later."

"So, what do you want?"

"A beachmaster."

"A what?"

"Our other one was damned near killed when his plane ground-looped. We have no backup, and you fit the bill perfectly. You're Navy. You know Navy talk and whatever it is that you Navy guys do. You know the Philippines. You know Amador. You even know Nasipit. And you're available."

"Otis, you've been drinking too much of that Australian dark beer."

The *Pembroke*'s captain and exec walked in and, seeing DeWitt and Ingram with their heads together, poured their coffee and discreetly sat at the table's other end.

DeWitt leaned forward and lowered his voice. "Actually, there's more to it."

"Go on."

Surprised he was perspiring, DeWitt decided against mentioning anything connected with Dezhnev and the Soviet Consulate in San Francisco. "She's come into possession of a very important document."

"What?

"It's about that torpedo you saw."

Ingram's voice rose. "You mean the Jap torpedoes on the bottom of Tulagi Harbor?"

The officers at the end of the table looked their way, then resumed talking.

"Shhh. Todd, damnit. This is top secret. A matter of national security. And we need it right now."

"How did she get mixed up in something top secret? And what the hell does national security have to do with Helen?" Ingram's fists clenched again.

"I'll tell you what you always tell me. 'Just shut up and listen.' "

Ingram sat back. "All right."

"Here's what I can tell you."

CHAPTER FORTY-FOUR

17 NOVEMBER, 1942
8° 48.2' N; 125° 33.4' E
MINDANAO, PHILIPPINES

Ingram looked out into the darkness. With the blister turret open, wind blasted in the PBY's cabin and he had to shout. "Are you sure we're there?"

De Silva, the young airman, chewed gum and squinted into the night. Tapping his earphones, he listened for a moment, then shouted back, "Yes, Sir, Commander. Skipper sez we just flew over it. Wants to know why you didn't bail out. What do I tell him, Sir?" De Silva, a kid of nineteen years, popped his gum and slammed the blister window closed, cutting the wind and engine noise down to a decent roar.

Ingram looked into the night and gulped.

"Sir?" asked De Silva.

The reason is I'm scared shitless. "Tell him we're ready," was all Ingram could think of saying. Then he reached in his pocket, making sure Helen's ring was there.

"Yes, Sir." De Silva spoke into his headset, listened for a moment. "Skipper says we'll take one more circle, then we gotta scram." De Silva clacked his gum and grinned. "So solly, Cholly. No mo gas. Skipper sez you better jump this time, or you get to play acey-deucey with me all the way back to Darwin." The PBY's skeleton crew of five had all played acey-deucey at one time or another on the long twelve-hour trip up.

Ingram looked at Seltzer also with a parachute strapped to his back. The boatswain's mate looked hard at De Silva and then drew a finger across his throat. "Remember who you're talking to, kid."

De Silva held up a hand. "Okay, Boats. Keep your shirts on."

Just then, the twin-engine PBY amphibian lurched, hitting an updraft, then began a slow, lazy turn to the left. "Commander?" asked De Silva.

Ingram looked down and tried to control his breathing. His pulse rate, too, and he closed his eyes, willing his heart to stop thumping so fast. They couldn't be more than two thousand feet above the Amparo airstrip. But with no moon, he couldn't see a damned thing out there. "Yes."

De Silva said, "I'd advise you to jump."

"What?"

"You already owe me two hundred thirty-five bucks. Who can tell how much further you'll be in debt to me if you have to stay for the return trip? Plus, the—"

Seltzer moved close and growled, "Knock that shit off, sailor."

De Silva, unfazed, waved his palms in the air, "plus, the skipper says we save gas if you guys jump. We have a much better chance of making it through that storm on the way back to Darwin."

Ingram nodded at De Silva's convoluted whimsy. They'd punched through a vicious weather front over Halmahera on the trip up. De Silva, he was sure, innocently mirrored the pilot's concern. The pilot was an intense, thin, tow-headed lieutenant (jg), four years De Silva's senior.

Ingram looked at Seltzer. "You ready?"

Seltzer betrayed himself, his Adam's apple bouncing up and down. "I'll go first, Sir."

"No, that's okay."

A moment later, the PBY straightened out, cut its engines, and began a long, shallow glide. "Signal light sighted, Commander," said De Silva, one hand to his earphone. He reached over and raised the blister window, the nighttime air once again blasting in the aft cabin, stirring up scrap paper and dust. De Silva held a hand to his earphones. "Ten seconds. Who's first?"

Ingram stepped up to a small platform and braced his hands over the bottom half of the blister window.

De Silva yelled over the air blast, "Could I have your address, Sir?"

"Why?"

"So I can send you a bill."

Ingram looked back. "You little—" That's when Seltzer grabbed his hips and shoved.

Ingram tumbled and spun from the Catalina and, like the drowning victim going down for the third time, his life over the past seventy-two hours flashed through his mind: DeWitt's quick sales pitch; Ingram's quick acceptance; Ingram's quick sales pitch to Seltzer; their long, boring flight from Brisbane to Darwin, only to climb right into the PBY and head for Mindanao.

DeWitt had said, "All you have to do is make contact with Amador. Two nights later blink the letters QQT, a flashing-light recognition signal at the *Turbot,* when she surfaces off Buenavista. Then you contact her by walkie-talkie, and conn her close to shore, where she off-loads five tons of supplies. Your reward: a return trip to Brisbane with Helen and, of course, her torpedo documents. Very simple."

Ingram pulled the rip cord and, "—Uhhh!" The canopy burst overhead, making his shoulders feel like they had jerked out of their sockets.

The sky was clear and moonless and it wasn't until he was nearly abreast of the trees that he realized it was time to tuck his—

"Oooff." Ingram hit the ground, pain shooting up his left leg. The chute didn't collapse, and a light breeze pulled him along over damp scrub brush for a moment. Then he managed to stand, pull on the shrouds, and collapse his parachute. But his ankle hurt, and he favored it as he walked forward, gathering his chute into his arm. Off to his left he heard a soft curse, which was soon followed by the squeaking of silk: Seltzer. And ahead, along the drop path, was the sharp crack of the supply pack plunging through trees and then thumping on the ground. Without that, they were lost: It carried radios, weapons, food, and medicine.

But then it became quiet. He stood for a moment and breathed deeply, taking in Asia's night air. It had rained within the last two hours and the odor of fresh water mixing with the soil and the tall grass brought back memories of two years ago, when he first reported for duty at the Cavite Naval Station on lush, green Manila Bay. There was also a tinge of lightning ozone—there must have been a thunderstorm. His ears popped and the sounds of Mindanao returned: wild monkeys screeching through the trees, and cicadas, and birds, and four-legged things of all sizes. All were prey to boa constrictors lingering in the tree's life-canopy, where they waited to fall and quickly twirl and squeeze their victims to death. Stoically, he mulled that he really was back in the Philippines, a place from which he'd almost paid with his life to escape; a place of phenomenal natural beauty and equally as phenomenal natural disasters, all seeming to mark time until the vicious political system that scourged the land was gone.

Twigs crackled behind him. "Meestair Ingram?"

Ingram spun, finding a shadow standing before him, whipping off a large planter's hat. "Yes?"

"How do, Sair?" The man bowed deeply. "I am Emilio Legaspi. Good welcome to Mindanao, by God." He bowed again and extended his hand.

They shook. "Th-thank you," said Ingram. "Is Don Pablo Amador here?"

"Todd, you're blinder than I thought." Amador emerged from the darkness, his white mane flowing in the night.

"My God." Ingram and Amador threw their arms around each other, hugged, then they stood apart, clapping shoulders. "It's good to see you."

Amador bowed deeply. "Welcome back, my friend. I only wish we could meet you in better style. Perhaps someday . . .''

"More than I expected."

Seltzer walked up, escorted by Felipe Estaque and Carlos Rameriez, carrying the supply pack. Brief introductions were made, they shook hands, then Amador said, "Only one supply pack?"

"Yes," said Ingram.

"Are you armed?"

Ingram pulled a Colt .45 from his holster, chambered a round, and made sure the safety was on. Seltzer did the same. "All set." He put his full weight on his ankle. It felt much better.

"Very well. It's time to get out of here. Hapons everywhere. They've been on the move for the last couple of days. So let's go." With Legaspi leading the way, they started walking west toward the Butuan Road.

"Same truck?" asked Ingram, referring to a battered truck Amador once had.

"Bicycles this time. The Hapons confiscated the truck. Then we blew it up for them and put it out of its misery."

"I'll miss that old wreck." Branches slapped at Ingram's face as they plunged deeper into jungle. Pushing them aside, he could barely see Amador's hair three feet ahead. Behind he sensed rather than heard Seltzer and Rameriez taking up the rear. Fifteen minutes later Amador negotiated some boulders and led them down into a gully, where they forded a raging brook. They slipped and fought their way up the other side, with Ingram grabbing on to tree roots to gain the muddy embankment, trying to keep his balance. Wheezing and gasping for air, he finally rose, covered with slime—and one or two leeches, he suspected—and followed Amador's white mane back into the jungle. Ingram's lungs felt as if they would burst, and Amador, now ten feet ahead, seemed to be virtually leaping through the bush. *He's into his sixties, and here I am with my tongue hanging out,* Ingram thought sheepishly.

After a while, they found a trail, the going smoother. Ingram caught up to Amador and whispered, "Uh, how is Helen?"

Amador chuckled softly. "She awaits you in Buenavista."

Soon they stepped into a clearing, with Amador holding up his hand, calling a halt. Legaspi emerged from the darkness and he and Amador drew together, speaking in a subdued Tagalog. Once in a while Ingram caught *Hapon*—Japanese—and *lechón*—pig. Legaspi spoke faster and faster, until Amador had to grab both the man's hands and silence him.

Seltzer joined Ingram, and the two moved up. Ingram whispered, "What is it?"

Amador whispered, "We're about fifty meters from the road, and Emilio swears he heard a truck. And he says he smells garlic, too."

"What's garlic have to do with anything?" asked Ingram.

Amador answered, "Koreans love garlic."

"I'm lost," whispered Seltzer.

In the dimness, Amador shrugged. "Many of the Kempetai are Korean thugs. They love garlic. Psst." He waved, and Felipe Estaque trotted up from the end of the column. Amador whispered to the *guerrillero,* who sniffed at the air and then shook his head. No garlic.

Seltzer said, "Something doesn't feel right, Mr. Ingram."

Ingram felt it, too. There was something . . .

With a hand in the air, Amador whispered, "The jungle is quiet. No screeching monkeys."

"That's it," Ingram agreed.

Amador jabbed a thumb over his shoulder, and wordlessly they crouched and began to step back, blending into denser jungle.

"Tomare!" Stop! A bright light clicked on twenty yards before them.

Then another light clicked from their left rear; another to their right. There was a guttural shout and a machine gun fired at them.

"Cross fire," screamed Seltzer, his face ashen white in converging beams.

Rameriez ran off to his left. Instantly a submachine gun and five or six rifles opened up, catching him at a full sprint, his body jinking and jerking in the frosted light. The *guerrillero* was dead as his body hit the ground like a sack of overripe tomatoes.

Cordite smoke rose around the clearing, and another guttural shout tore at the night.

Shadows rose from the bushes around Ingram. He crouched to run, but then a shadow dashed up, swinging a rifle. Ingram raised a hand to parry the blow when something crashed into the backs of his knees and he fell to the ground. Someone else kicked him in the ribs and he doubled up in pain. Screams around him meant the others were also being beaten. Bracing his hands under him, Ingram shoved to rise to his knees, but a split-toed sandal was braced on his head, another foot shoved the small of his back, and he crashed into a low bush. The man at Ingram's head twisted his foot, turning Ingram's face into the ground, forcing damp muddy soil in his mouth and nostrils. He couldn't breath and began to squirm and wiggle. Then a terrible crashing blow, shooting lights, and dashing bolts of pain . . . blissful darkness . . .

". . . Todd . . ." He bounced as the truck ground through gears, shifting into second, working its way up a steep grade. "Todd?"

Ingram lay on his side on the floor of the truck. Hog-tied, his hands were bound behind his back; another line was secured around his feet, tied to the line around his wrists. He coughed as the truck bounced again, his lungs shrieking in pain as he spat dirt from his mouth. "Todd?" He wanted to go back to sleep.

With a loud grind of its gears, the truck shifted to third and gained speed. From the corner of his eye, Ingram could tell he was in a covered truck, its canvas top illuminated by jinking headlights on a truck behind.

Slowly, as he regained consciousness, it hit him. Captured. Held by the Japanese. On his way to some torture chamber, for all he knew. God. He felt like he'd lose control. Then he wanted to vomit and fought to keep it down and ended up gagging.

Water splashed over his face and he opened his eyes to see a guard sitting above him, holding a canteen over his head, laughing.

Spitting more dirt out, he moaned. This was why he'd left Corregidor. To escape exactly this. *Oh, God, dear God.*

The Japanese had quickly overwhelmed their party. A setup. How?

"Todd?" It was a hoarse whisper, the voice right next to him.

"Pablo?" He whispered.

"How are you?"

"I've been better. You?"

"I think my arm is broken," said Amador, his voice weak.

"What happened?"

"A trap, I think," growled Amador.

"Jesus. How?"

"While you were unconscious, I heard two officers talking. I understand a little Japanese and . . . well, it looks like they've broken our code."

The truck bounced and Ingram tried to roll toward Amador. "The code? I thought it was airtight."

Amador's voice shook as the truck bounced over a rutted road. "I thought so, too. And I tell you, it couldn't have come from this end. Otherwise, how would they have heard the name Wong Lee?"

"The San Francisco Wong Lee? The restaurant guy?"

"Yes. How did you know? And more importantly, how did they know?"

Through the pain and haze, Ingram churned over that one.

Then Amador added, "Also, my friend, how would they have known of your graduation date?"

Ingram twisted further. "Me? My graduation?"

Amador hissed, "Yes. And who would know Helen's graduation date?"

A guard leaned over Ingram, shouted, and poured more water on him, making sure it ran up his nose. Then he kicked him and shouted again.

From pain, Ingram screamed loudly. But he extended it as much as possible to give the guard satisfaction, hoping that he wouldn't be kicked again.

The bucking stopped abruptly as the truck rolled onto a smooth asphalt highway, the humming of the tires making him drowsy. As Ingram nodded off, Amador's questions crashed through his mind, wrenching him awake, denying him sleep. Otis needed code authenticators back in San Francisco. He remembered recommending Helen's graduation date.

Outside of Helen and her parents, who would know about Helen's graduation date?

CHAPTER FORTY-FIVE

It rained as the trucks bounced onto the Nasipit wharf a little after daybreak. Ingram, Amador, Seltzer, and Legaspi were kicked off the trucks and prodded up the service barge's gangway at bayonet point. Once aboard, they were searched and then left to stand as rain came down in torrents. With the others, Ingram turned his face to the sky, letting the lukewarm tropical waters wash away muck and slime, accumulated during the night. Feeling better by the moment, he heard men shouting and grunting from the bow, and carefully stepped outboard to the deck edge for a peek. Five men worked on a set of chain-falls, loading a torpedo in a set of triple tubes. He watched with professional interest, and had to admit they were good. In fact, they were *very* good. Their movements were more efficient than the torpedomen on the *Howell,* or, for that matter, the crew he'd trained on a four-stack destroyer after his graduation from—

"My God," he whispered. Just forward of the service barge was an *American* four-stack destroyer, freshly painted, and looking as if it had just been delivered from the Bath Iron Works. But her color scheme was a darker gray than the U.S. Navy's, and a decorative white ring was painted around her forward stack. Her markings were Japanese, and the Rising Sun flew from a staff at the fantail. But unmistakably, she was an American four-stacker. Sailors walked about her decks, depth charges were loaded in racks on her fantail, and light brown stack gas rose from the number two and three funnels, almost as if the ship were poised to get under way. Even as he watched, a flatbed truck pulled up and more sailors ran down the brow and started passing crates aboard the ship. He caught Amador's glance and raised an eyebrow as if to say, *Why didn't you tell us about this?*

Amador shrugged, and Ingram perceived that the old man didn't realize this was an American destroyer.

An officer shouted. Two soldiers prodded Ingram toward a stairway at bayonet point.

"Pablo, don't worry if—" A rifle butt hit Ingram in the back and he went to his knees with an "Ooof!" He was dragged to his feet and Amador whispered, *"Vía con Dios,"* as he walked by.

With the two guards shoving from behind, he was marched up a companionway and aft, into a living quarters area. As he walked, he was astounded to see from the corner of his eye what was once Amador's proud lumber mill. The destruction of the three-story mill and warehouse was complete, with blackened wooden beams protruding a few feet above the ground.

Aft of the service barge was another surprise, a floating dry dock, her faded white hull number YFD-5, still visible. Ingram had seen this one many times in the naval shipyard at Cavite in Manila Bay, once the home port of the U.S. Asiatic Fleet until the war broke out. It hit Ingram that this barge was also an American war prize—a repair, berthing, and messing barge, an old YRBM.

Tied outboard of the YFD was a curious yard service craft: an ammunition lighter, another Cavite-based war orphan. A corrugated metal superstructure with sliding wooden doors and a peaked roof occupied most of her deck space. Her hull was black, and haze-gray paint peeled in great strips from her corrugated metal superstructure. A faded, grease-smeared white YFN-376 was still discernible on either side of the lighter's blunt bow.

They stopped at a stateroom, where one guard knocked, then opened the door and shoved him roughly inside. The room was empty and he was tied, hand and foot, to a sturdy brass stanchion decorated with scrimshaw. Then the guards turned and walked out, closing the door softly, leaving Ingram to blink and wonder.

Except for the rain pounding outside, it was quiet. He looked around, finding he obviously was in an officer's stateroom, with three large polished brass portholes giving a view on the harbor. The inboard side had a neatly made pilot berth. Mounted on the bulkhead was a gilded-framed picture of Emperor Hirohito atop a white stallion. Flanking the emperor were pictures of admirals, one he thought was Fleet Admiral Isoroku Yamamoto. The other admiral he didn't recognize and, ironically, dirty laundry was stacked underneath. In the stateroom's opposite corner was a desk with books and papers scattered about. A combination safe stood next to that, its double doors gaping open, more books and pages spilling on the deck. A gleaming brass Seth Thomas twenty-four-hour clock was mounted to the bulkhead over the desk. Even as he watched, it delicately chimed seven bells: 0730.

The rain roared harder, and with it the realization he was tired, the dull, sleepless hours from the trip north catching up to him. He sagged against his bindings, water running from his clothes and dripping on a polished hardwood floor. But the way he was tied, he couldn't ease all the way down. The hell with it. He'd slept standing up before. He closed his eyes; the rain drummed outside and he drifted . . .

The door crashed open, and two officers in blue uniforms with high collars walked in. One stepped up and ran his eyes up and down Ingram. He was older, bald, and a convoluted smile meandered across a long, crinkled face that seemed as if it had been at sea for a long time. He helped Ingram to his feet. "Welcome back to Nasipit, Commander Ingram. I understand you've been here before. My name is Warrant Officer Hisa Kunisawa. And I am to be your interpreter.'' He bowed to another officer standing beside him and said, ''Allow me to introduce your host, Lieutenant Commander Katsumi Fujimoto, captain of this vessel.''

Ingram's eyes flicked to Fujimoto, who cocked his right arm and yelled, *''Bakayaro!''* driving a fist deep into Ingram's stomach.

Ingram gasped horribly, lost consciousness momentarily, and sagged to his knees.

Kunisawa stepped back, pulled out a silver hip flask, and poured a slug in the gleaming cap. ''Ummm, Commander Ingram. He just called you a stupid bastard. I wonder why.'' Then he knocked back his capful and smacked his lips. Stowing his flask, he stepped up to Ingram, grabbed his elbow, and yanked him roughly up.

Wheezing, coughing, Ingram struggled for a breath that he felt would never come. Just when he thought he could draw one, Fujimoto grabbed his head and smashed a knee up into his face . . .

. . . Not realizing how long he was out, he woke up gradually, realizing they had tied his hands to a pad eye on the overhead so he couldn't sink to the deck. Water splashed on his face and he heard a voice . . . It was the warrant.

He yelled, ''Commander Fujimoto wishes to congratulate you on your promotion to lieutenant commander. Now you two are of equal rank.''

Ingram tried to steel himself against the fist that drove into his left kidney. The pain was as if lightning had detonated in his torso; a secondary shock like a thousand tiny pieces of glass dragged through his back and stomach . . .

''. . . I asked, 'Is this your picture?' '' said Warrant Officer Kunisawa.

He stood close, and Ingram tried to focus on the man. But the fog was thick, and everything seemed coated with red; his nose throbbed and blood ran from his mouth and from a cut above his eyes. A wet rag was roughly wiped over his face. He could see.

''Commander, look at this, please.'' Kunisawa stood close, and his breath smelled like alcohol. ''Is that you?''

''Huh?'' Through throbbing, shrieking pain, Ingram squinted, finally recognizing the *San Francisco Chronicle* picture of Spruance pinning the Navy Cross on him. ''Uh-huh.''

''Hei.'' Kunisawa bowed to Fujimoto.

Fujimoto wound up with his fist. Ingram tried to jerk his head away, but the blow smacked into his cheek, tearing open the scar from Corregidor. Blood gorged as pain ripped through his face, and then . . .

From two blocks away, Helen surveyed the barge through binoculars. She and her companions were in an abandoned grain and feed store, its contents long ago seized by the Japanese. Palms waved before her lens, the view further hindered by the rain and a single-story pineapple cannery, also abandoned.

''What is it, honey?'' Wong Lee reached for the binoculars.

"Bastards." She wrenched the binoculars away, her face pressed tighter to the eyepieces. "They hit him with a rifle butt."

"Is that your boy?" asked Wong Lee as the rain thumped on the tin roof.

"I . . ." Of course it was Todd. Helen had recognized him the moment he'd been shoved off the truck. *My God! Todd!* She couldn't believe it, and her pulse raced like a teenager's.

Todd. All her doubts faded the moment she saw him tumble, bound hand and foot, from the truck and hit the wharf. Amador, Legaspi, Estaque, and another American soon followed, bound the same way. All were yanked to their feet and marched up the gangway.

Then another body was pitched on the wharf. But he didn't move, bloody holes stitched across his back: Rameriez. Tears sprang to her eyes and she wiped at them.

"Come on." Using all his strength, Wong yanked the binoculars away and looked for himself. Soon he, too, moaned.

Helen turned to Manuel Carillo and Luis Guzman and said, her voice shaking, "Carlos didn't make it."

The two *guerrilleros* sucked in their breath. "How could this be?" growled Guzman.

"Another traitor?" Carillo hung his head; it had happened so many times before. A sellout. People talked about anything, sold scraps of information for food, especially in the more densely populated Misamis Oriental, Bukidnon, and Lanao Provinces to the west.

Helen looked at Carillo. How? So few knew of Ingram's arrival. "Don Pablo had a feeling. Maybe that's why he didn't let us come along." After receiving a message late yesterday afternoon about Ingram's arrival, Amador almost had to forcibly restrain Helen from going. "Somebody has to take care of the fort,' " he had said.

Wong repeated. "Well, honey? Is that your man?"

Helen watched them march Todd onto the second deck, then into Fujimoto's stateroom. She handed the binoculars over to Wong. "Yes, that's him. He's gained his weight back." Lord, he looks good. Oh God, keep him healthy. Don't let those pigs hurt him.

Wong hoisted the binoculars. "I don't doubt it. You're breathing kind of hard."

"That's not funny."

Wong Lee said. "I'm sorry, baby, I didn't mean to upset you . . . My God, Helen. What's wrong?"

Helen Durand's fists were doubled, her eyes narrowed and nostrils flared.

Wong had seen her like that once before. She'd grabbed a Springfield rifle, stood fast, and methodically pecked away at a squad of Japanese Kempetai chasing them up a hillside. On they came, until she'd carefully shot three in the head from twenty feet. The rest dashed back down to a roadside ditch, radioing for help while she escaped with Amador's raiding party into the jungle. "Are you okay?" Wong Lee asked.

"We can't just sit here and do nothing," she said in a cold fury.

Wong Lee dropped his binoculars in a gesture of futility and lit a cigarette. "How 'bout the radio? Call Australia."

"Even if I knew how to send code, they wouldn't recognize my fist. Otis would think it was a hoax."

Wong Lee's shoulders sagged. "We got nothing left."

Helen stared through him.

"What?"

"You ready to give up? You want to walk over there and turn yourself in?"

"Helen, I'm just a poor Chinaman who cooks for a living."

"What we have left is"—she patted a knapsack at her side—"a document that I worked like hell to get. And if I don't miss my bet, it's going to make a big difference when it gets into the right hands back home." She pointed to the wharf. "And there are people over there who have risked their lives for us. They deserve the chance to board the submarine as well as you and me. "Besides, Wong, do you know the recognition signal for the submarine?"

Wong Lee gasped. "Oh, my God. Doesn't Pablo?"

"No. He didn't have to. Only the beachmaster, Todd, knows the signal. Which means we have to get him out if we want to board that submarine."

He held his hands to his head.

"That's right. Don Pablo has always taken care of things. The first thing you should remember is your friends over there. When are you—Wait." She snapped her fingers. "What day is it?"

Wong scratched his head. "Tuesday, the seventeenth. So what?"

"That's right!" She clapped. "Here. Come here."

Wong Lee stood fast, not just a little frightened at Helen's countenance. "Anything you say, honey. God, I never seen you so mad."

She beckoned Wong Lee, Carillo, and Guzman around a crate. Picking up a scrap of cardboard, she scratched out a crude map of Nasipit. "Here's what we're going to do . . ."

CHAPTER FORTY-SIX

He woke up coughing, dully realizing they'd retied his arms to the brass stanchion, letting him sit on the deck, his legs splayed before him. He spat blood. Something fell out of his mouth and he looked down to see a red-gorged molar laying on his shirt. Ingram involuntarily pitched his head up and coughed again.

"Welcome back, Commander," said Kunisawa. You were out for ..." —he looked at his watch—it was Ingram's watch!—"for twenty minutes that time. That's pretty good."

Ingram spat blood. "So's your English."

Kunisawa stooped before Ingram, his breath laden with a bizarre combination of garlic and whatever he'd been drinking. "I speak English because I am a sailor of the world. And you should be thankful I've got it. You're going to have to deal with him through me."

Ingram wiped his blood-crusted mouth on his shoulder. "Why?"

"You don't know?"

"No idea."

"You're the sonofabitch that made him run aground," Kunisawa said a bit smugly. Then he said something over his shoulder. It must have been a question, for Fujimoto grunted in the affirmative.

"Ran what aground?" Ingram asked in an exasperated tone.

"Last May; his destroyer; the *Kurosio*." Kunisawa quickly explained, as Fujimoto stood close to Ingram, his feet planted apart, fists braced on his hips.

"Up, up, Commander." Kunisawa yanked Ingram's elbow, jerking Ingram to his feet. Bile rushed to his throat and he retched, nearly passing out. After a while, he felt better and opened his eyes, to see Fujimoto examining him clinically. It came to him that this was the pissed-off sailor Captain Falkenberg had spoken of in San Francisco—the one he'd outfoxed that night off Fortune Island just after their escape from Manila Bay in the 51 Boat. Ingram looked at the Japanese Lieutenant Commander with new eyes. Solidly built, he was five-nine or -ten, with sharp features. Yet he had an almost soft, kind face. A face he would have thought incapable of delivering the beating he'd just received. But navies are navies and skippers' careers are at risk when their ships run aground. Yes, he had probably lost his command, was terribly embarrassed, and consigned to this forsaken corner of the Philippines in shame. Fujimoto's father, Ingram recalled, was a retired admiral. He checked the pictures on the bulkhead; that must be him up there with Yamamoto; the two were somehow aligned. Something else tugged at his memory. What was it Falkenberg had said? Yes. Fujimoto had been aide to General Yoshitsugu Tatekawa, ambassador to the Soviet Union. Then what about—

Ingram screamed as Fujimoto drove another fist into his left kidney. He sank to his knees again and braced a hand to stop his fall. With another shout, Fujimoto stomped on his hand with the heel of his shoe, then kicked him in the ribs. Something cracked, sending him mercifully into . . .

"Up, Commander. Come on. That's a good boy," Kunisawa's voice reached the recesses of his whirling semiconsciousness.

Strong hands yanked at Ingram's elbows, jerking him roughly to his feet. Coughing and spitting blood, he sagged against his bindings, his chin on his chest.

"My, my, Commander. You're going to piss blood for a month."

Ingram opened his eyes, becoming aware that two guards propped him up. Kunisawa stood before him, sipping his schnapps from the silver cap, smiling. "Want a shot?"

"No, thanks."

Kunisawa snapped an order in Japanese. Ingram's chin was wrenched up, his mouth jerked open. Within an instant, fiery liquid tumbled down his throat and . . . it tasted good. It was liquor of some kind, sweet.

Kunisawa nodded toward the bow. "Kahlúa. Right off that destroyer. I found it in the captain's cabin. Can you believe that?"

The Kahlúa felt good, but his body still shrieked with pain. It hurt terribly to breath, and his ribs and left hand throbbed as if broken. His left side, especially the kidney area, felt as if it had been run over by an Army M-3 tank. Kunisawa wasn't far off the mark when he said he'd be pissing blood for a month. His kidney must be about the consistency of hamburger. Ingram coughed again. "Nice ship. Where'd you find her?"

Kunisawa waved his little hip flask at Ingram, his eyebrows raised.

"No, thanks."

Behind Kunisawa, Fujimoto sat at the desk and, looking at Ingram, massaged his bloody knuckles.

Kunisawa turned to Ingram. "Do you realize, Commander, why your Mark 15 torpedoes perform so poorly?"

Ingram was surprised at the abrupt change of subject. "What are you talking about?"

Fujimoto held up a drawing; it looked like a torpedo midbody. A little smile crept across his lips as he spoke to Kunisawa.

Kunisawa went, "Ahhh, ahhh," a few times, bowed, and then turned to Ingram. "Come, now, Commander. We know you have considerable expertise with naval weaponry, torpedoes included."

"No, I'm a supply officer." *Damnit!* It slipped out. He'd said that once before when captured by the Japanese. It hadn't helped his situation then, and he was sure it wouldn't help now.

Sure enough, Kunisawa relayed that to Fujimoto. Both laughed hilariously. Then Kunisawa asked, "How is it that a supply officer who deals in ordering . . . toilet paper and condoms, became executive officer of the U.S.S. *Howell* and distinguished himself at the battles of Cape Esperance and the Santa Cruz Islands?"

"They're hard up for people."

Kunisawa raised his eyebrows. "Hard up?"

"They're scraping the bottom of the barrel."

Kunisawa dashed off another translation to Fujimoto, both laughing again. Then Kunisawa said, "Kidding aside, you must understand Commander Fujimoto is a torpedo expert. He has, how do you say, reverse-engineered your Mark 15 torpedoes many times the past few months. We're very aware of the failures of torpedoes manufactured by Winslow River Corporation. Commander Fujimoto finds them horribly lacking."

In spite of his pain, Ingram raised his head to meet Fujimoto's eyes. "Is that so?"

"Yes, that is so. Well, get this, Commander. Winslow River's skin-mounted depth sensor is what's wrong. With your torpedo going thirty or forty-five knots, the velocity of water over the sensor gives a far different pressure reading than the . . ." Kunisawa stopped and asked Fujimoto a question. After an abrupt answer, Kunisawa said, "The actual hydrostatic pressure or real depth. Your error is proportional to the square of the torpedo speed; the faster it goes, the deeper it runs. Got it?"

Ingram was flabbergasted. "No."

Kunisawa poured another capful and started to drink, when Fujimoto grunted and waved a finger. "Sorry, Commander, this is my last one for a while."

Airplane engines roared overhead as Kunisawa screwed on his flask cap. Just then, the Seth Thomas clock chimed two bells: 0900. "Ahh, the Shōsō. Right on schedule."

After a moment, Fujimoto rose and looked out a port. Kunisawa joined him to watch a twin-engine flying boat touch down in the outer harbor and settle into the water, spray and mist shooting past its tail.

Looking at Ingram, Fujimoto spoke rapidly as he gathered papers and stacked them on the side of the desk.

Kunisawa offered, "The elegant solution, devised by Lieutenant Commander Katsumi Fujimoto, is to relocate the depth-sensing device to the free-flooding section inside the torpedo's midbody, where it won't be affected by velocity of water flowing over its skin. Thus"—Kunisawa snapped his fingers—"you have measurement of true depth, and the torpedo runs correctly and hits home. Bam!" He clapped his hands and then turned and bowed to Fujimoto.

Tightening his collar, Fujimoto gave a boyish grin and bowed back. Then he went to a basin, took the bandages off his hands, and began carefully washing up.

Ingram pondered what Kunisawa had just told him. Wouldn't George Atwell and Rocko Myszynski love to hear this? It confirmed their tests off Mooloolaba Harbor. And better yet, Fujimoto not only knew why they ran deep, he knew how to fix the problem. He wondered if there was a way he could get word back to Brisbane to Otis DeWitt and Rocko Myszynski. Maybe through Amador's radio, if it hadn't been confiscated. All he had to do was to figure a way. But then he wondered why they were volunteering this information; telling him, it seemed, everything. How could he be expected not to talk? "What do you want me to—"

"In good time, Commander. For now, we must go." Kunisawa stood before him and bowed. "You're going to be the star of our show today."

Ingram smacked his lips. "How 'bout some water?"

Kunisawa rubbed his hands. "Sure, sure, and then tonight we get to wipe out the *Turbot*. Boom!" He clapped his hands next to Ingram's ear, then reached for his flask.

"Hisa." Fujimoto stood before a mirror. He donned his cap and, inserting two fingers between the bridge of his nose and the cap's brim, made sure it was square. Then he grabbed a pair of white gloves and walked out.

With a sigh, Kunisawa followed, patting his hip pocket.

The *Turbot*? *What the hell do they know about that?* Ingram wondered, his stomach suddenly feeling leaden. *That means they know about tonight's rendezvous, and that means a trap. And how did this guy Fujimoto figure out the Mark 15 torpedo problems? For that matter, how did they know we were coming? How? How?*

The Seth Thomas clock had just chimed ten-thirty-five when the door banged open and the room filled with men, startling Ingram from a deep, dreamless sleep. His hands and feet were tied to the stanchion and he blinked from a half-crouch, unable to rise, his legs cramped and impossibly asleep. Kunisawa stepped up and, with the aid of another officer, pulled Ingram roughly to his feet.

They milled around for a moment, viewing him as if he were a caged chimpanzee, rubbing their chins, grunting in monosyllables. One was—he had to squint at the picture—yes, it was the same man, Fujimoto's father. His sleeves bore the two and a half rings of a rear admiral, a Shōsō, as Kunisawa had said.

The admiral stepped close and watched Ingram's eyes flick back and forth to his picture on the bulkhead, realizing that Ingram had put it together. He spoke quietly over his shoulder to his son, who bowed and nodded. Then he spoke some more and looked at Kunisawa.

Kunisawa cleared his throat. "As you can see, this is Shōsō Hayashi Fujimoto, father of Lieutenant Commander Katsumi Fujimoto. Uhhh, he wishes to congratulate you on your receipt of the Navy Cross. He also extends congratulations on how you saved your ship after one of our brave pilots crashed aboard in the Battle of the Santa Cruz Islands."

Kunisawa continued, "May I also present Lieutenant Yoshi Tomo, the Shōsō's aide and flag lieutenant." As Tomo bowed and clicked his heels, Kunisawa said, "This is Lieutenant Kenji Ogata, our repair officer and torpedo officer of the *Namikaze*. Just behind me is Lieutenant Koki Jimbo, our intelligence officer aboard the repair ship and new operations officer aboard the *Namikaze*." Each bowed and clicked his heels as he was introduced.

"It is to Lieutenant Jimbo that you owe your thanks for our hospitality. He's the one who has been reading your mail."

Ingram looked at Jimbo, trying to see behind his poker face. Then he looked them all over from right to left, and, too tired, let his chin fall to his chest. Just then there was a scuffle behind him, and he sensed a blow was headed toward him.

But the admiral waved it down and spoke. Kunisawa lifted Ingram's chin. "The Shōsō says he would like you to accompany him and Don Pablo Amador to Manila and spend a relaxed evening, with the two of you around the dinner table at Malacañan Palace."

Then the admiral cast his glance aside and spoke at length.

Kunisawa listened carefully, then bowed to the admiral. "Sadly, his son, Commander Katsumi Fujimoto, has spoken for you. And the Shōsō acknowledges this is as it should be. The Shōsō's real interest is in Don Pablo Amador. They have plans, apparently, of putting him to work in the Vargas government." Jorge B. Vargas had been appointed president of the Philippines after Manuel Quezon fled last March with General MacArthur. But now Vargas openly cooperated with the Japanese.

Young Fujimoto stepped to within a foot of Ingram and talked quietly.

After he was finished, Kunisawa interpreted, "That barge you saw tied up to the dry dock?"

Ingram turned, seeing Kunisawa's lifted eyebrows.

"Well, today, Commander Fujimoto intends to display to his father how your torpedoes work with the proper equipment. That is, my friend"—Kunisawa jabbed Ingram's chest with a finger—"with depth engines properly modified by Lieutenant Commander Fujimoto. Using live Mark 15 torpedoes, our target is that old ammo lighter back there."

A dark shadow passed over Kunisawa's face as he continued, "Those of us before you, including Don Pablo Amador, will observe the shooting from our newest addition to the fleet, the *Namikaze*."

Ingram's mind still wasn't working well. All he could think of saying was, "What's a *Namikaze*?"

"Your destroyer we salvaged, the *Stockwell*, which we found when we occupied Soerabaja. I towed her up myself. Now her name is *Namikaze*— *Wind on the Waves*. Her new commanding officer is Lieutenant Commander Katsumi Fujimoto. And I"—Kunisawa stood back and puffed out his chest— "am to be her executive officer."

Fujimoto applauded silently, making Ingram wonder if he understood English.

"And guess where you'll be, Commander."

A cold wave of dread and fear and abject loneliness coursed through Ingram.

"That's right, Commander, you and your buddies will be aboard the barge for a grandstand seat, where you can really see your torpedoes in action."

CHAPTER FORTY-SEVEN

16 NOVEMBER, 1942
CONSULATE, U.S.S.R.
SAN FRANCISCO, CALIFORNIA

Zenit shoved the message at Dezhnev as he sat. "Read," he ordered, then forked a heaping load of scrambled eggs in his mouth.

TOP SECRET—OPERATION KOMET—TOP SECRET
TO: A.) SERGEI (N) ZENIT, CAPT. 3 RANK NKVD, SFO
　　 B.) EDUARD I. DEZHNEV, CAPT. 3 RANK, VMF, SFO
16 NOVEMBER, 1942

1. TATEKAWA REPORTS MINDANAO OPERATION COMPLETE SUCCESS: PABLO AMADOR (SABOTEUR, QUEZON PATRIOT, RESISTANCE ORGANIZER) CAPTURED ALONG WITH ALTON C. INGRAM, LCDR USN, IMMEDIATELY AFTER SCHEDULED PARACHUTE DROP.
2. A BONUS WILL BE SINKING U.S.S. TURBOT TONIGHT IF SHE SURFACES AS PREDICTED.
3. SERGEI (N) ZENIT PROMOTED CAPT 2 RANK, EFFECTIVE IMMEDIATELY.

MESSAGE ENDS.

LAPTEV FOR BERIA

They sat at breakfast in a small staff dining room off the main kitchen, dishes clanking as the cooks prepared the morning meal. Zenit slapped the table with an open hand and grinned. "It's wonderful news, don't you think, comrade?"

Dezhnev turned the message over in his hand. The date-time stamp showed it had been received at 0447 this morning.

A waiter, one of the local domestic American workers, walked in and set a plate of scrambled eggs, bacon, and toasted bread before Dezhnev. "Coffee?"

"I said, don't you think this is a wonderful moment, Eduard?"

The waiter moved to Dezhnev's shoulder and tried again. "Coffee, Sir?"

"Don't let him see that," Zenit snarled, snatching the message from Dezhnev and hiding it under the table.

"It's in Russian," protested Dezhnev.

"Doesn't matter." Zenit pointed to the door. "Leave the pot and get out," he ordered.

"Yes, Sir," the man mumbled with a slight bow. After carefully setting the carafe on the table, he backed through the double kitchen doors.

Dezhnev fumbled for his fork. "You're not making friends, Sergei."

"He understands Russian. You see? He did exactly as I told him." Zenit pointed at the door.

"Anyone would have understood your tone of voice, Sergei. You made him feel like a dog."

"You have to teach these Americans their place in life."

Using his fork, Dezhnev pushed his food around the plate. Normally, he loved scrambled eggs, and the marvelous bacon, the toast, the Belgian waffles, and the fresh grapefruit and oranges they brought in. But now that message . . .

Todd Ingram: They were friends; they got pie-eyed together and sang songs. Now Ingram was most likely dead, or perhaps rotting in a cell somewhere, or maybe even now being strung up for hanging.

How could he look Toliver in the eye? Ollie had given him a new brass-tipped cane and they'd had dinner in the Top of the Mark Hopkins just two nights ago to celebrate his new duty assignment: ordnance liaison officer to Commandant, Twelfth Naval District, right here in San Francisco, a soft job in the American homeland, away from the terror of war in the South Pacific. For the dinner, Toliver had greased some palms and ordered an exquisite rack of lamb. And there was mint sauce and a chef to carve it right at their table. Dezhnev had had a spicy end piece. And there was vodka, with Toliver bringing along two girls. ". . . What?"

"I said, how do you like it?" demanded Zenit. He wore the collar devices of a captain second rank.

Dezhnev looked up with red-rimmed eyes. "Nice." *I wonder how long it will take him to have new rings sewn on the jacket?*

"I gave our tailor the jacket ten minutes ago. It'll be ready at four this afternoon. What do you think of that?"

"You work fast, don't you?"

"What?"

"Congratulations, Sergei."

Zenit gave a slight bow. "It's marvelous. This message is from Beria. It nearly ensures my transfer off the *Dzhurma,* you see. Possibly I can put in for a permanent position here. You must admit, the food is marvelous, don't you think?'' Zenit cast a friendly elbow at Dezhnev.

Dezhnev had betrayed Ingram. Zenit didn't care. It was almost as if the American were one of those political prisoners roasted in the *Dzhurma's* forward hold; someone to be spoken of at a distance. It struck Dezhnev that corpses were the only commodity that made Zenit's world go 'round and 'round; the more corpses, the higher the promotions. How many dead bodies would it take for Zenit to be promoted to captain first rank? Dezhnev felt like throttling the little bastard right where he sat. A sharp knife was within inches of his hand. One swipe across his throat and—

Zenit laid a hand on Dezhnev's forearm. ''You know, Eduard. You could do me a great favor.''

Cutting his throat would be too good for him. Tying him across a set of railroad tracks in the dead of night would be better; the freight train slowly grinding up a long, curving grade somewhere, its mournful whistle blowing, Zenit sniveling, pleading for his life; sweating and kicking and finally screaming as the train rumbled closer and closer.

Zenit continued, ''I would like to visit Wong Lee's. I've heard so much about it, the place where you broke this case wide open. Bring Toliver. I would like to meet him. Professional interest, you see. He won't know any better. Maybe some of his girls? Hmmmm, Eduard?''

''Shut up, you little twit.''

''What?'' Zenit sat straight up, his mouth open.

''I said, shut up.'' Dezhnev pushed away from the table and walked out.

''But your eggs, Eduard,'' Zenit called after him.

Ingram was chained to a pad eye on the barge's port side, sitting between Leo Seltzer and Emilio Legaspi. For some reason they'd kept Felipe Estaque on the barge. With only water to drink, they waited while the Japanese had an early noon meal. Then they watched as sailors lined up and stood at attention while Admiral Fujimoto boarded the *Namikaze,* followed by his son and the rest of the officers. Within minutes the destroyer's lines were singled up, while soldiers prodded a slump-shouldered Pablo Amador up the gangway. Then the brow was pulled in, her lines cast off, with Katsumi Fujimoto twisting his war prize clear of the wharf.

Expertly, he backed *Namikaze,* easing her alongside the ammunition barge. Thumping up the gangway from the wharf, three sailors boarded the barge and caught the messenger line that sailed over from the *Namikaze's* fantail. From that, they heaved the messenger, pulling the tail of the wire towline aboard. Soon they shackled it to a bridle at the barge's bow. As the other two headed for the gangway, the third sailor stooped briefly, checking the chains.

Seltzer rasped, ''Hey, buddy, sure you wouldn't like a round of acey-deucey? Poker? How 'bout blackjack?''

The man looked at Ingram for a moment, his face devoid of anything, his eyes dark, incomprehensible pools. With a last grunt of satisfaction and rattle of chains, he followed the others off the gangway to the dock. Soon the plank was dragged clear. Then they untied the barge's dock lines, threw them aboard, and walked back to the service barge.

The *Namikaze*'s fantail was abreast of where Ingram sat. Kunisawa stood by with the crew that would pay out the towline. He caught Ingram's eye, smiled, and pulled out his silver hip flask. "To you and your valiant crew, Commander. He looked furtively at the bridge, then took a long swig. "May this be your most memorable cruise." Froth kicked up under the *Namikaze*'s screwguards, and she began moving forward. The towline began snaking out and Kunisawa, satisfied the rig was proper, tipped the brim of his hat with two fingers, then walked toward the bridge.

The *Namikaze* moved ahead slowly, and soon the slack was out; the towline gently went taut, pulling YFN-376 into the main channel and on her way into Butuan Bay.

As they slid from the wharf, Ingram realized that the jungle across the narrow harbor was his last glimpse of land. He took a deep breath, smelling the earth, not fully heated for the day, a touch of dew still on the leaves before the sun evaporated it, turning it to a vapor that would return as life-giving rain later in the afternoon.

"They really trying to make a show for that admiral, huh, Sir?"

"What's that?"

Seltzer nodded his head toward the shed's open door. "AV gas, five-hundred-pound bombs, even a few boxes of dynamite. They want to make a big boom."

Ingram looked over his shoulder. He hadn't noticed the crates and barrels lurking in the shadows. It didn't matter. The Mark 15's six hundred pounds of torpex would surely do the job. What did it matter if the conflagration was aided by a few hundred gallons of gasoline, or five-hundred-pound bombs, or even dynamite? Dead is dead.

"Mr. Ingram?"

"Yes."

"I didn't sign on for this."

"I know. I'm sorry I talked you into it."

"No. I don't mean that. I'd just rather go down with my guns blazing. You see what I mean?"

Ingram admired Seltzer's control. On the other hand, all Ingram could think of was what was going to happen: a last ripping, flaming moment that would strike him from this life, like a crazed half-wit backhanding a porcelain urn with all of his strength.

To his right, Legaspi spoke in low tones; it sounded like Tagalog, and often Ingram heard the word *Dios,* his thumbs and forefingers intertwined, working a pattern with one another.

With some derision, Seltzer said, "Running his beads."

Ingram searched for something funny, even stupid to say. Instead, he stifled a sob. Finally he managed, "There are no atheists in foxholes."

"Yeah?" Seltzer stuck out his chin. "Where is God now, Mr. Ingram?"

"I don't think it matters."

As they pulled clear of the wharf, Ingram heard a truck quickly downshift and crunch to a stop. There were low moans and wailing; it sounded like women. One screamed and Ingram looked at Legaspi.

"Hapon sonsabits take our *dalagas* for to clean up their crap."

"Women?"

"*Sí*. They make them work for a week. Sometimes rape them."

They pulled farther from the wharf and the noise died out. Then it hit him. Helen. She had been waiting in Buenavista. But now she must be out there somewhere, possibly up in the mountains, or just across the harbor in the jungle, watching the barge slip from the pier. His cheek had been itching until that damned Fujimoto had hit him there, opening up the wound again. The bleeding had stopped, but the damned thing throbbed, like his hand and his ribs. And with the ribs, it was difficult to breathe.

They cleared the harbor on a cloudless afternoon with a duck-egg-blue sky. The seas were nearly flat, and the waters of Butuan Bay were crystal clear. As the barge gained speed, Ingram looked aft, into the lush, green richness of the Agusan's mountains, and once again he filled his lungs with Mindanao's torpid air.

Normally, the Filipinos would be napping. Not now. The times called for survival; anything to find something to eat. Steal your neighbor's chicken, his dog, even in broad daylight at—what time? The chain rattled as he looked for his watch, forgetting that Kunisawa had taken it—it must be about two in the afternoon.

An old seagull, a dark mongrel, rose from a piling and flapped alongside as they stood into Butuan Bay.

"Hi, Popeye."

The gull circled once, then landed on the barge's roof just above their heads.

"You'll be sorry," said Seltzer.

"You signed on the wrong ship, Popeye."

"Popeye, you're a loser," shouted Seltzer.

Ingram sat back, reached in his pocket, and fumbled at her ring. Thank God they hadn't taken it. On the other hand, maybe he should have given it to them. For soon it would be at the bottom of . . .

Helen. I hope you make it, honey. Vía con Dios.

CHAPTER FORTY-EIGHT

An hour later, the *Namikaze* steamed under a brilliant afternoon sun. Butuan Bay remained calm, with very little groundswell, a soft breeze blowing from the north. The ship's crew hauled in the towline and cast off the barge, setting it adrift. Then Katsumi Fujimoto put his ship through her paces with all four boilers on the line. Cranking up flank speed, the old *Namikaze* leaned gracefully into her turns, the helmsman spinning the wheel madly as Fujimoto ordered the rudder shifted from one side to the other, his father and flag lieutenant holding on to the starboard bridge bulwark with poker faces. Then he gave his father the conn. The old man's mouth split into a thin smile; wind ruffled his tunic as he shouted helm orders just like when he and Yamamoto were junior officers. They did figure eights, emergency stops, man-overboard drills, acceleration tests, more turns, with everybody from Lieutenant Togo to Hisa Kunisawa getting a turn at both steering and conning the ship.

After forty-five minutes of chewing up the ocean, Katsumi resumed the conn and rang up all ahead flank. At maximum speed—the knotmeter hovered at just under thirty-five knots—and raced by the ammunition barge, clearing it by no more than ten meters, everyone laughing as the barge violently heaved and bounced in their wake.

A shadow crossed Katsumi's face as he called, "Action stations, surface. Stand by for torpedo exercise." Then he turned the conn over to Kunisawa, as the crew ran to their stations. Walking aft, he joined the Shōsō and his flag lieutenant near the signal bridge. Noticing his father's raised eyebrows, Katsumi said, "Kunisawa is the best ship handler in the Navy. Let him make the attack. Besides, I've had my fun for the day."

The Shōsō nodded in agreement. "What type of approach do you intend?"

"Straight on."

"Ummm. Not much of a challenge."

"I agree, Sir, but the purpose of this exercise is to prove the depth-engine retrofit design. So I want to reduce the margin for error, and Kunisawa's exact conning is one way to ensure that."

"Ummm." The Shōsō scratched his chin. "I agree." Then he looked up with glittering eyes. "Katsi, you'll make a naval officer yet."

Katsumi nodded in acknowledgment of his father's backhanded compliment. He added, "Well, I—"

Just then they heard shouting on the main deck. The three of them leaned over the bulwark to see four sailors pulling aboard a struggling Pablo Amador from over the side. As they flung him to the deck and jumped on him, Katsumi cupped his hands and yelled, "Petty Officer Abe?"

Abe, a thin gunner's mate, looked up, while holding Amador's jerking right leg. "Yes, Sir?"

"What happened?"

"He jumped, Sir. We just caught his leg in time."

"Don't let him be harmed, Katsi. We need him in Manila," said the Shōsō.

"Yes, Father." Katsumi yelled down again. "Tie him to the boat davit. Make sure he can see the barge. Have a guard standing by to make sure his eyes are open."

Yes, Sir."

"You better give him some water."

"Yes, Sir."

"Very good, Katsi," said the Shōsō.

Katsumi was keeping score. His father, always remote, standoffish, forever distant, had complimented him twice today. *Amazing.*

The sound-powered phone buzzed. Katsumi snatched it from its bracket and snapped, "Captain." He listened, then said, "that's right, Ogata. Confirm twenty-five knots own ship's speed. Launch torpedoes at three thousand meters. Use high-speed setting on the torpedoes and set depth at one and a half meters. Now read that back to me. What? Yes. Set depth at four feet, then."

Katsumi nodded as Ogata repeated the instructions. "Very well." He hung up and called forward, "Carry out your orders, Mr. Kunisawa." In an aside to his father, he said, "You should have let the old man die. He's been a thorn in our side for months."

The Shōsō rubbed his chin. "You have your prize for the day, your Commander Ingram. I need mine. I need Amador in Manila. If the Filipinos think Don Pablo Amador is cooperating with Vargas, then the whole resistance movement will shatter; not just here, but on Luzon and Leyte, as well."

Katsumi held his tongue. He supposed his father was right, but he would just as well have seen Amador chained on the barge with Ingram.

Kunisawa opened out to ten thousand meters, then eased into a turn to port, reduced speed to twenty-five knots, and began his run in. Clean, white water peeled off the *Namikaze*'s bow as she steadied on course, her stern wake a straight, chalky, foam extending far behind.

Katsumi almost had to bite his lip as the barge grew larger in his binocular lens. The fact that the American was going to die far outweighed any proof of concept on the Mark 15 torpedo. That's why they were all here. To watch an execution. After all, Japan's Type 93 was far superior, so why worry? Katsumi knew his father, and judging from the way the Shōsō licked his lips, he felt the same way. Everyone wanted a big explosion, and damnit, that's what he would deliver. He propped his elbows on the bulwark, steadying his binoculars, to watch the problem develop. As expected, Kunisawa was conning a perfect run. A thousand meters to go, everything had been—"Damn-it!"

"What?" said the Shōsō.

"I forgot to give Ogata the gyro angle." Katsumi reached for the sound-powered phone.

The Shōsō reached and held his arm. "You trained Ogata?"

"Of course." He jerked against the pressure of the Shōsō's hand. "Please, Sir, it's almost time."

"Let's inject a variable element in this exercise, Katsi. Under normal conditions, Lieutenant Ogata is supposed to determine his own gyro angles. Correct?"

Katsumi jerked at the phone, but his father wouldn't let go. "Yes—correct."

"Then take it easy. You have nothing to worry about. After all, you trained Ogata. Let's see if he uses initiative and enters the correct gyro angle."

"Sir—"

"Isn't this what Kunisawa taught us? To be sailors? To develop our own initiative?"

"Yes, Sir." Katsumi let the phone go, then checked the range indicator. It was almost too late anyway, with the target range showing thirty-two hundred meters. Again, he raised his binoculars, trying to pick out the three figures chained to the barge's deck. One's head was on his knees. It must be the Filipino; he wore the blue denim *sinamay* of the defunct Philippine Army. On the other side was the sailor, also in denims, and the white hat of the U.S. Navy. In the middle was—

The forward torpedo mount coughed, a Mark 15 torpedo leaping from its tube, its counterrotating propellers already spinning as it hit the water with a soft splash. Two more torpedoes quickly followed at two-second intervals, leaving bubbling wakes that streaked directly for the barge.

Katsumi checked the range indicator. Perfect, three thousand meters.

"Looks good, Katsi," said the Shōsō loudly enough that all those nearby heard. "Lieutenant Ogata used his initiative. And he fired at the right time. Yes?"

"Yes, Sir," Katsumi muttered. He hated it when his father subtly crushed him in front of others.

The bridge was quiet as they watched the torpedoes race directly to the barge.

"Captain?" It was Kunisawa, a grin stretched across his face.

"Yes, Mr. Kunisawa?" Katsumi growled, louder than he intended.

Kunisawa reached for his flask, but thought better of it. "How close do you want to get to that thing before it goes boom?"

They were still on their firing leg, a course that would take them close to the barge. Yes, it was time to turn, and Kunisawa was being insolent. Katsumi ground his teeth, knowing he would have to deal with it later. Trying to sound as detached as possible, he said, "Please come left to a retiring course, Mr. Kunisawa."

"Aye, aye, Captain." Kunisawa ordered a gentle ten degrees left rudder, eventually steadying on a course to open the range comfortably, while still providing the Shōsō and his entourage a magnificent view of the fireworks off the *Namikaze*'s starboard quarter.

The three wakes, as if riding down an invisible guide-wire, continued their sprint directly toward the barge.

Ingram had said his prayers over and over. After a while, Seltzer joined him, and then sobbed as the *Namikaze* steamed toward them. Seltzer rasped, "The bastards have launched!"

Ingram felt cold, as if he were already dead, squinting to find the wakes, but they were too low to the water.

After a while, Seltzer jerked against his chain and cried out, "Jesus."

Ingram saw them, too: three missiles of death, spearing their way right toward them. "My God."

On they came, long white arrows, reaching at them from the horizon.

The destroyer eased into a shallow left turn to clear the impact area, and Ingram sobbed again. "Oh, God." If he had a machete he would have cut off his hands and legs and jumped clear. No! How can you cut off your hands and legs and jump?

He looked again, fascinated, as the deadly wakes grew larger. Here they—
Bong! Clunk!

The third torpedo missed the bow by two feet and raced on toward the Butuan coastline.

The ancient, mongrel seagull that had been sitting on the roof squawked and flapped its wings, rising to circle the barge, scanning the blue waters of Butuan Bay for a late afternoon meal.

"Look, it's Popeye," said Seltzer.

"It's like he knows more than we do." Ingram watched the gull rise and play off the little air currents eddying around the barge.

Seeing nothing of interest, Popeye squawked again and glided back to the roof, landing with a flourish. He shook himself, then tucked his beak under a wing, resuming his nap.

Seltzer clanked at his chains. "Sir?"

"Yeah?"

"The guy who said there's no atheists in foxholes really was right, wasn't he?"

"You bet."

CHAPTER FORTY-NINE

The machine shop was dimly lit and crammed with grinders, lathes, and drill presses. A set of double sliding wooden doors gave onto the bow and rumbled open and closed each time someone came in. For now, the doors were open and Ingram could see stars twinkling over Butuan Bay—a sight, six hours ago, he thought was gone forever. Another sight on the far bulkhead were three gleaming torpedoes sitting in racks. The top two were Mark 15s, fueled and ready to go, their warheads packed with six hundred pounds of torpex. Those two were the duds that had been fired at him today, grim reminders that the man with the dark robe and scythe had taken a twenty-four-hour rain check. The last torpedo had missed and sank at the end of its run. But the torpedo that replaced it was unlike anything he'd ever seen before. It was at least six feet longer than the twenty-four-foot Mark 15, and much wider. *Yes!* It was just like the torpedoes he'd seen on the bottom of Tulagi Harbor, the ones that had tumbled from the Japanese destroyer into the sand. The torpedo whose plans, according to DeWitt, were in Helen's hands.

Just then, a technician walked over to one of the American Mark 15 torpedoes and inserted a set of calipers into a nine-inch-diameter hole in the warhead. It was a cavity Ingram knew that contained the Mark 5 contact exploder. With a grunt of satisfaction, he returned to the bench, where Katsumi and three technicians muttered to one another as they flipped through manuals. Like a cadaver in the morgue, a Mark 5 exploder lay disassembled before them, its glistening little parts scattered over the workbench.

The two torpedoes had buried their noses a foot or two into the barge's side and failed to explode. The heavily compartmented barge was in no danger of sinking and an enraged Fujimoto sent over a crew of fingernail-chewing torpedomen, who tiptoed around, deadly afraid of jostling the torpedoes' arming devices. With Ingram, Seltzer, and Legaspi holding their breath, the torpedomen managed to rig a chain-falls, ease the two torpedoes out far enough, where, very carefully, the exploders were unscrewed, pulled from the torpedo warhead, and disarmed—no easy task, since the Mark 5 exploder weighed ninety pounds.

After that, the torpedoes were hauled out and hoisted aboard the *Namakaze*. Fujimoto sent over a diver, who slapped temporary patches over the two holes in the barge. Then the *Namikaze* towed them back to Nasipit, where the torpedoes were off-loaded for servicing.

And now, as Fujimoto and his torpedomen clanked their tools, Kunisawa paced before Ingram, his convoluted sense of humor gone. Perhaps he was too drunk, Ingram thought. He'd been hitting his flask all day. Even now he took another swig. "Today, we were shamed, and embarrassed before the Shōsō. And you know why?" Kunisawa pointed at the Mark 5 exploder. "It's because your torpedo is a piece of crap. Not only are your depth sensors faulty, your . . ." He asked a question of Fujimoto, who grunted an affirmative. "Yes, it's the firing pin blocks in that exploder that are all wrong." He pointed. "That damned exploder looks like it was designed by the Marx Brothers. No wonder you Americans are losing the war. Who's running things in Washington anyway? John Dillinger? Al Capone? I mean, this is so embarrassing, the Shōsō plans to return to Manila first thing tomorrow morning. He's disgusted with the whole mess. And damnit, so am I."

Ingram looked up from a bowl of rice to see Kunisawa's face was flushed, almost as if the warrant officer really cared about what was happening in the United States. Then Ingram took a long drink of water, shoveled some rice, and returned to rich chunks of *lechón,* roast pig, that Fujimoto's orderly had brought in.

Kunisawa saw Ingram's eyes flick to the Japanese torpedo. "You like it?"

Ingram nodded. "A monster."

"It's our Type 93. Goes like hell. Blow up a battleship. In fact, we sank your carrier *Hornet* with just four of these."

For a moment, Ingram scanned the Type 93. It was big, and it looked very, very deadly. "How big's the warhead?"

"About a thousand pounds."

Good Lord. No wonder the thing blew Toliver off the pilothouse. "That's nice."

Kunisawa ignored the remark, then bent over. "You know why you're eating so well, don't you?"

The *lechón* was good, and he resumed eating with the oversized wooden spoon. They had loaded his plate. They had also given him *basi* served in a delicate little cup. He'd set it aside, saving it for last. "Ummmmpf, thanks," he said around a mouthful of roast pork.

"You're welcome. The truth is, we want you to be healthy. To feel your best. Rather than a moaning, delirious derelict, we want you to be totally conscious when you see those torpedoes coming at you tomorrow. We want you to know you're finally going to get it," Kunisawa hissed, dropping to his knees, trying to catch Ingram's eye.

Ingram kept munching.

"How did it feel today?" Kunisawa took another swig.

With the food, Ingram felt a lot better, the sugar hitting his system like a shot of adrenaline. Yet it still hurt to breath, and his left side throbbed in the kidney area. But he couldn't resist the food and said through stuffed cheeks, "One torpedo missed. Crappy aim. Thought you were better than that."

"You." Kunisawa grabbed Ingram's lapel—

Fujimoto shouted and stood up grinning, triumphantly waving a small part in the air.

Kunisawa gradually released Ingram's lapel, as Fujimoto talked. Finally, he slapped his knee and shouted, *"Hei, hei,"* and bowed. Then Kunisawa leaned down to Ingram. "You hear that, Commander?"

"Every word," he said, his cheeks crammed with baked noodles.

"Very funny. Your firing pin blocks are too heavy. At the high-speed setting, they can't handle the inertial forces at impact."

Ingram stopped, his wooden spoon halfway to his mouth.

"I thought that would interest you, mister supply officer. The firing pin guide pins are made of steel. They're too heavy; their weight makes them bend and go cross-eyed when the torpedo hits the target. That means the firing pin can't reach the detonator."

Ingram took his bite.

"The fix is relatively simple. Tonight we're going to make a much lighter set of guide pins. Instead of steel, Commander Fujimoto has specified an aluminum alloy. Less weight, the firing pin can slide on the guide, as designed, hit the detonator, and *bam*!" Kunisawa whacked a palm with his fist. "Tomorrow we find out. Maybe you'll be lucky and something else will go wrong, and you will live another day. Then you can slop up more roast pig, ehhh?" He checked his watch, Ingram's watch, against the clock on the bulkhead. "Umm. Nine o'clock." He wound it and looked at Ingram, a thin smile playing across his lips. "Nice watch. Radium dial. Glows in the dark. Thanks."

"Have a good time, Tojo."

Kunisawa blinked and then spoke to Fujimoto. "Time for us to get under way, Commander." He picked up a flashlight and thumbed out Morse code for the letters QQT.

With great difficulty Ingram suppressed a flinch. QQT. It was the recognition signal he was supposed to flash to the *Turbot*. How did he know? Unless they had read the cheat sheet he'd packed with the supplies.

Kunisawa must have been enjoying Ingram's discomfort. "Yes. QQT. Thanks for being so thorough and writing everything down, Commander. Lieutenant Jimbo is on the beach now at Buenavista wearing a set of your khakis and cap, waiting to flash the signal when the sub surfaces. He speaks pretty good English, so he should have no trouble with the walkie-talkie. And after we've dusted off the *Turbot* tonight, you and your friends get to go for another joyride tomorrow."

Fujimoto came up and tested Ingram's chains and nodded to a guard, who stepped back. Then he looked at Ingram and spoke at some length.

"Strange," said Kunisawa. "Commander Fujimoto says he is no longer angry with you. He feels only pity, and sadness. He wants to respect his enemy. And you, he respected until he saw the shabby torpedo design. How can you be a proper warrior without the proper equipment? he wonders. How can you have a fair fight?"

Rage rose within Ingram. How could this bastard refer to his country's rape and murder of millions of civilians a fair fight? He swallowed rice and said quietly, "Are you asking me?"

Kunisawa nodded. "You could do him the courtesy of an answer."

Ingram's chains clanked as he shifted in his chair. "It's our own brand of chivalry. We'll outproduce you."

Kunisawa laughed, then translated.

Fujimoto must have understood, for he immediately smiled and then spoke in Japanese. Kunisawa bowed and said, "Please! Commander Fujimoto says. You can outproduce us with all the Mark 15 torpedoes you can make. But it still will not be a fair fight.' "

"No. We're going to do it with typewriters."

"What?"

"Typewriters, Tojo. We'll build so damn many that all we have to do is stack the crates thirty feet high on the beachheads. We'll crush you to death. Then, when the war's over, we'll have all these typewriters ready to go, instead of a bunch of surplus tanks."

Kunisawa chuckled and translated.

Fujimoto gave a wistful smile, stepped before Ingram, bowed, and gave him a small salute. Then he walked over to a lathe and looked over a machinist's shoulder for a moment, watching the man put finishing touches on the new set of firing pin guides.

Lieutenant Tomo, the admiral's aide, walked in and spoke with Fujimoto for a moment. Then he bowed and walked out.

"Well, it seems the Shōsō will join us after all and awaits aboard the *Namikaze*. It sounds like tonight's fun has just begun."

With a grunt of satisfaction to the lathe operator, Fujimoto took a last look at Ingram and walked out.

"Finish your meal in peace, Commander. Then they'll take you to the brig. Until tomorrow." He followed Fujimoto through the sliding door and thumped it shut behind him.

Ingram took a deep breath and pushed his food aside, a third of it unfinished, his stomach winding into knots. The *Turbot* tonight, the ammunition barge tomorrow. What did it matter? In the next twenty-four hours everyone would be dead. He held his hands before his face. Shaking. In fact, they had been shaking all evening, although he was damned if he was going to let Kunisawa or Fujimoto see. Then he picked up his cup of *basi* and knocked it back, letting the sweet, tender fire run down his throat. But instead of a soothing relaxation, it shocked him to the present; to the fact that over eighty officers and men aboard the U.S.S. *Turbot* were about to die, and there was nothing he could do. He sat, his head in his hands, rocking back and forth, frantically racking his brains for an idea. *Anything.*

Two guards wordlessly lifted him by the elbows and prodded him to his feet, his chains clanking. Across the room the technicians twirled their screwdrivers, seating the new firing pin guides. They were cool, efficient, professional, as they snapped the firing pin a few times. Grunting in satisfaction, they began to insert the Mark 5 exploder into the cavity in the torpedo's warhead.

Ingram stumbled as the guards dragged him through the doorway and into the moonless night. One guard pulled the door closed and they stood for a moment to acclimate their eyes, Ingram slouching against the triple torpedo mount, looking into the gloom.

He sensed something before he actually saw or heard it. Then the soft whine of ventilation blowers preceded a ghostly presence that eased its way down the repair barge's port side. He was enveloped in the heat of a twenty-seven-thousand-horsepower engineering plant; it seemed like an evil spirit in a decrepit eighteenth century slum.

Without running lights, the *Namikaze*'s black shape slipped past like a wraith in the night. Water bubbled softly along her waterline, and her tiny quarter waves slapped the barge. For a moment, he made out three figures grouped on the starboard bridge wing, their faces illuminated by the compass repeater's red light, one of them pointing ahead: father, son, and the ageless veteran who spanned both generations.

Then the *Namikaze* slowed and stopped at the harbor entrance, almost as if frozen in place. In the distance, Ingram heard a splash and the rattle of chain. Yes, she had anchored. The *Namikaze*'s silhouette blended into Mindanao's black landmass.

It came to Ingram that Fujimoto was content to stay right there, her nose barely poking from the harbor entrance, watching, waiting. At 0100, Lieutenant Jimbo, wearing Ingram's uniform, would flash QQT from Buenavista. The *Turbot* would rise three hundred yards off the beach. Then she would fling open all her hatches, bringing up five tons of cargo to load into twenty bancas scheduled to swarm around her. That's when Fujimoto would pounce. Cranking his ship up to thirty-five knots in complete darkness, he would be on the submarine in minutes and hit her without warning, blasting the *Turbot* to pieces with cannon and machine gun fire.

The guards prodded him and, with chains clanking, he rose and shuffled aft, his lower back shooting pain each time he stepped.

Behind him, he heard a loud groan. Then another grunt, followed by a soft splash. He turned to see a body tumble into the water between the barge and wharf. Four figures emerged from the blackness. Two stooped at his feet, fumbling with the chains. Before him was Amador's white mane, his arm in a crude sling.

Then suddenly a pair of arms wrapped around his neck. "Todd," she murmured.

Her arms were around him. "Helen?" It *was* Helen. She kissed him hard.

Amador whispered, "Please, they can't get to your chains."

Awkwardly, he stuck out his wrists, Helen still holding him with all her might. Keys jingled; the manacles and chains were softly eased to the deck.

He threw his arms around her and held her close, kissing her neck, her lips, her scent in his nostrils, her arms around him. His Helen. His sweet, sweet Helen. "My God."

"Enough for now," said Amador, prying them apart. "Please."

He couldn't help it, nor could she. They held one another, swaying and rocking as others pushed them into the dark seclusion of the midships passageway. They found themselves shuffling through a door and into a storeroom with just a seven-watt bulb overhead. "Two minutes," Amador whispered. The he closed the door softly.

Helen shook as tears ran down her cheek. And he wiped them with the back of his hand, only to discover tears ran down his cheeks as well.

She stroked his hair. "It's okay, honey."

He raised her head, seeing her for the first time in six months, the pale light notwithstanding: her face, her hair, and the whiteness of her teeth and the magnificent broad smile he had often dreamed of.

"Helen." He kissed her again and again.

She managed to whisper, "You really came back to me."

He stood away, realizing that he'd lost her twice. And there was something to say before anything else got in his way. He took her hand. "I love you."

"I love you, too." She squeezed hard, taking it and gently giving it back to him, something they would have forever.

Ingram dipped his head to her neck once again to smell her sweetness. She wrapped her arms around him.

"Owww." Pain raged through his back.

"What is it?"

He quickly explained and then ran a hand over her face and looked into her eyes. "Your mom and dad say hi."

"You met them?"

"Yes. They had me for dinner. I met Fred and they showed me your baby pictures." He cupped her chin in his hand and kissed her nose and ran his fingers on her cheek.

Helen touched one of her burn scars. "They haven't healed all the way."

"Didn't notice." He kissed her cheek again.

"Speaking of healing . . ." She ran a thumb along his cheek where his old wound had opened when Fujimoto had hit him. "Why is it still like that?"

"You threatening to stitch me up without anesthetic again?"

"If I have to."

Embracing each other tightly, they kissed again.

The door squeaked and several shadows filed into the room.

"Never thought I'd see you again, Pablo." Ingram slapped Amador's back. "How's your arm?"

"Helen set it a few minutes ago. Hurts like Vesuvius."

"Maybe you should lie down."

"No time," said Amador. "Listen. We hold the barge, but the Kempetai garrisons the town. It is their guards who patrol the wharf."

"What do we have outside?"

"Two at the gangway, four on the second deck, and two more guarding prisoners."

"How did they pull this off?" Ingram whispered.

"The Hapons made a mistake this morning when they conscripted women to clean the ship. What they got was Helen, Wong Lee, and eight other *guerrilleros,* all dressed as women and armed to the teeth. Even Carmen Lai Lai."

"Who's that?" Ingram asked.

Helen said, "Someone who came to our side. She helped with this." She opened her backpack and handed over a pouch to Ingram. "Here. The Jap torpedo stuff plus the page of notes."

Ingram was speechless as he thumbed through the Type 93 manual. All in Japanese, there were plenty of diagrams and mathematical tables. "Amazing. Rocko won't believe this. Neither will Bu Ord." He stuffed it back into her pouch. "How did you do this?"

Helen shrugged and restrapped the pouch.

Amador said, "The rub is we have to find a way out."

"What's the layout?" asked Ingram.

"With the destroyer gone, there is just a skeleton crew here. We've taken them all prisoner, including, by now, the men in the machine shop."

Two shadows joined the others. One of them spoke. "Evening, Skipper." It was Seltzer.

"Leo? You okay?" They shook.

Seltzer smacked his lips. "I'll make it."

Helen asked, "Who's this?"

"A guy off my ship." Ingram introduced them.

Seltzer said, "You didn't tell me she was so damned good-looking, Mr. Ingram."

"Hey, stand aside, buddy. She's mine." It was Wong Lee.

"Who's this jerk?" said Seltzer.

Amador said, "Meet Wong Lee, one of my bravest lieutenants."

"No, you don't, Pablo," said Wong Lee. "Hell, I just want to go home."

"You an American?" said Seltzer.

"You betcha."

Amador said, "Helen tells me it was Wong Lee's grenade that killed the Hapons conscripting women for the cleaning detail. His bravery paved the way for our rescue."

"We're not out of here yet, Pablo." Wong Lee shook with Seltzer, then reached for Ingram's hand. "Gotta cigarette, Commander?"

"Gave it up a long time ago. So you're the great Wong Lee. I'm Todd Ingram."

"That's me. Why? You been to my place?"

"Yeah. Great food."

"Did you meet my—"

"Later," said Amador. "We have to figure out what to do."

Ingram took a deep breath, finding his ribs still hurt. "We're like walking wounded."

Amador said, "Doesn't matter. We can all fit in that stake truck outside. If things go well, we can be in Buenavista in a half-hour, neutralize Lieutenant Jimbo, and warn the *Turbot* to come back in three or four days. Then we go hide in the mountains. The riskiest part is getting past the guards on the wharf. They're not fools."

"You need a diversion?" said Seltzer.

"Like what?"

"The barge. Let's blow it. They'll never know what hit 'em. With all that confusion, we can slip under their noses."

Ingram said, "I don't know, Leo. All that stuff, bombs, gasoline. That thing blows, and it may take us and half the town with it."

Amador said, "It may be our only chance."

Seltzer said, "Maybe we don't need to take the truck."

"What do you mean?" said Amador.

"There's that landing barge tied outboard of the YFD." When returning late that afternoon, they had seen a dilapidated forty-seven-foot wooden landing barge, chugging alongside the Shōsō's twin-engine Nakajima amphibian, loading boxes.

Ingram said, "How do you get past Fujimoto and his damned destroyer?"

"Hmmm." Seltzer rubbed his chin.

Just then the door burst open. A white-faced Legaspi thrust his head in.

"Emilio, what is it?" asked Amador.

Legaspi gasped, "Hapon sonsabits. Quick. Many out there." He dashed out. Just then, a single-shot rifle fired from the deck above. A machine gun on the wharf opened up in response, bullets thudding into the barge's wooden superstructure.

"Too late, growled Amador."

A searchlight snapped on, illuminating the passageway in a white hoary light.

Ingram grabbed Helen's hand. "Come on."

CHAPTER FIFTY

Ingram dashed outside and yelled, "Emilio. Get that light."

He needn't have said it, for Legaspi was on his knees, hoisting his Springfield to his shoulder. Machine gun bullets chewed the wooden bulkhead above his head as he squeezed off a round. With a crash of glass, the light fizzled out, plunging the wharf into darkness. The machine gun stopped firing and men cursed back and forth.

"That will slow them for a moment or two," puffed Amador.

In the relative quiet, Ingram couldn't help but think of the irony of their situation. "We've been here before, Pablo." They had been in the same fix five months earlier on the same wharf, barely escaping in the 51 Boat after dynamiting the lumber mill.

"There is one difference," murmured Amador in the darkness.

"Yes?"

"This time we have Helen."

"But we have no dynamite," Helen said.

"There must be a better way than blowing the place up." Ingram stroked his chin for a moment. "Pablo. How many men have we?"

Amador answered, "Carillo and Estaque guard the gangway, two more guard the prisoners. Carmen Lai Lai and nine others are stationed topside."

That left Ingram, Amador, Helen, Wong Lee, Legaspi, and Seltzer. Twenty against a garrison of perhaps a hundred. "Okay. Let's move forward."

A truck pulled up, the tires crunching over gravel. Men jumped out, their sandals thumping as they scattered along the dock. Someone yelled, and a truck-mounted spotlight snapped on, picking out Estaque at the gangway. The ex-Filipino scout instinctively threw up a hand, shading his eyes. The soldiers kneeling around the truck opened up, the rest of the soldiers in the burned-out lumber mill joining in, with at least twenty-five to thirty weapons firing at the same time. Estaque's arms clawed in space, his rigid body jinking up and down before he collapsed on the deck, his rifle clattering to his side.

"Felipe! Felipe!" Amador screamed. He stood, aiming a pistol with his good arm, methodically cranking off rounds, the muzzle blast flashing in the night. A machine gun round blew off his planter's hat, knocking him to the deck.

In panic, Ingram and Helen crouched beside him, Helen yelling, "Pablo?"

Amador raised himself to sit against the bulkhead and buried his head in his hands. "Felipe was the finest . . . like a son . . ." His voice drifted off, as Helen put her arms around Amador and rocked him.

Ingram patted him on the shoulder. "I'm sorry."

Amador shook Helen off and scrambled to his feet, broken arm and all. Picking up his pistol, he cranked out three more rounds. "These dirty Hapons. The only thing they know is wanton rape and killing and stealing another man's things."

Ingram grabbed Amador's wrist. "Pablo. Later." He'd never seen the Don so angry.

"Just look at my mill, my beautiful mill. It's been in our family since 1841," Amador yelled, pointing in darkness.

Ingram said, "That was my fault."

"Not your fault. It's these Hapons. These filthy, greedy Hapons, who must conquer the world so they can have their oil and their rubber and their . . ." —he waved toward his mill—"their lumber."

Then his voice resonated into the night, "Well, you're not going to get it, you cheap, lazy bastards. Not a peso worth." A bullet whanged off a stanchion, making everyone duck, except Amador, who kept yelling. "And after Felipe is gone, and after I'm gone, there still will be others to cut the heads off the snake. We'll dump them in your stew pots, you dirty—" Amador shook his fist as a machine gun stitched the wall close by. Ingram yanked him to the deck as Carillo and *guerrilleros* on the second deck fired back with their Springfields, smashing the truck's spotlight and scattering the soldiers.

Fifteen seconds of silence felt like an eternity. Wong Lee's voice shook. "Boy, oh, boy. I didn't count on this." He looked across the harbor. "Why don't we swim for it?"

Amador growled, "We might. But they could retake the barge, turn on a searchlight, and pick us off one by one."

"Better than getting picked off one by one here." Wong Lee began to unbutton his shirt.

"Hold on." Ingram called, "Where the hell is Leo?"

Just then Seltzer trotted around the deckhouse, a Springfield cradled in this arms. He handed Ingram a .45. "Sorry, Skipper. Took me a while. I found this rifle and two grenades."

"Where?"

"Machine shop. Doubles as an armory."

The Japanese at the truck began firing, and soon they were joined by other riflemen on the wharf.

"Jesus. How'd they get so close?" asked Seltzer.

Ingram snapped, "The truck. Lob one on it right now."

Seltzer needed no urging. "Got it." He yanked the grenade's pin, stood, and with a grunt hurled it into the night, while the others dropped to their knees and covered their ears.

A blinding flash was followed by a ripping explosion on the wharf. An eerie quiet descended, punctuated by two prolonged groans.

"That will give them something to think about," said Ingram.

"Damnit. Missed the gas tank."

Wong Lee said, "Now's our chance. Let's scram."

"How about crocodiles?" said Helen.

"I'll take my chances. Better than getting shot by Japs," said Wong Lee.

"Hold on," said Ingram. "What about the landing barge?"

Seltzer checked his Springfield's clip. "The thing's a junk heap, but it might work. All we need is to get the engine started."

Legaspi said, "I know that banca. Diesel. Sixty horses. Runs real good. I'll do it."

Ingram rubbed his chin. "Maybe . . ."

"Where would you go?" asked Helen.

Ingram said, "There's still plenty of time to get to Buenavista and warn the *Turbot*. Maybe even set up another rendezvous time. Where's it tied up?"

"Outboard on the port side," said Seltzer.

Even in the darkness, Amador's eyes grew bright. "It just might work. And yes, Emilio is good with boats."

"Okay. Leo, you and Emilio go try and get the thing started. We'll hold off the Japs until you're ready."

"Got it." Seltzer stood.

A green flare shot from behind the lumber mill and hissed up into clear blackness, where it popped a parachute and then gently floated down. "What the—?"

Another searchlight, far brighter than the others, blazed at them from the harbor entrance.

Wong Lee shaded his eyes. "Aw, shit."

"Down, everybody," said Ingram.

Like an enraged tenement dweller probing for a cockroach with a flashlight, the *Namikaze*'s searchlight flicked over the barge. After a moment, the long shaft of light slowly swept across the harbor to the jungle on the opposite shore. As if it had a mind of its own, the beam swept back to the barge, peering into windows, corners, seeking the enemy. That was soon followed by rattle of rifles and automatic weapons from the wharf, cordite smoke hanging in the air like a London fog. Bullets chewed up bulkheads and clanged against machinery. "Coordinated attack. They must be in radio contact with the destroyer," Ingram muttered.

As if in confirmation, the ship fired a fifty-caliber machine gun in three-shot bursts.

Helen peeked over the rail. "We're trapped."

"That's it. I'm going." Wong Lee started to unbutton his shirt.

The others made to follow, but Ingram said, "Look at that."

"What?" said Amador.

"They're shooting high. They're afraid of hitting something down low. On the first deck—That's it! Emilio. Do you really think you can start that landing barge?"

"Yes, Sair."

Seltzer said, "Skipper. That piece of crap don't look like an option anymore."

Amador turned and looked at Ingram. "What's on your mind?"

Ingram squinted into the night. "They'll spot us when we jump from the ship and start swimming. After that, the Japs will rush aboard and it will be a shooting gallery." He pointed at the *Namikaze*'s silhouette laying astride the harbor entrance. "Look at that damn thing, just waiting."

A machine gun thumped from the wharf, blowing bits and chunks of wood as it swept down the barge. "Duck!" said Ingram.

Someone screamed in pain topside. Framed in a spotlight was Carmen Lai Lai, standing now, firing a single-shot Springfield.

Several Japanese weapons responded, red splotches bursting on Carmen's massive chest. She finally plunged through the rail, crashed to the main deck, and was still.

"Carmen," Helen mouthed.

Amador squeezed her hand.

Seltzer's voice squeaked, "Mr. Ingram, damnit. What do we do?"

"Over here and I'll tell you." Ingram ducked through a passageway and dashed over to the barge's port side, pain shooting up his back. He stopped and waited, panting and wheezing, as bullets thunked into the thin walls of the deckhouse on the starboard side. On second thought, it seemed desperate, scatterbrained. Would it work? And as they gathered around, he sensed their eyes upon him, searching his face. Like freshly caged animals, they were in near-panic, searching for a way out of this hellish trap, its walls slowly squeezing in.

Quickly he explained what he had in mind.

"Seems the only way," agreed Amador.

Nobody had a better idea, so Ingram started forward. While Legaspi headed aft for the landing barge, Amador softly called instructions to his men on the second deck, telling them they had to hold the Japanese at bay for at least ten minutes.

Ingram and the others stepped into the machine shop. After closing the doors, Ingram fumbled for a light switch and snapped it on. Then he said to Seltzer and Wong Lee, "Okay, you two look for the impulse charge."

"Right." The pair dashed to the aft bulkhead, finding a row of double-locked cabinets with chains through the handles. Seltzer stooped and grabbed a length of pipe and began prying off the hinges. Wong Lee ripped open a drawer, pulled out a crowbar, and attacked the other end.

Two fifty-caliber rounds punched through, throwing splinters and smashing a lathe, shrapnel flying in every direction. Ingram and Helen fell to the deck, where he threw an arm over her. They waited for a moment, then Ingram wobbled to his feet. "Anybody hurt?"

The others stood, dusting themselves off, surprised they were okay.

Helen gasped, "They must not realize we're in here."

"Let's hope our boys topside keep them bamboozled just a little longer." Ingram reached up and swung a chain-falls assembly along an overhead track until it was over the Mark 15 the Japanese torpedomen had modified earlier that evening. Reaching over to the workbench, he found a pair of hoisting lugs and tried to screw one in. But his fingers shook and it fell clanking to the deck.

"Here." Helen eased him aside and twisted the lugs tight.

Ingram snapped in the hooks, then shouted over his shoulder, "Leo. Any luck?"

Seltzer muttered, "Not yet. Shit, lookit this. Cotter pins, swivel shackles, a year's supply of machine screws, nuts, and bolts—Damnit." With a growl, he yanked a carton marked WASHERS off the shelf and flung it aside, the contents jingling on the deck.

Suddenly there was a roar from the wharf as small arms concentrated on the aft section of the barge. The return fire from Amador's *guerrilleros* on the second deck seemed pathetic by comparison. Amador stepped out the port side door and shouted up. Soon he stepped back, saying, "Three dead and another two seriously wounded up there. How much longer?"

"A minute." Ingram wheezed as he set the stanchions. Then he dropped the torpedo skids into place, the sections leading from the torpedo rack to the double doors. A bolt of pain shot up his left side. Everything seemed to turn a hazy red, and he had to bite his lip and concentrate on staying conscious. When the wave passed, he called to Helen, "You about done?"

"Set." Helen looked at him. "You look awful."

He blinked a couple of times, wiping blood off his split cheek. "I feel awful."

She walked over and pushed him toward a chair. "Here. Sit."

"In a minute." Ingram rolled slack out of the chain-falls. The chains became snug and finally began to lift the torpedo from its rack. Helen, Amador, and Wong Lee moved in and helped hand-over-hand the chains. Soon the Mark 15 torpedo rose from its cradle and hung free.

A fusillade roared at them. Wong Lee screeched, "These bastards don't care what happens to their barge, do they?"

Everyone fell to the deck again and covered their heads, their knees fetal, all wishing for a hole to climb in. Bullets ripped through the bulkhead; splinters flew, machinery and boxes and crates shattering above their heads, sharp, jagged pieces jabbing, bouncing off their clothing. The air thumped their ears as the bullets crashed about, almost as if each one were a macabre drumbeat.

Miraculously, none hit the torpedo. During the roaring cacophony, someone yelled in abject human terror. Impossible for Ingram to tell if it was Helen or Wong Lee or Amador or Seltzer. Or even himself. More shells crashed in the machine shop, mixing with the terrified screams. This time Ingram's throat was raw; he'd been screaming, too.

CHAPTER FIFTY-ONE

17 NOVEMBER, 1942
SERVICE BARGE 212, NASIPIT, MINDANAO
PHILIPPINES

An explosion roared outside, and miraculously the gunfire trickled to nothing, a blissful silence descending on the smoke-filled room. Ingram was wedged under a drill press, his arm around Helen. He raised to an elbow and looked into the blinking face of Wong Lee just three feet away under a workbench, his hands over his ears. "You okay?"

"Huh?"

"I said, are you okay?"

"Y-yeah." Wong Lee sat up and flicked splinters and broken glass shards off his shirt.

Ingram looked down to Helen. "How 'bout you?"

She stared wildly for a moment, then nodded and gasped, "Yeah."

"Pablo?"

Something tinkled on the far side of the room.

"Pablo?" Ingram shouted.

"We were blessed." Amador rose from a pile of pipe fittings.

Suddenly Ingram remembered—the torpedo! He swung to see it untouched, still dangling from the falls.

The door on the port side squeaked open and a breathless Seltzer dashed in, holding up a grenade pin. "Last one," he gasped, looking around the room. "Jesus. Everybody okay?"

"Looks like it." Ingram scrambled to his feet and hobbled over to the torpedo.

"What are you doing?" asked Seltzer.

"Making sure." Ingram ran his hands over the Mark 5 exploder. Yes, the Japanese technician had snugged the flush-mounted bolts properly.

Wong Lee returned to the back of the room and started pawing through the wreckage. Suddenly he yelled, "Hey!" He thrust a brass canister over his head. "How's this?"

Ingram yelled back, "Yeah! That's it."

Seltzer said, "Where'd you find it?"

Wong Lee walked up and handed the canister to Ingram. "A case of four. First cupboard you looked in."

Seltzer groaned.

Ingram turned the impulse charge in his hands, examining the primer cap on the base. "We're in luck. It's percussion."

"Is that it, then? We all set?" Wong Lee's voice squeaked like a sixteen-year-old on a Saturday night.

"Help me with this first." Seltzer and Wong Lee joined Ingram at the torpedo, helping him whip the chain-falls to lower the torpedo. With a clunk, the 3,841-pound Mark 15 fell to the skid. "One more thing." Ingram quickly unhooked the chains and unscrewed the lifting lug. "Ready."

Ingram searched their faces as they gathered around the torpedo, breathing hard, their faces ashen, afraid to move; afraid to commit to the next deadly step. He tried to think of something profound, even heroic to say; something that would make them laugh or give them a sense of purpose. He wiped at his eyes and looked at them looking at him. *Damn.* They could all be dead in the next sixty seconds, and yet, all he could think of was . . . nothing.

Ingram raised his hands and slapped his sides. "All right. Here's how we do this. Wong Lee, you kill the lights when I give the word. Then slide the doors open and come back to give a hand with the torpedo. Leo, you and I will lay down the last two skids as soon as the doors are open."

They stood rooted to their places, waiting for someone else to say something or make a move.

Ingram shrugged. "Well, let's go. You have to die of something."

Wong Lee stepped to the light switch. "You'd make a wonderful insurance salesman, Commander."

"Thanks." Ingram grabbed a torpedo skid. "Ready?"

Seltzer picked us his skid and nodded.

"Go!"

Wong Lee flicked the lights, plunging the shop into darkness. With a grunt, he gave the doors a push and they slid open, thumping at their stops. One by one, Ingram and Seltzer quickly laid the skids on the stanchions, the pathway now leading directly to the bottom right torpedo tube. While Seltzer yanked at the breech locks, Ingram gathered with the others at the back of the torpedo. "Go!" he barked.

They pushed. Ingram pushed with them but saw only grays and darker grays as the torpedo moved away from him. Blackness swarmed through his vision and he felt as if Fujimoto had kicked him again. When he refocused, he found he'd dropped to his knees, the torpedo out of sight. He blinked for a moment and found that they had pushed the missile down the skids almost to the tube breech.

"Hold it." Ingram groaned, heaved to his feet, and stumbled to the breech, checking the tube lug. Satisfied, he flashed a thumbs up. With growls and groans, the others shoved the Mark 15 into the tube until it was fully seated. Then Seltzer slammed the breech door and dogged it. "Sonofabitch," he puffed.

"Okay." Ingram reached for the impulse charge, but . . . he looked up with a foolish grin. He just couldn't move.

Helen stepped over and held Ingram's shoulder. "Let someone else do it."

As if in a dream, Ingram watched Seltzer shove the impulse charge home, lock the chamber, and arm the firing pin. Then the lanky boatswain's mate climbed into the mount-trainer's seat and peered through the sight as he cranked the train wheel.

But the wheel spun freely, the mount not turning. "Shit," Seltzer muttered.

"Shift to manual," Ingram wheezed.

"Check." Seltzer reached behind him and fumbled at a lever. It was a task for the mount captain, whose position was behind the mount trainer. It was too awkward for Seltzer and he couldn't uncage the lever from where he sat. Ingram tried to reach, and groaned with pain.

"Let me." Helen pulled over a box, stepped up, and lay across the tube, grabbing Seltzer's hand and placing it on the lever.

"Thanks," he mumbled. With a yank, he uncaged the lever and swung it up into position. He tried the train wheel again; the torpedo mount squeaked right a few degrees. "Got it."

"It's all yours," puffed Ingram.

Seltzer hunched over the sight again and cranked his wheel. "My, oh, my. Look what we have here."

"What do you see?" asked Amador.

"Tojo smack-dab in the crosshairs."

"What's he doing?" asked Ingram.

"Target angle two-seven-zero. DIW," reported Seltzer.

"What the hell does that mean?" snapped Wong Lee.

Seltzer cranked in the fine adjustment to the train wheel. "That means the little bastard's port side is facing us like a frigging barn door, and he's dead-ass in the water."

Ingram rasped, "Must be still anchored. Too bad. Okay, Leo. Set high speed. Depth four feet. No gyro angle." His lungs seemed as if they were on fire. It hurt to breath or even talk, and once again he swam on the edge of darkness, except this time nausea welled and he had to work at choking it back.

"Ready." Seltzer pressed his eye to the sight.

Then Ingram remembered something. "Leo. What's the range?"

Seltzer's eyes grew wide and his face turned as white as the destroyer's searchlight beam. "Shit."

"What do you think?"

"Three, four hundred yards, maybe. I can't tell." He looked down at Ingram, both aware the torpedo would have to travel at least 350 yards before the Mark 5 exploder armed itself. Anything less and the torpedo would not detonate. "What now?"

Ingram peered into the night.

"How 'bout disconnecting the arming mechanism?"

"That means pulling the torpedo from the tube and taking out the exploder, and doing things to it I'm not sure would work. Besides, there's not enough time." Ingram took another breath. "Maybe if they weigh anchor and open the range?"

"I dunno," said Seltzer.

"What's wrong?" asked Amador.

"Shoot the damned thing," Wong Lee demanded.

Just then, the aft four-inch mount on the *Namikaze*'s fantail opened up. A shell whistled overhead and landed on the floating dry dock, blowing away half the port side. "Fujimoto has guessed what we're doing," Ingram wheezed. As he spoke, the *Namikaze*'s whistle blew six short blasts and a clanking noise ranged across the water. "They're raising the anchor."

"Who cares? Shoot that goddamned torpedo," screeched Wong Lee.

"What do you think, Mr. Ingram?" Asked Seltzer.

"We have no choice." Ingram turned to Amador. Pablo, could you step over here, please?"

Amador moved up. "Yes?"

"See that?" Ingram pointed at a gleaming brass trigger grip mounted on Seltzer's train wheel.

"I do."

"One for the Hapons." Ingram nodded at the wheel, his face grim.

Seltzer sat back, locked the train wheel, and lifted his hands. "It's all yours, Sir."

"Thank you. I believe I will." Amador stood on the little box Helen had used, reached over, and squeezed the trigger.

The mount belched as the impulse charge kicked the Mark 15 torpedo out of the tube, where it hit the water with a splash and disappeared from view.

Ingram did some rough math, figuring the torpedo run would be only about fifteen seconds at forty-six knots.

Seltzer hopped off the mount and crossed his fingers. "Here's hoping the range is over three-fifty."

Ingram shot back, "Here's hoping Tojo knows how to fix depth engines and exploders."

Another four-inch round whistled in, landing fifty yards before them and twenty-five yards to the left, raising a tall water column.

"They've got our range," said Amador.

Seltzer turned. "What if they—"

Whack! The night turned to day. *Namikaze* sailors spun up into the air. The old four-stack destroyer rose from the water as if her midships were pried by an enormous lever, the ship cracking in two, bow and stern falling away. A much louder detonation followed, bringing a thunderous, eardrum-piercing roar, as the *Namikaze*'s magazines exploded.

The shock wave struck like a giant hand before they could take cover, flinging them backward to the deck . . .

The night sky. That was the first thing he saw: a cluster of stars; gently sloping hills on one side, and the service barge rising above him on the other; all under a marvelous velvet night sky, the dew kissing his face, wetting his lips with a soft, sweet assurance that he was alive, that he could feel, and that he could see and enjoy what was to come . . .

He knew he was prone because something was propped under his head for a pillow, a lifejacket, perhaps. His ears were ringing, and several heads were gathered around, some he didn't recognize. A white mane of hair. Amador, close, his brow furrowed, then looking up, calling to someone. Another figure scrambled down a crude ladder into . . . ? It was the landing barge. He couldn't hear, but he knew by the *thump-thump-thump* vibration under his back and the rich odor of diesel exhaust that the engine was running. He raised a hand to his face, and someone bent over.

Helen. She wiped at his cheek with a rag.

"My God, you're beautiful." Then, "What are we waiting for?"

She smiled and he heard her beautiful voice. "Wong Lee and Seltzer are still in the torpedo shop."

"Why?"

"Lots of stuff on the shelves. The Jap's exploder notes. Manuals, technical pubs, comic books, take-out menus, everything." Helen took the pouch off her shoulder and held it before Ingram's face. Stuffed with documents, it was much fuller than when he first saw it.

He lay back and released himself to the sweet darkness . . .

They must have been under way, because the boat rocked gently and the engine vibrated with purpose.

"Welcome back." Helen bent down and kissed him on the forehead.

The ringing was gone. It was her voice. It really was Helen this time. His own sweet girl, not the voice of his dreams, or even the voice of her mother. But Helen. He reached up and stroked her hair. "Almost forgot."

"What's that?"

The boat jolted as it plowed into a wave, slapping water in the air where it flew over their heads. His side came alive, sending electric jolts as if a demon were nested there. But something *was* different. A rigidity. Somehow, Helen had taped his ribs. When he took a breath, it didn't hurt as much. Not bad. But his throat was dry. Never mind. She looked wonderful in the night, leaning over, her hair grazing his face. He pulled her head down and kissed her, ignoring the pain.

"No sudden movements," she said.

He kissed her again, and she gently wrapped an arm around his head.

After a moment, he reached in his pocket and handed over her class ring. "Your mom and dad wanted me to give this to you."

She recognized it at once, then slipped it on the fourth finger of her left hand. She ran a hand over his cheek. "I knew it was coming."

"What? How could you?"

"When Pablo told me about the new date on the authenticator, I knew you'd been up to something."

"Oh. For a moment I thought you were being clairvoyant."

"Not me. That's Mom's specialty."

"I'm not so sure," Ingram croaked, feeling tired again.

"Did she really show you my baby pictures?"

"Ummm."

"And you met Fred?"

"Purred like hell, then went to sleep in my lap."

"Amazing."

Ingram's eyelids fluttered.

"I guess we'll have a long time to talk about it."

"You bet." Then he fell asleep.

You shall judge of a man by his foes as well as his friends.
JOSEPH CONRAD
LORD JIM

*The Lord gave us two ends to use: one to think with and one
to sit with. The war depends on which we choose—heads
we win, tails we lose.*
FLEET ADMIRAL CHESTER W. NIMITZ
TO ADMIRAL WILLIAM F. HALSEY

EPILOGUE

21 DECEMBER, 1942
GOLDEN GATE PARK
SAN FRANCISCO, CALIFORNIA

The man shifted his weight on the cement bench, the cold burning through his overcoat like an acetylene torch. The morning had brought low, thick clouds, the park nearly deserted on a Monday. His bench was on a hill near Stow Lake, where one enjoyed a view of the Golden Gate Bridges' twin orange towers. But squalls tumbled across the peninsula, obscuring the towers as rain whipped his face, smearing his glasses. He looked at his watch: ten-thirty. His contact was a half-hour late. He stood and paced around the bench again, checking his watch, oblivious to the rain.

The cold felt better, Ingram ruefully admitted to himself, than the miserable malaria-laden humidity of the Solomons. Another gust whipped through, almost carrying away his little fedora, rain blasting against his overcoat and dark gray slacks. He reached up and tightened his polka-dot tie, then drew the overcoat lapels close around his neck, a vain attempt to keep out fiendish little rivulets of rain that worked their way inside his shirt to run down his back.

His Naval Academy ring was back on his fourth finger and Ingram twisted it absently as he reviewed again who he was supposed to be: Doctor John Mickaeljohn, a physicist at the University of California at Berkeley. Through wiretapping, Dr. Mickaeljohn had been overheard collaborating with Leonard Strong, a local Communist cell leader. Today was the day Mickaeljohn was to meet his Soviet control and turn over the first batch of documents for a project called VOSTOK. All they told Ingram was that VOSTOK was a major Soviet espionage mission aimed at the U.S., and that the real Dr. Mickaeljohn and Comrade Strong had been arrested earlier this morning. There remained only one more thing to do.

A twig snapped behind him. Ingram turned to see a mufti-clad man in a hat walking stiffly toward him, using a cane with a shiny brass tip. Ingram figured he'd been watching from the thicket for the past half-hour or so.

Eduard Dezhnev walked up with extended hand. *"Privert, Doctor Mickaeljohn."* Hello, Doctor Mickaeljohn. Dezhnev's grin was wide, his voice the same rich baritone.

Ingram waited until Dezhnev stood face-to-face with him. Then he took Dezhnev's hand with both of his and squeezed, hard. "Hello, yourself, you two-timing sonofabitch."

Dezhnev's grin disappeared, as if whipped away by the squall. His mouth dropped, his lips working open and closed. His voice quavered as he said, ". . . You. It's . . . thought you were . . ." He tried to jerk his hand away.

"Thought I was dead, you bastard?" Ingram squeezed harder.

"Owww." Dezhnev brought up a knee, trying for Ingram's groin. Just in time, Ingram twisted, parrying the blow. He threw a swift backhand across Dezhnev's face, flipping the Soviet agent's hat in the air, where it sailed away on the wind.

Dezhnev managed to rip his hand free and step back, wiping a little rivulet of blood running from the corner of his mouth. "How did you . . . Look, Todd. I'm sorry. They made me do it. You are my friend. I didn't want it to come to this."

"Bullshit."

Dezhnev whipped a small automatic from his pocket. It looked like a .22. He raised it to hip level and flipped off the safety. "What can you do? I have immunity, you know."

Ingram nodded at the pistol. "You really going to use that thing?"

Dezhnev sighed and put the pistol away. *"Do svedaniia."* Good-bye. With a curt bow, he turned and walked away. He got no farther than ten steps before finding himself surrounded by four men, who quickly disarmed him and snapped on handcuffs.

Dezhnev turned and looked at Ingram. His dark red hair was plastered to his forehead, water running down his face. "Todd, I'm really sorry. Perhaps we could have been friends in another time."

"Perhaps."

Three men led him down a path, one stooping to pick up Dezhnev's hat and jam it on his head. The fourth man—Ingram knew him only as Agent Cassidy of the FBI—walked back up to the bench.

"Is that it?"

Agent Cassidy nodded. "Yes, that's it. Look, I'm sorry. I didn't know he'd be packing a pistol. Kinda dicey there for a moment, but everything worked out. You okay?"

Ingram's back ached and there had been a jolt of pain when he'd twisted to backhand Dezhnev. "Not bad."

"It's cold. We better get you back." They started walking, their feet crunching on the gravel path.

At length, Ingram asked, "How did you figure this out?"

"Lucky, this time. We had a man posing inside the consulate as a waiter. Heard some juicy stuff."

"You mean we're spying on our allies?"

Cassidy shrugged. "You should see what they're doing to us."

They rounded a clump of trees and stepped into a cul-de-sac. Three police and four unmarked cars were parked around a four-door drab olive Plymouth sedan with black U.S. Army markings on the door. Dezhnev sat in back, his hands cuffed behind him. His lips were tightly pressed, a tiny bit of blood trickling down his chin. Unblinking, his gaze was fixed straight ahead. Another man with a long nose, thin mustache, and dark curly hair sat beside Dezhnev. His expression was as dour as Dezhnev's, and it was obvious he was cuffed also.

"Ever see the other guy?" asked Cassidy as they walked by.

"No. Who is he?"

His ID says he's Sergei Zenit, an agricultural attaché. But we know he's Captain Second Rank Sergei Zenit of the NKVD."

Ingram turned his head. "Good God. NKVD?"

"Yes. He is Dezhnev's control. And there's another. Their driver. Georgiy Voronin, an NKVD enforcer. Unlike Zenit, he spotted our stakeout and took off. We'll pick him up before he gets to the consulate.

"What happens to them?"

"Persona non grata. Their ship, the *Dzhurma,* was here for overhaul. She's ready now and sails tonight for Vladivostok. Just before they get under way, we're going to shove those three bastards up the gangway, hands tied behind their backs, deportation orders pinned to their lapels."

"Um." Ingram removed the glasses and handed them over. "I won't need these anymore."

"Thanks. You sure you don't need a lift?"

"I'm fine. See you later." Ingram turned to walk the quarter mile to where he'd parked Toliver's Packard. It was raining now, but he didn't mind. He wanted time to think. Just then a virulent zephyr struck, bringing with it cold, hard rain. "Uhhhh-rah."

Cassidy called after him, "What?"

Ingram shook his head. He had an errand to run, and to do it right, he had to forget what was behind him. "Let the dead bury the dead." He walked down the hill, the rain turning to a soft mist.

*　　*　　*

Ingram pushed through the revolving doors of the St. Francis Hotel. The gilded lobby felt warm, and as usual was full of uniformed officers clamoring for rooms. At the check-in counter was Toliver, surrounded by a mountain of luggage and obviously registering, most likely for his twelfth-floor suite paid for by the Manhattan law firm of McNeil, Lawton & Toliver. He called, "Ollie!"

Toliver waved back, finished signing in, and tipped a bellboy. With his brass-tipped mahogany cane in hand, he hobbled over, his greatcoat and combination cap still dripping with rainwater. "Todd? What the hell? You dressed like an undertaker?"

Ingram grabbed Toliver's hand. "Ollie. Welcome back. How was Washington?"

"Too much brass. No place to sleep. They made me stay in a BOQ. Me? Can you imagine that?"

Ingram chuckled. Although they'd talked on the phone from Honolulu, it was the first time he'd seen Toliver since that day on the *Zeilin* two months ago. His face was flushed. He'd gained weight, and from the way he'd just walked across the lobby, he seemed okay on his feet. In his new job as Twelfth Naval District Bureau of Ordnance representative in San Francisco, life seemed to be agreeing with him. Ingram clapped Toliver on the shoulder boards. "You're looking okay, Ollie. How's the hip?"

"They took me off the crutches a week ago." Then Toliver beamed. "Say, how's my car?"

"No dings yet."

"Good. Doctor says I can drive now. I can't wait." Then he smiled at Ingram. "You're looking well, too, Lieutenant Commander. How're the ribs?"

"Still a little sore, but fine."

The *Turbot* pulled into the Pearl Harbor submarine base on December 2. In a drugged bliss, Ingram was unaware of an armed courier waiting for the submarine to dock. No sooner were the *Turbot*'s lines doubled up, then the courier took custody of the Type 93 torpedo manual and Fujimoto's Mark 15 notes. Immediately, he boarded a four engine PB2Y Coronado amphibian, which delivered him eighteen hours later to the Twelfth Naval District Headquarters on Treasure Island in San Francisco. From there, Lieutenant Junior Grade Oliver P. Toliver III took custody of the documents and personally delivered them to the Navy's Bureau of Ordnance in Washington, D.C.

Meanwhile, Ingram was taken to the hospital where he spent a week. Then, for five days, Admiral Spruance put him up at the Royal Hawaiian Hotel. Normally reserved for submariners, it was located on the pristine sands of Honolulu's Waikiki Beach. And now, Ingram had been a day in San Francisco to meet Toliver who had just returned from Washington, D.C.

Toliver said, "Well, commander, it's time for another wetting-down party."

"Maybe."

"Uhhhh-rah."

Ingram stared at the polished marble lobby floor.

Toliver's smile faded. "It's true, then? All I've heard about Ed?"

Ingram nodded.

They were being jostled, so Ingram drew Toliver to the side near the concierge's desk. "The FBI arrested him this morning. His cronies, too. That's why the getup. They asked me to play the part of a contact to lure him in."

"Jesus. I thought I was a good judge of character. I trusted that bastard. He was Navy, like us. Shot it out with the enemy, just like . . . us. We had good times. Shit." He reached over the concierge's desk and dropped his brass-tipped cane in the wastebasket.

Ingram watched it rattle around. "You remember saying anything to him?"

Toliver raised his hands and let them flop to his sides. "Tidbits. That's all. Stuff about you and Helen . . . hell, I don't know."

"Anything on torpedoes?"

"No. That was before your Nasipit stuff came through. That was too hot to tell anyone, I'll say."

"Good." Ingram took off his raincoat. "Now, how did it go at BuOrd?"

"I don't think the Winslow River crowd had any idea about how good the Jap Type 93 torpedoes are. Even when I slapped Helen's torpedo manual on the desk. And you should have seen the battleship boys. They just sat there, their lips flapping in the wind."

"What did they say about Mark 15s?"

Toliver said quietly, "That Japs' notes hit like a ton of bricks. Last time I saw, the Winslow River people were slinking around, lower than dogshit. Especially when we started diagramming depth-engine sensors and exploder foul-ups. Then they went to a closed-door session and kicked me out. The word is that it's not just the Mark 15 torpedoes that are screwing up. It's all of our torpedoes. Aerial torpedoes, and especially the submarine Mark 14 torpedoes. Apparently they're having terrible failures."

"You think our stuff did some good, then?"

"No doubt about it. They had no idea the Jap torpedoes were so lethal and that ours were so crappy. Combine that with the Japs' excellent night tactics, and you can see why they're kicking our ass in the Solomons."

"So they're taking in the whole picture?"

"They're giving torpedo design and naval doctrine a serious look. Maybe leadership, too. Too many peacetime 'cover your ass' types afraid to get out there and take chances."

Ingram rubbed his chin. "That's basically what Spruance said."

"Atwell invite you to play golf?"

"He's gone. Fired, I think. Someone commissioned him as an Army captain. He's now supervising Quonset hut construction in Greenland."

"Out of sight, out of mind."

Toliver nodded. "Nobody wants him talking.

"Look, Todd, come on up to my room and I'll tell you all about it while I change. Then we'll go out, get loaded, and pick up some broads."

"You're nuts."

"Back in a minute." She walked across the lobby and stood before the St. Francis's large revolving doors. Seconds later, Kate and Frank Durand burst through. With squeals of delight, they wrapped their arms around their daughter.

Ingram said, "Come on over and meet them."

"Hang on." Toliver wiped at his eyes.

Ingram watched the threesome hugging in front of the revolving doors, impervious to grousing captains and colonels who had to squeeze past.

Toliver's voice cracked. "God. She looks so much like her mother. It's uncanny."

"Ummm."

"And she knew Helen was waiting right there, didn't she?"

Ingram pulled a handkerchief and blew his nose. "Cold in here, damnit."

"Yeah."

Just then, Frank Durand spotted Ingram from across the lobby. He grinned and waved.

"Go," said Toliver.

Ingram moved, then stopped. "See you tonight, Ollie?"

But when he turned, Toliver was gone.

"I—"

Toliver snapped his fingers. "Say, I forgot. Did you see Pablo? And . . . and . . . how *is* Helen?"

"Right here, Ollie." Helen stood close, wearing a broad smile and a smart new dark blue dress.

"Holy cow." Toliver spun. He kissed her, then held her at arm's length. "My God, you're beautiful as ever. And lookie here. High heels." He whistled. "Where did you get those nylons? Snazzy." He took her in his arms and kissed her again. "Ummmm. Welcome back, honey. What're you doing tonight?"

"Looks like I'm going out to watch you get loaded and pick up broads."

Toliver gave a lopsided grin. "Hell, you know what I—"

She nodded. "I know just what you meant, Ollie."

"I was speaking figuratively."

Helen asked, "Can my folks come, too? They're due any moment."

Toliver stared at the floor for a moment. "Well, fine. I guess I could—"

Ingram said, "How about Boom Boom, too? They're ready to discharge him from Oak Knoll. You two guys can go out later and paint the town."

"What's he up to?"

"Doing fine. He's about ready to head out for the *Howell*."

Toliver nodded. "The old girl sails again." He looked to Ingram, the question unspoken.

"They're taking me back as exec. And there's talk of a command. They haven't made up their minds yet. I have to say, their confusion suits me just fine." He wrapped an arm around Helen's waist and pulled her close.

She asked, "How was Washington, Ollie?"

"Great. In fact, those guys are amazed you were able to get that stuff out. How did you do it, anyway?"

"I . . ." Her face darkened. "Excuse me. I have to check the desk." Helen dashed off.

Ingram said, "The Army caught up to her."

"Ahhh." Toliver called after her. "Hey, Helen. All that back pay. How 'bout a loan?"

She waved over the top of her head.

Watching her go, Toliver said in a soft voice, "I think I upset her."

"Don't worry about it."

Toliver persisted, "What did I say?"

"I don't know. She just doesn't want to talk about it."

"Really?"

"Like us, she hasn't regained all her weight. And she has nightmares. But when I try to get her to tell me what happened, she clams up."

Toliver nodded. "I still dream."

Ingram forced a smile. "Me, too. But not so much now as before. It takes time."

Toliver sighed. "How about a drink in the Mural Room before dinner?"

"Okay. Right now I'd like to head to our room and take a quick shower."

"*Our* room?"

"Right."

Toliver mused for a moment. "You know? We could have dinner at Wong Lee's. I've been dating this girl who works there."

"Suzy?"

"Yeah, you remember. Turns out she's a junior at Stanford. I've been helping her with her homework."

"I'll bet."

"No, really."

"You getting serious with her?"

"I don't know."

"Well, get a load of this. Guess who we brought back with us from Mindanao." He told Toliver about Wong Lee, who had boarded a fleet oiler after landing in Honolulu, and was home within a week.

Toliver snapped his fingers. "Yeah. I saw the guy just before I went back East. Smokes tons of cigarettes?"

"That's him."

"I don't know if he'll like the idea of me chasing his daughter. Maybe we better have dinner in the Mural Room."

Ingram smiled. "Wong Lee will be glad to see us, I guarantee." He glanced over to see a clerk at the registration desk hand Helen a thick brown manila envelope. She turned and started tearing it open.

Toliver took Ingram's elbow. "Yeah. Look, Todd, are Helen's folks really coming up?"

Ingram looked at his watch, a new Bulova. "Should be here any minute now. She's on pins and needles."

"Why?"

"We couldn't meet them at the station. I was doing this deal for the FBI and she had to go over to Fort Mason, drawing uniforms and paperwork stuff. They just sent over her orders and—" Ingram looked at Toliver. His smile was gone, his expression somber. "Ollie. What is it?"

Toliver's voice was low. "Todd, look. I know this is the twentieth century and these are modern times and all. But jeez."

"Jeez, what?"

"You said her dad is an ex-Marine. What's he going to do when he learns you've been . . . well, you know, shacking up with his daughter and all that."

Ingram broke out laughing.

Helen walked back, preoccupied with her envelope.

Toliver asked, "Damnit. What's so funny? Didn't you say you were going up to *our room*?"

"Ahhhh. I did say that. Here." Ingram held up Helen's left hand.

She smiled, displaying a gold band on her fourth finger. "We didn't have a proper ring, so Pablo loaned us his."

"Holy cow. You're . . . you . . . congratulations!" Toliver grabbed Helen and kissed her again.

With a broad smile, Helen said, "Thanks, Ollie."

"When?"

Ingram said, "We waited up in the mountains for the *Turbot*. I had an infection and ran a temperature of a hundred and three. I . . . we wanted to do something, because, I'll tell you, I thought I was going to die. So Pablo ran down to Agusan, rousted a priest out of bed, and we were married at two in the morning. Helen kept me stable until the *Turbot* showed up. Then the shanker mechanic got me going with penicillin."

"That's wonderful." Toliver shook Ingram's hand, then hugged Helen close. "God, it's good to see you again."

"You, too, Ollie." She kissed him on the cheek.

Ingram looked at Helen's envelope, his brow raised.

"Fort MacArthur Army Hospital. San Pedro, California," she said.

Ingram nodded. "Not bad. When?"

She looked inside the envelope again. "Report no later than twenty-two February 1943."

"Sixty days. Enough time to pick some avocados."

"Enough time to get married again."

Ingram turned to Toliver. "We're sealing it with a church wedding in Ramona, Ollie. How 'bout being my best man?"

"You bet." He gave Helen another peck. "Too bad you didn't check with me first."

Ingram said, "All you had to do, Ollie, was bail out of a PBY in the middle of the night."

Toliver thought that one over, then said, "No, thanks. Speaking of [ ] how is he?"

Ingram said, "They had to drag him on the submarine. Convinc[ ] come back with us until the place cools down. So he flew on to [ ] family in New Mexico." He reached in his pocket and mutter[ ] me. Might as well do this now. Before Kate and Frank show[ ] Frank *may* beat the crap out of me, like Ollie says. All these [ ] Here." He pulled out a dark blue box labeled I. MAGNIN [ ] and held it out to Helen.

"Oh." Helen gasped at the gold wedding ring capp[ ] carat diamond.

Ingram eased it on her fourth finger. "Back pay [ ]

Helen held it up to the light. "It's beautiful." T[ ]

"Ahem. See you in a while." Toliver started [ ]

Helen tensed. "Mom and Dad are here."

"What?" Ingram looked across the cro[ ] streaming through the revolving doors. "[ ]

"She's here, I tell you."